The Chosen People

MASTERWORKS OF MODERN JEWISH WRITING SERIES
EDITED BY JONATHAN D. SARNA

Academic Director of the Center for the Study of American Jewish Experience
Hebrew Union College—Jewish Institute of Religion

The Chosen People

BY SIDNEY L. NYBURG

With a new introduction by
Stanley F. Chyet
Hebrew Union College—Jewish Institute of Religion
Los Angeles

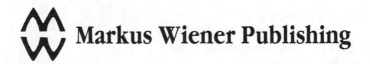 Markus Wiener Publishing

Published in arrangement with Harper & Row Publishers.

First Markus Wiener Publishing edition 1986

For information write to:
Markus Wiener Publishing, Inc.
2901 Broadway, New York, N.Y. 10025

Cover design by Cheryl Mirkin

ISBN 0-91029-47-9

Library of Congress Catalog
Card No. 85-040729

To
H. L. N.

CONTENTS

INTRODUCTION
by Stanley F. Chyet

Sidney Lauer Nyburg (1880-1957) was a native of Baltimore and scion of a comfortable family: the Nyburgs, Lauers,
and De Wolfes had been settled in Baltimore for a good part
of the nineteenth century and, along with his wife's family,
the Laupheimers, Nyburg belonged to the local gentry. Having studied at Baltimore City College, Nyburg earned a law
degree at the University of Maryland in 1901 and over the
years built a practice concentrating on corporation and mercantile law. He appears always to have been attracted to civic
concerns and, in addition to his service as a board member
of the Associated Jewish Charities in the city, served on the
boards of the Peabody Institute, the Maryland Historical Society, and the Peale Museum, and served also as a member
of the Baltimore Rent Control Board during World War I. A
knowledgeable bibliophile, he was able to acquire a good
many rare books, largely editions of Elizabethan and post-
Elizabethan writers; the collection was divided at his death
among the Enoch Pratt Free Library, the Peabody Institute,
and the Historical Society.[1]

The Chosen People (1917) was not Nyburg's first book. He
had already published two works of fiction (*The Final
Verdict: Six Stories of Men and Women* in 1915 and *The Con-
quest* in 1916) and would publish two more in later years (*The
Gates of Ivory* in 1920 and *The Buried Rose: Legends of Old
Baltimore* in 1932). Only *The Chosen People* is of particular
Jewish interest.

Nyburg, a product of the Progressive Era, took seriously
the challenge offered American life in those years by William Jennings Bryan, William James, John Dewey, Thor-
stein Veblen, William Dean Howells, Clarence Darrow, and
other notable social critics. Social conscience is at the center

I

of *The Chosen People* and of his outlook. His novel with its focus on economic injustice and social inequity in Baltimore supplies ample evidence of Nyburg's disdain for the socially irresponsible laissez-faire capitalism which typified an America in rapid passage from old agrarian-commercial to new industrial patterns. An article he wrote for the *Menorah Journal* some months after *The Chosen People* was published bears independent witness to his indignation:

> Our world has not been a just world. Our industries have not been administered in the interest of the whole people. It is the crying disgrace of our civilization that as the nation has grown ever richer misery too has increased its toll on our citizens. All of us have smiled complacently while we tried to forget how within walking distance of our comfortable homes were thousands of fellow Americans huddled together in hovels unfit for occupancy by cattle.[2]

The Chosen People belongs to a larger genre of American novels all documenting the labor strike as–in Georges Sorel's stark phrase–"a phenomenon of war."[3] These novelists included undeservedly obscure writers like Edward King (*Joseph Zalmonah*, 1893) and Isaac Kahn Friedman (*By Bread Alone*, 1901), somewhat better known litterateurs like James Oppenheim (*The Nine-Tenths*, 1911) and Elias Tobenkin (*Witte Arrives*, 1915), and celebrated fictionists like Jack London, (*The Iron Heel*, 1908) and Upton Sinclair (*The Jungle*, 1906–*King Coal*, 1917, shared a publication year with Abraham Cahan's *The Rise of David Levinsky* and Nyburg's novel.)[4]

Baltimore provided Nyburg with a splendid basis for his expression of social protest. The garment manufacturing enterprises which the Wiesenfelds, Friedenwalds, Greifs, Sonneborns and other Central European Jewish immigrants began in the city during the 1840's and 1850's had fifty years

II

later ripened into a major industry, recognized as such not only in Maryland but in the United States as a whole. Baltimore in the early 1900's ranked fourth or fifth in the production of men's clothing; Henry Sonneborn's firm, founded at mid-century, dominated Southern production of men's clothing by the century's end and employed 2,500 workers in an eight-story factory. As much as 70 percent of Baltimore Jewry depended for a living on the clothing industry. From 400 sweatshops in East Baltimore came more than half the clothing produced in the city as the new century began.[5]

Of course the expansion and muscularity of the Baltimore clothing industry owed a great deal to the Eastern European immigrant Jews who, settling there after 1880, constituted an exceedingly convenient—and initially docile—labor source. Unionization had been strenuously attacked by the garment manufacturers in Baltimore as early as the 1870's and 1880's—"Take your scissors and go home!" was an employer's rejoinder to striking workers in 1880; "talking union" was still grounds for dismissal twenty years later.[6] Nyburg's empathic comment on the immigrant situation is worth underscoring: "These immigrants had brought from their native lands across the sea a wholesome terror of the [secular] Law, and its inevitable disasters for poor folk." [*The Chosen People,* p. 142] Even so, the unionizing urge persisted.

The years 1901-1918 have been called a "golden age" for the Jewish labor movement in America, and in Baltimore as well as elsewhere a series of garment industry strikes answered the manufacturers' determination to combat unionization. There was nothing simple about this violent conflict; not only were employers pitted against workers and against one another, often enough workers too were divided. Particularly noteworthy were the Baltimore strikes of 1909 and 1914, which culminated in a bitter rivalry between the conservative United Garment Workers of America and the new, more radical, more immigrant-oriented Amalgamated Clothing Workers of America (ACWA).[7]

Besides being sympathetic to labor, Nyburg, it is obvious from his book, wished to champion women's rights. He created in *The Chosen People* two strong women characters as intelligent as they are attractive, the non-Jewish socialist Ellen Stewart and the Jewish capitalist Ruth Hartman. Both may have been shaped by what he knew of Dorothy Jacobs, an immigrant garment worker in her early twenties who had organized the Baltimore buttonhole makers in 1909, helped in 1914 to direct the strike against the Sonneborns (whose firm is the model for Nyburg's fictitious Pioneer Company), and by 1916 been elected to the ACWA General Executive Board.[8]

His pro-labor sympathies notwithstanding, Nyburg was capable of understanding the anti-union outlook as well and of representing it at least fairly, as he did in the passionate apologia he attributes to a Baltimore clothing manufacturer in Chapter XVI of the novel. Nyburg's characters on either side of the barricades are victims of circumstance and of their own myopia rather than dedicated manipulators and cynics. Such "evenhandedness" on Nyburg's part makes for a remarkable presentation of social reality.

The Chosen People is remarkable on other counts as well. In his novel, Nyburg asserts no explicit Zionist commitment, though the book is likely to be the first American fiction—in English at any rate—to represent a kind of cultural Zionist view sympathetically. In the *Menorah Journal* article cited above, he speaks of Zionism, "right or wrong, wise or wholly an illusion," as "a splendid example of Jewish idealism—a joyous devotion . . . to a task utterly removed from self-interest" and even goes on to reflect a vision it would be no misstatement to describe as an Ahad-Ha-Amist cultural Zionism.[9] What this suggests is that Nyburg's "ra-

IV

cial" thinking—seventy years later we would prefer to say, his notion of ethnicity—has a marked influence on his approach to Jewish life in Baltimore. Nyburg emphasizes "a racial difference between the Jew and the non-Jew." He is rather at a loss "to define it, to put it into the definite crystallization of hard and fast words but it exists none the less." He believes "Jewish idealism" to be "one of the distinguishing marks of this racial fibre."[10]

His standpoint is clear enough in the pages of *The Chosen People*, as when, for example, he imputes to Philip Graetz a certainty "that behind the mask of indifference [to Jewish tradition], the racial spirit of the Jew was still living and throbbing, and he meant . . . to awaken it to vigor," or when he assigns Ruth Hartman "the faculty—perhaps racial—of being roused to a state of keen emotional excitement, while her critical judgment remained judiciously unaffected." [*The Chosen People*, pp. 11, 87] In another context, Nyburg says of the pro-unionist lawyer David Gordon:

To the lawyer, with his Nationalistic ideas, the Jews were a Race whose duty it was to work out their own destiny and develop their own peculiar characteristics as best they might. The Christian might approve, disapprove or ignore—as his fancy happened to dictate. Through all the centuries he had never helped, and after this lapse of time, he could not hinder. [*The Chosen People*, p. 191]

No wonder a non-Jewish writer in *The Nation* was inclined to salute Nyburg as "a Jew . . . proud of his race, and whose pride exacts much of that race," and as "an American . . . who desires that American life may be strengthened and ennobled by her Jewish citizens."[11] Given such an understanding of the Jews—whether "Westernized" or enduringly "Oriental," whether "German" or "Russian," whether Orthodox or Reform or atheist, whether employer or worker—as con-

V

stituting a "Race," it was in Nyburg's opinion the more scandalous, the more wounding, that so puny a measure of racial solidarity bespoke itself among them. The antagonisms boiling within Baltimore Jewry—between the comfortable mansions of Eutaw Place and the East Baltimore ghetto—troubled Nyburg far more than gentile policies of anti-Jewish social exclusion.

All in all, the world of *The Chosen People* is a decorous and philistine world, one seen more from an upper-class "nativist" or "German" than from a lower-class immigrant or "Russian" perspective, but either way viewed critically. And it is a world in which religious modernism finds a—somewhat uncertain—role and voice.[12]

The year 1917 saw also the publication of another novel that made a memorable addition to the catalogue of American Jewish imaginative literature: Abraham Cahan's *The Rise of David Levinsky*. Cahan's novel is "the unrivalled record of a great historical experience," the settlement in turn-of-the-century America of two or more million Jews from Eastern Europe, and a novel which, though "created in English and cast in a Russian mold, . . . contained the essence of Yiddish culture and experience"; it is, moreover, surely "among the best novels of American business" and thus, "in the guise of fiction, a critically important chapter in American social history."[13] Cahan accomplished in *The Rise of David Levinsky* something quite unprecedented in American literature: a portrait—in one and the same character—of a Jewish industrialist and a (more or less) emancipated Jewish intellectual.

Nyburg, while less innovative, also produced something unprecedented: a portrait of an American Reform rabbi, possibly modeled on the young Savannah-born Morris Samuel Lazaron (1888-1979), who in 1915, a year after his ordination at Hebrew Union College in Cincinnati, became rabbi

VI

of the Baltimore Hebrew Congregation. The portrait is on the whole an appealing one, though Rabbi Graetz is depicted as a man of astonishing naivete: Sheldon Blank, reviewing *The Chosen People* in June, 1917, for the *Hebrew Union College Monthly,* accused Nyburg of a "mistake in assuming that so thoroughly incompetent a man could be elected to serve a Baltimore congregation."[14] Nyburg also invested his rabbinical protagonist with an impressive fund of moral earnestness, but the reader may very well detect in Nyburg's views of "Classical" Reform Judaism, its institutions, its clergy, its pattern of worship, its values, its Victorian *Schmalz,* an obliquely, yet invincibly satiric note: "It was Philip's misfortune to be cursed with a craving to live his sermons – and to make others live them, too." Temple Beth El

had all the characteristics of what is termed the reformed wing of Judaism. Its creed had been purged of all except a simple monotheism; it had cast aside most of the forms and ceremonials of the older faith; its ritual, so its members believed, was rooted in absolute rationalism.

If one had strayed within its walls he would hardly have been able to state with positiveness wherein, save for an occasional phrase or response spoken in the ancient Hebrew tongue, its worship differed from that of the Unitarian . . .

In these precincts the rabbi prays: "Help us . . . , the children of Thy martyr people, to be loyal also, to our great heritage!" [*The Chosen People,* pp. 199, 11, 13]

The Chosen People still belongs in mindset to the nineteenth century; that much seems evident from its genteel style, the indirection with which relations between men and women are treated, its pre-Freudian psychology, its consciousness of respectability. At the same time, in terms of its themes, the novel exhibits a decidedly modernist cast; it instructs and questions at least as much as it diverts and entertains. From the point of view of American Jewish literature, then, this is a transitional work—fittingly so, since it appears on the very eve of America's entry into World War One, and just as a new generation of American Jewish writers, the children of immigrants, stands ready to emerge.

Hebrew Union College—
Jewish Institue of Religion,
Los Angeles
November, 1985

NOTES

[1] See *The National Cyclopaedia of American Biography,* Vol. 47 (N.Y.: James T. White Co., 1965), p. 582.

[2] "Jewish Ideals in a Changing World," *Menorah Journal,* Vol. IV, No. 2 (April 1918), p. 69.

[3] *Reflections on Violence* (Glencoe: Free Press, 1950), p. 301: the French original dates from 1906 and 1908.

[4] See Walter B. Rideout, *The Radical Novel in the United States, 1900-1954* (Cambridge: Harvard University Press, 1956).

[5] See Isaac M. Fein, *The Making of an American Jewish Community: The History of Baltimore Jewry from 1773 to 1920* (Philadelphia: Jewish Publication Society, 1971), pp. 134, 166; Nina Asher, "Dorothy Jacobs Bellanca: Women Clothing Workers and the Runaway Shops," in Joan M. Jensen and Sue Davidson, eds., *A Needle, A Bobbin, A Strike: Women Needleworkers in America* (Philadelphia: Temple University Press, 1984), pp. 198-99, 207.

[6] Fein, p. 167; Asher, p. 204.

[7] Introduction to a reprint of Edward King, *Joseph Zalmonah* (Ridgewood, N.J.: Gregg Press, 1968), originally published in 1893; Asher, pp. 199, 203-204; David Brody, *Workers in Industrial America* (N.Y.: Oxford University Press, 1980), p. 31.

[8] See Asher, pp. 197 ff.

[9] *Menorah Journal,* Vol. IV, No. 2 (April 1918), pp. 71-72.

[10] Ibid., p. 65.

[11] April 5, 1917, cited in *Book Review Digest: 1917,* pp. 417-418.

[12] *Hebrew Union College Monthly,* Vol. IV, No. 1 (June, 1917), p. 29.

[13] Introduction to the Harper Torchbook edition (N.Y., 1960), pp. v, vii, xi.

[14] Vol. IV, No. 1 (June 1917), p. 29. The Cincinnati rabbinical student Sheldon H. Blank (who would become Professor of Bible and a major figure on the Hebrew Union College faculty), thought Nyburg's novel "excellently conceived and artistically constructed" and applauded it for offering "a fairly accurate analysis and statement of some of the problems of American Jewry," in particular "the fissure between Reform and Orthodox Judaism, the disagreement between the German and the Russian Jew, the problem of intermarriage, assimilation, the place of religion in business, and the Jewish mission."

THE CHOSEN PEOPLE

CHAPTER I

A Prophet in Israel

" On this day shall ye be forgiven and cleansed from all your sins: before God ye shall be pure!"

The solemn words of the young Rabbi were at one and the same moment an earnest command to future holiness and a promise of the Divine Compassion. He seemed, as he spoke, a fitting prophet of God's word. His slender young figure quivered with a noble enthusiasm. His dark handsome face was aglow with that light which comes to a man who believes himself to be dedicated with all his strength and vigor to a sacred cause.

The Great White Fast—the Day of Atonement, the holiest day in all the year—was nearing its close. Through the stained glass western windows of the Temple Beth El, the setting sun cast great pools of crimson and purple upon the floor of the synagogue. The vast congregation sat silent and responsive under the spell of this youth whom they had called from his little Western village home to be their guide.

As for himself, all through the long day of prayer he had, in his exaltation, given no sign of the sense of achievement so normal to a man of twenty-four, suddenly called to become the minister of the largest and wealthiest synagogue in Baltimore,—a city where American Judaism had already acquired something of a tradition.

Throughout his prayer, as in his eloquent sermon of

the morning, he seemed aglow with the fervor of a youth into whose hands had been placed a holy charge. These were to be his people! He would use them for God's purposes! Through him there should come to this community an era of nobleness and largeness of vision possible only to men and women moved by the spirit of the Faith he knew to be the Truth.

From time to time as the organ tones pealed out, he had eyed his parishioners almost wistfully. Some were old and grizzled, some had features almost stolid in their unimaginativeness; all appeared prosperous and but too well contented with the world as it then was. Would he ever be able to make them see the vision that was constantly before his eyes? But as the day wore on he found, or thought he found, the most sodden become kindled by the flame of his own enthusiasm, and he cast his doubts aside.

Even though softened by years of ease and affluence, these were still God's people,—descendants of the stern men who had followed Moses through the bitterness of the Wilderness, and had, centuries after, withstood the fires of the Inquisition. In this later day of opportunity the mission of the Jew was still to be fulfilled, and he, Philip Graetz, among these men and women, would not fail to do his share.

Since early morning the throng in the stately building had been held under the spell of this youth's passionate fervor. Philip knew only too well that the enthusiasm of this great Fast was no fair test of the daily measure of his congregation's interest. With the loosening of the bonds of orthodoxy the daily visit of the faithful to the synagogue had long since become a thing of the past, and only on great festival days did one witness the vast out-pouring of men and women, seemingly indifferent to their faith on all other days of the year. Beth El had all the characteristics of what is termed the reformed wing of Judaism. Its creed had been purged of all except a simple monotheism; it had cast aside most of the forms and cere-monials of the older faith; its ritual, so its members believed, was rooted in absolute rationalism.

If one had strayed within its walls he would hardly have been able to state with positiveness wherein, save for an occasional phrase or response spoken in the ancient Hebrew tongue, its worship differed from that of the Unitarian. The men and women were seated side by side in defiance of the orthodox convention; the Rabbi and his listeners were uncovered. Professional musicians of both sexes filled the Temple with melody whose beauty was in no way characteristic of the Jewish tradition.

Of all this Philip Graetz approved. Yet he believed that the true essentials of Judaism were still inherent in this simplified form. He was sure that behind the mask of indifference, the racial spirit of the Jew was still living and throbbing, and he meant, with all his soul, to awaken it to vigor and to a commanding influence in the daily life of this old city.

He believed in himself and in his work. He was already compelling these well-dressed, comfortable creat-ures to think and to feel. He would make Religion—their own Religion, Judaism—the dominating force in the intimate lives of these people,—these unformed youths, these delicate featured impressionable maidens, the young husbands and wives,—and even among the old! He could not afford to doubt his own success. His mission was too

11

important for failure. He, in his humble way, was to be God's prophet.

The words of the stately ritual fell from his lips as though they had been phrased to meet his very need:

" Oh, consecrate our hearts unto Thee, and make them Thy living altars, whereon shall burn the holy flame of devotion to Thee, oh Merciful God."

Amid the exultant notes of the organ the service drew to its end, but Philip seemed to feel, somehow, as though he could not let these,—his people—go. His very soul yearned to make them know all his purposes toward them, the help he meant to bring to them, the wounds he meant to heal, the consolation and strength he meant to bring to the heart of each of them. As he rose to pronounce the benediction, suddenly, almost without volition on his part, moved, as the Rabbi would have said, by God Himself, his tense emotion broke forth in unpremeditated prayer.

" Great Spirit of the Universe," he cried, " whom none of us may comprehend, but whose presence fills our lives, it is our ardent prayer that the inspiration of this hour may never vanish from our hearts. Be with us as we return to our homes so that each of them may be happier, purer and richer, in the beauty of earnest manhood and womanhood!

" Be with us through the long and difficult years that are to come, filling our souls with strength and purpose to mold this vast world into harmony with Thine own Justice.

" Help us in the daily struggle of the counting-room and the market place, to thrill with the warm human love of all mankind, which is the one great law of our Holy Faith.

A PROPHET IN ISRAEL

"For the dim vision of Thy Divine Love, O God, our fathers and our fathers' fathers for twenty centuries have smilingly embraced the rack, the scaffold and the stake, and Thou hast marvelously preserved them through all the ages that Thy Spirit might not perish from the earth.

"Help us then, the children of Thy martyr people, to be loyal also, to our great heritage! In these days of enervating ease, keep us true to the ideals for which our fathers blithely suffered and died.

"May we, too, be staunch and brave and true to our tradition, and remain unshaken in our resolve to bequeath to our children ever more and more of Thy Divine Spirit than we have ourselves received, as the birthright of the Jew.

"And for myself, who have come into this strange land to minister unto Thy people, give me, I pray, a full measure of vigor and courage to interpret Thy mysterious Word. Let me not fail in the great work of making Thy Love and Thy Purpose manifest unto each of these men and women who shall look to me for guidance. Make me clear of eye to see the Truth, and dauntless of spirit to strike at evil without one thought as to how great be its strength, or how perilous the encounter.

"Help me to work Thy will among this, Thy people! Make of me with all my youth, with all my ignorance, with all my weaknesses, the instrument of Thy irresistible inspiration.

"Like David, God's servant of old, I am but a stripling, and as my people look upon their feeble and untried leader and think of the work I am yearning to do for them and with them, remembering the scoffing, skeptical, practical army of men and women who are girt round about

13

us, mocking at virtue and holiness and Love (human and divine)—our hearts may well grow faint, and sink within us. But, like David, I shall go forth in the name of the Lord God of Israel, strong in the knowledge that the battle I am to wage is not for myself and my own poor glory, but for Him and His Divine Service.

" Help us then, oh Father, each according to his pitiful needs, so that in the end we may become truly Thy priest people; that through us, Thy Truth and Thy Love may encompass all the Earth, as the waters that cover the sea."

Slowly, thoughtfully, in striking contrast to its usual heedless habit, the huge congregation filed from the great white structure. Even in the Autumn twilight, amid the trees and shrubbery of the hill-side parked street, they did not find it easy to emerge into the commonplaces of daily unexalted life. There was something different about this new young Rabbi. One or two young men smiled tolerantly and wondered how long he would be able to maintain this attitude of rarified exaltation, but they met with little response from their sobered friends.

Among the throng there walked slowly and silently an unusually pretty, dark-haired and dark-eyed girl, whose face seemed still to be reflecting the emotion of the young minister. After a few minutes she turned to her older sister and said impulsively, " Isn't he wonderful, Bess? Isn't he wonderful ? "

" Yes, Ruth, wonderful," her sister answered, " I'm sorry Rob didn't get there; I think even he would have been impressed."

" Why didn't Rob come ?" the girl asked; " he usually comes to Temple at the end of Services on Atonement day."

"Operating, I suppose," his wife answered, with a hint of dissatisfaction in her voice. "A surgeon never gets anywhere. But I wish he could have heard Dr. Graetz. We must have him to dinner one night next week."

The girl made an impatient gesture as though her generous enthusiasm had been suddenly chilled, but she did not answer, and the two walked silently down the hillside to their home.

CHAPTER II

MRS. FRANK ENTERTAINS

It was considerably after six o'clock, and Mrs. Frank was beginning to display signs of restlessness. The children had received their good-night kisses, together with appropriate bribes and threats, cunningly devised to stifle any noise which might disturb their mother's carefully planned dinner. Her own becoming toilet was complete; but her husband had not come home. It was a ghastly task, trying to do anything gracefully if one happened to be the wife of a busy surgeon. She had extorted a score of solemn promises that he would forget all other claims for this one night, and she had invoked upon him every possible form of vengeance if he should fail her. She did want, above all things, that the dinner she was giving in honor of the new Rabbi should be a real success. And if she must begin by explaining her husband's absence—

But even as she glanced nervously at the clock, the doctor's rapid step was heard running up the stairs and, without going through the ceremony of tapping at the door, he burst into the room.

Mrs. Frank had always intended, sometime, to have a room of her own. She knew that good taste was tending in that direction, and besides, if a man would allow his sleep to be shattered by midnight telephone calls, there was no reason why his wife should suffer. But the house was too small to provide her even with a dressing room, and the doctor, indulgent in all other things, refused firmly her plea for a home in the suburbs. He found

16

it hard enough to care for his practice living here as they did on Eutaw Place. He had offered, by way of compromise, to rebuild the present dwelling; to purchase the adjoining house and build a big home of her own designing, but acceptance of this offer meant a permanent abandonment of her hopes, and so the months went by and she remained just where she was.

"Hello," the doctor called to her, boyishly, "you're all dressed, I see! My, but you look festive. Give me a kiss and help me get into my dinner clothes. Aren't you going to say anything nice to me for being an obedient husband? I promised, and here I am, on time to the dot."

She smiled at him indulgently and pointed warningly to the clock on her dressing table.

"Oh, lots of time, lots of time," he assured her. "You've put all my togs out for me, haven't you? That's an angel. If I hadn't sworn to you I'd be here, I'd have cut. I surely have been busy today."

"You always are," she answered, "if you were a sea captain or an Arctic explorer, I'd see you oftener than I do."

And as if to illustrate the text, the telephone next to the bed broke suddenly into an insistent clang.

The doctor sprang toward it, but she intercepted him.

"Listen, Rob," she commanded with a hand on his arm. "You can't go, no matter who wants you. If it's the President he must wait, or get somebody else. Just this one night,—please!"

He was already holding the receiver to his ear and exchanging greetings with the man at the other end of the wire.

"Oh, Dr. Deeming! * * * No! I'm sorry. I'm

afraid you'll have to let another man see him. * * *
Try Sorrell. * * * Yes, he can do it better than I
could. * * * Yes, he can! * * * Well, you see
if I go out now I'll have a divorce proceeding on my
hands. * * * Oh, divorce takes up more time than
a dinner party. * * * Yes, it's something special.
You think he could wait? * * * Midnight? * * *
Yes — I'll meet you then * * * Church Home
* * * Oh, yes, I'll surely be there. * * * They
better had be gone by midnight! Good-bye!"

"There," he said hanging up the receiver and going on
with his dressing, "there's nobody else in the world but
you, Bess, for whom I'd have refused to come when Dr.
Deeming called."

"You're not really going out at twelve o'clock tonight?" she asked, handing him now and then some
necessary garment as she talked.

"I surely am," he insisted, gaily. "What do you
care? Even a new Rabbi will be talked out before then.
I can go and do my little bit of surgery in peace."

"You know, Rob," she complained, "I don't believe
you ever think of anything but your nasty old work. I
never can get you to take me anywhere. We never spend
a peaceful hour together. Morning, noon and night,
you're at one hospital or another. The children barely
recognize you. And I wouldn't mind it so much if you
really had to do it. But we could manage just as comfortably if you didn't earn a penny." In his grotesque
disarray, he made a gesture of impatience.

"I know," she went on quickly, anticipating his protest, "you're going to say I'd hate being married to a man
who didn't do his work well enough to be in demand, and

that one can't practice a profession unless he puts his whole self into it—and all the rest. I've listened to it before. But it leaves me somehow stranded!"

He crossed the room, half dressed as he was, took her in his arms and kissed her heartily.

"Stop!" she cried, without, however, trying to free herself, "you're mussing my best bib and tucker."

"Well," he said as he returned to the prosaic task of putting on his collar, "it's hard on you women, I know. I'm sorry for you; but I don't know what to do about it. You married me because you wanted a man who wasn't keen on drifting along, doing nothing. You had plenty of chances to marry the other kind. Now here I am—I can't do things by halves, and that's all there is to it. You've got a job. There are the kiddies."

She sighed. "Children aren't much of a job for people with money, Rob. Barbara looks after them better than I could. When they get older, there will be governesses, and schools and things."

"Oh, well," he answered with masculine cheerfulness, "we won't settle the woman question now. Maybe we'll lose all our money and you can cook and clean house like your grandmother did. I believe you'd do it pretty well, and be a lot happier. Meanwhile, who is coming to dinner besides the holy man?"

"Don't sneer at him, Robert," she ordered. "Why do all you men feel so superior to a minister?"

"I suspect it's because we think he gets paid for being good, Bess, which is another way of saying 'He's good, 'cause it pays him.'"

"He isn't!" He gets paid for making us good."

"Gosh," answered the doctor hurriedly brushing his

hair, " then he hasn't earned anything on my account. No wonder he has to go out to his meals. Who else will be here?"

" Well," his wife said, " there'll be Clarence and Florence, of course."

" Of course," he repeated, " he'll tell me how well America could be run if it were managed like his factory, and Florence will explain how she is going to get thin again next year."

" Is there anyone who measures up to your level, my dear? " Elizabeth asked with a smile.

"There are such people," he retorted, " but we don't seem to have them to dinner."

" Well, there'll be Arthur Kahn," she went on, " he has brains, hasn't he?"

" Yes, but he's smug. Good Lord! but he is smug. Even your dear Uncle Clarence has trouble out-doing him. If Ruth marries him, I shall take out his appendix with fatal results the first time her fudge disagrees with him."

" Then be nice to Dr. Graetz," she advised him meaningly. " Ruth is going to marry some one, you know. Maybe you'll like Dr. Graetz better."

" I do, I do," the doctor assured her. " Whatever he's like, he has my vote. Anyone else coming? "

" Rose Behrend and Frieda Stern—Ruth wanted them," Elizabeth went on.

" Good," Robert said, " put Frieda next to me, if I must have one. She amuses me. I like them impudent. That's how you won my heart, Bess, dear. Now tie my miserable white tie and I'll be a thing of beauty. Isn't your party one man short?"

20

"No," Mrs. Frank answered as she deftly knotted the scarf. "The last man will be David Gordon."

The doctor suddenly stopped smiling and emitted a low and prolonged whistle.

"David Gordon! How in the devil did you chance on him, and still more, why did he say he'd come? He's not the dinner type. He's more like me."

"Don't," Elizabeth protested, indignantly, "he's not like you. He's horrid. I don't care if he is a 'big' lawyer, —I didn't want him. I'm sure he is going to spoil my whole party. Ruth asked him."

The doctor raised his eyebrows inquiringly. "Ruth! I didn't know she'd been cultivating Gordon."

"You never do know what's going on in your own house," Elizabeth stated with resignation. "Gordon did some legal work for the social service group of Ruth's Alumnae Association,—some Child Labor Law or something. He must have done it particularly well; he made a tremendous impression on her. He didn't do it like any gentleman would have done, just because he was interested. He charged them a good stiff fee."

"Is that why you call him horrid?" the doctor asked. "He got them what they wanted, didn't he? And if they are all like Ruth, they were able to pay."

"Of course," his wife admitted, "but you know it wasn't 'nice' to treat a group of girls that way. He should have entered into their own spirit of enthusiasm, or made some excuse for doing nothing at all."

"I see," her husband observed, "I think you are wrong, but I never did know much about the ornamental side of life. Well, since then, I take it, Ruth finds him interesting, and you find him dangerous?"

Mrs. Frank nodded. "That's one way of putting it," she said, "of course, I don't know just what Ruth thinks about him. I've no real reason to be so serious about it, but he is clever, and ambitious, too, I suppose, and Ruth is rich and pretty. I don't like it."

"You'd better let Ruth meet a live man once in awhile instead of these conventional, college-made Cash Registers like Arthur Kahn," Robert cautioned her. "A husband lasts a long time and the docile dainty ones are worse, if anything, than the men you can't manage. If she wants Gordon, thank your particular God she knows an intelligent human animal when she sees one, even if he doesn't reek of money. Ruth has enough, and Gordon isn't the type who'll want to dangle around spending his wife's income."

"I'd rather he were," Elizabeth said with spirit, "then he wouldn't interest her, or if he did, he'd spend his life trying to please her."

"He wouldn't succeed," the doctor proclaimed dogmatically, "any decent woman would soon be disgusted by a man who spent his life trying to satisfy her whims."

"Perhaps," Elizabeth said doubtfully, "but this one surely wouldn't make her happy. I want her to marry what you call a live man. You're live. But you're nice, anyhow. He isn't."

"Why not, Bess? I never heard any harm of him. He ranks as the most prominent lawyer of his age in town. He's building a splendid practice. There's no Jew of his age in the city who has done so much, having so little to start with."

"We can't really call him a Jew at all, if you drag that in," Elizabeth urged, "he doesn't believe in anything."

" No more do I," Robert replied cheerfully, " it doesn't seem to bother you."

" He talks unpleasantly," his wife continued, seeming to find genuine delight in enumerating the faults of her prospective guest. " He makes you feel uncomfortable. He seems to take a real joy in making all our little foibles seem absurd. He doesn't fit in with any of our habits,— Ruth's habits either. Naturally, I don't want my sister to encourage a man who will estrange her from all of her friends, and mine."

" All of which, translated," Robert insisted impatiently, " means that he's a Russian Jew, instead of having been born here with German Jews for grandparents."

" Well if you will have it, then," Elizabeth conceded, " I'm willing to put it on that score. He's a Russian, and that means he's somehow uncouth,—at least to us. He isn't delicate. I'm willing to suppose he's honest, and brilliant, and has all the virtues you want to claim for him, but he isn't one of us, and he never can be."

The eminent surgeon laughed patronizingly.

" Don't be a snob, my dear. It's particularly silly in a Jewess—any kind, American, German, or Russian. There's a lady in Roland Park tonight, saying just your own words about you."

" But it isn't true of me," Elizabeth protested indignantly, " so I don't care if she says it or not. Of the Russians, it *is* true."

Once more her husband laughed. Then he spoke slowly.

" You do care, Bess. Why should you pretend with me? You certainly wish every one could be judged on his own merits whether he be Jew, Christian, or Mohammedan. It hurts you when you find yourself treated discourteously just because you are a Jewess. How can you expect a mere Christian to learn tolerance, if you haven't it yourself?"

"I don't want to begin to learn by using my only sister as an experiment," Elizabeth answered. "It isn't as though there were no other men worth while besides Gordon. Now, if she should happen to like Dr. Graetz——!"

"Ah!" the doctor murmured. "I begin to see. We are going Rabbi stalking. In how many homes in Baltimore tonight do you suppose webs are being spun to entrap this poor, innocent boy into mixing up his ideas of Sacred Love with profane?"

Elizabeth smiled. It was her turn to be tolerant.

"It won't hurt him," she asserted. "If I were a man, I'd rather like to be married to Ruth. Besides, you know, he must marry sometime. Even you, my dread Lord and Master, couldn't escape, and after all, are you so much the worse for it?"

"I'm much better," he assured her gallantly, as he led the way to the staircase, "but think of your own fate! And your interest is in Ruth, not in the child Rabbi."

"I find you reasonably bearable," she said, making a grimace at him, "at least, on those rare occasion when you honor me with your presence."

"Maybe that's why you do find me bearable," he retorted gaily, as they descended the stairs arm in arm. "Now, the holy man, you must remember, only works two days in each and every week."

CHAPTER III

THE FEEDING OF LIONS

IN many ways Philip Graetz was younger than his actual age would have indicated. From his early youth he had felt himself destined for the ministry, and the years he might otherwise have spent in careless contact with chance companions had been devoted to diligent study and preparation. At college and later, at the theological seminary, his absorption in fitting himself for his mission had left him little time, and still less inclination, for frivolity. His intimates were few, and principally students who shared his own unearthly enthusiasms. His parents had died during his childhood, leaving him a legacy which would have seemed small to most men, but which was ample for his purposes. Such few relations as he had, looked askance upon his ambitions, and his choice of a career. Indeed, one of the few quarrels he could remember had occurred between himself and his paternal uncle, when he had insisted upon refusing that gentleman's benevolently meant offer of an interest in a flourishing department store in a Western City.

It followed then, that his knowledge of men and women—the actual clay out of which he was to mold into tangible form the visions of his religious ecstasy—was based altogether upon his own imagination, and the books he had read. He really loved his fellow creatures ardently, meant to live for them, and had necessity arisen, would not have shirked dying to serve their needs. None the less, in the commonplaces of every-day life, he felt inexpressibly shy and ill at ease. To enter a drawing-room full of people was to him an actual ordeal, to be avoided, if possible, and to be dreaded if no escape were to be found.

One cannot remain unconscious of such a malady as this, and Philip, realizing what a handicap his self consciousness might become, had determined to accept the advice given him by a well-loved teacher in his divinity school who had recognized his youthful talent as a thing too precious to be wasted. He had, therefore, urged young Graetz, after his graduation, to devote an entire year to aimless travel, learning to meet and to mingle with chance acquaintances. Events had moved too swiftly to permit this plan to be put into practice. A committee from the Baltimore congregation, seeking an incumbent,—and preferably a young and enthusiastic one—for Beth El's vacant pulpit, had heard the youth preach his farewell sermon at the college chapel. Philip was never self-conscious in the pulpit, and the committee, to a man, had succumbed instantly to his eloquence and winning sincerity. He wanted, above all things, to be put to work. In Baltimore, the representatives of the Temple told him, was a field where his talents would be appreciated as they deserved. It was the opportunity of a life time. His results were to be limited only by his own qualities. Here was a congregation, wealthy, old and comprising among its members some of the most influential men in an important, interesting city.

He forgot all else in his joy in a task which was to prove his prowess, and with never a doubt of success in his ministry, he had flung himself upon his duties.

Tonight, however, as he sat in the place of honor at

this his first dinner party in Baltimore, the idea was borne in upon him with overpowering weight that a minister's activities were social as well as religious. He was among the men and women who were to be his friends and associates in his all-absorbing work. He was here this evening because they wanted to make him welcome,—to be kind and hospitable; yet as he realized how absurd he would appear, had he begun to talk of any of the things which seemed to him worth discussing, he wished with all his might he had found some excuse for remaining in his own study. He possessed none of the small change of conversation, and apparently, to tender bills of larger denominations would be to make himself a bit ridiculous.

Nevertheless, no matter what he may have felt, he emerged rather well from the awkward instant preceding the dinner, when introductions and formal greetings were exchanged. His well-bred manner, his grave courtesy, his good looks and youth were eloquent in his favor—all the more because he had not yet learned to reckon upon them as assets.

Even gaunt, forbidding-looking David Gordon, with his occasional smile—terrifying and cynical—had turned toward the new Rabbi a glance of unconscious approval. And now, seated at Mrs. Frank's beautifully appointed table, with pretty Ruth Hartman at his right, and Mrs. Frank, herself, at the head of the table just next to him, he was aware that, so far, all had gone fairly well.

There had been a minute of suspense during which Philip wondered whether he would be called upon to ask a blessing, before the meal was served.

The young minister was an advocate of this ceremony,

—true to his belief in linking together his religious faith with each and every happening of the daily round of life—but he was selfishly pleased to find it was not the custom in the Frank household, and he breathed a sigh of relief, because for the moment, at least, he need do nothing conspicuous.

Dr. Frank, seated at the foot of the table, smiled his tolerant smile of good-natured amusement as he noticed the first course provided by his wife. She had ordered oysters to be served,—perhaps, as thoroughly characteristic of Baltimore's good cheer. The surgeon obtained a secret whimsical joy in observing these dainties—anathema to the orthodox Jew—being consumed contentedly by every one of the guests, including the new Rabbi,—with the single exception of David Gordon, who flatly proclaimed his agnosticism, but would not, or could not, conquer his aversion to the forbidden food.

Meanwhile, Ruth, with half unconscious art, was speedily putting the bashful Philip at ease, by talking to him in low tones of the happiness and inspiration she had found in his Atonement Day service. His diffidence fell from him as he answered eagerly her intelligent questions about his studies of the past, and his plans for the future.

Just opposite Philip sat David Gordon. He eyed the younger man for the first few minutes with that searching, intent manner which had often preceded his famous cross examinations. He gave the impression of being able and anxious to read through the very hearts and souls of men and gloatingly to pluck out their guilty secrets. Philip engrossed with Ruth, was, as yet, unaware of this scrutiny, and Elizabeth Frank was a sufficiently experienced hostess to attempt without delay, a diversion of her uncomfortable guest's interest.

"Well, Mr. Gordon," she began, " I ought to count myself particularly lucky to have you here tonight. It isn't often one can capture two lions in the same evening."

The supposed lion should, by all the rules, have purred gracefully, but his answer partook much more of the nature of a polite roar.

His tones were suave enough, and his manner betrayed nothing to which a lady might take definite exception, but he retorted quickly:

"You are too flattering, Mrs. Frank. I am an ordinary barn-yard animal. I'm no lion. Certainly not, if Dr. Graetz is an example of the king of beasts."

"I'm sure you're a lion," she answered, mildly displeased, but determined to punish him without betraying any consciousness of her intention. "Everyone tells me you are. It must be Dr. Graetz who is not the authentic animal. Would you mind informing me just what characteristic makes you the sole representative of lionship at my poor board?"

He saw at once how ridiculous her question tended to make him appear, and he extricated himself as best he could by another remark of almost definite rudeness.

"If I've any claims to lionhood among this group," he rapped out, "it's because I seem to be the only specimen here who has hunted and brought down all his own prey since he was a cub."

Elizabeth was silenced for an instant. He had balked her, somehow, in her design of making him absurd, but he had done it at the expense of what seemed to her, good breeding. It was not " nice " for a man to gloat over his past poverty, or his present riches, and she secretly scored another black mark against the man whom she had liked not too well at the beginning.

He smiled at her suddenly, and seemed anxious to relieve her embarrassment.

" That was a silly thing I said," he told her with such apparent sincerity as to force a smile from her in return. " It's as stupid to feel proud of having been born poor as having been born rich. It's absurd to be proud of being born at all, isn't it? So many people seem to get born."

" Still," she resumed, not to be outdone in generosity, " there must be something in having done things for one's self."

" It depends altogether how well they manage to get done, I guess," the lawyer answered. " Sometimes, a self-made man is really lucky in having had only one bad teacher, instead of two dozen. He has less to forget."

They were silent an instant. Then David Gordon said: " I suppose I snapped at you because all this talk of lions seems to me particularly harmful. You charming women make men do things so that afterward they may come to you and be admired, instead of doing them just because they feel an impulse of their own. Now, there's that pleasant boy of a Rabbi,—he thinks he came here to serve what he calls God. He would, too, if he could be sentenced to life imprisonment in his own Temple. But in ten weeks he'll be serving three hundred goddesses instead of one God. The change will do you ladies no good, and will do him a lot of harm."

Elizabeth was once more antagonistic, but in spite of herself, interested.

THE FEEDING OF LIONS

"Why do you say that?" she asked. "None of us wants to do anything which may injure his usefulness and if we did, how could we?"

"How can you help it? would be a fairer question." David replied. "You women have become too intelligent and too attractive to be ignored. You're the only articulate people in any congregation. The men don't care a rap about the Rabbi just so long as he does nothing to make them uncomfortable. How often, in a year, does your husband go to Temple?"

"Most years, once; some years, not at all," Elizabeth admitted. "But Robert is an unusually busy man and——"

"We all are," the lawyer interrupted. "Our tasks aren't all as important as Dr. Frank's, or as well done, perhaps; but we're all busy. Meanwhile, you ladies aren't busy at all. You are thirsting for something to do which will keep you interested. So lots of you will try Religion, —particularly now, when you have a charming young man for a stimulus. He'll pose to please you. He'll become feminized. No man can stand that process. He'll lose whatever fighting instinct he has, and then he'll be just an agreeable manikin, to be played with by grown-up girl-children."

Elizabeth gave vent to an indignant exclamation of protest; but David Gordon raised one hand in deprecation.

"Don't get angry," he commanded, good-humoredly. "I hope I'm wrong. It will do you no harm to be warned of his danger even if it turns out to have been exaggerated. But you'll see! If you cast your eye down the table at this very instant, you'll see Miss Behrend, whom I've been neglecting, waiting, on conversational tip-toes, for an

31

opportunity to ask Dr. Graetz what he thinks of Baltimore. If he were a brute like me, he'd ask in return, what in the name of all the devils he could know of this City after living here two weeks. But he'll tell her it's perfectly lovely, and his damnation will have begun."

Sure enough, at the next pause in the flow of words between Ruth and Philip, Rose Behrend asked the unlucky question, though in a slightly less hackneyed form than the lawyer had predicted. David smiled maliciously at his hostess, as Philip began his reply.

" So far, everyone has been amazingly kind to me," he answered. " I'm sure I shall be very happy here."

It was Elizabeth's turn to smile triumphantly at David. Certainly, the Rabbi's answer had not been as puerile as the lawyer had prophesied.

It was part of David's equipment as a lawyer, and a good one, to lose a point, now and then, with grace. In his gesture and smile, he rather magnified whatever right Elizabeth might have to believe her young champion had falsified his own prediction. He struck into the general conversation by saying pointedly:

" Bravo, Dr. Graetz! I'm glad you're too wise to be betrayed into generalizing from your first impressions of this City. On the surface, it seems like almost any other city—except perhaps, a bit less excitable,—but it has surprises in store for you. Baltimore has an atmosphere of its own."

" What do you mean by atmosphere? " demanded Mr. Kaufman's deep, harsh voice. " I think this town is just like others except, as you say, it's deceptively quiet. We're curing that, though. The activity is really here, only, up to this time, we haven't had sense enough to talk about it, while other cities have. Our business has suffered."

David looked at the prosperous merchant with a glimpse of contemptuous pity which he took no trouble to conceal.

"I wasn't thinking of the clearing house statistics," he announced in the curt tone which left Mr. Kaufman, and his wife too, vaguely conscious of a stinging rebuke, without knowing just why it was merited.

Dr. Frank, in spite of a secret satisfaction at the conversational mishap of his wife's uncle, felt constrained, as a good host, to come to his rescue.

"I suppose," he remarked genially, "Clarence means the business situation here, to be taken as typical of other things. Our activities in science, in political betterment, and in the art of living are perhaps more intensive, and less openly displayed than in other cities. What do you think, Arthur?"

Arthur Kahn, who prided himself on being at one and the same time a thorough man of business and a fastidious patron of all the cultured arts, replied leisurely:

"We're a manufacturing City and a University City at the same time. Our lives are busy ones but we live them under the shadow of the Johns Hopkins. I think that is the distinguishing characteristic of our City."

The Rabbi looked puzzled. David Gordon smiled sarcastically.

"Don't," he urged with exaggerated caution, "accept any of their tabloid explanations. After you've really sensed the intangible atmosphere of this town, you will know better than to attempt to define it. Baltimore is

THE CHOSEN PEOPLE

like a well-loved woman. You will find yourself most fascinated by the qualities which exasperate you most."

"Oh," called Frieda Stern, from her end of the table, "such a knowing thought from a bachelor! You must have revelations to make, Mr. Gordon, about well-loved women!"

"The more reason, then, for not making them, Miss Stern," he replied, "but I will assure you of one fact— every bachelor knows more about the subject than any married man. He can afford to allow his imagination more play."

Philip seemed to feel some duty to bring back the subject to its starting point.

"You seem, Mr. Gordon, to have very definite ideas about the City," he ventured. "I need these more, just now, than theories about lovely ladies, but you say I can't get them second-hand. How long must one live here to sense its meaning? You've lived here all your life, haven't you?"

"No!" David answered bluntly, and as though he meant nothing less than a deliberate challenge, "I was born in Russia."

Mrs. Frank hastened a bit too patently to the rescue of what she feared might become an awkward situation.

"But you are virtually a native of Baltimore," she insisted promptly, with an insinuating smile, "you came here as a mere child. You're not able to remember your birthplace, are you?"

"I wouldn't be able to remember it were it not for the kind jogs given to my memory by my friends of German descent," David announced, seeming to take a perverse pleasure in the embarrassment he was causing. "As it is,

I sometimes find it difficult to remember anything else!"

For a full minute there was a dead silence. Then the offended Elizabeth turned deliberately to Dr. Graetz and began talking to him in a low tone about some totally unrelated subject. The conversation broke up into little eddies and scraps of talk, among pairs and trios, and it was not until the dinner was almost finished that another remark was tossed across the table. It was the irrepressible lawyer, who, once more, returned to the charge.

"Dr. Graetz," he said, " I've been letting my thoughts play with the idea you expressed a few minutes ago about feeling sure you'll be happy here. I rather hope you'll think better of that wish, because if you're going to do good work in Baltimore, you are going to be made miserably unhappy. I'm serious in wondering which of the two paths you'll choose."

The two men faced each other earnestly, while Elizabeth nervously waited for the coming of another storm.

The Rabbi responded gallantly to the lawyer's challenge.

" If I must decide between duty and happiness, I hope you will have no doubts as to my decision. When I said ' happiness ' I wasn't thinking of mere pleasure. Why do you believe I can't have both?"

"It depends on your idea of work," David answered. "What do you want to do here?"

"Dr. Graetz told us that very beautifully on Atonement Day," Mrs. Frank said, foreseeing the outbreak of an uncomfortable religious discussion, and determined to avert it at every possible hazard.

But Philip was definitely interested, and had no wish to take refuge behind any woman's petticoat.

THE CHOSEN PEOPLE

"I want," he stated, "to translate our ideals of ethics and spirituality into the conduct of daily life."

"Of men as well as women?" asked David crisply, and irritatingly.

"Of men as well as women," Philip repeated, firmly.

"Well, that's a dangerous programme," was the lawyer's comment, "unless you are going to emasculate it. If you mean to urge husbands and wives to be reasonably kind to each other and to the children, and neither to steal, nor kill,—you'll be safe enough. Most of us live up to those ideals now. If you mean justice between man and man—down town, as well as up town—in less than a year, you'll wish yourself dead."

"I mean just that," affirmed Philip, his exaltation seizing him in its grasp. "I shall mean nothing less no matter what happens."

"Then you have my intense admiration—and condolences," announced David. "You belong to the race of martyrs."

"So does every Jew," replied the Rabbi, with quiet dignity. "I won't shirk my share."

"You won't be allowed to," asserted David with cheerful confidence. "Your own congregation will arrange your torments."

By this time, Mr. Kaufman, still smarting under the wound sustained by him during the earlier minutes of the dinner, felt called upon as President of Beth El, to repel the attack made by this presumptuous alien.

"My dear Dr. Graetz," he announced patronizingly, "you must not permit yourself to be alarmed by Mr. Gordon—who has never, I believe, been a member of our congregation, or of any other, for that matter. You shall have our earnest support. We are not in the habit of making martyrs of our Rabbis."

"You have never had one who made you take him with enough seriousness," was David's manner of tossing Kaufman aside. " When he begins to interfere with your business, you'll cultivate the habit."

Arthur Kahn, at this point, apparently convinced that Respectability needed a younger and more virile champion, took up the gage.

" I presume, Mr. Gordon," he said superciliously, " it is hardly Dr. Graetz's intention to drag his religion through the mire of business and politics."

"You do find them pretty dirty, then, I take it?" asked the lawyer blandly.

The young Rabbi felt that should the discussion become dissipated in trivialities or personalities, his silence might appear to have committed him to a course of inaction foreign to his beliefs. He therefore gently interposed his own idea.

" If you will pardon me for interrupting," he said, "my position seems to me very simple. I have no desire to intrude my own views regarding business or politics upon my congregation, except where I find a clean-cut question of moral right and wrong. On such issues, I shall certainly expect to take a definite stand—and a vigorous one."

The ladies beamed upon their courageous young minister, but David Gordon still frowned dangerously.

" Questions of right and wrong are subtle," he argued. " My right is your wrong. When you try to force your own theories on others, your ordeal will begin."

" You forget," was Arthur Kahn's comment, " the factor of personality. Dr. Graetz," he continued, with pointed emphasis, " fortunately is not altogether devoid of tact. He will be able to say and do things which certain other people could venture only at the risk of riot."

The lawyer who should have been completely over-whelmed, merely laughed.

" Tact," he repeated, " we do find it a great help some-times, don't we, Mr. Kahn? Now, let's see. You stand, Dr. Graetz, for spiritual values—particularly Jewish ones —even in business, but like Mr. Kahn, you will cultivate a tender regard for tact. Let's see how it works out. Mr. Kaufman is engaged, on a huge scale, in making gar-ments. He's a Jew and a member of your congregation. The bulk of his laborers are likewise Jews, although they have not the inestimable advantage of being members of Beth El Temple. Still, the relation between employing Jews and laboring Jews is a field where one might expect to bring Jewish idealism to bear, isn't it? "

Everyone at the table except the Rabbi seemed to feel a sense of tension. But Dr. Graetz answered without an instant's uneasiness:

" Undoubtedly."

" Well then," the lawyer resumed, " let us suppose a struggle to arise between these two classes of your fel-low Jews. Suppose the usual pleasant details—sullen men on the verge of violence, starved women, dying babies. And suppose, in addition, the almost impossible: Imagine Mr. Kaufman and his partners to be in the wrong—a thing, I take it, which has never occurred in the past, and is extremely unlikely to occur in the future. Still, it's possible. How will your tact help you? "

Even Dr. Frank, who delighted in seeing his wife's smug family made vaguely uncomfortable, felt things had gone too far, particularly now, since this innocent young man had become involved, but before he could come to the rescue, Ruth anticipated him.

"Now, Mr. Gordon," the young girl exclaimed, with a hint of generous indignation in her voice, "you must realize what an unfair thing it is to expect a stranger in our City to say, off-hand, just what he would do under such trying conditions!"

"Ruth's right," Dr. Frank added, more smoothly. "You're asking what I think you lawyers would call a hypothetical question, of a man who hasn't had time to make himself an expert."

Dr. Graetz, once more, refused to be extricated from his dilemma.

"I do not wish," he began with an appealing sincerity, "to evade Mr. Gordon's question. It's true I don't know the local conditions, but I do know what I conceive to be my own duty. If I believed Mr. Kaufman's position to be unethical, I should go to him frankly and explain just where I thought he was in error. I should be perfectly sure he would be as anxious to do what is right as I would be to have him do it. If I were misinformed, he would convince me. If he were in the wrong, I should be able to make him understand why he ought to change his course, because he'd know I wanted absolutely nothing but simple justice."

There was a moment's silence. David was about to retort with some sarcasm, but looking into Philip's flushed, earnest face, he seemed to think better of it, and said nothing. Finally, Mr. Kaufman, touched by the young Rabbi's boyish faith in all human goodness, said heartily:

"You would be quite right, Dr. Graetz. If you came

to me, I'd meet you in just your own spirit. We all want to be fair. To be anything else would not only be doing wrong—it would be bad business policy, besides."

The Rabbi smiled at him confidingly. But the lawyer and the surgeon exchanged a smile of a somewhat less innocent quality.

Just then, Elizabeth, breathing a sigh of relief because this uncomfortable dinner was, at last, ended, rose and led the way to the living-room. Often she had indulged vague intentions of inaugurating in her home the custom of leaving the men at the table, to follow the women after a discreet interval. She had never done so because she knew and feared the opinion of those of her dear friends who would view her innovation as an evidence of sheer affectation. Tonight she congratulated herself on her informality. What would have become of these men, without the restraining influence of gentle woman, was a problem upon which she could not dwell without horror.

CHAPTER IV.

POST-PRANDIAL

CONVERSATION is always a dangerous pastime, except among people whose mental equipment qualifies them to talk glibly, without saying anything. Elizabeth had no such confidence in her guests tonight. Yet the polite fiction that men and women meet to exchange ideas is one which cannot be too blithely ignored. Had Elizabeth's dinner party occurred twenty-five years earlier, the men would have retired to some convenient card room to forget all irritating abstractions in " pinochle," while the deserted women would have solaced their loneliness with amiable chatter about domestic mishaps. In this enlightened year, 1915, however, such childish solutions were no longer feasible. None of the men present played cards at all, except Mr. Kaufman, who would have found the stakes and conditions of play, in this home, absolutely uninteresting, even could he have been provided with companions.

Still, these unruly males must not be allowed to drift once more into unlicensed talk. In this dilemma, Elizabeth's quick wit contrived the expedient of ending the evening by an appeal to music—not so much because of the traditional power of melody to bring peace to ruffled souls, but because well-bred men and women (or even moderately ill-bred ones) cannot possibly commit the crime of speech while someone else is singing. And this is true, no matter how bad the music may be, or how witty the phrase which trembles tantalizingly upon one's own lips. Besides, Ruth's singing was by no means bad. She sang, as she did everything, not remarkably well, not with any originality, but gracefully and acceptably. Her voice was not one of great volume, and now and then her method showed traces of a sad laxness of discipline, but on the other hand, she chose simple ballads which were not calculated to over-emphasize her defects.

Above all, she looked amazingly pretty as she sang, a fact of which she was not entirely unaware, and of which the more experienced Elizabeth was still more definitely informed.

Therefore, the remainder of the evening passed placidly enough. None of the group—not even David Gordon —was without some measure of that ardent love of music which is part of the Jewish heritage, and the sight of a pretty girl singing just such songs as could be lazily enjoyed without the faintest mental effort, brought a pleasing sense of contentment.

On the whole, Elizabeth, as she dismissed her guests, was not altogether displeased with the result of her evening. It was easy to see that Philip had gone away steeped with pleasant recollections of his hostess' charming young sister, whose kindness and beauty of face and voice, he would not soon forget. After all, the rest didn't much matter.

To her husband's hurried question, asked as he made ready to drive to the hospital:

" Well, didn't I behave like a pattern host out of the *Ladies' Home Journal?* " she had responded with a laugh and a good-night kiss, and sent him off without reproaches to do his " bit of surgery " as he had put it.

As for David Gordon, it did not occur to her to imagine what his impressions of the evening had been, and had she known, she would have cared very little.

After declining Dr. Frank's hearty invitation to drive him to his home (which he could easily pass on his route to the Hospital) David walked briskly down the tree-lined length of Eutaw Place, in the crisp Autumn night, wondering if he, too, would have become smug and complacent if his life had been cast among these dainty creatures who steadfastly turned their eyes away from all repulsive things. There was Ruth, of course;—she was still young; she had possibilities; she and her position could be made useful, too; but a life time full of artificialities was something of a price to pay for anything existence could offer. In the midst of the reverie, he found himself directly opposite Temple Beth El, its stately white lines standing out clear and utterly cold in the moonlight. How amazingly incongruous its classic beauty and simplicity of design seemed to the life of these men and women, who, casting aside their own racial genius and artistic cravings, had hired some Christian architect to fashion his alien dream into the marble they had bought. How like a mausoleum it appeared in its deserted grandeur! Could the religious impulse buried in this tomb be quickened again to life, even by the ardent enthusiasm of a Philip Graetz? A Graetz, confronted and hemmed in, ever and always, by a score of Clarence Kaufmans, waiting at every turn to translate generous poetry into the deadly prose of practicability? Then, there flashed into David's mind the idea of a Herculean statue of Clarence Kaufman, dominating the great portico of the synagogue. He almost saw it there, in the shadow, gross, insistent, earthy, and irresistibly menacing. He laughed aloud at his whimsical fantasy and hurried on.

CHAPTER V

The Fashion in Prophets

One of the most mysterious causes for speculation in a world not too intelligible at the best, lies in wondering how a fashion suddenly arises in a community, and like the Pied Piper, leads an entire population of grown-up children joyously dancing in its train.

The Pied Piper himself (if he had been truthful enough to admit it) was no doubt somewhat puzzled by his spectacular popularity, and maybe indulged more than one secret misgiving regarding the next tune he would choose to pipe when his youthful audience should at last find itself slightly bored by his unconventional quickstep.

During the few months following Mrs. Frank's dinner, Philip Graetz without knowing just why or how, became something of a fashion. He was overwhelmed with invitations to dinners, luncheons and teas. He was fêted whenever he could produce no legitimate excuse, and upon every conceivable occasion, he was forced to deliver an address. He found himself talking almost without cessation. Women's Clubs, Amateur Societies for the cure of all Social ills, Students' Leagues, Bible Study Classes— all these and many more claimed the privilege of listening to this tall, dark youth with the flashing eyes and rich vibrant voice, who had a trick of making all women and many men suspect the existence in themselves of some vague thing which he called spirituality.

Nor was this enthusiasm confined altogether to members of Philip's own race. He was constantly receiving and accepting invitations to talk before groups composed partly or completely of non-Jews, and his reception at such times was no less hearty and inspiring than among his brothers in the faith. For all that, the young Rabbi did not fail to perceive, without much effort, how rigidly his intercourse with Gentiles was restricted to activities occurring elsewhere than in their own homes. When he lunched down town, he was deluged with the cordiality and good fellowship of Protestants and Catholics, as well as Jews. A few non-Jews of a more skeptical tendency than his own mind approved, found him well worth while, and sought permission to visit the modest bachelor quarters he had established in a quiet hotel near his Temple; but neither Protestant, Catholic nor Agnostic asked him to dine with his wife and daughters. He received invitations to exchange pulpits with Christian ministers but not to exchange visits among their families. They found it necessary, apparently, to maintain an exclusiveness in their own homes which could safely be dispensed with, in the House of God. Philip was not hurt at these mild manifestations of a social exclusion. He accepted them as a matter of course, and like many another man who has had much less encouragement went steadily on talking. He did it exceedingly well, and had he not had a fair appreciation of that agreeable fact to begin with, he must have come to discover it, without delay. Everyone, Jew and Gentile, told him how inspiring he was; how eloquent; how purposeful he made life seem. The ladies told him this with much more wealth of detail than the men, which was an economic waste, because at twenty-four (and for an indefinite period thereafter) a man invariably finds one word of feminine praise worth a score of compliments of prosaic masculine origin. Philip, however, was lucky or unlucky enough to have both varieties from which to choose.

Altogether he kept his poise surprisingly well—all the better perhaps because, now and then, he was troubled by some dim suspicion that he was being acclaimed much, but followed little, if at all. At most times he succeeded in pushing these doubts aside by reminding himself that he stood at the very threshold of his ministry and that the task he had set himself was one which would certainly demand a life time of endeavor. Meanwhile, he went on drifting comfortably with the rapid current of petty events, tending without knowing it to become just a little more disposed to accept his parishioners' flattering views of himself; just a trifle more complacent, and ready to fit himself into the niche which was waiting expectantly for him.

His congregation had never a doubt regarding his well-regulated and respectable future. In the natural course of events he would cease to be a novel figure in the life of Baltimore's Jewish community, but he would lose none of his prominence. He would be asked to talk less often, but his influence would be stronger because of his ever-widening circle of personal friendships. He would find time for some leisurely seminary work in the Semitic department of the Johns Hopkins University, and would ultimately be awarded the degree of Doctor of Philosophy without having neglected in its pursuit any of his ministerial duties. He would affiliate himself, as a matter of course, with the proper number of organizations for Social and Civic Betterment. He had already accepted membership upon the Board of Directors of the Jewish Charity

THE FASHION IN PROPHETS

Organization Society. He would lead a useful, untroubled life of pleasant routine—and above all things he must, of necessity, and without undue delay, marry and establish a hearth and home of his own.

Perhaps many of the fair communicants of Beth El gave to this phase of their Rabbi's career far more earnest thought than they were able to bestow upon his plans for spiritualizing the City's commerce and social life. The religious cravings of more than one devout maiden might have been translated by a brutal masculine spectator into terms of indefinite dreams regarding a handsome, thoughtful youth, with graceful manners and a startling gift for sympathizing with all one's woes and hopes. True, this sympathy was secretly voted to be a shade too indiscriminate. Judith would have appreciated it far more had not Miriam, Eve and Jessica—to say nothing, alas, of Max and Joseph—tasted also of its soothing qualities. It was commendable enough to love all mankind, but applied to womankind as well, too much of virtue seemed little less exasperating than a vice; all the more of a vice, because it was a thing to which one was forced in mere decency, to give, in public, an apparent approval. There was no end of conjecture expended upon this seemingly inevitable event in Philip's life. Not a few of the fair prophetesses who purported to speak with authority found their calm, judicial judgment somewhat warped by an uncontrollable desire to shape, as well as to foretell, the course of coming events, and in more than one case there was a definite belief in the utter futility of faith without works; but in the opinion of most observers who had no personal hopes or fears to color their decision, it was agreed that Ruth Hartman would sooner or later become

47

the minister's wife. It would be such a suitable union!
She was pretty; she was young and her income was amazingly huge. There were few girls who worshipped at Beth
El who were not fairly wealthy, but Ruth was unique in
being, at the same time, unusually rich and without any
living parent to exercise uncomfortable veto powers upon
a girl's freedom of action. It was easy to see how much
of an impression she had made upon Philip. When he
found himself with rare evenings to spend as he chose, he
usually drifted to her home, and she, for her part, had
no scruples about capriciously breaking whatever engagements she might have accepted, to fit Philip's unpremeditated plans.

She had found Arthur Kahn much more than endurable, because, supercilious and impressed as he was with
his own supreme importance, he was pliant in her hands;
she had been keenly interested in Gordon,—partly because
he seemed resolutely determined to be betrayed into no
entangling alliance with a girl of another and a hostile
class, and partly because she knew he was for her a forbidden creature, who might with much art be forced,
against his will, to play a sour, cynical, yet intellectual,
Romeo to her highly decorative Juliet. There were many
other men, besides, who had hovered about this rather
spoiled young Ruth and from among whom she had
intended, in her own good time, to choose, at last, a fortunate and obedient mate. But Philip, from their first meeting, seemed to her to be made of other stuff than the clay
of which the men she knew were molded. He was
totally oblivious of all considerations of money, and that
she liked tremendously, with the enthusiasm of a girl who
has never known the logical consequences of poverty, and

who had been too well warned regarding the attractive qualities of her own dowry. He refused to accept with seriousness her little qualities of selfishness and lack of consideration for others. He neither defied her imperiousness as David Gordon had done, nor obeyed her whims as Arthur Kahn still did. He assumed with a smile, her intense desire to do, think and say the sweet and lovable thing which must be characteristic of herself. Sometimes she almost became what she believed he thought her, and whenever this occurred Ruth felt more tenderly toward her spiritual guide. A gracious lady owes no small debt of gratitude to any man who can cause her, without the slightest discomfort to herself, or the sacrifice of a single one of the pleasant things of life, to feel nobler, purer and stronger. Ruth showed no unwillingness to pay her debt.

He was fortunate, also, in being too busy to be ever at her beck and call. She could never be perfectly sure he would appear when he had promised, though he never failed to send some message telling of a claim upon him which he had been forced to obey " knowing she would have been disgusted with him had he shirked his duty, even to be with her." It gave a tinge of uncertainty to whatever hold upon him she possessed; and, again, of necessity, there were scores of other women—attractive ones too—with whom in the very nature of things his relations must be constant and intimate. The much-wooed Ruth was more than once as near the verge of jealousy as a well-bred, college-schooled maid can permit herself to wander, and always and most irritatingly, without the shadow of a plausible excuse in Philip's conduct.

She found herself thinking about him, more often than

she cared to admit. She could not but notice how well the two of them looked together; she found a real pleasure in observing how much more interestingly he talked than most of her other acquaintances; how much more enthusiasm he possessed; how clean and wholesome were his thoughts,—often impracticable, certainly, but all the more boyishly charming, she told herself, with that mature wisdom upon which very young girls always pride themselves until their years actually justify its possession.

Perhaps he appealed to her most strongly because she knew there was something fine and precious in him which she would never understand. For Ruth, deep below the habits of thought and action which were born of much wealth and little discipline, loved without knowing just why, what seemed to her beauty of character, no less than she loved beauty of line and color.

Had he asked her to marry him during those first months of his ministry she might have pretended to weigh the question gravely, but there would have been no doubt of her favorable reply. Week after week went by, however, and still he did not speak to her of marriage. Each of them seemed to find a genuine pleasure in the other's presence. Each made opportunities for as many meetings as could be arranged by these much-sought young people. Sometimes, on late afternoons they strolled slowly through the Park—forgetting to notice its austere December beauty as they exchanged confidences upon the myriad subjects which lose their importance for us as we become older and wiser, and color-blind to the delicate shades of self-revelation possible only to Youth.

Sometimes she drove him far into the Green Spring Valley, or into the Hills of Howard in the trim little motor car she prided herself upon managing better than any mere man could do. These fragmentary excursions were supposedly to exhibit to Philip something of the charms of Maryland, but the attractions of his dainty guide completely obscured those of the country-side, and Ruth was far too intelligent to have anticipated any other result. When the musical season began, she persuaded him to become her guest at the series of concerts given by the Boston Symphony Orchestra and though her box seated six persons with comfort, she constantly neglected to issue other invitations, or if she did remember, her guests by some strange fatality, always failed her at the last minute.

She was perfectly well aware that she was causing their names to be coupled together in the gossip of the huge whisper gallery of the Jewish community. She did not care. He, being only a man, and one not yet accustomed to the peculiar qualities of Baltimore's echoes, was less keenly conscious than she of the construction which would, perforce, be placed upon their companionship; nevertheless, his thoughts on the subject were far more troubled than hers. For unlike all heroes of romance (though perhaps the phenomenon is more common in daily life) Philip was not perfectly sure he wanted to marry Ruth. He could not have told why. He found her charming to talk with, a delight to his sensitive love of beauty, and quick to understand and appreciate his enthusiasms and hopes. But while he was always glad to be with her it did not cause him an iota of unhappiness to be separated from her, and this circumstance awoke in him a definite uneasiness. He had never before had much time for girls, and his views regarding love and marriage were mostly borrowed from books. He had read what the

Divine Passion ought to do to a man, and as he scanned himself he failed to identify the classical symptoms. It would be pleasant to marry Ruth, certainly, but he felt constrained to admit that should she fling herself into the arms of another, he would not find life the empty, mocking void conventional under the circumstances. He would still remain intensely interested in his own work and his own plans. This was not the fine, all-satisfying rapture of which he frequently spoke when he was called upon to officiate at marriage ceremonies, bringing by his words deep thrills to the imagination of brides, and a sense of bewilderment to less introspective grooms.

Therefore, in his own case, he was willing to let the weeks glide into months while he awaited some stronger urge than he had hitherto experienced. Nor was Ruth sorry because of his delay. She found this stage of something more than friendship, inexpressibly sweet. It must, of course, transform itself, before long, into the definiteness of a betrothal. Meanwhile, its very illusiveness lent it charm.

Ruth's sister, Elizabeth, however, failed to share the girl's contented patience. She desired this marriage keenly, not as her husband pretended to believe from a " sheer weariness of having no other lives to arrange save his own, and the children's," but because she really felt the Rabbi would bring a happiness and a steadiness into Ruth's life. She knew she had indulged and petted the little sister left in her care, far more than was good for her. Since she had ceased to be a child, Ruth had taken quite naturally to indulging and petting herself. Elizabeth, now and then, gave way to a nervous spasm of dread lest the girl should, some day, marry in the same impetuous way in which she bought the pictures or motor cars which happened to catch her fancy. Mrs. Frank was seeking in Philip someone who should, with the most perfect mildness, correct her own mistakes in dealing with Ruth. This might be a bit inconvenient for Philip, but he would find compensations.

Dr. Frank never listened with seriousness to his wife's forebodings. He was nearly as fond as was Elizabeth of his pretty young sister-in-law, but his greater detachment gave him a fairer estimate of her practicality. His fears for Ruth tended in precisely the opposite direction from those of his wife. Ruth knew values. The pictures she purchased, however impulsively, were usually worth what she paid for them, and the automobile she had bought proved far more reliable than Dr. Frank's own car. The surgeon believed Ruth would always arrange her life to serve her own comfort and what he dreaded for her was a consequent degeneration into a flabby worthlessness of mind and spirit. He wanted her to choose something difficult and fight it through. He would have liked it better had her accomplishments come to her with less facility. He thought he knew just how unwieldy of body and clumsy of brain she would be at forty if she married some eminently suitable person, like Arthur Kahn. He had not scrupled to enlarge upon this idea with much annoying detail to both Ruth and Elizabeth. Regarding Philip, he was more doubtful. Ruth might really throw herself, whole-heartedly, into her enthusiast-lover's dreams, and rise to higher stature fighting his hopeless fights,—provided, always, the man really intended to do anything but talk. If he were merely going to be a fashionable social ornament, he would be the worst possible husband for a girl who was herself all too prone to such a fate. Meanwhile, he stole covert glances at the progress of the idyll, and implored his wife to cease from trying to play Destiny.

Incidentally, he amused himself more than a little by watching Elizabeth's burning impatience.

He came home late one night in December after a day of unusual effort—even for him—and was about to enter the living-room when Elizabeth beckoned him toward the library.

"Dr. Graetz and Ruth are in there," she whispered.

"Well, suppose——," he answered laughingly. "Your grandfather would have walked in boldly and insisted on knowing what his intentions happened to be. Life was simpler in those days."

"Indeed it was," his wife sighed fervently. "Now-a-days girls do these things for themselves—and badly."

He lifted her hand to his lips and then pointed significantly to her wedding ring.

"Not always so badly," he smiled, "not always!"

"Of course, my dear," she retorted good-humoredly, "when I succeeded in ensnaring you, I was an unusually lucky woman. You thoughtfully remind me of it, now and then. But it doesn't change the rule. Now Ruth——"

"How far have they got?" Robert interrupted. "Last time I eavesdropped they were talking glibly of plans for advancing the Brotherhood of Man. It struck me as malapropos. The Fatherhood idea should have been in this young man's mind——."

"Robert!" his wife exclaimed, "I believe you're growing positively coarse!"

"Perhaps," he conceded. "All day long I've been tinkering with people's insides. It makes one elemental.

I never once thought about making them noble. I was merely concerned in keeping them alive, if possible. Preachers and women see these things from one angle, ploughmen and surgeons from another. Is Ruth really going to marry him, jilt him, or keep me out of my living-room forever?"

"I don't know," Elizabeth admitted. "I can't get her to talk about him at all."

"Oh," the surgeon announced easily, "then we might as well discuss wedding presents. If she won't talk about him, she really wants him, and if she wants him it doesn't matter what his views are."

"I don't know," Elizabeth repeated. "Things with them seem about where they were more than a month ago."

"It doesn't matter, Bess, if Ruth has really made up her mind!" was Robert's final comment. "Of course, he would be a bit languid, being a chap who makes a living by mere talk. Anyhow, all men are potterers by trade except physicians and surgeons. Now that I think of it, even physicians potter some."

CHAPTER VI

The Brotherhood of Man

THE first incident tending to unsettle Philip's faith in himself and his work was so totally irrelevant, so completely unrelated to his own life or to the interests of his congregation, that it might easily have left a man of more phlegmatic temperament absolutely undisturbed.

About eleven o'clock one night in January he was slowly and deliberately making ready for bed. Although weary of body he was more than normally pleased with himself. He had made, this evening, at a public Emergency meeting, held in the vestry rooms of Beth El, a well-conceived and beautifully delivered plea for funds for the Jewish Charities—whose treasury had been strained almost to the point of bankruptcy by demands resulting from the violent economic changes caused by the European war. He had pictured eloquently the unendurable misery existent in the city, although his only knowledge of its actual details had been obtained from the routine reports of the Society's paid workers. The tangible results of his words in Dollars and Cents had been amazingly gratifying—even to the Society's skilful managing director, who had shrewdly decided, as he put it, "to play the new Rabbi as a trump card." Philip had done a good evening's work. Many unfortunate creatures would escape lack of food and shelter, because of the compelling force of his thought and imagination. Incidentally, this virtuous deed had been one which would entail pleasant personal consequences to himself. There are few of us—however contemptuous in theory of the shallow admiration of our fellows—who could have returned home from such a meeting without a comfortable glow of self-satisfaction—and Philip was only twenty-four years of age—and had believed ardently in the lovable qualities of all men, even before they had begun to demonstrate these virtues by extravagant praise of himself.

The reaction after his speech left him unusually worn, and he had hurried home from the Temple to enjoy what seemed to him a well-earned night of sleep. Just as he was in that debatable stage where one is neither properly garbed nor disreputably negligee, the telephone bell rang sharply and he sprang to obey its summons.

It was a woman's voice who spoke. " Is this Rabbi Graetz? " she demanded.

When he assured her of his identity she continued in the measured tones of a competent subordinate, performing a routine duty—not unimportant—but one which demanded no display of undue excitement.

" This is the Johns Hopkins Hospital," she announced. " The Resident has ordered me to ask some Rabbi if he could come here at once to see a man in the accident ward. The patient's injuries will probably prove fatal, the doctor thinks. We know nothing of the man except that he keeps asking to see a Rabbi. Will you come? "

" Certainly," Philip answered, " immediately! I'll order a taxi. What shall I do when I reach the Hospital? "

" Go to the desk in the entrance hall and ask for Miss Watts," he was told, after which the voice extinguished itself promptly, with a business-like click of the telephone instrument.

It was certainly characteristic of Philip that he had not indulged in even an instant's hesitation before accepting his duty. There were many extenuating circumstances he might have urged as excuses for inaction. He was tired, not because of mere frivolity, but because he had been engaged in work for the good of others. It was a night of sudden and penetrating cold after a day of dull rain, and the streets were covered with a thin and treacherous sheet of ice. As a matter of fact, one of his older brothers in the Rabbinate had been given priority by the Hospital nurse in her telephoned request, and had promptly pleaded a convenient indisposition. It was to this worthy man's thoughtful consideration that Philip owed his present necessity for a hurried trip to the opposite side of the city.

After summoning a taxi-cab, by telephone, he hastily replaced his discarded clothing and descended to the vestibule of the Hotel, there to await the arrival of the automobile. It seemed abnormally long in making its appearance, but when it finally drew up to the curb, its chauffeur explained how impossible it was for any machine, even if it were equipped with chains, to make rapid progress on such a night. Philip peered through the frosty windows of the cab as it threaded its deliberate path through unfamiliar streets. He noticed with a sense of growing depression row after row of small, monotonous homes, each one exactly like its neighbor. Through his mind, in unison with the steady throb of the motor, coursed somber and unconnected fancies. He thought of his errand, and the next minute found himself wondering into which of these staid, uncharacteristic little structures Death would make his next raid, bringing into the drab lives of its occupants, perhaps, the only touch of dramatic dignity they would ever know; and next his imagination was deciding what words he could find to say by way of consolation to the strange man to whose aid he was hurrying, and who, perchance, by morning would be far wiser than himself and all other living men, with a new-found knowledge of the mysteries of Life and Death.

At last the machine came to a stop before the great pile of Hospital Buildings, and Philip dashed up the steps, and into the vast rotunda of the central building. Breathless, and taken completely by surprise, he found himself face to face with Thorwaldsen's great white statue of the Christ, the arms outstretched, the face filled with Divine Compassion. So significant was this huge mass of eloquent marble that there was scarcely need for the chiselled inscription—"Come unto Me, all ye who are weary and heavy laden, and I will give you Rest."

The young Rabbi unconsciously paused, and paid full and heartfelt tribute to the memory of the Great Rabbi of Bethlehem, who has been chosen by millions as the symbol of Infinite Love, yet whose name has been invoked by myriads of false followers in justification of deeds of fiendish cruelty. "He too was a Jew, and a teacher of our faith," was the thought which flashed into Philip's mind, immediately to give place to his own characteristic idea. "After all, it is we, who will not believe Him to be more than He truly was, who understand Him best,—who can best teach the world what He meant it to know." Filled with such emotions, he remembered his own mission of helpful ministry, and making his way to the desk, introduced himself and explained his purpose. The night clerk promptly telephoned to some mysterious personage and very shortly thereafter a trim, tall, young woman, dressed in stiffly-starched blue, came to his side and beckoned him to follow her. It was difficult to believe one could walk so great a distance without passing beyond the confines of the Hospital. Along many corridors, Philip was led by his guide. Each hall, with its dim lights reflected upon the brightly-polished floor, seemed almost deserted, yet somehow pervaded by an uncanny air of being ever watched by tireless attendants. He had never before entered this, or any other great Hospital, and the impression created in his mind was almost one of awe. Behind each of the doors Science was at grips with disease and death. Every instant was pregnant with Fate for scores who lay in their neat, white beds, unaware whether they should return again to take up their petty, engrossing anxieties and ambitions, or mingle themselves with the dust from which they had sprung. Now and then, a nurse or orderly would glide swiftly and noiselessly into some patient's room. Once they passed a physician garbed in spotless white linen, hurrying quickly upon some duty of apparent urgency. They paused at the turn of a hallway to avoid interference with two orderlies bearing upon a narrow litter the inanimate form of a patient still drugged with ether, on his way from the operating table to some place where he would await the mysterious return of the soul, which had somehow left his body untenanted during its hour of supreme ordeal. Yet all this intense drama was enacted in an atmosphere of abnormal quiet, like the death struggle of a mouse imprisoned under the glass vacuum bell of an air pump. The Rabbi felt oppressed, impotent, his own importance completely crushed out among these silent creatures who dealt without a shadow of excitement with the issues of health and agony, existence and eternity.

During all this time the young nurse had spoken no

word. Philip, as he followed her, gave another swift thought to the possibilities of the interview which lay before him. It was an unusual thing for a Jew on the threshold of Death to seek the aid of a Rabbi. A teacher in Israel is not believed by the most credulous of his followers to possess any greater power than any other poor mortal, to pardon sin or to intercede on behalf of a conscience-stricken penitent, with an offended and outraged God. Some very practical errand, or last message, no doubt, was to be entrusted to him by a forsaken, friendless creature whose desire for a Rabbi was based upon the knowledge that in such a man he could not fail to find a Jew—and therefore, a brother.

Philip's opportunity for conjecture came to a sudden end, for his conductress turned suddenly from the corridor into a small office where at a study desk there sat, apparently awaiting the Rabbi's entrance, a vigorous young doctor dressed in the white Hospital uniform.

"You're Dr. Graetz?" he began, motioning Philip to a seat, and speaking in brisk but not discourteous tones. He did not give Philip opportunity to reply before going on to say:

"I'm Dr. Manning. I'm in charge here till morning. It's not such an appropriate night for being dragged across town, is it? Still, I thought I ought to do something about this chap. He's a Hebrew." The doctor paused slightly before using the word, as though he were anxious to choose a term bearing the least offensive significance.

At another time the minister would have explained tolerantly his preference for the word "Jew," and repelled the idea of anyone of that race being anxious to escape its implications; but now he merely nodded, and the physician continued:

"He's an accident case. Slipped tonight, on a crossing at Baltimore Street, and one wheel of a heavy auto-truck passed over his abdomen."

Philip struggled unsuccessfully to restrain a shudder of horror, and the man of medicine noticed it with professional contempt.

"You needn't get squeamish. You won't see anything to shock you. He's covered up all right!"

"It isn't that!" Philip protested feebly, but there was a definite lack of conviction in his tones.

"Well," Dr. Manning said, "they brought him in here and took him into the operating room, but the house surgeons said, at the first glimpse, he hadn't a chance. He's sure to "go out" pretty soon, and meanwhile, all we can make out of him is the word "Rabbi." He says it over and over again. He's still conscious, but we can't learn his name or anything else. If he'd been an Italian or an Irishman and had called for a priest, he'd have got one, so I thought if he wanted a Rabbi I ought to try to find one for him."

"I thank you very much," Philip responded. "I hope I'll be able to make him more comfortable. Does it matter how long I stay?"

"Not a bit," the physician answered coolly. "He's got no chance anyhow. I took him off the ward and into a private room because I didn't want him to disturb the other patients too much. So make yourself as comfortable as you can, and if you want anything, ask Miss Watts to send for me. She'll take you to him at once."

The nurse, who had remained silently standing in the presence of her superior, and who would have been shocked rather than gratified had the doctor suggested her being seated during the interview, now betrayed prompt signs of returning animation.

She opened the office door significantly so that Philip would have had no reasonable opportunity for further questions even had he meditated them, and without delay, led him once more upon his quest.

A minute later she ushered him into a small room with one great window through which there was visible, against the cold brilliance of an electric street lamp, a great wind-tossed tree, every twig of which was covered with a beautiful garment of glistening ice. The gray walled room was utterly bare except for a bed, a chair, and a tiny table bearing upon it a glass of water and a nurse's chart.

The form upon the bed was covered to the chin with a white sheet, but a long, nervous, ill-kempt hand lay wearily on either side of the patient's body, and on the pillow was the head of a man whose every feature proclaimed the Jew. Not the Jew one would have expected to meet at Beth El Temple, or in Mrs. Frank's elegant living-room, but one who had known misery and hatred in the Old World, and who had fled from it to experience hardship, privation and grinding poverty in free and boundless America. His long and untrimmed beard was coarse and of the blackness of charred wood. It accentuated to an almost ghost-like whiteness the deathly pallor of his brow; but his eyes, in his hour of mute despair, were fine—great, dark, intelligent eyes—which seemed haunted with a tragedy the man himself could never have expressed or understood, even when he had been vigorous and full of abundant life.

The eloquent eyes rested inquiringly upon the intruders, and the nurse spoke with the slow distinct accents one uses to children, and to men who cannot comprehend the only language one can talk.

" The Rabbi," she announced, pointing to Philip,— " the Rabbi."

The dying man's eyes lighted up with an expression of eager hope, unspeakably touching to his young visitor. This broken creature was poor, helpless and unlettered. The life he was yielding up had been sordid and unbeautiful, but still this forlorn immigrant shared with himself the wonderful traditions of the Martyr Race, and in his crude way had borne all too heavy a share of its agony. He hurried to the bedside, and grasped the weak, useless hand in his own.

Then the mangled man on the bed began to talk in harsh dry tones spoken almost in a whisper, but with headlong feverish haste. The nurse was about to leave them to their confidences, but Philip stopped her with a gesture of consternation.

He was unable to understand one single phrase the poor creature was racking his soul to utter!

Why had he not thought to ask what tongue this man could speak, or why had not the Hospital authorities made sure before sending for him, of his primary qualifications for the task? Now and then Philip caught the sound of some familiar, though mispronounced, word of Teutonic origin, but the sense of what was being told to him was utterly lost.

The Rabbi spoke German—bookishly, it was true— but nevertheless, fluently. With Hebrew also he was perfectly familiar. Of the Yiddish dialect he knew nothing at all. Had this immigrant's vocabulary been composed almost entirely of words borrowed or corrupted from the Hebrew and German tongues, Philip might have succeeded in piecing together the significance of the torrent of words which issued from the lips of the sufferer. But unfortunately, Yiddish is a varied and fluid mode of speech. In the mouths of wanderers from some sections of Europe, it may easily be mistaken for an ungrammatical and degenerate form of the German language. Other Jews, however, speak the dialect with so many infusions of words and accents appropriated from the Russian, as to make it totally unintelligible to anyone uninitiated in its baffling perplexities.

The patient, who was now staring desperately into the Rabbi's face, had come to the scene of his death from the wrong Russian village!

Frantically, Philip began talking to the man in his own grammatical German and instantaneously, the light of intelligence left the patient's eyes, and a look of dumb, puzzled misunderstanding appeared in its place.

Again and again Philip tried his utmost to find some method of communication with the injured man. He only succeeded in awakening in this mind, to which he had intended to bring peace and comfort, a reflection of his own excitement. The guttural whisper became sullen,—almost angry—and the one word which the Rabbi could understand in the immigrant's outbursts of despairing protest was the contemptuous syllable " goy "—which he knew to be this dying man's pitiless judgment upon himself as one who was in truth no Jew at all—a stranger and an alien.

" It's no use," Philip said helplessly, turning to the nurse. "I can't find out what he wants to say. He speaks nothing but Yiddish. You should have sent for a downtown Rabbi—a Russian."

THE CHOSEN PEOPLE

The nurse, quick to repel any blame which might be imputed to her in this unexpected dilemma, replied quickly:

"I had to use the telephone directory. Down-town Rabbis can't afford telephones. Besides, I thought any Rabbi would do."

Her voice expressed a polite contempt for a religion so loosely organized to aid its distressed communicants. Had the man been a Roman Catholic the first priest she had summoned would have been fully equipped to cope with the situation, or at least to find prompt assistance, if for some reason he had found himself unprepared for his task!

"We must find him a Rabbi who is a Russian Jew, at once," Philip announced.

"I'll take you back to Dr. Manning," replied Miss Watts, evidently determined to become entangled in no further responsibilities.

The dying immigrant had relapsed once more into his former state of despairing apathy. Philip cast upon him a last glance of mingled compassion and self-reproach and returned to Dr. Manning's office. There new perplexities confronted him. The young doctor apparently considered Philip to be disgustingly ill-equipped for his duties, and had neither comprehension nor tolerance for these delicate distinctions between various kinds of Jews. To Dr. Graetz's demand that a Russian Rabbi be procured at once, the physician responded by giving him *carte blanche* to summon as many as he chose, but this permission merely disclosed another bit of deplorable ignorance on Philip's part. He was compelled to confess he did not know the name of a single minister of his own creed in the city, except those of the few fashionable

66

up-town Temples—no one of whom he had a right to suppose more proficient in Yiddish than himself.

Dr. Manning's smile savored slightly of amused cynicism. Philip, growing more miserably embarrassed every moment, yet feeling he dared not ignore his debt to his dying brother Jew, continued to rack his brain for some available solution.

"It needn't be a Rabbi, then," he urged. "Surely there must be some one in this big Hospital who can understand Yiddish."

"There is no one of your faith on the resident staff at this time," the doctor informed him patiently, "in the day time one of the young women in the Social Service Department could interpret for you, but they're all off duty now, and even if I wanted to drag one from her home at this time of night, I wouldn't know for which one to send."

"There must be plenty of Russian Jewish patients here," Philip insisted.

"There certainly are," Dr. Manning agreed, "but we don't catalogue them by race; I can't send someone through the wards waking up sick people to ask if they can talk Yiddish. I'm afraid I've done all I can."

Philip remembered suddenly that Dr. Frank had told him how often he was called to the Johns Hopkins in the small hours of the night, and it occurred to him to announce his acquaintance with the surgeon and to suggest the possibility of his aid. The young resident thawed slightly at the mention of Robert's name.

"Dr. Frank is a member of the Visiting Surgical Staff," he explained. "He's only here when he's operating or giving after care to his patients. I'm pretty sure he isn't here now, but I'll make certain."

Miss Watts, once more pressed into service, soon reported that Dr. Frank had been in the Hospital earlier in the evening but was not expected again until morning.

The thought of Dr. Frank awoke in Philip's mind some recollection of David Gordon, whom he had not seen since the night of the dinner at the surgeon's home. Here was a man who was himself of Russian birth, who could doubtless speak Yiddish, and who would, in any event, know just what should be done.

He asked permission to use the telephone and after a few anxious minutes succeeded in awakening the lawyer, and telling him excitedly the whole distressing story. Gordon was silent for an instant after Philip had completed his narrative. The young Rabbi, fearing the telephone connection had been interrupted, exclaimed impatiently: "Hello! Hello! Are you still there? Can't you tell me what to do?"

"I'm here," was the reply he heard, "let me alone a minute. I'm only a lawyer, I have to think before I can give advice." Then a minute later he was told:

"Lubowitz would come. He lives on Albemarle Street near Pratt, but he's got no telephone, and his English is so bad you'd never make him understand what you wanted if you went for him yourself. Same thing with all the others. I could give you a dozen of their names. If you think it needn't be a Rabbi, I'll come myself."

Philip's thanks were almost incoherent in their fervid gratitude, but David Gordon cut him short with rude decision.

"All right," he snapped, "you needn't make such a fuss about it. Telephone for a taxi while I get into my

68

clothes. My address is 1086 Madison Avenue. Sure you've got the number? Better write it down. I'll be right over."

The lawyer rang off without more formality, and Philip, after arranging for Gordon's transportation, reported to Dr. Manning the result of his efforts. The doctor had never met Gordon but knew of him as one of the city's most successful lawyers. He secretly wondered at the strange quality of these Jews who were willing to leap eagerly from their comfortable beds at the call of some pauper with no claim upon them except the tie of a common race. "And when they get here," he thought, "they haven't an idea what's to be done! Still it's odd how they stick together!"

If the dying man, less than a hundred yards away, could suddenly have awakened to health and intelligible speech, he might have expressed some doubts as to the accuracy of this Gentile generalization relating to the Solidarity of Israel. Or had the physician remained to chat with the Rabbi while they awaited Gordon's coming, he might somewhat have modified his judgment, but he had hardly motioned Philip to a chair before he was called away to a distant part of the Hospital upon some mission which appeared to permit of no delay.

"Help yourself to a book or a magazine," he suggested. "There are cigarettes on the table if you smoke. I'll be back as soon as I can. I'll tell the ward nurse as I pass, to keep an eye on your man."

Philip, left to himself, found the minutes dragged wearily. He had never learned the solace of tobacco, and the books on the doctor's shelf seemed painfully technical. He ran his eye hurriedly over their titles, only to find text books treating of every disease of which he had vaguely heard, and a few whose acquaintance he hoped never to make. Among all this mass of medical lore he found in a corner a volume written by William Osler, bearing the title "Aequanimitas and Other Essays." It was impossible to have lived in Baltimore even a few months without gaining some hearsay knowledge of the great physician whose name and whose personality had become a tradition, no less potent since his removal to a foreign land than when he had been part and parcel of the city's life. Philip pulled down the book with its title so oddly at variance with his own mood. He tried to read, but the words made no impression whatever upon his confused, jarring thoughts. Equanimity seemed, like many other desirable attributes, a thing one might well exalt when one happened to have it, but which was not to be procured for the mere desire. Sometimes the dark face of the injured immigrant stared up at him with great accusing eyes from the printed page, as though asking what right he had to pose as a teacher in Israel who had no comprehension of the wants of those who would stand most sorely in need of aid. Sometimes Philip was swept by wholly ignoble emotions of damaged self-esteem. He had been made to appear supremely ridiculous, he felt,—ridiculous to himself, to this business-like sprig of a doctor, and to David Gordon, who would be none too sorry to confirm his previous scoffing beliefs regarding the inefficiency of preachers in general and himself in particular. It was unfair that he, who had meant so well, should be placed in such an absurd position. He had been fed on praise ever since he had entered this hospitable city, and had unconsciously learned to shrink from the very thought of mockery.

For a minute he forgot the plight of the sufferer he

had come to aid, in his boyish resentment against every one and everything connected with his unheroic situation.

He tossed the book upon the table. Equanimity was not for him, he decided, as he began nervously to pace the floor. It certainly did take Gordon a long time to make the trip across town, he thought, until his watch convinced him to the contrary. He began once more to indulge in vain conjecture as to what this man who was about to die could have to impart. Nothing, in all probability, of any real consequence. Still, it would seem vital to a man about to set forth on this last mysterious voyage. To die among men whom one had never seen before and whose every action proclaimed their utter indifference to the personality one was about to lose— it *was* hard, it was worse than hard; it was robbing a man of one of those few emotional consolations which are the birthright of all of us—rich and poor—learned and stolid. Fantastic visions of his own death invaded the young minister's mind. He had always thought of his end as something impressive, dignified, as nearly approaching the sublime as was consistent with standards of restrained good taste. Now he could not repel perverse pictures of himself, stretched on some rude bed in a foreign country, dying as the result of some grotesque mishap, among strangers to whom his last words of profound significance and burning eloquence were merely a confused jumble of uncouth noises. Never before, since his childhood, had Philip feared Death. It was a climax, according to his faith, to a triumphant purposeful life. Now, however, as he strode from wall to wall, he felt actual terror at the thought. How could one sustain his beliefs in the supreme dignity of human

71

life and death as one remembered the mangled mass
of aching flesh in the near-by room, whose career had
seemingly been a painful quest across half the world for
bread to fill an empty belly, and whose end was the
unnoticed and matter-of-fact death of a worn-out animal?

The minutes ticked themselves away. Philip, whose
nights had never before been tempestuous, wondered
why he had failed to realize what an eternity of time
stretched between the hours of sleep and waking. Yet
there were nurses here—mere girls—who kept solitary
vigil every night! He stole to the door almost as though
he were about to attempt some actual crime, and opening
it, peered out into the long, silent corridor. If someone
would only make a noise, something loud, discordant,
human! But no, there was nothing to relieve this overpowering sensation of suppressed, watchful but coldly
unsympathetic, activity. It was like an unearthly, hideous
pantomime.

The Rabbi turned again into the office and the door
swung silently closed. He was once more the solitary
prisoner of his sense of duty. In the hope of distracting
himself with a new sensation, he seized from the table one
of the doctor's cigarettes and with some awkwardness,
succeeded in lighting it. He drew into his lungs a few
experimental puffs of smoke. The adventure only added
to his discomfort. Without feeling actually ill, he was
conscious of a slight sensation of uneasy dizziness and
confusion. Remembering the necessity of possible action
when Gordon should arrive, he tossed the cigarette into
the ash tray and resumed his solitary pacing of the room.

It was in this state of mental and physical wretched-
ness that Gordon found him. The lawyer, seemingly as
alert and as fully master of himself as though it were

noon-day, instead of two in the morning, came briskly into the office with Miss Watts.

"Hello, Dr. Graetz," he said, "you see I'm here. Where's the patient?" he demanded of the nurse with a hint of sharp aggressiveness.

She seemed more deferential to David Gordon's crisp authority than to Philip's studious courtesy.

"I must see Dr. Manning first," she explained, almost apologetically, "then if he says so, I'll take you in at once."

But when the doctor returned, it was with unexpected news. He introduced himself to the lawyer, and without the faintest apparent emotion went on to say:

"I'm afraid you've had your night's sleep disturbed for nothing. I've just had a look at your patient. He's gone into coma. You might wait around awhile if you like, but I'm pretty sure he'll never come out."

David shrugged his shoulders without making any comment. He was, in fact, watching Philip narrowly, being perhaps more interested in noting his reaction to these tidings than in the information itself. The Rabbi was horrified, it seemed to David, out of all proportion to the magnitude of the event.

"You mean," Philip stammered, "he's going to die! going to die, without being able to talk again?"

"That's about it," Dr. Manning answered. "'He showed more stamina, at that, than the average, else he'd never have rallied after the ether."

The three sat silent for a few minutes. Such an outcome of the night's sordid tragedy seemed incredible to Philip—now that he had succeeded in bringing the capable David to his aid. He had nerved himself to the thought of his apparent absurdity and incapacity. He was no longer able to think boyishly of himself as a being of almost supernatural power, scattering balm and spiritual peace among the poor and hopeless of his brethren— not without some remote resemblance to the compassionate Christ whose sculptured presence dominated the entrance hall below. But that it should all end in complete and final disaster—a disaster which left another to pay for his own ignorance—this was more than he felt himself able to endure.

"Pull yourself together," David ordered in a stern whisper. Then in his normal voice he said: "After all, if he's unconscious the poor devil isn't bothered about what he wanted to tell. Perhaps it's just as well."

Courteously declining the doctor's suggestion of cigarettes, and calmly proffering his own well-filled case of black cigars, he proceeded dexterously to entangle Dr. Manning in a long and intricate argument regarding the value and veracity of medical experts in legal proceedings, and the consideration—or lack of it—accorded them by courts and counsel. So absorbed did the doctor become and the lawyer appear that the Rabbi's silence seemed entirely unnoticed. Philip had only garbled impressions of what they were discussing. He was plunged into a passion of the deepest self-reproach. He knew how illogical, how morbid, he had become; but he was unable to free himself from the memory of the unhappy man who had weighed Philip and his whole life in a single instant, and condemned them with one burning word of scorn.

He never did know exactly how long the lawyer and the doctor went on talking, but at last a nurse made her way into the room with a whispered message to Dr. Manning, and Philip understood that the man was dead, and that he and David Gordon were expected to go home.

David managed the details of their departure with the same easy authority he had displayed from the minute of his appearance. It was he who expressed the appreciation of both of them, of the doctor's kindness; it was he who procured a taxi for their transit, and who piloted Philip safely through the mazes of his farewell.

When the two men were at last seated in the machine, rumbling away from the Hospital, David lapsed into silence, as he puffed meditatively upon his cigar. Perhaps he thought nothing he could say would be of much help to Philip, and the best service he could render would be to give him time to regain his poise; but when the machine halted for a minute in the bright electric glare of a street crossing, and the lawyer observed how drawn and pale was the Rabbi's face—almost as though he were in physical pain—he turned to the young man impulsively.

" Look here," he said in his decided manner, " don't let yourself get maudlin about this affair. It was neither you nor I, you know, who ran over the man, and if we'd chosen to spend the night in honest sleep we couldn't have been indicted. It's not your fault the people at your Seminary chose to teach you the Higher Criticism instead of Yiddish—and maybe they knew what they were doing, at that. If your worthy President, Mr. Kaufman, could know what you are thinking, he'd decide he was squandering your salary on a madman."

The Rabbi perceived the kindliness concealed behind the lawyer's brusque words, but he shook his head despairingly.

" I know," he answered, " you think I've behaved like a child——"

" Not a bit," David answered. " I think all the better of you because of the things you're ashamed of. Of course, you've no sense of humor, but if you had, you couldn't be a Rabbi at all."

Philip's eyes widened with distress at the idea of anything humorous being mingled with the night's grim happenings.

David laughed a curt, dry laugh as he read his companion's thought.

" Never mind," he said, " you'll feel better, remembering what a heathen I am."

Once more Philip shook his head.

" You can't see! " he began, " I didn't come here to talk only to rich men. I wanted to help. It isn't just this one poor fellow. I——"

" Never mind," David repeated, laying his hand on Philip's shoulder, as the machine drew up to the Hotel where the Rabbi was to alight. " I see what you mean, and you're a good sort. But there's more to it all than you thought. It wasn't only the Yiddish! You and this Russian never could have understood one another, anyhow."

CHAPTER VII

Public Penance

HEALTHY, vigorous self-esteem is not unlike a normal human body. It can endure blows of the most painful violence, and yet retain the blessed quality of healing its own wounds. Sometimes one feels all the more self-reliant for the injuries from which he has triumphantly recovered. Having fought our way back to health after catastrophes which, we like to believe, would have crushed, for all time, a man of weaker fibre, we become convinced we are not to be conquered by any series of events unless their weight be almost supernatural.

Some such salutary process promptly began to act upon Philip Graetz. He awoke late, the morning after his visit to the Hospital, his spirits bruised and lacerated by the memories of last night's experience. He still wondered how, after having failed so lamentably in the doing of an elementary duty, he could have the brazen effrontery to attempt the ordering of the lives of others. But presently, he arose and looked through his window at the crisp winter sunshine, noting with his quick, approving eye the ice-clad trees and the trim beauty of the parkway leading down the slope of Eutaw Place and up the ascent in the distance to Druid Hill. As he gazed, life once more began to offer compensations even to a young man who has been honestly and woefully disappointed in himself. Surely in a world of such definite loveliness as the one to which he had awakened, there could not fail to be work, and stimulating work, for such a man as he was!

The morning papers brought him additional consolation. Each one had at least a column devoted to the speech he had delivered in the earlier and happier hours of the night, and made admiring mention of the magnificent response which he had evoked. "The Sun" even allowed its enthusiasm to display itself in an editorial, praising the proverbial eagerness of the Jew to care for his destitute co-religionists without the slightest aid from non-believers. The editorial also referred, in glowing terms, to Philip, and quoted, with extravagant praise, a sentence or two from his address.

After a long and careful search, Philip found in an obscure corner of only one newspaper, a five line item briefly recording the death at the Johns Hopkins Hospital of an unknown man who had been run over by an automobile truck at the corner of Baltimore and Frederick Streets. The chauffeur of the truck, the article stated, had been released by the authorities,—the accident, apparently, having been unavoidable.

The young Rabbi, as he sat comfortably at his solitary breakfast, began soberly a new appraisal of his powers and shortcomings.

Here was a man whom he should have been able to understand, and yet could not. There was a large measure of truth in David Gordon's dogmatic statement that his lack of comprehension was complete—not a mere matter of language. Philip subjected himself to a hasty self-examination and was forced to concede his almost complete ignorance of the lives, the work and the hopes of the poor of all races, and particularly of his own. He

PUBLIC PENANCE

knew them only through literature and his vivid imagination. Well, that was bad, to be sure, and something he should have thought of earlier. On the other hand, with all this lack of knowledge, he had, within a few hours of his subsequent disaster, succeeded in procuring a sum of money which would bring comfort during the whole winter, to hundreds of men no less important than the forlorn immigrant whom he had so signally failed in his death hour. At the worst, he had his uses.

The minister, however, was not content with so prosaic a conclusion of his stock-taking. It was virtually an admission of the truth of David Gordon's scathing estimate of his worth to the community. He was not going to become a mere "apostle to the genteel" of his own race. He twisted uneasily in his chair at the idea.

He was the product of faulty ideals of rabbinical training; his congregation, who expected nothing better of him, were no less blind than he had been. Still, it would be his own fault if he were not quickened to a passionate desire to teach himself the things he must learn if he meant to accomplish his Divine Mission of Brotherhood—yes, and to teach it to his congregation, too.

He decided that, tragic as had been the fate of this mangled creature at the Hospital, his death must not be allowed to become purposeless. It should serve as a milestone in the important life of Philip Graetz. He saw nothing grotesque in one man thus dying obscurely, in order that he, himself, might live in a blaze of heightened spiritual splendor. He did not, in fact, consider that phase of the situation at all. On the other hand, if his reflections were saturated with egotism, no one could have been less conscious of it than he. He was consumed, as the first step of his renewed vigor and use-fulness, with a desire to make full atonement for his presumptuous ignorance. He wanted to acknowledge his fault and proclaim its pitiful consequences. He intended to seek helpful guidance in learning to become more useful—no matter how distateful the lessons might be. He would not be content with the easy adulation in which he had basked. He would even conquer his aversion to David Gordon's unconcealed assumption of superiority, and crave at his hands whatever help the lawyer, with his intimate knowledge of conditions among Russian Jews, might have to offer.

Because his vanity had been so sorely bruised by this unfortunate adventure, and he shrank timidly from the ridicule of which he judged himself deserving, Philip decided his penance ought to include some public recital of his failure to translate his ideals into actuality. His congregation had witnessed each of his small triumphs. The community would be buzzing this morning with comment upon the success of his appeal for the relief funds. They should hear, no less publicly, of the disaster wrought by his feebleness. It would not be an easy task, but he would do it. And he did do it, too. On the next succeeding Sabbath he preached what was certainly the least conventional sermon which had ever been delivered in a Jewish Temple within the memory of any of his listeners.

Without the faintest effort at self-exculpation, he told, with unaffected earnest eloquence, the entire story of his visit to the Hospital. He omitted no detail of the immigrant's pathetic reliance upon him and of his despair when he had discovered himself, all too late, to

PUBLIC PENANCE

be a victim of the fact that the world of Jews is made up, even to a dying man, of rich and poor, of native-born and aliens. Under the spell of Philip's gift for pregnant words, the simple happening became epic with a compelling pathos and irresistibly significant in its wider import.

All this had occurred because he, Philip Graetz, had not known the elementary duties pertaining to the common bond which knits together all men born of women, and most of men, all Jews whose fathers stood together, shoulder to shoulder, in their death-defying struggle to preserve God's Truth to the world.

He, their Rabbi, meant in all humility and recognition of his past wanton neglect of duty, to learn these things, so that his faith might be more than idle words. He implored the men and women who looked to him for guidance to join with him in the difficult tasks he meant to accomplish. There must be developed, first in this city to which he had dedicated himself, and thereafter throughout the earth, a comprehension and a sympathy, between all Jews—no matter what the land of their birth, no matter how poor and unlettered, or powerful and wise, they might be. And when Israel had set its own house in order, how could it be otherwise than that this universal talisman of love—at once human and Divine—should be eagerly claimed by all mankind!

" Out of Zion should go forth the teaching proclaimed by Moses of old that Man should love his neighbor as himself."

Philip had sincerely intended his sermon to be a frank confession of weakness. He had unsparingly yielded himself up to criticism and scoffing. With unalloyed sur-

6   81

prise, he observed the effect of what he had said. He could have spoken no words which would have brought him a more genuine tribute of his congregation's reverence and affection. His very boyishness and unassumed contrition regarding a circumstance they could not consider a very grievous lapse raised him to a loftier eminence in their regard. Never before had he seemed to them so thoroughly good, and free from the vices they recognized in their own hearts, as today.

It was a tragic little story to which they had listened, and as he had told it, it had made a poignant appeal. There was many a self-satisfied tear shed during the recital. Philip naively accepted these tears without any doubts, but really, they were tokens of the type of grief one thoroughly enjoys as a proof of his own unusually delicate sensibilities; such unrestrained emotion as we love to display under the spell of a great tragedian.

The congregation, itself, was not too prone to self-analysis. In a manner it actually *was* moved. Had Philip's sermon closed with another appeal for funds, many of his auditors would have willingly deprived themselves of some pleasant little luxury by way of response to his plea. The men and women who had heard his words were, for the time at least, profoundly sympathetic toward their less fortunate brothers and sisters. They would, in fact, have made any sacrifice to bring them happiness—provided, of course, it was not unreasonable, and had no tendency to disturb existing economic conditions or the niceties of social distinctions.

CHAPTER VIII

Concerning Love—Sacred and Profane

Philip hardly knew whether to be glad or sorry when he realized how the public penance to which he had condemned himself had been transformed into another petty triumph. It was certainly pleasant not to have forfeited the affection and admiration of these adoring people. On the other hand, if they were so blind when his failures were called to their attention, would he find them alert and helpful when called upon to act as lieutenants in his long and arduous campaign of regeneration? Meantime, however, he was not unwilling to content himself with the knowledge of having fulfilled to the utmost his duty of open confession.

He did, however, feel that between Ruth and himself some clearer perception of actual values should exist. He was vaguely looking forward to a possible marriage with this girl. She ought, he believed, to have a definite knowledge of what was in his thoughts, if for no other reason, so that her choice of him might be the true expression of her nature. So young was Philip Graetz!

He found her, at their next meeting, lounging luxuriously amongst a great pile of vividly-colored cushions in the Frank living-room. She had been reading when he was announced, and though she expected him, she chose to hold out her hand in greeting, without changing her extremely becoming posture. Still, her smile made up in warmth whatever was lacking in the cordiality of his reception.

Ruth, since last Saturday's sermon, had been doing her share of thinking regarding her young minister; and the more she thought the more puzzled she grew. She realized how much his enthusiastic, spiritual knight-errantry appealed to her. It was that which had caught her fancy at the beginning. She would not wish him to lose it now. Yet he should not be permitted to make a really "uncomfortable person" of himself, and much as she had thrilled at the artistry of his sermon, she became, for the first time, dimly apprehensive lest further progress in the path he proposed might lead him to the verge of distasteful fanaticism. Bayard and Sir Launcelot were delightfully graceful figures of chivalry; Don Quixote was no less noble, surely, yet his performances, perhaps just because of their deadly sincerity, had become ridiculous. So far, Dr. Graetz's feats of prowess had been colorful without transcending the limits of good taste. Ruth meant to conserve, if she could, all his ardor for the betterment of the world—by which she meant making it conform to her own standards of living—without letting him become injured or coarsened in the process. She was not doing this merely to mold her possible husband along lines which should make him a pleasant mate with whom to spend her life. She was actuated by a genuine desire to help him to hold fast to his own happiness, much as many a well meaning mother urges her little boy not to be lured by the neighbor's children into fisticuffs or rough sports, from which, at the best, he will emerge disreputably dirty, and at the worst, with a blackened eye and a bleeding nose.

She plunged without delay into the topic uppermost in her mind.

CONCERNING LOVE—SACRED AND PROFANE

"That was a brave sermon of yours, Philip," she began. They had reached the stage where it seemed more natural to them to use first names than to be more formal. "But did you stop to think before you preached it? If you had done it a shade less beautifully, you'd have hurt yourself seriously with the congregation. It was your way of telling your story which turned things in your favor. You'd better not tempt Providence again."

It is hard to become vexed with a pretty girl who seems filled with solicitude for one's welfare. Yet Philip was distinctly not pleased.

"Don't you see, Ruth, what you feared was exactly what I was trying to bring about? I meant them to blame me. They ought to. I deserved it."

"I knew you would think so," she answered. "But I don't like people to blame you. There are so many good things about you which they can never discover, that it won't hurt them not to learn of the one or two things they might censure."

He smiled tolerantly as he shook his head. This was not good doctrine either for him or for the girl who might become his wife, yet the incense burned before his shrine by this charming young priestess did, in truth, have a pleasant fragrance.

"I wasn't thinking so much of the congregation as of myself," he explained. "I was disappointed in myself. I wanted to make a fresh start. That seemed to me the logical way to begin. Now I am committed to something. I'll have to do something definite whether I want to or not. I can't feed myself on words."

For her part, she had no fault to find with his stimulating, thoughtful "words." They were the greatest of his charms.

"I don't understand," she said with gentle dissent. "We've talked, again and again, you know, about your ideals. I thought it was your theory that the world was to be moved by personal influence. You were to stir us to become more worth while, and each of us would in turn, influence his companions. How can this be done except by what you call 'talking.'"

"We've got to act some, too," he insisted. "I've decided words have no influence if they aren't coupled with deeds. I've got to do some of the things I urge other people to do."

"You mean personal service work among the poor?" she inquired doubtfully. "That's what your sermon really implies, doesn't it?"

It made the young Rabbi wince to hear his vision called by this bedraggled name. Yet he could think of no better phrase to express his idea.

"Something like that," he conceded, "but with a different spirit. We've been trying to help the poor, and particularly, the immigrant poor, because we felt it to be an unpleasant duty. That's why we've never made any progress. We ought to do it because we really care, just as you'd want to help me if I were unhappy, or I, you. I couldn't go home tonight to my warm, cosy room and be comfortable there, if I knew you were wretched and I could help you. Yet there are thousands of men and women whose lives haven't even a memory of happiness in them, and we amuse ourselves,—and forget!"

Ruth was sincerely stirred by the passionate words he spoke, and the true emotion that rang in each syllable.

Yet she was not convinced. She had the faculty—perhaps racial—of being roused to a state of keen emotional excitement, while her critical judgment remained judiciously unaffected. At one and the same instant, she realized how fine and lovable were Philip's unselfish aims, and how sad was the inevitable disillusion which lay before him.

If he could only find it possible to hold his beliefs unimpaired, and to continue to speak of them with his peculiar ardor, without ever putting them to the cold test of actuality! But a sharp and sudden flash of comprehension warned her that even if she could find it possible to divest this man of his intense romantic idealism, he could never become the graceful hero she desired who would issue commands without himself entering the dusty fray. He would become, instead, a conventional creature of grandiose phrases, not much better than the really efficient Arthur Kahn. It hurt her to realize that she could spare him unhappiness only at the expense of the quality in his nature she was learning to love. She was not a girl greatly given to shielding others from pain at her own expense. She had no illusions about her own unselfishness, but at this moment she was filled with an intense desire to bring happiness to this boy whom she believed so much better and so much less wise than herself! She had no room for vexation at the irksome dilemmas into which, as his wife, she would be continually forced. She was entirely willing, for the time at least, to follow in his path, saving him as well as she could, his share of the briers, even though she believed his road led to irretrievable disaster.

When she roused herself to speech, her words reflected these thoughts. She would not quench the flame which glowed in his spirit, no matter what befell.

"If anyone can do the things you hope for, you can do them," she said with a genuine humility. "You're better than most of us—men or women, either. Oh, yes, you are!" she exclaimed, anticipating his protest. "Now, I couldn't do anything for anybody but myself," she went on, resuming her natural tone. "I've tried it, and I know. So your hopes are based on all men and women being less selfish than I am."

"Don't jest about it," he urged seriously. "I don't believe you're selfish. It's just that you haven't thought of such things before."

Ordinarily, Ruth would have smiled her pretty smile which she had always found far more convincing of her complete loveliness of character than mere sober virtues could ever prove; but in tonight's mood she was possessed by a pale reflection of Philip's own rigid determination to seem nothing other than what she truly was. She desired so greatly his affection for the real Ruth, with all her human frailties and shortcomings, that she feared to have him bestow his love upon an imagined Ruth of fanciful perfections. So she replied half in mirth, yet with a rueful spirit of contrition underlying her words:

"You're wrong. Robert says my only true religion is expressed in the creed 'Thou shalt love thyself, thy God, with all thy heart and with all thy soul and with all thy might.' And I'm afraid he's right."

"I have a relative or two myself," Philip interposed. "My uncle's mildest judgment on me is that I'm a low-grade imbecile."

"Oh," laughed Ruth, "but Robert adores me—vices

and all. I have to be demure, all the time, to keep Bess from growing jealous."

Philip's eyes seemed to find some justification for the alarm of the surgeon's wife.

"Well," he concluded, "if you force yourself to be demure, you've one long series of unselfish deeds to your credit."

"That's neat," she retorted, "but unconvincing. It's really no effort for a girl to be demure, if she finds it becoming. I do,—or at least I flatter myself so far. But to go back to where we started, I have done personal service work, and I made a flat, utter failure of it."

"That just bears out what I said," Philip argued. "It was because you thought of it as a duty. If we go among our fellows, full of a spirit of comradeship, how can we help making them understand?"

"I managed to keep them from it," Ruth answered, "and I don't believe I felt this work to be a duty. It was in my senior year at Goucher and I imagine I wanted to play Lady Bountiful."

She wondered why she felt impelled to tell unpleasant things about herself to this man whose admiration she wanted above all things to win, but she continued steadily:

"It was mostly vanity; and they didn't like it;—at least, none of the worth-while ones did. I didn't like it, either. Those who were respectful were cringing frauds, and those who were self-respecting human animals seemed to resent the way I behaved toward them. They irritated me as much as I did them. I got along better with the Gentiles than the Jews. They behaved as though I owed them a debt and was pretty slow about paying it. After awhile I grew tired of it and stopped. It seemed like pouring water into a sieve. One never saw any tangible results. Here and there we helped someone, but we couldn't really change conditions——"

He was roused at once to vehement protest.

" We can change conditions. We must. We will win the confidence of the men and women who are poor and unhappy. Then we'll learn from them what is the real cause of it all and when we once know what to do, there will be no one who won't want to make things better. No one likes to think he is responsible for another person's misery."

" No," she agreed, " but it's not so simple as you make it."

He was reminded unpleasantly of the parallel between her phrase and David Gordon's.

" The poor are miserable because they haven't enough money. If you give them more it must be ours. Most of us aren't vicious, exactly, but we don't see how it will better the world to make everyone's life ugly and monotonous because most people's must be."

" I don't want to," he replied, " I want, on the contrary, to make everyone's life as beautiful as yours. There must be some way to do it. We will find it when enough of us really desire it ardently. The world has always found what it felt it must have."

" It's a task for a mathematician," she concluded, and then perceiving acutely that he was not entirely satisfied with her, she added quickly, " or a prophet, and I'm coming to believe you are something of a prophet. Only remember the multitude have a habit of stoning their prophets. It's that I was thinking of."

" I'm not afraid of that," he proclaimed sturdily.

" I know," she answered, " that's why I'm afraid of it for you."

He was surprised to find himself more gratified by this girlish attitude of solicitude for his safety than he would have been by her prompt acceptance of his plans. She was quick to note this, and was glad. She had found it possible to be her own self without repelling him. She pushed her advantage a step further.

" You know," she went on, " it's a woman's nature to be interested in the individual happiness of the few people she cares about. I'm afraid whatever enthusiasm I have in your ideas, is altogether because they're yours. If they mean danger for you, I'd rather the people you want to aid went without it. If they mean your happiness, I want to help! "

" They do mean my happiness," he answered, deeply touched at the devotion he had awakened in this generous girl who seemed to him so pliant and so much his own. " I shall count on your help."

She pledged it with her irresistible smile, and both of them were illogically happy as their thoughts turned to more personal topics. She had discovered her inability to sway him as she would, even to serve what she considered his own needs. If she were to win his love, it must be done at the price of her submission. She was willing to pay that price—was even filled with joy at the thought. He, for his part, had misunderstood her true character tonight more than ever before, in spite of her earnest effort to reveal herself to him. He mistook her solicitude for timidity; her confession of imperfection for evidences of an almost morbid conscientiousness; her surrender of her views to his own, as the frank acceptance of his superior wisdom. Yet despite this total lack of comprehension, he left her home feeling more strongly than ever bound to her. She had asserted with gentle but compelling force, a claim he was unable and unwilling to resist. It had been clearly revealed to him how much he had taught her to entwine her thouhgts and her fancies about himself. She was willing to adapt her own theories to his. She became unhappy at the thought of his disaster. It never occurred to the young minister to suppose all this had not been his own handiwork. He fancied he had found Ruth young, impressionable, and without a definite idea regarding marriage, and he had without any such intention, stamped his own indelible image upon the white innocence of her imagination. This being accomplished, it could never be erased—and he was not at all sure he would wish it to be. She was a dear girl—not a heroic helpmate for a prophet, to be sure, but none the less sweet for her feminine lack of Spartan firmness.

It gave him curious sensations of pride and awe to recall with what frank freedom from coquetry this beautiful young girl displayed her deep affection for him. He did not intend to fail her. He could not delude himself into investing her with the almost goddess-like qualities of mind and spirit of which his dream-wife had been blended. But there would be compensations in her adorable dependence upon his protecting strength and courage. He smiled to himself as he pictured their future, and at that same minute, in her own luxurious room, Ruth, all aglow with strange and delicious anticipations of a lifetime of self-sacrificing devotion, was smiling, too.

CHAPTER IX

CONCERNING JEWS—REFORMED AND INCORRIGIBLE

PHILIP'S first effort toward understanding his less fortunate brethren naturally took the form of lessons in Yiddish. He was essentially a student, and when he found himself incompetent for any special task, he instinctively turned for help to a book or a teacher. He discovered among the undergraduates at the University a young, impecunious Russian Jew possessed by a fierce resolve to secure a bachelor's degree, and forced by grim circumstances to earn his bread and tuition while he studied. Philip made arrangements to receive this youth in his study on two afternoons of each week and surprised his boyish tutor—whose name was Israel Rubin—by volunteering to pay him a much larger sum than his services were actually worth. Philip was justly confident of acquiring speedily a proficiency in the dialect he had determined to master. He had a definite feeling for the shadings of language, and he was sure his fluency in the use of German would make his task an easy one.

He hoped, also, to learn from this boy much more than Yiddish, but in this expectation he was promptly disappointed. Rubin was distressingly deferential, and respectfully conscientious in the instruction of his distinguished pupil. But he made absolutely no response to Philip's attempts at more intimate exchange of thought. The lessons took the form of conversations in which Rubin would ask some simple question and correct whatever blunders Philip's answer might contain. The boy, however, seemed insistent in confining the questions to impersonal matters. He could not but perceive how alert the older man was to grasp whatever he tried to impart, but in spite of this fact, he appeared to consider the Rabbi an odd specimen, whose eccentricities must be tolerated with patience because he was, after all, almost a Christian and, therefore, not to be judged by the same tests as other Jews—and also because he was amply able to afford the indulgence of his curious whims. Rubin never could decide why a man who had a job among English-speaking people—a job, too, commanding a salary considered fabulous by this poor boy—should want to learn Yiddish, when he could already speak with amazing fluency four other languages—real languages—the kind one had to know to win college degrees. The friendliness of the minister's intentions to the boy did not bring them closer together. On the contrary, it probably made their relations more formal. At the end of the first lesson, Philip, supposing vaguely that Rubin's home was not too well provisioned, had ordered a dainty tray to be sent from the Hotel kitchen to his room. Afternoon tea was not one of Dr. Graetz's habits, but with delicate good breeding he allowed it to appear so, in order that he might offer refreshment to his young guest and teacher. He was vastly amazed at the boy's embarrassed refusal and a little chagrined at the prospect of consuming, without aid, the English muffins for which he had no appetite and the tea he loathed. He pressed Rubin for some explanation. It was then the turn of the Rabbi of a heterodox Temple to become embarrassed, for the inexperienced boy, unlearned in finesse, blurted out his unwillingness to partake of food which was not " Kosher "

—not prepared according to the dietary laws set forth in the Scriptures. An awkward moment followed. Philip could not take offense at Rubin's position, yet he, the teacher in Israel, was certainly made to feel rebuked at this greater rigidity on the part of a young Jew, with whom one could not and ought not to argue. The situation was all the more uncomfortable because Rubin did not know whether it would be wiser to remain, and manufacture conversation, while Philip was served, or to abandon his host immediately after declining his hospitality. He elected to remain, and they suffered together—their stilted conversation proving as distasteful as the despised tea.

After this experience, Philip's hopes of gaining, through Israel Rubin, any real insight into down-town Jewish conditions grew perceptibly fainter. After equipping himself with a working knowledge of the dialect, he would be able to go out on his own voyages of discovery, but this would involve delay, and painful gropings in the dark. He resolved to appeal to David Gordon for guidance. He did not come to this decision without misgivings. He knew he would find in the lawyer a total absence of the pleasant deference and esteem he had grown accustomed to expect during his short career in Baltimore. Still, Gordon seemed to Philip to be a man of brusque sincerity, given to brutal speech, but not unkind, in spite of his manner. At any rate, he must know the very things Philip desired to learn, and the Rabbi would be committed to nothing as the result of an interview.

He therefore telephoned Gordon late one afternoon and asked if he might call on him at his rooms that night, or any other night convenient to the lawyer.

David Gordon replied with a question of his own:

" Is there anything I can do for you? "

Philip felt slightly rebuffed in spite of the cordiality of the question. Most of the men and women he had met, appeared to feel honored at his desire to cultivate their acquaintance. It was not entirely gratifying to have his advances thus weighed and debated. Still, he stifled his slight annoyance and responded:

" Yes, I want some advice."

" Professional advice? " demanded the lawyer.

" No," the Rabbi replied with audible impatience. " Personal advice. Why do you ask? Do you object to having me visit you? "

He could hear, over the wire, Gordon's indulgent laugh.

" My dear Dr. Graetz," he was told, " so far as I'm concerned, I'll really be glad to spend an evening with you. It was yourself I was thinking of. The sheep you tend won't like it. They would really object less if you were discovered in the home of a disreputable woman. I'm considered a bad influence."

Philip was hurt at David's words and manner and there was real dignity in his answer:

" I think, Mr. Gordon, I must have shown you only my worst qualities. I'm not entirely the coward you seem to suppose. I'm here to try to teach my people what seems true to me, not to be the slave of their whims,— and I have asked you for the courtesy of an interview."

" Well, well," the lawyer answered, in a tone of good-humored raillery. " What a gift for misunderstanding you Rabbis have. I never took you for a coward. One doesn't waste his breath warning cowards of danger. You know I'll be glad to see you. Come tonight, by all means. But the best advice I can give you is to take no advice of mine."

After David's mocking taunt about the possible injury to the minister's popularity which might follow any companionship between this oddly assorted pair, physical violence could not have prevented Philip from keeping the appointment. He was really a brave man and the greatest of his few fears was the dread of some day betraying a lack of courage. In his adolescent days, his constant anxiety to prove to himself his indifference to danger had led him into queer situations. If David had been animated by a consuming desire for his presence, he could have chosen no better method of bringing him to his door.

The house on Madison Avenue where the lawyer lived had evidently been, many years before, the homestead of a family accustomd to spacious and luxurious living. It was a large and grim brick building, square and uncompromising, set back from the line of the street and boasting a strip of lawn on one side, almost as wide as the house itself. When the tide of fashion had swept from this section of the City the wealthy old residents who had made their homes there, this house had sunk from its former eminence into a crowded and ill-cared-for boarding-house. It was then that it first sheltered David Gordon—when he decided to live up-town instead of in the congested quarter of East Baltimore where he had spent his boyhood and youth. Its location pleased him none the less because it was unfashionable, and threatened to become more unfashionable every year. So loath was he to locate elsewhere that he had several times tided the shiftless proprietress of the house over financial difficulties which threatened to result in her eviction, and consequently, his also. When she had finally demonstrated her complete inability to meet any and all of her duties, Gordon, whose practice had been proving more and more lucrative, and who had nothing but contempt for the customary methods of disposing of one's surplus income, suddenly bought the house, and building an addition in the rear, transformed the structure into an apartment-house. It looked very much like what it was—neither a home, nor a building originally designed for its present purpose, but David was totally unconcerned regarding its æsthetic properties. After reserving the entire first floor for his own use, he nevertheless found his investment reasonably satisfactory.

Gordon's rooms, Philip decided, were not uncharacteristic of the man himself. The furnishings seemed selected with an eye solely to utility. They were substantial—evidently of solid workmanlike excellence, not exactly ugly, but with no pretence to beauty, either. A negro boy who had appeared in answer to Philip's ring ushered the Rabbi into the lawyer's study which was at the extreme rear of the building, away from the noises of the street. Three sides of the big room were lined with dark oak sectional book-cases. Philip had a book-lover's affection for the built-in open shelf, but Gordon had apparently desired to preserve his volumes as securely as possible from dust. Philip's books mingled among each other according to some mysterious law of elective affinities of their own choosing. His copy of Browning was next to his edition of Whitman. His Tennyson and his Shelley belonged together, he knew not why; but Gordon's library was trim in its evident obedience to classification. Two of the walls were devoted exclusively to law books; the third side to books of a more general interest, among which Philip noticed with surprise that books of a scientific and philosophical nature, such as those of Huxley, Tyndall, Darwin, Spencer and James, struggled for numerical supremacy with works on purely Jewish subjects.

David Gordon was seated in the center of the room at a huge table, covered with open law books and orderly little piles of documents. As Philip entered the room, he carefully and deliberately closed the volume he was studying, after inserting a blank slip of paper between its leaves,— and motioned the Rabbi to a chair on the opposite side of the table from himself.

He glanced at Philip for an instant, with his searching half-amused smile before saying:

"Well, you're here! I'm afraid you've come to the wrong shop, but I'm glad to see you, anyway. You don't smoke?" he added, indicating the cigars and cigarettes at the end of the table, and selecting a fresh cigar for himself.

"No," Philip answered, with his conciliating smile. "It's one of the things I mean to learn, some day."

"I would," the lawyer said, as he lit his own cigar. "It's a great help to a man who believes in brotherhood. Nothing draws men together so surely as the possession of a vice in common."

The lawyer was a trained observer of witnesses, and he found it easy to see Philip's sensitive, shrinking repugnance for this jibe at his pet ideals. He replied to Philip's unspoken protest by saying:

"You and I shall never get on together if you're going to take offense every time I violate your standards of good taste. The conventional forms of amusement,—cards, theatres, athletics—don't appeal to me. I get my relaxation by saying whatever I happen to please—except, of course, regarding matters of business. I even talk impudently to myself, when there's no one else to stir up. So take it as a matter of course; let it be understood you think me a malicious boor, and we'll have a comfortable basis for fellowship."

Philip did not know whether to smile or to frown. He had met young men at college with an overweening desire for impertinence, but they were adolescents unseasoned by the responsibilities of life and work. But Gordon was a man well over thirty, and a busy and successful lawyer.

"Would it be rude," Philip inquired, "if I were to ask how, with your peculiar views on sport, you managed to acquire, and hold together your clientele?"

David smiled approvingly.

"Yes, rude, and therefore, interesting. I'm glad you show faint signs of being infected. I treat my clients as they deserve. I do their work as they want it done, and make no pretences of hiding my contempt for them. The theory works out. A business man dearly loves to bully people and he respects only the fellow who can bully him. I've made a study of it—I can even make that chap you met at Frank's—Arthur Kahn—uncomfortable sometimes. The consequence is, they all pester me to do their work for them. When you take medicine you never believe it's any good unless it's bitter."

Philip decided it would be wiser to smile, after all.

"Very well," he urged, "bully me; though I came to you for advice before I knew your philosophy."

"Oh, you saw it in practice," David insisted. "However," he went on, "my job is law. I don't know much—

and I warn you I don't care much—about fine theories of sugar-coated life. It seems a pretty crude and cold-blooded proposition to me. With this pleasant introduction, I'm at your service."

Philip hardly knew, after hearing David's blunt words, how to approach the topic upon which he wanted help. He was an artist in the use of phrases when his auditors were sympathetic and receptive. In the face of the lawyer's cynicism—real or assumed—he was embarrassed and tongue-tied.

David promptly came to his assistance with a series of terse, irreverent questions.

"What's the matter? Have your male sheep been hectoring you? Or are the ewes making too many sheep's eyes? Aren't you as happy here as you expected?"

Philip remembered David's words at Dr. Frank's dinner and the recollection gave him his cue.

"I've been much too happy," he burst out, "and too useless, just as you prophesied, if you remember. I want to get down to some real work and I don't seem to find it possible."

David scowled. "Exactly what do you want to do?" he demanded sharply.

Philip settled himself to a lengthy explanation:

"The people of Beth El are all rich, or at least comfortable," he said, "that seems to be the case in all the up-town Reformed temples. But they are only a handful of the Jews in the City. There seems to be a complete barrier between them and the others. My congregation ought to be put to work making things right among the down-town people. They seem to need help badly enough.

THE CHOSEN PEOPLE

Everyone says so. We're the powerful ones, yet we do nothing. I don't know what ought to be done, and the East Side doesn't send us any message to tell us."

"Do you mean charity?" David asked impatiently. "You have your Relief Society. You scrape money together. Let that satisfy you."

"It doesn't satisfy me," Philip answered vehemently. "I'm not a child. I know the alms-takers can't be representative of a majority of the Jewish population. I want my people to co-operate with the others. If our culture is superior to theirs, just as our wealth is, we ought to be willing to diffuse it. I want the members of my congregation to make friends of the less fortunate Jews; to work with them in solving their problems—to make their religion an actual thing. I know you are a skeptic and don't share our beliefs——"

David broke in curtly:

"You're right. I certainly don't!"

"I've no quarrel with that," Philip resumed, "but you've got to reckon with the people who do believe. Here's all this force, power and intelligence going to waste because no one familiar with the conditions on the East Side is willing to show me the proper point of attack. I came to you because you do know these conditions."

The lawyer laid down his cigar and looked straight into the eyes of the younger man.

"I don't see why I should bother to save you from the trouble you seem resolved to find. But I can't help it, and I'm going to tell you the ugly truth. You don't know East Side conditions, but you could learn them, with or without help. The trouble with you is, you don't know the conditions on your own side of the town. And

102

you never will learn them till it's too late to save your skin. Anyhow, I'll tell you a few. Your congregation likes to hear you indulge in vague talk about human brotherhood; the merest semblance of the actual thing would horrify the women, and enrage the men. The down-town Jews are Russian. The up-town Jews are American by birth, and German by descent. The one group is above the poverty line—employers mostly. The other group is on the border line or below it, and they're employees. You and your crowd give some sort of an allegiance to a denatured Judaism. I and mine, so far as we have any religion left, are rigidly orthodox. So there you have a whole catalogue of reasons for hates. Your group has had all the best of it so far,—easy lives, easy faith, easy education and an easy superiority. Mine has barely begun to become conscious of itself. Only yesterday it stopped being meek and began to take stock of its own grievances. Your men are beginning to be afraid of us. They notice we no longer accept their Divine right of lording it over us. They think our uncouth, immigrant ways do the Jews in general, and particularly, their comfortable selves, no good among the Christians. And now you come with bland words asking the upper dog to release his grip! If you try to force him, he'll turn and bite you!"

"Let him bite, then!" Philip shot back at him. "I stand for Justice. Are you satisfied with the picture you draw?"

"I state facts as they are, not as they ought to be," the lawyer affirmed. "Will the fight stop after you're bitten? Certainly not. And don't flatter yourself you'll get any help from the other side. To them you're as alien as they are to you, for all your patter about a common religion. Keep on good terms with your own clan,—talk to them pleasantly, and do gracefully what they pay you to do. There's nothing to be ashamed of in such a life. On the other hand, if you try to meddle with something too big for any man to deal with, you'll do more harm than good, and get torn into shreds, besides."

The lawyer replaced his cigar in his mouth with an air of finality, and relighted it after a gesture of annoyance at finding it had gone out during his harangue.

Philip sat silently thinking a moment before returning stubbornly to the attack.

"Our point of difference," he decided, "lies in your belief that men will be unaffected by the teachings of their Religion. That's natural for you who have no beliefs, but hard for me to imagine. Even if things are as hopeless as you say, what's the value of a faith unless it sets to work to remedy them?"

"No value at all," David replied cheerfully, "you can't quarrel with me on that score."

"If I accepted your conclusions, I'd resign from the Rabbinate tonight," Philip declared.

"That would be a pity," the lawyer responded. "You have a real gift for oratory, and it's become an obsolete art among lawyers and politicians."

Philip, stung to real anger, forgot his habitual dignity and tolerance.

"Fortunately," he blazed, "I have some gift for sincerity, too. That isn't obsolete in my pulpit whatever it may be at the Bar."

David, instead of becoming correspondingly angry, laughed admiringly.

CONCERNING JEWS

"You're an apt pupil," he said, "now listen. I don't doubt your sincerity. It's your common sense which seems to be lacking. You speak of the force of Religion. I believe that force to be almost extinct. You don't. But you must believe Religion, even in its prime, was weaker than human nature. You've read history. Here's a state of war—an economic struggle, a class consciousness, a race hatred, a fight between aristocracy and democracy, all bundled into one, and you come along telling passionate men—who are in deadly earnest—to forget what they want and what they hate,—in the name of Judaism! Bah! And it isn't even an authentic Judaism you offer them. It's a pale sentimental imitation of Christianity, with the Christ left out."

David silenced sternly Philip's horrified exclamation of dissent at this crowning blasphemy.

"Don't try to debate it with me," he commanded, "I don't want to convince you. What difference does it make which of us is right, if I and my people feel as I say,— and we do feel it. We think your soft talk about loving the man you sneer at and underpay, is just part of a bad imitation of that Christianity which has conquered the civilized world by abandoning its own cardinal teachings. We think you, yourselves, are only more or less successful imitations of Christians—in your lives, in your studies and in the culture you're so proud of, though nobody knows why. It never can be as good as the original, and the original doesn't fill us with any thrills of admiration."

"You're talking unutterable nonsense," Philip exclaimed hotly. "Just because you're too blind to see virtue in any religion—Reformed or Orthodox——"

"Don't get excited!" David interrupted. "You're

105

right, though not in just the way you mean. It's silly for me to let this talk degenerate into a barren discussion about dogmas, and superior and inferior cultures. The vital part is this: to every East Side Jew, except the handful who have made enough money to belong in spirit in your own camp—you are the hired man of Clarence Kaufman and his kind. As such, they'll have no more to do with you than if you were a Roman Catholic. On the other hand, if you tear yourself adrift from your well-to-do congregation, and go down alone among these unfortunates who can get along just as well without you—you will have cut yourself off from your base of supplies,—of money, influence and Christianized culture. You have nothing to offer them but the pleasure of associating with your exceedingly well-meaning self. You needn't take my word for this. You have only to make the experiment."

David was talking soberly and impressively now, and Philip pondered for several minutes before replying. Finally, he said:

"I know you are trying to tell me what you think is true; yet I'm sure you must be wrong. You manage to have friends in what you call both camps. Why can't I?"

"Friends?" repeated David grimly. "Clients, you mean. During working hours, the lawyer is a free lance. He fights fairly, and without pretences for the man who employs him; meanwhile, he is really serving himself. Besides, I don't want to be taken with absolute literalness. You can make a fair sprinkling of East Side friends, if you use tact and meet them on a purely personal basis. What you want is to let loose on them your well-fed, uptown flock. You can't do it. If Savonarola and John

Knox could be rolled into one and turned Jew, the combined prophet couldn't do it."

Philip sat silent, his attitude one of dejection, but his lips set in a line of stubborn determination.

"It's no fun killing people's enthusiasms," David remarked, with some effort at consolation, "but I'm not much given to chasing rainbows, and you would know what was in my mind."

Philip's composure had by this time returned and he was able to smile pleasantly.

"I'm afraid you are not altogether a successful murderer," he observed, "the corpse has yet to be convinced of its demise."

"Yes," David replied dryly "enthusiasms are like cats or lies, in the number of deaths they can survive."

Philip laughed.

"You see," he explained, "I came here to ask the question 'how' and you merely answered 'don't!' It isn't responsive. I suppose that's why I can't accept it as final."

"It's final so far as I'm concerned," David answered. "Let's talk about something else."

"In one minute," Philip said eagerly. "I think I owe it to you, and to myself, to tell you why I wouldn't adopt your view-point even if it's true—which I can't believe. It would make me perfectly indifferent to Life. If there's nothing on the earth worth-while, we have to pretend there is. According to you, my congregation are all smug hypocrites—consciously or unconsciously—and the Downtown Jews are merely different instead of better. The world is all made up of hatreds, Religion is a silly superstition, and my own place in it is to be a sort of intellectual vaudeville artist. I couldn't go on with existence on such terms. If everything were just as you say, I'd want —as I do now—to fashion my own vision, and work to make the dream come true,—even if I killed myself in the effort. Hasn't everything worth-while in history happened because some man had a vision more beautiful than the sordid odds and ends of facts, which practical men mistook for the whole of life?"

"You poor 'kid,'" David exclaimed. "You're incorrigible! Well, go earn your martyr's crown, if you will, and never have it assayed to make sure it isn't brass. Perhaps you're lucky, after all!"

"I am," Philip affirmed exultingly. "As for you, you must be miserably unhappy. Don't you see any hope for the Jew at all?"

"Yes," David said with decision, "Zionism!"

Philip broke into a peal of hearty laughter.

"I suppose there must be a joke, if *you* can see it," David observed coldly.

"Pardon me," the Rabbi said, "I'm not laughing at Zionism, though I don't believe in it. But you are surely an amazing man! You are too sophisticated for any Religion. You think the various classes of Jews can't be kept from each other's throats, even in a well-governed, established, old community like Baltimore. Yet you want to pour them into an unsettled land of dangers like Palestine. You would urge these bitter enemies to join forces in the building of a new state, to conserve the Judaism which you say is obsolete."

"Not to conserve the Religion!" David replied promptly, "the race! There's something distinctive,—something worth saving, in the race. It has lasted all these centuries because persecution kept us sheltered from outside influences. Then came freedom, and the only difference between Jews who have lived two generations in America and England, and the Christians, is based on the blessed fact that the Christians won't accept you as part and parcel of themselves, no matter how hard you pretend to be. We Zionists want to have a land where the race can develop its own possibilities, before all the Jews get to be as worthless as the Congregation Beth El."

The long discussion had at least taught Philip not to blaze up at David's taunts. He was secretly glad it was his turn to be superior, and therefore, he could afford to be good-humored.

"You laugh at my visions," he said, "your's seem to be a thousand times less practical. While you're still telling me I'm a young fool, for daring to believe people can learn common kindness, you calmly propose that these very people attempt the impossible. And for no sane reason that I can see. America's good enough for me!"

"The difference between us is clear," David replied. "I believe men can't be made to do anything which is against their real interest. For the tribe of Kaufman and his wage slaves to slobber over each other is not only puerile, it's a direct handicap in their eternal game of cutting throats. But Zionism is for the real advantage of every Jew. Men can do the impossible if they are forced to choose between a great gain on the one side, and Death on the other. The Jew can't keep alive without Zionism, and no race wants to become extinct."

"Of course," Philip interjected. "Anyone can argue, if he begins by assuming the very thing he wants to prove. We non-Zionists are American in all our hopes for ourselves and our children. We don't want a Jewish country, any more than we'd expect to see the Baptists or the Presbyterians go off and establish a country of their own. And we don't think we're dying, either."

"The most hopeless consumptive always thinks he's getting better," David replied. "As a matter of fact, all the Jews except the Zionists are Christian in everything but race. You will talk Religion when you ought to be talking Race. Religion won't help you. The only difference between you and a Unitarian lies in the fact that he can join the Maryland Club, and be a guest at a good summer hotel, and you can't. That's what you rely on to save Judaism. No, sir!" he concluded, "you have your choice of two roads and only two; complete assimilation of the Jew among the other races of the world,—and Zionism."

Philip anticipated with keen pleasure a contest on terms of something like equality with this older man who had been calmly taunting him, all evening, with his youth and inexperience.

"You completely ignore——" he began, loftily.

David interrupted him:

"I intend to keep on ignoring it, whatever 'it' happens to be. I've passed the debating society stage. I can tell when a man isn't to be convinced, if you can't; I'll help you by telling you that your eloquence, applied to me, is as hopeless as mine with you. Each of us may safely assume the other to know the stock arguments, and as for making any sort of an impression, unfortunately, we lack an audience. Why squander perfectly good words?"

Philip, still good-humored, though not completely free from a trace of chagrin at the conduct of this unceremonious and arbitrary host, arose to go.

"I didn't mean you to get out," David assured him, in the tone of one who is teaching a child rather than apologizing, "there are plenty of other things to talk about."

"No," Philip said; "it's late, and as it is, I've kept you a long time from your work. It was kind of you to see me at all. I'm coming again, even if you don't want me."

"I do want you," David replied. "I've always wished I could spend the last night with one of the Christian martyrs,—his last, I mean—not mine. That's the way I feel about you,—Christianity and all. Come soon, before the lion gets you."

"I will," Philip promised, realizing perfectly that behind David's words lay a subtle, and kindly-meant repetition of the warnings he had given earlier in the evening. "But don't be too sure," he added, "maybe I shall eat the lion."

David sighed with an exaggerated assumption of despair.

"After all the natural history I've tried to teach you! Well, well, a man should never be betrayed into an argument except in Court—where he gets paid for being misunderstood."

CHAPTER X

A Prophet in Search of Employment

INTELLIGENT debate upon abstract topics is not without some definite value, in spite of what David Gordon's views on the subject may have been. Though we invariably find it impossible to convert our opponents, the ingenuity and logical force of our own arguments rarely fail to produce the most profound impressions upon ourselves. A little well-distributed opposition can do more to make us sure of our positions than unlimited acquiescence.

This is what happened in Philip's case. He had gone to David in quest of advice. He came from the evening's interview doggedly determined to prove, both by word and deed, the error of the lawyer's opinions.

The first fruits of this resolve took the form of a series of scholarly sermons upon the Origin and Purposes of Reformed Judaism—the necessity for its advent, what it had already accomplished, and what its mission was to be in the future. These sermons, preached at Beth El to an admiring congregation, were promptly published in a Jewish weekly which enjoyed a national circulation. They created some little stir throughout the country, being cordially applauded as the most coherent and persuasive statement which had yet appeared of the advanced reform position. Philip had hoped he might become involved in a literary controversy, with ample opportunities for demonstrating how well-prepared he was to sustain the theories he had chosen to defend. But unfortunately, the orthodox never read the magazine in

which he had printed his articles, any more than Philip
himself took the trouble to examine their journals. He
was therefore forced to content himself with observing
his own Board of Directors' ill-concealed fear lest his
new-found fame might cause congregations in New York
and Philadelphia to envy Baltimore the possession of its
brilliant young Rabbi, and to make efforts to lure him
hence.

Philip promptly sent copies of these sermons to David
Gordon. Each one had been aimed directly at the skeptical lawyer. They must surely succeed in making some
impression upon him! The only response elicited, however, was a note typed on David's office stationery, which
read:

DEAR DR. GRAETZ:

I hope you won't think my praise fulsome, when I tell you
I consider your sermons no worse than most of my briefs. It
puzzles me a little to understand how a mind sufficiently keen to
evolve your arguments can be guileless enough to join with your
audience in accepting them as valid. My own position is less
cruel. If I can delude a court into agreement with me, I need
not worry about my own beliefs.

Send me some more sermons of the same type. I shall welcome them as evidence that you are busily engaged in keeping
out of mischief.

Yours sincerely,
DAVID GORDON.

When Philip first read this note, he did not realize
how much truth was hidden in its last sentence. The
preparation of these sermons had consumed much time.
As a necessary consequence, he had been forced to defer
his projected tours of exploration into East Baltimore.

THE CHOSEN PEOPLE

It was now February and he sometimes reproached himself with the random recollection that he was no less ignorant of East-side conditions than on the day he had first entered the city. But he was busy,—feverishly busy —with a thousand details of his congregational and social activities, and, after all, there was no special haste. His delay indicated, he was sure, no weakening of his purpose.

In this way it came to pass that Destiny made Philip the victim of a rather malicious bit of irony. While he sat in his study calmly setting forth, upon neat sheets of paper, the aggressive duties enjoined upon him by his religion, in case certain calamities should ever occur, the events he dreamed of were actually being enacted, almost within sight of his window, and he was too much engrossed in his work, either to hear or see.

Since the beginning of history, man has been engaged in an unsuccessful effort to give to actual life, at least a trace of the color and intensity so prodigally splattered over the crudest works of friction. The worst of it is we can never rid ourselves of the idea that the drama is really there if we could only rearrange the details, and the sequence of events.

Philip knew precisely how a strike should burst upon an industrial community. There had been no factories in the village where his early youth had been spent, and later he had been too much occupied with books and teachers to know whether or not there were labor troubles in his collge town; but he was perfectly aware how such things ought, in all artistry, to be staged. There should be first a low rumble of unrest among the workers—a fiery letter or two printed in the daily press, complaining of intolerable grievances, and an adroit but unyielding reply by the employers, setting forth their side. Then there should appear frantic appeals by disinterested citizens to both factions not to embroil a quiet city in the horrors of conflict. This would be the psychological moment for the entrance upon the scene of an inspired young prophet of the religion of Brotherhood, whose part in the drama would be to bring to these enraged men a peace based on exact justice and human fellowship. In unfortunate communities where no such mediator was at hand, this prelude must, in due course, be followed by the bursting storm. The factories would be idle, hunger would promptly breed violence, riot would stalk through the city, the wealthy would be haunted by all too plausible fears for their safety, while the whole civic life would be menaced by the fury of the contending camps. Finally, there would come the militia, or at least a small regiment of special constables,—who would crush out all disorder with a ruthless disregard of the real merits of the conflict.

To one who knew so well each and every one of the elements of suspense and climax necessary to the proper development of such a tragedy, it was more than disconcerting to discover that, in defiance of all the proprieties— with never a signal to herald its advent or progress to Philip—a strike had actually been in force in the factories of the Pioneer Clothing Company for a period of over four weeks. It was bad enough for any such occurrence to steal into a community without detection by the spiritual sentinel, but the guiding spirit of the Pioneer Company was Mr. Clarence Kaufman, the president of Beth El!

Nor did it come to the Rabbi's knowledge, even at this late day, because of any special vigilance on his part, or because of any visible disturbance of the City's normal life, but through the sheerest accident.

Philip's salary was liberal and his expenses modest. Even had he possessed no income save his earnings, there would still have been a fair surplus to his credit. As it was, he was surprised—for his interest in such matters was slight—to find, one day, after repeated insistence from his bank had forced him to have his pass-book balanced, that his savings now amounted to nearly two thousand dollars. He knew just enough about money, and its care, to realize the advisability of investing this sum, and anxious to have no further concern about the matter, went directly from the bank to the brokerage office of Arthur Kahn, determined to ask him to purchase on his behalf whatever security he might think judicious.

Arthur received him with his wonted air of polite condescension. It was impossible not to observe what a busy and important man he was, and how much of the City's financial stability was dependent on him. Still he was more than happy to be of service to a scholar like the Rabbi, whose infinitesimal business interests were more than counterbalanced by his value as a spiritual and social factor. The choice of an investment was quickly made, Philip being totally innocent of any knowledge on the subject, and admitting the fact blithely. He allowed Arthur to direct him unquestioningly, and the broker promptly arranged to purchase for him such an ultra-conservative security as he would have recommended to an unsophisticated widow whom he had determined to protect from unscrupulous promoters of oreless gold mines. Philip, after expressing his thanks, was duly bowed out of Arthur's private office, and was about to wipe the whole transaction from his memory—at least, for the present—when he paused in the general lounging-room of the brokerage office to bestow a passing glance upon a scene, which, to his unaccustomed eyes, was novel and somewhat interesting.

One side of the room was occupied by a long blackboard. On this there was painted, in white, mystic combinations of letters of the alphabet. Philip did not know their individual significance, but correctly supposed them to be abbreviations for the names of various corporate stocks. A boy stood before this blackboard with a bit of chalk in his hand neatly tracing, under each symbol, various figures. At one side of the room, a telegraph instrument, reposing under a glass top, steadily disgorged a long strip of paper tape, and a clerk bent over it calling out numbers to the boy at the blackboard. These activities appeared to create an unusual degree of interest in a half score of men who sat in deep, comfortable leather chairs, puffing vigorously at cigars and intently watching the chalk marks. The Rabbi recognized several of these men, and bowed to them genially. He reflected how bored he would be if it were his duty to spend his days guessing what numbers would appear on that wall—even if he were well paid for doing it. The men to whom he had nodded assumed, for their part, that he had called on Arthur Kahn for the purpose of securing funds from him for some pet charity, and secretly pitied him for having to spend his time at such an unpalatable task.

While Philip stood there, deciding he really must go, in another minute, one of the most intent of the critics of the blackboard, remarked to his neighbor, as though resuming an interrupted conversation:

"If you want a good local industrial, why not buy ' Pioneer Clothing '? "

"Don't like it," was the prompt response. "I hate ' one-man ' companies."

"It's always paid its dividends regularly," the first speaker insisted. "All our local companies are ' one-man ' companies, only you don't usually know it. ' Pioneer ' is selling low just now because of the strike. It's due for a rise."

"If it wins this strike," his companion added, significantly.

"Oh, I'll gamble on Kaufman," the first man proclaimed confidently, "he always wins his strikes."

Philip did not wait to hear more. He was profoundly troubled. He had what he knew to be an absurd feeling of being unfairly treated—of having been taken unawares. Even now, when he had learned of the existence of a strike in the factories of his own parishioner, he had no idea of its cause or merits, nor how he ought to set about obtaining the desired information. He had a luncheon engagement with a small group of young men, and he was, therefore, unable to give any concentrated thought to the matter, but throughout the meal-hour he was preoccupied, silent and uninteresting—a surprising contrast to his usual self. When he succeeded in tearing himself away from his companions he deliberately set about getting light upon the situation in the Pioneer factory. His first steps were unavailing. It did not seem politic to him to ask Mr. Kaufman for the desired information. Any subsequent investigation of the accuracy of his statements might prove embarrassing. Several other possible sources of knowledge he rejected because he could not rid himself of a definite sense of humiliation at being compelled at this late day in the strike's progress to go from door to door begging odds and ends of data upon a subject regarding which he felt he should have been fully advised. It was for this reason he steadfastly refused to appeal for guidance to David Gordon, who would, he reflected with chagrin, have, at his fingertips, all the details of the controversy.

After a number of fruitless demands at public libraries, at police headquarters, and elsewhere, the obliging young lady in charge of the inquiry department of one of the newspapers suggested to the Rabbi a visit to the State Bureau of Industrial Statistics. It was the duty of this office, she informed him, to collect and classify all facts and conflicting claims pertaining to strikes, lock-outs, and boycotts, and to place them at the disposal of any person with an inquisitive turn of mind. Philip thanked the girl with fervor, wondered why this idea had never occurred to him, and hurried off to put her plan into practice; but when he reached the office he was confronted with a neat sign explaining how many less hours, a day, of labor a paternal State demands of its employees than is required by any other business enterprise. The Bureau would not be open until next morning, and Philip was forced to postpone his investigation until then.

He was in no mood to spend the evening with Ruth, as they had planned, but he could think of no adequate explanation for absenting himself, so he found himself at her home a little later than his usual hour of arrival.

His delay had caused Ruth some slight impatience, which she suppressed artfully when she noticed the dejection and preoccupation of her visitor. Philip was one of those transparent natures who are ill-equipped to conceal their emotions. If he were happy or miserable, enthusiastic or depressed, he promptly displayed signals of his state, in his words or manner.

"What's the matter?" Ruth demanded with flattering solicitude, as soon as they had exchanged greetings.

He answered her question with another!

"Did you know there was a strike at the Pioneer plant?"

Ruth was not normally one of those inflexible worshippers of literal Truth, whose nobility is so commendable and uncomfortable. She knew, too, how much better would be the effect on Philip's perturbed spirit if she were to assert a total ignorance of all recent happenings in the business career of her inconvenient Uncle. But she was in the throes of a new emotional experience. Her fondness for Philip was tangled in her thoughts with hosts of rosy-colored beliefs about his delicacy of moral perception, and her own ardent desire to adapt herself to his standards. She could not bring herself, therefore, to lie to him, although she would have cheerfully done so to anyone else.

"I did know of it," she admitted, almost apologetically.

It is, perhaps, not unjust that one who craves the fine moral glow which follows a virtuous deed should be willing to pay for it with some corresponding loss of comfort. Unfortunately, the moralists have falsely taught us to expect a reward instead. When the reward bears all the outward semblance of a punishment, we feel cruelly defrauded. The first instalment of Ruth's price for her devotion to the truth was promptly demanded. The balance she was to pay long after, without knowing just how, and when. For her silent and concealed knowledge of the existence of the strike, ranged her in the Rabbi's thoughts—although he hardly realized it himself,—among the partisans of Clarence Kaufman.

"You should have told me, Ruth. I ought to have known," Philip said with grave reproach in his voice.

Ruth was distressed. Never before had he seemed so definitely displeased with her. Yet her conduct throughout had been directed by a pure, disinterested care for his welfare and happiness. The Ruth of a year before would have been astounded could she have seen the Ruth of today, grown almost unselfish. Still more would she have been startled at the meekness with which she submitted to this undeserved reproof.

"I hoped it would straighten itself out," she explained eagerly, her pretty face filled with an earnest appeal that he should smile upon her again. "There's some trouble at the Pioneer works nearly all the time. It usually clears up by itself. I hoped it would this time. Maybe it still will. I thought there was no use in worrying you, unless things grew really serious. Are you angry with me?" she asked, finding he showed no signs of returning serenity.

"No," he replied soberly, "not angry,—of course not, Ruth. But I wish you had told me. I ought to have been at work, trying to see if I could help. Do you know what this strike's about?" he demanded peremptorily.

"No," she said simply, then adding quickly in the

hope of being restored to favor if she proved her value.
" I can find out all about it if you want to know; I'll ask
Uncle Clarence, or Arthur."

He shook his head forbiddingly.

" I shall have official information tomorrow," he said,
slamming this door of hope in her face. But he went on,
unconsciously venting on Ruth all the vexation he felt
at his own lack of alertness. " Don't you think you ought
to have been interested in finding out why the men
were fighting?"

Ruth's mood of unwonted patient submission still
held its sway.

" I suppose," she pleaded by way of justifying herself, " if this strike had been an isolated happening, I'd
have been curious to find out all about it. But, you see,
there's always some sort of quarrel going on in the factory; mostly about trifles, too. If I tried to keep in touch
with all their squabbles I wouldn't have time for anything
else."

" But you're interested in the company financially,"
he insisted uncompromisingly, " you're a stockholder. It's
your business to know how the men who work for you
are treated!"

Ruth's new-found attitude of patience was not sufficiently matured to endure such undiluted rebuke without
some noticeable strain. For a minute she forgot her position as a lowly disciple, and turned sharply on her stern
monitor.

" You have some investments of your own, I suppose,"
she said. " Do you know the policy of each company
toward its men?"

Philip was silenced; he remembered the bond Arthur

A PROPHET IN SEARCH OF EMPLOYMENT

Kahn had purchased for him only that morning, and was forced to admit to himself how completely he had ignored this phase of the situation, not only in this specific instance, but applied to all the sources of his small income.

Nevertheless, he was not greatly delighted to find how easily Ruth had succeeded in putting him in the wrong, while she proceeded to push her advantage further by adding, when he failed to reply:

"Of course you don't! And I have more excuse than you! Even if I disapproved of what was being done, I couldn't take any action. My money is all held in trust for me. I only get the income till I'm thirty. My hands are tied. Don't you see it isn't my business?"

By this time, Ruth's temporary irritation had exhausted itself, and she was, once more, anxious to pour balm upon the wounds she had helped to inflict.

"Of course," she went on, "I've learned from you that we all ought to give thought to such questions. What I meant was, I'm no more to blame than everyone else for not having done it before."

"No," Philip admitted honestly, though without enthusiasm, "you are right. I've no right to throw stones. I've got to admit I've been pretty remiss. Still," he continued, turning to a more inviting side of the problem, "the main question is not what we ought to have done, but what we're going to do now. That's why I wish you'd told me about this strike earlier. I've been losing time while it gained headway."

She perceived she had gained nothing by her successful attack. He still blamed her. She attempted another and more feminine mode of conciliation.

"I'm sorry," she said simply, "I was trying to spare

123

you. I thought if you could be led to ignore the little quarrels, you'd have all the more influence when the really serious troubles began."

This was decidedly better. Philip was unable to remain completely oblivious to her evident contrition and desire to be useful. She then skilfully led him to explain his plans for gaining a complete knowledge of the questions at issue between Mr. Kaufman and his employees, and his intentions, when he should discover a just solution of their difficulties, to demand its acceptance by both sides.

Try as she would, she could not blind herself to the certainty of much discouragement and unhappiness in store for Philip when he should thrust his boyish, but lovable, idealism between these grimy, infuriated fighting men.

In spite of the resolution she had formed to follow the path he was destined to tread,—no matter through what perils it might lead,—she was possessed by a woman-like desire,—now that the approach of danger was imminent—to defer, if only for a brief interval, the actual encounter between his cherished theories and the crude realities.

It was for him she feared, much more than for herself. Even at the risk of intensifying his exasperation, she felt she must attempt to divert him from his rash adventure.

"But you said, Philip," she urged, "you would not interfere in such matters unless you found a clean-cut issue of right and wrong. You still believe that, don't you? You're not going to try to dictate mere matters of policy?"

A PROPHET IN SEARCH OF EMPLOYMENT

"No," he answered. "I still believe that. But," he added with aggressive determination, "I'm reasonably sure if there's constant friction, as you say there is, it can't be due to a mere question of policy."

Ruth, before replying, looked thoughtfully into the wood fire blazing on the hearth. It occurred to her that this youth, with the ardent temperament, could find a question of right and wrong in a multitude of matters where she could see nothing but problems of expediency. She experienced a quickly-suppressed spasm of heresy, while she wondered how a world, keyed to so intense a pitch, could possibly endure. She brought herself back to a consideration of Philip's idea. She knew more about the Pioneer Company and its policies than he had supposed. Ruth always was surprising Philip by betraying a definite knowledge he had not believed her to possess, yet he had never learned to anticipate anything from her but pretty helplessness.

"I can tell you right here and now," she informed him, "the main cause of the friction. It's because the Pioneer will have nothing to do with the Unions. Some of the Baltimore factories employ both Union and non-Union labor. In others, the Unions have practically forced out non-Union men. Uncle Clarence is the only manager who has succeeded, so far, in refusing to deal with Unions altogether. That's what they fight about, with a thousand variations, of course. I can see how a man might argue either side, but I don't see how you could ever convince Uncle Clarence, or the men, that they were morally wrong."

Philip was somewhat baffled at this statement of the situation. He had supposed he would be confronted by a

125

more appealing demand for a higher wage, or better working conditions. Ruth began to feel she had chanced upon the fortunate charm by which she could, at the same time, keep him inactive without crushing either his faith in himself or his fondness for her.

" You see," she went on, bringing her alert intelligence to bear on her task, " why I was, and am, so anxious to prevent you from committing yourself too hastily. I don't want to try to influence your final judgment. I know I couldn't, even if I tried, but I really don't want to. You wouldn't be yourself if you didn't have your wonderful sense of duty. I don't want you to waste yourself. The question of Unions isn't one where all good men take the same side. At college we had one teacher of Economics who saw nothing good about them and one who saw nothing bad. I'm sure I don't know what to believe. But this I do know: If you take sides for, or against the Union, just because you happen to think that way, you'll never be able to make men like Clarence Kaufman, or the labor leaders, credit you with any desire to be fair to both parties."

Philip found no escape from the conclusion of Ruth's logic—yet he was definitely dissatisfied. She was right; he admitted it; still, he was disgusted to find himself here, and everywhere, condemned to an inglorious inaction—to an appearance of prudent timidity, all the more exasperating because he knew himself to be restrained by no cowardly fears for his own welfare. There were always perfectly valid reasons for remaining comfortable and conventional! And now Ruth had allied herself with the irresistible forces which shackled him. She was good, of course, and only striving to serve what she considered

126

his needs. In this case, she was painfully wise, too. None the less, she appeared to him at that minute as a Delilah, without Delilah's guilt, making with all her fascinations, common cause with those who planned to bind him, hand and foot, dim his vision, and prostitute his strength to the menial labor of the millstone.

At this uncomfortable juncture, Ruth found an unexpected ally in the person of Robert Frank. He had just entered the house and had paused at the door of the living-room for a smile and a nod before going upstairs to Elizabeth, when Ruth gracefully arranged a soft cushion and a comfortable chair for him and daintily tempted him to sit with them for a while.

The surgeon was a reasonably observant man—whenever he found opportunity to bend his attention upon anything other than his work. Ruth had never before exhibited any marked inclination toward sharing Philip's company with other members of her family, and the pair seemed to his eye more solemn than the most impersonal lovers ought ever to be. He knew she must be in need of some sort of moral support, and all his principles of non-interference urged him to go straight upstairs to his wife, and leave Ruth to grapple with her own problem. Nevertheless, the appeal for aid of a pretty girl, even if she happens to be a sister-in-law, has, somehow, more potency than any mere principle. Robert stretched himself lazily in the chair and awaited developments.

" Anything wrong?" he asked with a cheerful lack of finesse, which would have made his wife shudder could she have heard him.

" Yes," the girl replied, deciding she could never introduce the subject indirectly with only Robert to help. "Philip is troubled about the Pioneer strike."

"The Pioneer strike!" the surgeon repeated, "I do remember hearing something about it—but anyone who starts to worry about your Uncle Clarence and his strikes is as unfortunate as a woman who's annoyed about the color of her hair. It's a life job."

"Oh, no, Rob," Ruth answered saucily, "a woman's hair sometimes yields to persuasion." She was not sorry to relieve, if she could, the tension of their somber conversation. Besides, her own splendid hair would seem none the worse for a few thoughts devoted to the subject.

"The hair may change somewhat," Robert retorted easily, "but the worry remains! So do Clarence's little tilts with the labor question. What's wrong this time—do either of you know?"

"No," said Philip, "we don't, and we think we should have known long ago."

Robert began to understand why Ruth had arranged a cushion for him.

"I suppose a good citizen would have known all about it," he admitted with a genial good-tempered raillery, "but there is no such animal. If one doesn't look these things up, he is a bad citizen, and if he isn't too busy to look them up, he's a parasite. So there you are. Anyhow, I plead guilty. Tell me what little you do know."

"We don't know anything," Philip began, disgustedly.

"But we suppose it's just the old question of the Union," Ruth interrupted.

"It can't be acute," Robert decided. "The dispensary records haven't begun to show any unusual increase in broken heads and black eyes."

Philip's own eyes grew wide with a horrified interest.

A PROPHET IN SEARCH OF EMPLOYMENT

" Do they have battles with the police? " he inquired eagerly.

" No, with one another," the surgeon informed him, nonchalantly, " strikers and scabs. Not battles, either. Plain ordinary street brawls—nothing spectacular. The common or garden variety of drunken husband or wife does much more damage."

Philip was not inclined to accept this matter-of-fact view of such occurrences.

" I haven't seen anything about such affairs in the newspapers," he insisted, " I haven't seen one word about the strike printed."

" I suppose it's been there," the surgeon observed, " but not stressed too heavily. You see that's the Baltimore attitude. No suppression of the Truth, of course, but gentility, calmness, no hysteria! If you listen to our newspapers and public men, we have no slums, no poverty to speak of, and no labor disturbances except among a few disorderly foreigners. Even our thunder storms have better manners than those in Boston or New York! "

" But if there really is actual violence," Philip persisted, " people ought to be made to take notice—whether the newspapers think so or not! "

Robert smiled pleasantly at the younger man, whose generous emotionalism appealed to him. He meant to be particularly careful not to say anything which might dull the edge of Philip's unsophisticated eagerness. Yet he must not allow the minister to make himself ridiculous, either. This was, probably, why Ruth had called for his help.

" You see, Dr. Graetz," he said, " one can't allow his sense of proportion to be swamped—can he? All this

129

isn't ' violence,' if you use the word as we've been using it. It really isn't even disorder. Both Ruth and I drive about town as we always did—nobody hurts us. The men who want to work and those who don't, merely exchange bodily compliments, now and then. After all, it's human nature, isn't it?"

Philip pondered the question as though it had really been intended to evoke an answer. Then he replied with decision:

" No, Dr. Frank, I don't believe it is. These men, strikers and scabs, really belong on the same side. They're ' Labor ' as opposed to ' Capital.' There must be something artificial which sets them to attacking one another."

The surgeon, who had been busy with his own surmises, bent a sharp glance on the earnest, likeable boy. After all, he concluded his mentality was anything but negligible.

" Well," he conceded, " maybe you're right. Perhaps it isn't natural, but it's usual. Nothing happens so regularly as the unnatural," he went on, smiling again. " The practical fact is that when you have a flat question like Unionism, men will differ, whether they line up according to their true interests or not; and when they differ they will fight."

" But we who believe there is something better for men than fighting and hating, oughtn't we do something?" Philip demanded. His voice gave his question the character of an indictment.

" I do what I can," the surgeon answered easily, " if they come into my hospital service, I patch them up."

" Perhaps that's enough for you," Philip said, " but the rest of us ought to do something to keep them from needing to be patched up."

A PROPHET IN SEARCH OF EMPLOYMENT

Robert had no wish to pluck this thought from Philip's mind; he wanted Ruth's husband, as he expected Philip to become, to be a man of action; but he also wanted these actions to be the result of mature knowledge. His point of view was not identical with Ruth's. He regarded the dangers of a hot, desperate encounter between the Rabbi and his congregation, as a thing from which no one who really cared for the young man's welfare should deter him. He believed it could not be avoided, if Philip were really worth-while. He desired it also because in his opinion the stress of such a trial was exactly what Ruth needed. Still, he thought the minister should not be allowed to enter the lists in his present state of ignorance of the forces with which he had to fight. It would be sending a mere youth out to lead an army. Even in the doubtful event of a victory, he would not know how to make a wise use of his power. Robert was pervaded by the scientist's distaste for untrained men. He meant, if he could, to stimulate Philip's courage and determination while he, nevertheless, delayed the critical hour, until the untried fledgling should be properly equipped.

"You're right!" Robert exclaimed heartily. "Don't ever let anyone persuade you that something oughtn't to be done about these things, or that you're not the man to do them! I believe you're the very man to attempt such things right here in Baltimore."

Philip beamed upon him, while Ruth wondered what perverse Fate had led her to put her faith in her unreliable brother-in-law.

"But," Robert went on, suddenly changing his tone, "it isn't enough, merely to do something! You've got to do the right thing. As yet you don't know what it is, do you?"

131

"No," Philip answered honestly, "but I want to find out—and now!"

"Good for you," Robert continued, "but don't make the blunder of mistaking a 'guess' for a 'know.' The most pitiful thing in my line of work isn't the silly self-satisfied doctor who looks at a patient and fails to see he ought to be operated on at once. It's the man who isn't well-trained, and who knows something ought to be done without delay, but for the life of him doesn't know what to do!"

"But," Philip urged, "suppose the patient's state is desperate. Oughtn't your surgeon do the best he can, even if he isn't sure just what?"

"No!" Robert replied vehemently. "Nature at her worst can't do a patient as much harm as a surgeon whose intentions are good, but whose anatomy is wobbly. Your job is to study, and to think about these conditions you want to remedy. Later on, when you're sure you know, act—no matter who tries to stop you!"

He paused; then he went on, with a return to his former lightness of manner:

"I'm sure I don't know by what right I began to lecture you, Doctor. I'm afraid we're all preachers at heart; but hurling sermons at a minister is something like carrying coals to Newcastle. You'll have to forgive me."

Philip was sincerely moved by the older man's unusual burst of serious encouragement. Even though his counsel was one of delay, it was a delay pregnant with hope.

"Indeed," he said with the grave air of frank courtesy which his congregation found so charming. "I owe you, not forgiveness, but more gratitude than I can put into words. I think your students must find you a wonderful teacher. You've made me see things. I'm going to make a better job of my work some day because of what you said."

The minister had indeed shaken off his mood of dejection and doubt. He was his enthusiastic self again. Ruth, happy at having gained, at least her immediate end, threw her sweetest smile at Robert, and the surgeon prudently resolved to leave them to their own devices before his laurels should have begun to lose their freshness.

"Well," he said, rising and extending his hand cordially to Philip, "I've an idea you'd make more of a success as a pupil than I do as a teacher. We don't often have to hold our students back. Good luck to you! I think I'd better run upstairs to my wife and listen to a preachment or two myself."

When he reported to Elizabeth, her first demand was: "What on earth have you been doing down-stairs, all this time?"

"I've got a new profession," he told her gaily.

"I hope the hours are better," she said significantly.

"When you learn about it, you won't stop to count the hours it takes," he assured her. "I'm to become a Prophet manufacturer! History is full of King makers from the original Warwick down to the late Marcus Hanna. But to turn a man into a prophet—a Messiah, maybe,—is unique. You ought to be a proud woman, my dear."

"I hope you haven't been putting ideas into Philip Graetz's head," Elizabeth exclaimed sharply.

"Of course," he laughed, "I know you ladies would

prefer him without any. But he is a 'nice' boy, isn't he?" Robert added irrelevantly.

When the 'nice boy' returned to his rooms at the end of the evening, his faith in himself and his mission was stronger and more buoyant than ever. Yet there was but one point upon which there was absolute agreement among his three most interested counsellors. David Gordon, with his flat assertion of the utter impossibility of Philip's purposes, Dr. Frank, with his encouraging insistence upon a long course of rigorous preparation before action, and Ruth, with her unheroic desire to save him today, tomorrow and always, from any and all peril and unhappiness, were in perfect accord in their ultimate conclusion:

For the present, at least, Philip should do nothing.

CHAPTER XI

A LITTLE MATTER OF HOMICIDE

WHEN Philip, the morning after his discussion with Ruth and Dr. Frank, visited the Bureau of Industrial Statistics and was there placed in possession of whatever official information had been collected regarding the Pioneer strike, he found Ruth's surmise to have been substantially correct. It appeared from the documents on file, and from the more informal chatter of an obliging young clerk, that the Pioneer Clothing Company was the only plant in Baltimore of any considerable size which had made no concessions whatever to Union Labor. There seemed to be no complaint regarding the physical condition of the factory, which was, in fact, declared by Philip's informant to be almost perfectly fitted, both in architectural design and in its methods of maintenance, to meet the hygienic needs of its occupants. The papers, he explained, were full of allusions to a vigorous dispute regarding a recent change in the scale of wages for " piece work." Apparently, the entire working force was paid upon a " piece work " basis instead of receiving definite weekly salaries. Both the former scale of wages, and the one put into effect immediately before the beginning of the strike, were among the papers placed at Philip's disposal, but he found them totally incomprehensible. To him they were a hideously complicated jumble of unfamiliar names and figures. He was glad to toss them aside with the comforting thought that this phase of the controversy was altogether irrelevant, for one reason because, according to the clerk's

135

version, the Pioneer's rate of wages was, if anything, slightly higher than the sums paid by other factories; and for another, because at the commencement of the negotiations between the Company and its laborers, Mr. Clarence Kaufman had unconditionally offered to submit all questions relating to wages and working hours to an arbitration committee of three, of whom one member was to be selected by himself, another by the employees, and the chairman to be the Professor of Economics in the Johns Hopkins University. Nothing could be fairer than such a proposal, Philip concluded, yet it had been peremptorily refused.

The entire conflict, therefore, as Philip was able to understand it, resolved itself into a clean-cut issue of Unionism. There had been many previous efforts to establish Union conditions in the Pioneer plant—all of which had proved unsuccessful. Clarence Kaufman had steadfastly refused to employ Union labor, and had heretofore defeated all the numerous efforts designed to compel his abandonment of this position. The Company, although the largest clothing manufactory in Baltimore, the best equipped from all physical standpoints, and the one which seemed to pay the highest wages, was certainly the least popular, not only among the workers but among its capitalistic competitors. The garment makers seemed to regard its higher rates of payment and excellent shop conditions as bribes to induce them to abandon their just right to organize, while other Clothing Companies apparently considered Kaufman's methods of escaping the annoyance of Union interference by devices which tended to unsettle the working conditions in other factories, as positively unsportsmanlike.

A LITTLE MATTER OF HOMICIDE

Curiously enough, though the Pioneer Company in employing operators invariably rejected those who were affiliated with any Union, a persistent craving to join such organizations would manifest itself from time to time among the men and women in the factories. The most prominent in such movements were with machine-like regularity found guilty of some infraction of discipline,— to all appearances completely unrelated to these attempts at organization,—and discharged. The Pioneer had never before flatly thrown down the gage to Unionism by stating it would refuse to retain in its employ men who were definitely affiliated with organized labor; nevertheless, such unruly workers mysteriously disappeared, and so efficient was the Company's system of manufacture, that it did not seem to suffer appreciably by reason of the constant changes in its operating force.

In January, a new "piece work" scale had been quietly put into effect, without much prior announcement of the Corporation's intention. This change,—Mr. Kaufman and his associates insisted—was in the direction of equalizing the opportunities in the different departments, and upon the whole, so they asserted, involved an appreciable increase in payments—rather than a diminution. They said the workers were too illiterate to perceive this, and Philip, whose brain ached from his own efforts to compare the two scales intelligently, was prepared to admit, ithout reserve, the entire possibility of their misunderstanding. He even indulged secret doubts as to whether Clarence Kaufman knew perfectly what it meant. Here, however, Philip was in error. Mr. Kaufman had a perfect comprehension of its most delicate implications. Nevertheless, whether it was correctly interpreted or not, it created a vast amount of dissatisfaction and unrest. Just because each employee felt himself unequal to the task of intelligent scrutiny, it was vaguely felt that their combined ignorance might be equal to the feat. Among the men, there was one of much more than average force, named Israel Ginzberg, who had been born in this country of Russian parents. Fortunately or unfortunately for him, he was able to speak and write both English and Yiddish with fluency and a certain crude, emotional eloquence. He had gathered together a number of his fellows, and proposed, once more, the formation of a branch of one of the nation-wide Unions. The first steps were taken in carefully-guarded secrecy, but the movement spread through the plant with the speed and vigor of an epidemic. Then the inevitable happened. Ginzberg found in his pay envelope a politely impersonal note announcing the ability of his employers to continue their commercial careers without further aid from him; but, this time, the revolt had gone too far to be crushed in so simple a manner. The great bulk of the Pioneer's employees abandoned their posts with their leader, and completing the details of organization, they prosecuted their strike with determination and an unexpected degree of resourcefulness. The National body with which they affiliated came to their assistance, with advice and funds, and Ginzberg who under normal conditions might have plodded obscurely along at his machine a whole dreary life-time, was developing under the burden of his new responsibilities a quality of real leadership. Philip read some of his manifestos with a genuine interest. The man was certainly too prolix—much too intemperate, also. He hurt his cause by his constant habit of over-statement, but his work was certainly human, and saturated with a compelling passion. The statements and arguments submitted on behalf of the Pioneer Company were never, Philip decided, the work of Mr. Kaufman. They were composed by well-paid lawyers and advertising men, skilfully conceived and phrased, and knit together with threads of irresistible logic. There was no answer to them, yet Philip laid them down with a feeling of coldness—almost of distaste.

As the Rabbi bundled together the documents in the case and prepared to go, the clerk who was surprised and curious at finding any disinterested person willing to devote an entire morning to so strange a pursuit, remarked:

"Come in again, Sir, from time to time, and I'll bring your information up to date. We'd get along better if more people took an interest in these affairs."

"Don't many people?" Philip asked.

"Not in this town," the clerk told him with a shrug and a smile. "You're the first man without an axe to grind who's asked us a question. Are you writing a paper on the subject?"

"No," Philip said, "just trying to find out things—and you've helped me a lot."

"There's going to be a mass meeting of the strikers on Wednesday afternoon at Eastern Hall," the clerk volunteered, "you might find it interesting, if you want to hear their side."

Philip thanked him again and hurried off. He debated seriously with himself the wisdom of attending this meeting. His presence there would certainly lend itself to misconstruction. He was not afraid of being reproached for the passive countenance he might appear to give to the

139

cause of the garment workers, but it troubled him to reflect they might consider his purpose to be one of hostile espionage undertaken on behalf of Clarence Kaufman, the President of his synagogue, and, in a sense, his paymaster.

Besides, he had an engagement for that afternoon. A great soprano was to give a song recital at the Peabody Institute, and cards of admission were few and not easily procured. Ruth had season tickets for all performances at the Institute, and Philip had eagerly accepted an invitation to be her escort. Of course, he could explain his inability to keep the appointment, but then he really wanted very much to go, and as for the mass meeting, he was not sure it was a sensible adventure for a man in his equivocal position. It would be interesting, certainly, but on the other hand, nothing would be said there which he had not already read among the documents at the Bureau of Statistics.

The soprano won an easy triumph in this contest, and Philip and Ruth enjoyed the concert with keen zest, and without a single premonition of the happening of events which were to change the color of both their lives. The great singer awoke in them such delicious thrills as she sang tenderly of the joys and woes of lovers and warriors of a by-gone age, that they had no thoughts to squander upon Israel Ginzberg and his followers, who at that very instant, in a dingy, smoke-laden hall, were declaiming in shrill, passionate voices about the more sordid but none the less intense sorrows of the modern factory worker.

While Ginzberg in East Baltimore talked bitterly of the intolerable brutality of his more fortunate brother-Jew, Clarence Kaufman, and while Philip and Ruth at Mt. Vernon Place drank in the melody poured forth by

A LITTLE MATTER OF HOMICIDE

the famous singer (congratulating themselves without knowing exactly why, because they knew her to share with them the bond of Race)—in still another quarter of the city, alongside the huge buildings of the Pioneer Clothing Company, one more scene in this dull gray drama was being enacted.

Around and around the factory structures, which occupied an entire city block, there marched a procession of men and women, moving very slowly but without pause,—like a long, black caterpillar. From inside the factory could be heard a steady whirr and clatter which announced to the men and women on the pavement the presence at their machines of unsympathetic strangers filching their bread from them. Now and then as the twilight grew deeper a flurry of chill rain fell, but the patient little regiment continued unceasingly its endless circuit of the walls. They were pickets. They had been told the law in force in this land of absolute equality to rich and poor. They knew it was their privilege to speak with strike breakers if they did so peaceably, and to persuade them, if they could, of the grievous wrong they were doing to their more courageous comrades. But they had also been taught—and compelled by police justices to pay for the information—the somewhat inconsistent duty of refraining from obstructing the side-walks in the slightest degree. It was rather difficult to reconcile these interesting principles of our Jurisprudence, but the ingenuity of the descendants of the Talmudists had not proved unequal to the labor. As long as the group kept in orderly motion it could not be said to be causing an impediment to traffic. There was no City Ordinance which could abridge their right to pass and re-pass any designated place upon the

141

public streets. Moreover, the sight of these dejected men, with their dark, woe-begone faces, and the women, ill protected from the rigors of the weather, was not without a definite dramatic appeal. The strikers realized this, and the procession of unemployed at the factory door had become a daily incident of the closing hour.

About the wide entrance to the plant was grouped a file of blue-coated policemen, no less patient and far more alert in appearance, than the strikers they had come to observe. These men had no grievance of any kind against the rebellious garment workers. If they had any prejudices on the subject they were mainly against the " scabs." Still, a policeman's primary duty is to preserve order and to obey the commands of his superiors. Therefore, the policemen on duty stoically accepted their service here as part of the day's work and were grateful the strikers were mostly Jews and Slavs, instead of upstanding Irishmen like many of themselves. Indeed, they ordinarily found the former employees of the Pioneer Company rather docile. These immigrants had brought from their native lands across the sea a wholesome terror of the Law, and its inevitable disasters for poor folk. There were often murmurs of remonstrance, but never definite defiance of constituted authority. Now and then, bitter words between some striker and strike-breaker would develop into an interchange of blows. Twice during the course of the trouble, angry gusts of passion had swept over the crowd, and stones had been thrown at the strike-breakers as they left the buildings. But the police, up to this time, had never been resisted. When they decided to make an arrest there were no attempts at rescue. Some difficulties had been anticipated on account of the volatile nature of those strikers of Italian extraction, but less violent Jewish and Slavic comrades had held them in leash. The police captain in charge extended heart-felt congratulations to himself whenever he reflected upon the credit he would probably receive as the result of a task whose difficulties were few.

The dusk had almost faded into night when the rhythmic throbbing of the machinery within the buildings ceased. The adjoining streets, however, remained under the blue-white glare of the electric lamps no less bright than in the day except for the sharp shadows around the angles of the walls. Under this cold piercing light the weary line of marchers continued to make its monotonous progress—as though, like their fathers of old, they believed the walls of this new Jericho must fall when they had made the prescribed number of circuits, and sounded their trumpet call of justice.

A few minutes later, the file of policemen displayed signs of a greater activity, the space about the wide doorway was cleared, the gates opened, and a number of men issued timidly forth and hurried away. There were few women among the operators who were now at labor for the Pioneer Company. The first of those who emerged were permitted to go without interference, but soon, the pickets appeared to pluck up courage, and groups gathered about the departing laborers, gesticulating excitedly, and raking them, fore and aft, with vigorous arguments setting forth the iniquity of their behavior. At least two or three of the strikers invariably talked at the same time and the result was an incoherent jumble of mere syllables. Now and then, however, such expressions as " scab " and " robber " would float for an instant upon the surface

THE CHOSEN PEOPLE

of the noisy confusion of words. Most of the strike-
breakers entered into no rejoinders but elbowed their way
out of the crowd assisted by the police. A few remained
to toss back the same quality of abusive argument they
had received and a little passion-stirred group became sta-
tionary upon the pavement. Two policemen hurriedly
approached.

"Here," one bawled roughly, "you've got to move on.
You can't block up the street this way."

One of the strikers, evidently a spokesman, answered
respectfully, but firmly in English grammatically perfect
in spite of a marked accent.

"We have a right to talk to them provided we don't
threaten. Judge Perkins said so."

"Ye've got no right to make them stand and listen
to ye, if they don't want to," the policeman answered,
and assuming without further parley a disinclination to
listen on the part of the strike-breakers, he repeated
roughly his command:

"Come,—move on—clear the path!"

He began none too gently, but with no ill-will, to push
the crowd away. Several other patrolmen came to his
assistance. The group receded with irritating slowness.
It seemed hard to them to have waited in the drizzle all
these hours for a word with the men who were stealing
their jobs, only to be cheated at the end in this unfeeling
manner. They did not resist, but their obedience was
sullen and incomplete.

Just then, the crowd began to grow perceptibly larger.
The strikers who had spent the afternoon at the mass-
meeting, listening to Ginzberg's fervid recital of their
grievances, and growing mad with self-pity, had made

their way up-town to the factory almost in a body. They pushed closer to the entrance, to discover the cause of the disturbance, and the retreating current of obstructionists forced back by the police, was carried forward again by this new and stronger impetus. Meanwhile, more women and men were issuing from the factory, only to become wedged in the throng. One of the pickets slipped and fell upon the wet pavement, and those on the outskirts of the crowd, unable either to see or hear clearly, believed he had been deliberately felled to the ground. The temper of all, —the strikers, the strike-breakers, and the squad of officers —became ugly. Each faction was sure some real injury was intended to it. The Captain ordered his men to draw their clubs and called to the crowd to stand back.

"We are going to clear the street!" he shouted, "stand back! You'll get hurt if you don't."

Those nearest the factory door would have been only too glad to escape, but their efforts in that direction were effectually blocked by the new-comers in the rear, who were themselves well out of reach of the dreaded clubs, and who in addition were still seething with the emotions of the afternoon's meeting. Meanwhile, the blue-coated file pressed irresistibly forward. They were as considerate as they could possibly afford to be, remembering their primary duty to clear the street, but it was inevitable that some unfortunates should be tightly wedged in the struggling mass. Screams, of women as well as men, began to mingle themselves with threats and curses. Several more men lost their footing and fell, and above all the noise there was heard the blood-curdling shriek of one tortured creature who was trampled upon in the confusion. By this time, there was an uncontrollable frenzy of fury and terror among the men who had marched up town from the meeting, where they had been told how lightly their lives were valued by their oppressors. Their masters were finding starving them too slow a process. They were about to have them crushed to death under the feet of their own comrades, or the brutal clubs of the police. It was a game at which two could play. Suddenly above the heads of the struggling men, and into the doorway of the factory, there was swiftly hurled a well-directed fragment of brick. Those near the entrance heard a sharp, hideous, cracking noise as the missile crashed squarely against the head of a man who was in the act of crossing the threshold. Without a single cry or murmur, he swayed unsteadily for an instant, crumpled up and fell, lying half within and half without the building, a dishevelled, grotesque bundle of garments and bruised flesh.

The crowd seemed awed by this sudden manifestation of its own desperate mood. The deadly, though still shapeless thoughts which had been finding lodgment in the minds of many, had without warning been translated into deed, like a prayer of unthinking hate, too promptly answered. The result lay there, uncomplainingly, in the entrance way to the factory, the blood slowly trickling from the wounded head. How badly the man was injured, or what results might follow, it was impossible to foresee. Enough—perhaps far too much—had been done for today! The crowd began rapidly to melt away. But not before the keen-eyed police-captain had called to two of his men:

" That man with the brown derby! on the curb, see? Get him, and the man on each side! It was one of those! "

Ten minutes later the street was almost deserted. A

stray policeman was to be seen here and there, by way of an excess of caution. The factory had completely disgorged its workers and had settled down to a night of well-guarded quiet. The strikers had returned to their homes, with a confused realization of having, somehow, put themselves in the wrong.

Philip driving home with Ruth after the concert, found his afternoon's enjoyment unmarred by any echo of the unseemly little incident. If any rumor regarding it drifted up-town, it did not appear sufficiently important or dramatic to be worth repetition. The newspapers, next day, gave it scant consideration, merely printing the barest details, and stating that the physicians at the Mercy Hospital feared the injured man—whose name was Rosen—had sustained a fractured skull. It was also added that a striker named Isaac Clutsky, after three hours of rigid questioning in the office of Detective MacBurney, had admitted throwing the brick and was being held by the authorities to await the result of Rosen's injuries.

The following day the newspapers printed nothing at all about the occurrence, but on Saturday there was an obscure paragraph in both morning journals, telling the public of Rosen's death.

After which things resumed, once more, their accustomed course. Perhaps the pickets at the factory were somewhat fewer and more cautious, the detachment of patrolmen slightly increased in number, and more vigilant. The dead man, who had come from Rochester to find work and death, in Baltimore, was duly buried, and apparently, forgotten. If any hearts were stricken because his life had been so suddenly shattered, they beat in far-away cities, and no one here seemed either to remember or to care—no one, except Clutsky, caged like an animal in a grated cell, brooding dumbly on the infinitesimal instant it had taken him to tear down forever the whole fabric of his happiness; but Clutsky was a negligible creature, esteemed little by his comrades or his former employers. His fellow workmen scornfully decided his ruin had been principally the result of his own stupidity in consenting to talk to the detectives. If he had held his tongue and awaited the coming of a lawyer, no one could have proved conclusively whose hand had hurried Rosen out of the world.

Nevertheless, in spite of appearances, the dead strike-breaker was not entirely forgotten. It was his fate to be remembered most by men who had never seen him in life and who would have turned from him disdainfully if he had entered their presence.

While the strike continued to drag its length wearily along, and the Pioneer's stockholders to indulge in faint murmurs, and while the garment workers' Union took note with increasing dread of its rapidly diminishing treasury, three very exclusive night conferences were held at the home of Mr. Clarence Kaufman. The first night, his guests included only an eminent lawyer and a ragged furtive-eyed Russian Jew, who was commonly reputed to be one of the loudest-voiced partisans of the rebellious workers. The second night found Mr. Kaufman's library polluted by the blighting presence of four unkempt residents of the East Side, whose words were dignified by the minute attention of three members of the legal fraternity, and recorded in the form of swiftly-pencilled hieroglyphics by an expert stenographer.

On the third night, the entire executive board of the

A LITTLE MATTER OF HOMICIDE

Pioneer Clothing Company remained until a late hour with Mr. Kaufman and his attorneys, talking long and earnestly in subdued voices as they filled the room with expensive cigar smoke. Two days later, a deadly mine was exploded in the camp of the enemy when the Grand Jury " Upon their oaths presented Israel Ginzberg," the heart and soul of the strike, because " before said murder and felony were committed, he did at a place of public assembly, in said City of Baltimore, known as Eastern Hall, unlawfully, maliciously and feloniously, incite, procure, counsel, and command the said Isaac Clutsky to do and commit said felony and murder; against the peace and dignity of the State of Maryland."

CHAPTER XII

How a Popular Hero is Made

It was about half past four in the short winter afternoon when two men in "plain clothes" met Israel Ginzberg on his way home from a meeting of one of the strikers' committees, and quietly insisted upon his accompanying them to the Central Police Station. The choice of this hour was not mere accident. The last editions of the evening newspapers were then almost ready for the presses; Judges and Magistrates, with inconvenient notions on the subject of bail, had long since gone to their homes, and there was a fair possibility of a convenient night devoted to pleasant and illuminating conversation between a prisoner with a nervous temperament, and a detective or two with inquiring minds.

It was about half past eight on the same evening when David Gordon, carrying a leather brief bag in one hand, walked briskly into the Station-house building, and up to the brass rail, behind which the Lieutenant in charge sat writing laboriously in a ponderous book of records.

"Good evening, Lieutenant," the lawyer said crisply, "my name's David Gordon."

"Good evening, Mr. Gordon," the Lieutenant replied deferentially, looking up from his desk, "maybe you remember me. I was a witness for the Railroad Company in the Atley case."

"Of course I remember you," David answered easily. "If you weren't a policeman, I'd expect you to harbor a grudge against me. But you fellows have better sense. You know it's all part of the day's work."

A genial, tolerant grin overspread the Lieutenant's honest face.

"Yes, Sir," he agreed, "of course. But really, the accident did happen just the way I told it."

David nodded.

"A Jury is like one's wife," he smiled, "we know she's talking nonsense, but we have to do what she says."

The Lieutenant's laugh was heartier than the lawyer had dared to hope. When he relapsed into official gravity, he inquired:

"What can we do for you, Mr. Gordon?"

"You've got a client of mine locked up here—Israel Ginzberg. I want to see him."

The lieutenant twisted around uneasily in his chair.

"It's a serious charge, Mr. Gordon,—accomplice to murder. Captain MacBurney said he wanted to talk with the man before he saw anyone else."

It was evident that the Captain of Detectives had decided a few hours of solitude might put the accused into a more pleasant frame of mind for the proposed interview.

"If I let you see him," the Lieutenant went on doubtfully, "I'm going to get into trouble."

"I wouldn't want to get you in trouble," David remarked with evident concern, "but for all that, I've got to see the man. I'll 'phone MacBurney. Is he at home or at headquarters?"

The Lieutenant, happy at shifting this inconvenient decision from his own shoulders, promptly put his superior into telephone communication with the lawyer, and listened eagerly to David's end of the conversation.

"Hello! Captain! This is David Gordon. I'm at the Central, and I want to see a client—Israel Ginzberg. Yes, I said *David* Gordon * * * Well, I suppose I may amuse myself with a criminal case once in ten years if I choose * * * No, I mean to see him *now,*—at once, —immediately * * * We both know what the law is, Captain, and I'm accustomed to taking all it gives me * * * Well, you know I can always manage to get hold of a Judge or two, even in the night time; besides, it's only three blocks to the nearest newspaper office * * * You bet,—I'm just pining for a chance to give a sob story to a reporter * * * Oh well, you musn't take it that way, Captain * * * You're a fighting man yourself * * * If I ran away when you barked at me, you'd never hire me next time you got into a mess!"

He beckoned to the Lieutenant to take the telephone receiver.

"He says I may see Ginzberg," David announced, "he wants to tell you so."

Without further delay, a turnkey led the lawyer toward the lock-up in the rear of the building. The structure had originally been a school-house, and in happier days, had echoed the pleasant treble voices of boys and girls, intent on devoting themselves to as little work and as much play as their watchful teachers would permit. When the slowly rising tide of commerce had crept northward, the children had been transferred to a more remote section, and the ugly brick building had degenerated into this grim machine for drilling into the less pliant minds of adults, stern—if somewhat hazy—lessons regarding the attitude of the Criminal Law toward the outcasts ensnared in its meshes. The first and most striking principle to be absorbed by these hapless pupils seemed to be that in this world of punishments, men are bitterly cruel to one another. This elementary truism was proclaimed in unmistakable manner by the rows of barred iron cells, each (with its wooden bench and its concrete floor, within which were locked, pending further experimentation, the men and women who were, under our humane and scrupulous jurisprudence, presumed to be spotlessly innocent until a jury of their peers should in its sapience think wise to continue the rigors they had already tasted. The steel cells had been erected in the large hall which had once been the school's assembly room. Here the little scholars had gathered together on Friday afternoons to "speak pieces," and on less important days to listen to official announcements of petty weal and woe. The most unmanageable of the children had been sent to this room to be disciplined by the principal, instead of by their own teacher, and many an anxious boy or girl whose former bravado had singularly melted away during the long minutes of detention, had awaited with trepidation the inevitable hour of reckoning.

Men and women, no wiser than their childish predecessors, were now being " kept in " after another fashion, within the same walls. The lighting of the cell-tier, though dim and sepulchral, was amply sufficient to enable the guards to observe the behavior of each of the prisoners. It was still early in the night, and many of the cages were, as yet, untenanted. In several, men to whom this experience was no novelty, lay stretched out serenely on their benches, sleeping composedly, if not always noiselessly. In another cell, a hopelessly intoxicated human animal declaimed indignantly, though incoherently, against the tyranny of all constituted authority, his maudlin ravings being now and then interrupted by disgusting paroxysms of nausea. In the women's section at the opposite side of the room, a slatternly creature sat all huddled together, her shapeless body quivering with harsh racking sobs; but for the most part, the inhabitants of these grated tenements kept silent vigil, crouching stolidly, each on his bench, looking out through the bars with dull, hopeless eyes. They had blundered into a trap; there was nothing much to be done about it except to submit to whatever infliction the successful hunters might find fit to impose. Meanwhile, for tonight, they must wait. Over the whole room, despite the open windows, there hung a sickening odor of mingled disinfecting solutions and the stenches for which these attempted remedies had been devised. David Gordon, although not unduly fastidious, sniffed rebelliously, as he followed the turnkey.

He was led to a cell at the end of the room furthest removed from the entrance. The lawyer's quick eye noticed at once the absence of any neighbors in the cages next the prisoner. Mr. Ginzberg, it was evident, was thought by his instructors in practical ethics, a proper subject for searching and uninterrupted communion with his own soul.

"That's him!" the turnkey announced, pointing with his thumb.

David did not need to be introduced. He and the labor leader had exchanged words before, besides which the lawyer had taken the trouble to learn many details regarding his new client,—his temperament, his habits and his unfortunate diction. An ability for unusually rapid work, and a curiosity about seemingly irrelevant details were part of David's equipment, and he had been devoting his energies exclusively to this matter for the past three hours. He had made a mental wager with himself to the effect that Ginzberg's composure would by this time be completely shattered, but he had not expected to find him so utterly unmanned.

His cell was sufficiently roomy to enable its occupant to indulge in three uninterrupted paces. In this restricted space, however, Ginzberg must have traveled many miles during the few hours of his confinement. He had been unable to remain seated. He had darted restlessly to and fro, dramatizing for himself the bewilderment and anguish of his wife, wondering why none of his men came to his help, and how many more hours he could endure this torture before the mental confusion he already felt would become downright lunacy. He was weak from hunger, yet he could not think of food without a positive physical qualm of illness; he felt feverish and faint; his features worked convulsively, and more than once he was guilty of unconcealed tears.

The turnkey looked at the man with open scorn and thanked the God who had created him an Irishman without superfluous nerves.

David came directly to the grating and grasped Ginzberg's hand.

"I'm Gordon," he began with a reassuring directness. "You recognize me,—don't you? Some of your friends have employed me to take care of you. I've seen the Union people, too."

"Oh, thank God, you've come!" exclaimed Ginzberg, too unstrung to indulge in pretences of fortitude. "I couldn't have stood it another hour. I was going mad. You must get me out of here! My wife's been here. The guard told me. She was crying; they wouldn't let her see me. I don't know how she'll get along without me—the children, too! And what have I done they can lock me up for? Nothing! For God's sake, Mr. Gordon, get me out of here!"

David gripped the man by the arm and spoke to him sternly, though almost in a whisper:

"I came here to find a labor leader for a client, not a baby. Pull yourself together, man! If you're going to send each one of this riff-raff out of here, to tell how you sat down and howled like a whipped cur, nobody will be able to help you. Don't worry about your wife. I'll look after her. You and I have a man-sized job before us! Stop whining, and let's get down to work!"

Ginzberg's expression was one of actual astonishment to find such brutality and absence of sympathy in the behavior of his new-found ally. Nevertheless, the lawyer's sharp words had the desired effect. Ginzberg became silent, and at least outwardly, collected, although his most pronounced emotion at the minute was one of angry disappointment.

Meanwhile, David, noticing an inquisitive face peering through each cell door, and presuming a pair of ears to be attached to each face, called to the turnkey.

"Go tell the Lieutenant," he ordered, with the calm assurance of one who anticipates no doubt of the granting of his requests, "I can't consult with this man out here. Tell him I want a private room. There are papers to be signed. It isn't light enough to read them here, and I'm not used to talking through bars. Say I'll be responsible for the man's safe keeping."

A few minutes later, David and his client were seated in an upstairs room before a small table. Except for the two chairs and table the room was bare. The windows were covered with an iron grating and its heavy wooden door had been ostentatiously bolted from the outside. Nevertheless, it was a private consultation room. It was a relief, if only temporary, from the abhorrent cell, with its loathsome neighbors. Ginzberg began to reflect with some feeling of reassurance that if his mentor was ungentle to him he was correspondingly forceful in his behalf.

The lawyer laid his brief case on the table, and unlocked it, disclosing a mass of papers and a compact, but rather inviting little bundle, containing luncheon.

"To begin with—eat that!" he commanded. "The meat is ' kosher.' I s'pose you haven't had any supper!"

"No," Ginzberg said, secretly tempted, but feeling the necessity of maintaining his pose, "thank you just the same, but I don't think I can eat in here, Mr. Gordon. You must fix it so I can go home!'

"You can eat when I tell you to, or do most anything else," David insisted, without one sign of weakening. "Hungry men take longer to think, and I've no time to waste. Whenever you can't manage to obey orders you can get one of the small fry to look after you. I do my fighting with the other side—not with my own clients."

The overawed Ginzberg began to munch the sandwiches with docility.

David went on with his dictatorial and uncompromising remarks.

"You've got to get this idea of going home out of your head," he announced, "you're going to get out of here in the morning, but you're not going home. You're going to Jail!"

Ginzberg laid down the half-consumed sandwich and once more showed signs of collapse.

"I won't!" he wailed, "I can't! I can't stand it! I'll be crazy in a day. Besides, there's my wife, and the Union, too. There must be some way to get me out! For God's sake, try!"

David eyed him with apparent unconcern, while he motioned him pitilessly back to his food.

"Now listen," he began, "don't be a baby! This job we're going to do isn't one to be begun by whimpering because your wife has cried a little. I'm going to see her when I leave here, and I'll bet she's behaving better than you are. She isn't going to starve. I'll take care of that. Meanwhile, the fiercest labor battle that ever happened in this State is going to be fought about you—Israel Ginzsberg—and you sit there snivelling like a scared child. You haven't even a chance to say whether you want to fight or not. If you don't win, the Pioneer crowd will smash you as though you were a cockroach."

The simile seemed trying to Ginzberg's none too robust appetite, and David, perceiving he had been too vivid, made a wry smile of discomfiture and went on.

"So we've got to win. There's nothing else for it. And I can save you; perhaps some other lawyer couldn't, but I can—that is, if you do precisely as I bid you. As I'm working up this defense, you're to be a popular hero. You can't blubber the words I'm putting into your mouth through your tears!"

In spite of these serious words, or perhaps just because Gordon seemed perfectly willing to face a bad situation without illusions, his client found a definite solace in his lawyer's strength.

"But," Ginzberg urged, "you could do all this better if I were out of here—if I were home! couldn't you? And it must be easy to get bail for me. I haven't done anything. Any Judge can see that!"

David shook his head peremptorily.

"Any Judge couldn't see that. I can't see it myself. You don't seem to understand the seriousness of this affair. Were you playing with words all the time? Did you think you could begin a war with people like the Pioneer, and then when they began to strike back at you, call out like a little boy that you didn't want to play any more? There's a man dead! You're accused of inciting a murder!"

"I didn't kill him," Ginzberg protested excitedly. "I didn't even go with the men to the factory. I was miles away. What did I have to do with it?"

"You did kill him!" David insisted sternly, "I don't say you did wrong, and I'm going to save you from any punishment, but you did kill him. You crushed his skull with the speech you made! You can't toss dynamite around and pretend surprise when it explodes. Are you going to say you didn't expect anyone to take you seriously? Everyone will laugh at you! Nobody will believe you! You've got to be a man and give your action some dignity, whether you want to or not!"

The lawyer was observing his client narrowly, and noted with the artist's pleasure in his workmanship the invigorating effect of his words.

Ginzberg was silent for a minute. "Then I can't get bail?" he asked, but he put the question without weakness.

David gave him a look of definite approbation.

"I don't know," was his frank admission, "whether I could get bail for you or not. In the absence of special reasons, persons accused of murder are not admitted to bail, in any amount—no matter how large. But I don't intend to try. I've found out what you said that day at Eastern Hall. You went pretty far! I know you didn't mean to. It's a weakness we talkers have."

For the first time, David smiled good-humoredly at Ginzberg, before he went on: "Well, there's no use in bothering about that now, but technically, I'm afraid you couldn't put up a very strong defence. We've got to arouse a public sentiment. I am going to exhibit you as a noble martyr, fearlessly facing death for the cause of suffering labor. That's why I've been yelping at you to keep a stiff lip. A martyr must never appear to be frightened—no matter what happens. Look heroic! Hold your tongue! Let me do the talking for you, and I'll make a national figure of you; people from one end of the country to the other will read about you and the brave fight you're making. In the end, when the case comes to trial, no Juryman will be able to think about you without getting a lump in his throat. On the other hand, if you show the white feather, you're done for. You'll just be a pitiful, stupid baby. Your own men will go back to their jobs and make you the scapegoat. The best you can hope for is a few years less in the Penitentiary. You won't have a friend left in the world."

David faced him squarely across the table, looking searchingly into his eyes.

"You're all right now!" he announced, in a tone of absolute finality, "you've had your little spasm, and you're through with it. I'm glad MacBurney put off seeing you. I can fill the newspapers with tales of your courage tomorrow, can't I? You're sure of yourself?"

Something of David's resolution had infected the labor

leader; besides, the thought of the coming flood of newspaper publicity was not without the appeal to Ginzberg's vanity which the lawyer had anticipated.

"I'll play your game," he answered. "You're sure you'll pull me through, though, aren't you?"

"Yes," David assured him, curtly, "if you do as I tell you. Now, remember! no interviews of any kind with anybody. Tell reporters you will give out signed statements. Tell the Detectives, David Gordon said he'd have them before the Police Board if they tried to make you disobey his orders. They'll know I mean what I say, and besides, I'll tell them the same thing myself. Here's some money! Send out for books and newspapers; read; amuse yourself as best you can, and don't talk, don't get intimate with other prisoners and above all,—don't whine! If you see Clutsky in Jail, avoid him as if he had smallpox! We can't afford to burden ourselves with him! When you think you can see your wife without losing your nerve, I'll send her to you. Don't bother about her, or the Union, or anything else, but keep quiet, let me talk for you, and enjoy the sensations of being a hero!"

"I'll try," Ginzberg promised.

"You can do it," David said encouragingly, "besides, there's money in it for you—lots of money. When you get out, you can write a book about it, and give lectures, and people will tumble over each other to pay you. If you can't write the stuff yourself, you can hire someone at eight dollars a week."

Ginzberg's pleasure in this distant smile of fortune was somewhat tempered by David's unfeeling aspersions on his capacity for authorship; but, without giving him time for remonstrance, the lawyer, drawing a number of documents from his bag, continued:

11   161

THE CHOSEN PEOPLE

" Here are three statements—one is to the Public generally, setting forth your outrageous treatment; the second is to the Garment Workers, exhorting them to be firm, no matter what your cruel fate may be; the third is to the Jews of Baltimore, asking as one Jew to the others what their religion means. All three will be on the front page of the morning newspapers. They'll make a magnificent splash, and the papers won't feel any worse toward you, when they think of the receipted advertising bills. Sign them!"

Ginzberg took David's fountain pen, and signed obediently.

" You may read them if you want," Gordon said indulgently, " they're good stuff."

The imprisoned Garment Worker took advantage of the lawyer's permission. He would not have worded any of the statements in the form in which he found them. His own style was somewhat more florid. Still, he had enough native shrewdness to realize the value of his lawyer's efforts, and began to congratulate himself on the lucky chance which had sent him this adroit champion.

The statements had been rather hastily dictated by Gordon, but all of his work was done at high speed, and he did not feel he could have improved much on his first drafts by labored revisions. He knew his phrases bore no resemblance to those of the man who was to sign them, but he knew also how few people in the entire City would be able to recognize either Ginzberg's characteristic style, or his own.

The statement to Ginzberg's co-religionists had received the largest amount of David's attention. The paper read:

HOW A POPULAR HERO IS MADE

" To the Jews of Baltimore:

I am a Jew, like yourselves—at least, like some of you, for I have always been poor, and always worked for my bread, with my hands. It was for Jews that I worked. They were rich, and I was poor, but I had read in the Law of Moses that they were my brothers. I believed it. Tonight I am sitting alone in a cell, and I am not so sure. I have broken no law, either of God or man. I have striven to make things easier for my comrades; I have never injured anyone, yet it is Jews who have locked this iron door upon me, and Jews whose wealth and talents are devoted to sending me to my death, or still worse, to a life behind prison walls, separated forever from my wife and helpless little children.

"They do this thing because I had the courage to tell them they were not dealing justly with the men and women who labored unceasingly, in poverty and misery, so that they, their fellow-Jews, might be gorged with gold. I said no more than every teacher of such subjects, in every college, knows to be true. I said no more than each of you knows, in his heart, to be true; if you doubt one word of it, leave your own comfortable homes and come down to the hovels, where we drag out our miserable lives, and then read my words again.

"But we asked no help at your hands to cure these cruel conditions. It was our own task. Without education, without money, without anything but the knowledge that we fought for Justice—we struggled for the coming of a happier day. We would have gained our end. I believe—whether I shall live to see it or not—we shall still gain it. But, meanwhile, our oppressors—Jews, like ourselves—sought for a weapon to punish the man whom they had not been able to silence. They found it in the desperate deed of a poor wretch, crazed by his wrongs. They, who created the conditions which inflamed his disordered mind, are the true perpetrators of his deplorable crime—not I, who merely pointed to the work of their hands.

"I wish I could bring Samuel Rosen back again to life. He was a fellow-worker, however mistaken, and a fellow-Jew. But the owners of the Pioneer factory shook with devilish glee when he died. It gave them a chance to kill another man—another Jew—whose presence on earth was inconvenient. It did not matter whether the man whose blood they sought was innocent as his

163

children, or guilty as themselves. It did not matter what he had
taught. They will find ways—never fear! to twist and distort his
plain words. He must be stoned like the prophets of old. who
dared to tell the truth to their wicked kings!

"I am not concerned about my own fate. No matter what
happens to me, I shall find strength to bear it. But there is one
thing I do want, here in my prison, to learn. I want to know
what your religion means to you! There isn't room in the
same Judaism for men like my oppressors and myself. I am
told the President of the Pioneer Company is also the President
of one of your most important synagogues. I want to know if
there is still space under the dome of that Temple for the men
who think it no crime to kill another, unless he will buy his
life at the price of slavish Silence. I want to know if you are
just mumbling words when you talk of Loving your neighbor
as yourself. I want to know if your Religion is only a theatrical sham. If it is, I and all who think as I do, want to cut
ourselves loose from you as though you were polluted! If it isn't,
if your creed means anything, if the God you worship isn't
a hollow mockery, you have got to take sides against the men who
claim to be part and parcel of your Holy Faith, while they scheme
and plot to revive for the mere lust of money-making, the perse-
cutions their own ancestors endured because, like me, they would
not cease from proclaiming the truth."

As Ginzberg finished reading the paper, a film of
moisture spread over his eyes—so deeply was his self-pity
moved by the recital of his woes, and the nobility of his
cause. The author smiled cynically, as he estimated
the effect of his passionate statement on the man who
signed it.

"Cut it out of the newspaper," was his half-mocking
command, "and read it now and then. It makes you
wear just the face you need;—sort of combination of
Holy Martyr and gallant Captain of the sinking ship!
Well, that's about all! I must see your wife and the
newspaper men before I go home, so I'd better be off."

HOW A POPULAR HERO IS MADE

He rose and bundled his papers together and prepared to knock at the door for the turnkey who was to liberate David and conduct Ginzberg back to his cell.

"One thing more, Mr. Gordon," the garment worker said with some hesitation, " I know you don't often take criminal cases and that your fees are always big, I haven't any money, and you know how the Union's fixed, —what about your pay, and all these advertising bills?"

David shrugged his shoulders impatiently.

"Don't you bother," he replied brusquely, "I'm not working for nothing. A very philanthropic gentleman," an elusive smile played about his lips for a second, " who desires to remain unknown, has become interested in your case. He's determined you shan't suffer, even if you are poor. He's paying me a good stiff fee, and isn't stinting me about expenses. See that you hold your tongue about this, too."

Ginzberg looked at the lawyer with a very perceptible uneasiness.

"Well!" David demanded sharply, "what do you care? Any time my services don't please you, you have only to say so. Did you ever hear of any client of mine who didn't get a little more than a square deal?"

"Oh, no! Mr. Gordon," Ginzberg protested, in almost abject fear of having given offense.

"Then you needn't be afraid I'll begin with you!" David snapped out, and turning, beat impatiently upon the heavy door.

CHAPTER XIII

The Appeal to Organized Charity

David Gordon certainly knew his public. His advertisements did not fail to cause the " magnificent splash " he had predicted. All next day the town echoed his phrases, and Israel Ginzberg, before noon, became the most-discussed citizen of Baltimore. He was the victim of a detestable plot, or a shrewd, unscrupulous agitator— according to the sentimentality, youth, politics and bank account of each one of his half million judges. Since more citizens of Baltimore are distressed because of an occasional or chronic scarcity of funds, than those who suffer because of an excess in that respect, and because even among the latter there are many who have purchased with their wealth and leisure a well-stocked equipment of sensibilities and genteel radicalism, the tide of Public Opinion was strongly in favor of the imprisoned labor leader.

The newspapers, which up to this time had treated the strike and everything pertaining to it, with languid disdain, now swerved to the other extreme,—not, to do them justice, because of their receipted advertising bills, as David had cynically predicted, but because such a bitter quarrel, with the promised excitement of a dramatic criminal trial as a climax, was " news," and good circulation-feeding news, at that. A steady stream of pathetic little memoirs of the chaste family life and communal activities of Mr. Ginzberg, trickled from Mr. Gordon's office into the reading columns of that unshackled press which gives the public exactly what it wants.

166

THE APPEAL TO ORGANIZED CHARITY

There was much surprise expressed at David Gordon's connection with the case. The employment on Ginzberg's behalf of one of the City's foremost lawyers, whose clientele for a number of years had included some of the wealthiest and most influential members of Baltimore's financial group, occasioned curious surmises—many of them decidedly unfavorable. David met this situation with another statement, repeating to the Public substantially what he had told Ginzberg himself. An extremely wealthy and public-spirited gentleman, believing a cruel judicial wrong was about to be perpetrated, had retained his services to make sure the legal rights of the accused were fully safe-guarded. For his own part, David Gordon added, he had accepted eagerly the opportunity thus offered to defend the cause of an innocent and injured co-religionist and former neighbor,—regretting only his financial inability to devote his time and whatever skill he might possess, to gratuitous service.

This statement proved extremely effective. If David had said he was serving without any compensation, the assertion would have been greeted everywhere with incredulous smiles, such being the guileless nature of Man. If David Gordon had been poor and unknown, he might reasonably have been expected to break a lance on behalf of wounded and oppressed Truth. He would then have been credited with a praiseworthy and enterprising thirst for legitimate advertising; but all of us value Success much too highly to believe it capable of stooping to the depths of such a vulgar, irrational emotion as sentimental unselfishness. Therefore, when David had calmly an-

167

nounced the presence of a generous fee jingling in his pocket, the public's respect for him, and incidentally for the man he had not neglected to link with himself as a " co-religionist and former neighbor," increased in direct proportion to the supposed size of his " retainer."

While all the City was buzzing with confused assertions and denials regarding the merits of the strike and of this prosecution, the Pioneer directors, beginning in repent, perhaps, of the hornets' nests they had unwittingly stirred up, but deeming it impossible to retrace their steps, made the further mistake of publishing rejoinders to the Ginzberg advertisements. They were, like all the Pioneer statements, models of logic and coherence. They set forth the physical advantages of the plant, the payment to the employees of the largest wage consistent with a reasonable profit, the prompt offer of the Company to submit to a partial arbitration of their differences, and the arbitrary refusal by the strikers of this proposal. They quoted and emphasized the fiery and intemperate language used by Ginzberg in his speech at Eastern Hall, and insisted that after a man's life had been wantonly sacrificed, the original merits of the strike had become a subordinate issue, and the prosecution had become necessary in the interests of the public safety.

The morning after, found the front page of the newspapers plastered with the reply David Gordon had delightedly prepared. It eluded all the strong points of the Pioneer Company's case. To prove the inadequacy of the wages paid, graphic little pen pictures of the homes of the employees were drawn, citing in each case, the street name and number of some wretched dwelling. It argued from the long number of prior strikes in the

factory the inability of the workers to deal with their
employers unless they were permitted to organize. The
flat refusal of the Company to include this disputed point
in the proposed arbitration was set forth in full detail.
The statement openly accused the Pioneer Company of
misquoting Ginzberg's speech, adding that the true text
was withheld only to baffle the designs of certain witnesses
for the State, who at the best, would prove none too
scrupulous. It next proceeded to quote from the most
prominent text writers and teachers of economics numerous statements far more radical—though possibly
more tactfully worded—than those imputed to Ginzberg.
Lastly, the personal note was again artfully sounded.
There was a burst of rhetoric, pitilessly excoriating the
relentless persecution of the imprisoned labor leader and
the despicable hypocrisy of the factory owners.

The statement was a little masterpiece of special pleading, done into the language of the "man in the street."
If it was not perfect reasoning, it was something more
effective. Even Mr. Kaufman's friends were somewhat
shaken by its merciless vehemence. Ginzberg began to
acquire a respectable number of partisans, up-town, as
well as down-town.

Among others whose emotions were profoundly stirred
by this bitter war of words, was Philip Graetz. He
felt more than ever the helplessness of his position,
doomed as he was by the irony of his training, and his
apparent leadership of his people, to an indecision and
inactivity against which his very soul rebelled. His
well-trained intellect forced him to note the fallacies
in Ginzberg's pleas, but his quick, generous sympathies
were all with the starved natures who had dared—with

or without warrant of law—to snatch hungrily at the rich prizes of life which had been his own unquestioned inheritance. He found but little encouragement in this attitude from Ruth, who was still the victim of her new-found inability to conceal her real sentiments from Philip —even to win and hold his affections.

They pored over the advertisements together, and when Philip gave vent to an expression of heartfelt pity, Ruth exclaimed impatiently:

"Oh! of course, he's clever—diabolically clever!"

"Who—this poor Ginzberg creature?" Philip asked wonderingly.

"No—not Ginzberg—you don't suppose he wrote this stuff! It's David Gordon's. I can recognize him in every word, can't you?"

"Yes, I suppose he did the actual writing," answered Philip, impatiently. "What difference does that make, if the ideas ring true?"

"But they don't," Ruth retorted rebelliously, "at least, not to me. And it isn't because I have any sympathy to waste on Clarence Kaufman, or because I've got some money locked up in his factory. I wish every penny of it was gone, so I wouldn't feel responsible. But here's the point—and David Gordon is just keen enough to dodge it—it doesn't matter whether the things this Ginzberg man said are true or not, or whether he and his men had a real grievance. If he repeated the multiplication table, and knew when he did it, he was likely to cause a riot, he should be punished. That's plain, ordinary, common sense. If you don't concede that much, nobody's life will be safe in the streets."

Philip felt himself roused to a direct antagonism,

although he had argued much along the same lines in his debates with himself.

" There's something more important in the world than peace," he declared. " A peace founded on injustice may be worse than riot and bloodshed. I don't want to justify violence, but if you carry your theory to its conclusion, no one could ever protest against any existing evil—no matter how outrageous—because some irresponsible person might get drunk from the thought of his wrongs."

" You can't carry any theory to an extreme," Ruth answered. " You must use some degree of judgment—or stand the consequences."

" These men are the victims of the system people like ourselves created," he asserted. " How can you hold them to your own sophisticated standards? It isn't fair ! "

" My standards would have saved Rosen's life," she could not resist saying, even though she knew she was exasperating Philip by her words.

" But they've cost the life of many a laborer's wife and baby," he rejoined. " It seems we are never going to help these people to wholesome happy lives. If they want such things they've got to break the rules we chain them with."

Their repeated debates brought them no closer to agreement. On the contrary, Philip began to distrust Ruth's motives. Her thoughts were too cogent, he decided, to be her own. She had, perhaps unknowingly, absorbed them from the class-conscious clique among which she moved. The chasm between the pair began imperceptibly to widen.

A week after the date of Ginzberg's arrest a noon-day meeting of the directors of the United Hebrew Organization Society was held in a private room of a clubhouse in the heart of the business section. It was not an infrequent thing to hold such meetings around the luncheon table. One could discuss comfortably, over a well-cooked meal, the problems of the underfed, and thus combine duty, pleasure and economy of time. Today, however, the digestion of more than one director was threatened with peril, since David Gordon had requested in writing, and had been granted, the privilege of appearing before the body. His coming boded no good. Several of the officers of the Society had opposed receiving him, but the majority had urged the unwisdom of playing directly into his hands, by a refusal to learn, at least, the nature of his desired communication.

The Board of Directors was composed of some fifteen men,—supposedly representative of the best element of the Jewish community. They were all busy men who sincerely wished to devote some skill and energy to alleviating the condition of the Jewish poor. The main outline of their system had been acquired from their remote predecessors. They collected from the well-to-do, the largest sum which could be wheedled from them, and distributed it among such applicants for relief as their investigators reported to be worthy. There was never quite enough for a complete and adequate division, but they did the best they could. Meanwhile, it troubled them vaguely to find their work grew no less onerous from year to year, but if any member became too sadly discouraged, he quietly withdrew and gave place to some younger and more sanguine opponent of Poverty.

The most recent recruit to this directorate was Philip Graetz. He had, so far, been more of a spectator than an actor in the Board's deliberations—since he had not yet overcome a feeling of being imperfectly informed regarding the problems to be prudently solved—and then solved all over again some months later. Most of the members were prosperous business and professional men. Some, however, were considered promising, rather than prominent, in the community-life, and their mild radicalism was treated with a tolerant indulgence.

Into this group, after routine business and less monotonous food had been duly discussed, stalked David Gordon. He was no stranger to many of its members. Some of them, such as Philip and Arthur Kahn, he had met socially. He had been counsel for several others, in legal matters more or less important. All who knew him had a wholesome appreciation of his dangerous force, and perhaps those who oftenest made use of his talents, were the ones who felt least friendly toward him.

The President, whose name was Seligman, and who was the sole proprietor of a large and flourishing department store, rose courteously as David entered, and motioned him to be seated.

"May I order lunch for you?" he asked hospitably.

David declined both the vacant chair and the proffered food.

"Thanks!" he answered, "I never eat during business hours. However," he went on, standing at the head of the table and speaking with a grim smile, "your invitation is nevertheless most appropriate, because I did come to ask you for something to eat—not for myself, though! I want it for Mrs. Israel Ginzberg."

THE CHOSEN PEOPLE

Nobody said anything, but the atmosphere was definitely hostile. David had expected no other reception, but he was none the less contemptuously angry at their instantaneous reaction of antagonism to his words. They all seemed to expect David to say something more, so he continued without the faintest effort at conciliation:

"Those of you who are superior to the vulgarity of the newspapers may require some further explanation as to the lady's identity. She is the wife of my most spectacular client, and the mother of two highly interesting young children. Her husband, due to the abundant zeal of a friend of some of you, is at present enjoying the hospitality of the State. Our paternal government thoughtfully provides him with an abundance of food—of what quality I can't say—still the quantity is ample. Through some oversight, his wife and children receive none whatsoever. Curiously enough, their grief at the removal of the head of the family has not completely deprived them of all appetite, as I presume our somewhat sentimental lawmakers anticipated would happen in such cases. The children, in particular, illogically enough, seem to desire food at regular intervals. It's distressing to find such callousness among the young, but then they're uncultured animals—no fine instincts, at all! I felt constrained to humor them, perhaps because I, myself, am incurably low and common in my tastes. I have bought them meals for a week now, but it has occurred to me to consider the gross impropriety involved in a bachelor, like myself, thus maintaining the wife and children of another man. I decided to seek help among more representative persons whose respectability, unlike my own, was so far above reproach as to make slander impossible. My first thoughtless impulse might have brought me to accept alms for her from some non-Jew, but then I was fortunate enough to remember your Society. I understand it exists solely to give food and shelter to anyone lucky enough to be of your own faith, provided the applicant is reputable and in actual need. Mrs. Ginzberg possesses all these qualities. You only have to see her and hear her talk to know she's a Jewess. She hasn't the price of tomorrow's breakfast, and her virtue is unquestioned, except in so far as it may have been tarnished by her acceptance of petty cash at my hands. Gentlemen, opportunity awaits you!"

David Gordon, having thus delivered himself to his own satisfaction, if to no other person's, seated himself comfortably. His listeners did not share his sense of ease. Some of them, like Arthur Kahn, were ablaze with suppressed anger at the lawyer's insolence; a few were incapable of complete comprehension of his sarcasms, and were stupidly puzzled, while others, too astute to give way to indignation and too well acquainted with Gordon's reputation to suppose he would thus prejudice his own plea, for the sake of indulging his humor, groped about in their minds for the correct explanation of his conduct. Mr. Seligman was the first to break the silence.

"Mr. Gordon," he stated, "we are seldom asked to pass upon the question of relief to strikers. It is customary for the Unions to which such persons belong, to supply their needs."

"Oh, yes," David replied, "I have been told so, but in this case the 'local' which my client attempted to organize, is almost as poverty-stricken as Mrs. Ginzberg. In case you grant my first request I may become encouraged to apply to you for relief on the Union's behalf. It is also needy and Jewish—at least mostly Jewish, like ourselves. If you don't consider it entirely worthy, you maintain, I believe, a department for delinquents."

This time Mr. Seligman was seriously affronted.

" I understood, Sir," he blurted out, trying desperately and successfully to restrain himself from unparliamentary conduct, " you came here at your own desire, to discuss a serious matter. Your manner——"

" It's bad," David interrupted solemnly, " I admit it. I strive constantly to improve it, with what poor success you've noticed. But I mean to be serious. Israel Ginzberg has resigned his position as President of his 'local,' and with it his membership, under their peculiar by-laws, also became suspended. When a man at the head of an institution is accused of crime, it is considered praiseworthy on his part to step aside from his post of leadership until he's been exonerated. An odd conventionality, perhaps—particularly among poor folk—but one much in vogue among statesmen, ministers of the Gospel, rabbis and priests, as Dr. Graetz, I am sure, will cheerfully testify. These creatures have chosen to imitate their betters. Therefore, Ginzberg's family is not entitled to relief from the Union."

" I should call that a quibble, Mr. Gordon, if you won't take offense at my words," Mr. Seligman remarked.

" No offense in the world, my dear sir," Gordon assured him. " On the contrary, I think you're entirely right, but under our not infallible system, quibbles occasionally win cases. Then they become principles, either of law or of conduct. Now, I'll be frank enough to say this noble attitude of scrupulous care for his comrades' interests seems to me a rather good card for my client to play. Therefore, it shall be played. I don't often inject my own word into such matters, but if it helps you in your decision, I'll tell you this: The Union Treasury is in sore straits. I shall not allow Ginzberg to be a drain on it; even if they choose to vote him funds to which he has no legal claim, the Ginzberg family will not get one cent from that source, even if it starves. So there's your problem. You can't evade it by any hopes based on the Union."

At this point, Arthur Kahn turned to the lawyer and began to speak in his characteristically deliberate manner, carefully selecting each word, and perfectly enunciating each syllable.

" Mr. Gordon," he demanded, " I understand from the newspaper statement bearing your signature that you are being adequately compensated for defending Ginzberg? "

" Your recollection is accurate, Mr. Kahn," David replied, " it is not given to all of us to be philanthropists."

" And the newspaper advertisements," Kahn continued, " are not, I presume, a voluntary offering on the part of the managing editors? "

" Once more, Mr. Kahn," David said suavely, " the accuracy of your perception does you credit. In the matter of space rates, if no where else, the Pioneer Company and Israel Ginzberg were created free and equal."

" Well then," Kahn persisted, pausing to give his argument additional force, " why doesn't it occur to you to curtail a percentage of these enormous legal and advertising bills and devote the proceeds to feeding the wife and children of this prisoner? "

David turned full around in his chair, the better to bestow his peculiar smile on the questioner.

"My dear sir," he replied, "you seem to forget one important factor. Everyone does not share your utter indifference to my unfortunate client's fate. These expenses are incurred to save him from hanging, or a long term in the Penitentiary. You must suppose Mrs. Ginzberg is a cannibal and wishes to dine upon her husband's flesh!"

Arthur Kahn was stung to inquire angrily:

"Since when, under our code of laws have innocent men been forced to try their cases in the newspapers?"

"I should say," was David's bland retort, "it became necessary immediately after private corporations learned to punish personal grievances in the Criminal Court. If you want the exact date, it coincides with Mr. Clarence Kaufman's election to the Presidency of the Pioneer Company."

"Gentlemen," Mr. Seligman interposed, tapping on the table, "all this talk is leading us nowhere——"

"One minute, Mr. President," Arthur Kahn called out. "I'd like to ask one more question. Would it be an impertinence, Mr. Gordon, if we inquired of you the name of the gentleman who is defraying these expenses?"

"It would be so gross an impertinence, Mr. Kahn," David answered, "as to be impossible from any such scrupulous gentlemen as yourselves."

"But," struck in somewhat timidly a fat, jolly-looking young architect named Straus, "if you find it impossible to be frank with us, how can you expect us to grant your request, and vote relief to this woman?"

This question seemed to voice the general sense of

the Board, and David turned upon them, this time, with entire seriousness.

"I'm going to be frank with you,—brutally frank," he said. "You gentlemen are business men, and good ones at that. Let us save time by assuming that we all possess some brains. Then you must have guessed from what Mr. Seligman would term my unfortunate manner—and quite properly, too,—my utter indifference regarding your decision in this matter. I'm not making any request, Mr. Straus. I'm giving your Society an opportunity to carry out the objects for which it was supposed to be incorporated. I want to put you on record one way or the other. However you vote, you'll serve my purpose."

"I presume you mean," another member ventured, "we must choose between making ourselves obnoxious to our largest contributors or to your newspaper audience."

David Gordon smiled again.

"That's the business man's translation," he conceded. "Dr. Graetz would have said, I imagine, your choice is between your duty and your comfort."

"Not so fast, Mr. Gordon," the President rejoined, "we can't assume it's a duty to help this woman. Her husband is accused of inciting murder."

"I pledge you my word the children were not accomplices;" David retorted, "the youngest can't talk."

"And," went on Mr. Seligman, "you could get funds elsewhere if you chose, while we often have no money to spare for the worthiest applicants."

"Indeed, I can get the money elsewhere," was David's cheerful comment. "This interview is a prelude to getting it by popular subscription, solicited from the general public. I don't want you to be able to deny I gave my own co-religionists the preference. Your reasons for refusing to help this family, while interesting and perhaps perfectly convincing to reasonable men like yourselves, will look to the vulgar, unthinking multitude as mere excuses put forth by satellites of Clarence Kaufman."

Everyone kept silence for a minute. The Board was in a delicate position and relished neither its dilemma nor the cold-blooded attitude of the man who was calmly proceeding to take advantage of it.

Mr. Straus suddenly rose from his seat and faced Gordon almost pleadingly.

"Look here, Mr. Gordon," he urged, "you've got us into an uncomfortable corner—there's no denying it; but is it worth while? You're a successful man, of course, but you're still young, and you expect to keep on living and doing your work in this town for many years. Is it worth while making all of us your enemies?"

David's eyes contracted into two slits and his jaw became squared, but his voice was as suave as ever.

"I shall expect more charity than that at your hands; but even if you disappoint me I must serve my own client. That's a lawyer's obligation, no matter how many friends it costs him. Besides, since we're being frank, let me tell you this: I'll get a lot more business from you men now sitting around this table, if you find I can do what I set out to do, than you'd ever give me if I good-humoredly let you twist me around your fingers. When you hire a lawyer, you're looking for a man who gets what he's paid to get, not one whose manners are charming. Now, I'm going to get Israel Ginzberg out of Jail. If I had to set the City on fire to do it, I'd trouble you, Mr. Straus, for the match!"

"But what good will it do your client?" Mr. Seligman demanded. "It seems to me you're only hurting us, without helping him. If this woman really needs help, you can get money for this family in a dozen ways. If you'll treat it as a confidential matter, I will, individually, give you all the money you want for her, right now."

David shook his head.

"That's decent of you, in a way," he said, "although it isn't exactly brave. Anyhow, you may trust me not to repeat it; but it doesn't serve my turn. As a representative Board, you have got to decide whether you're trustees for the hungry Jewish women and children of Baltimore, or merely an employers' association for keeping mendicants from troubling you on the streets. The public,— Jew and Gentile—and the newspapers, particularly, want to know!"

"Won't you tell us," Arthur Kahn asked, "why you want to stir up gratuitous trouble? That seems to be your object."

"Gladly," was the lawyer's rejoinder, "you can take my answer back to Mr. Kaufman himself, if you desire. I'm going to split this town—and particularly the Jewish community—wide open. I'm going to give wounds that will leave scars. Up to this time, these petty labor troubles have meant agony for the strikers and their families, and a mere topic of conversation for you intelligent folk uptown. This time there shall be no one—man or woman —who shall escape a fair share of the pain. I mean to make such fights so miserably uncomfortable that you won't let your Kaufmans go into them in this care-free, swash-buckler fashion. I mean to placard your cruelties and your weaknesses on the walls for every street ragamuffin to see and jeer at. I mean to let everyone who can read know exactly what your virtue and your charity are worth!"

"You're a Jew, Mr. Gordon," Philip Graetz said, for the first time breaking silence, "I believe you are prouder than many others of your essential Jewishness. Don't you care whether you discredit our Race and our Religion before all the world? Don't think," he added, "I am out of sympathy with your client and his family, but we Jews ought to settle these things among ourselves; we ought not to furnish an additional pretext to the Christian for sneering at the Jew, and discriminating against him. It isn't as though there were no such unhappy quarrels among non-Jews, but we are forced to be more careful than the Christians. We ought to settle these things among ourselves!"

"Very true, Dr. Graetz," David agreed, imperturbably, "but you didn't settle them. Mr. Kaufman chose to drag this quarrel among Jews into a Christian court. We don't propose to let you drown Anti-Semitism in Ginzberg's blood."

"So whatever we decide, you mean to report to the newspapers?" the President inquired.

"Just so!" said David, "together with such personal comment as seems to me proper. If you care to vote this relief, I shall say the best representatives of Baltimore Jewry have indignantly repudiated Kaufman and his methods! If you refuse, the line is sharply drawn, among the Jews, between the rich and the poor, the native-born and the immigrant, the capitalists and their hangers-on, and the workers. We shall carry the case to the whole community."

Seligman looked significantly from face to face, around the table.

"The newspapers," he murmured meaningly, "may be persuaded against such a campaign.

"Never believe it!" Gordon smiled. "I realize what large advertisers you gentlemen are, but a newspaper is a paradox. It must print the things the advertiser hates, in order to keep the circulation the advertiser demands."

"It's war, then, you propose," Arthur Kahn announced. "There's only one answer to be made to a declaration of War!"

"You're wrong, Mr. Kahn," David answered. "I come here telling you of a war, actually in progress. You have your choice as to which banner you will follow. There is only one path you can't choose. That's neutrality."

"And that," Straus remarked, "is just the road we'd like to explore."

Gordon rose.

"I presume you gentlemen would prefer to deliberate, relieved of the incumbrance of my presence."

"Must you have a decision today?" Seligman suggested. "This is an important problem you've given us."

"Today," David repeated relentlessly. "I have an appointment this afternoon with the newspaper men. I shall tell them whether you have granted, refused or postponed the question of relief. You'll find it no easier to make up your minds tomorrow."

"Mr. Gordon," Seligman said, "I think you have

treated us with absolutely no consideration whatever, but we know your personal word is good. For my part, you are at perfect liberty to remain and listen to our discussion, provided you will consider our individual opinions as matters of confidence."

David bowed.

"I appreciate your courtesy, Sir," he said, "and I should certainly not abuse it. Nevertheless, I believe it would be wiser for me to withdraw. Among a thousand other infirmities, I find it exceedingly difficult to be silent while other men are talking. I'm sure you'll pardon me. I will await your message in the ante-room."

"You're sure," Seligman called as David stood with his hand on the door knob, "you won't accept my proposal of a private contribution—a liberal one, mind you— your own figure, in fact."

David smiled again as he shook his head decidedly, and left the room.

"Well, gentlemen," said the President, "whatever we do, we're in for a bad time! What's your pleasure?"

"If we yield, we shall cut the Society's income in half," the Treasurer remarked sententiously.

"If you don't yield, your influence among the people you want to help will be cut to zero," one of the younger and more radical members replied.

"We ought to do what is right, irrespective of the consequences," someone said, as though half ashamed of his courage.

"Well then," Kahn said, "it's right to refuse the application. The man's a dangerous law-breaker. The woman's plea isn't made in good faith. Gordon practically admitted it. She doesn't need our money. He wants to make trouble. No decent man likes to be black-mailed. I, myself, am ready to vote against relief and to spend, out of my own pocket, whatever sums may be necessary to point out to the community the motives behind this request."

" I can't agree with Mr. Kahn," said another member. " If we had an application from a stranger, supposedly starving, we'd grant emergency relief, and set a paid investigator to work to discover if help were actually needed. It's not our business to take sides in this strike —no matter where our money comes from. I vote we grant emergency relief, and issue a statement explaining our conduct. Without committing ourselves, we shall have taken this action because we were unwilling to accept the possible responsibility of this family actually going hungry."

" What do you think, Dr. Graetz? " Mr. Seligman asked deferentially. " That is, if you care to express an opinion."

All eyes were turned on Philip, who was known to everyone to be the Rabbi of Kaufman's temple. He responded to the test without a sign of flinching.

" I want tremendously to bring about Peace. I think this relief would be extending an olive branch. I don't think the woman's entitled to it as a matter of right, but that's all the more reason why we should be generous. I think we ought to extend aid, with a full statement of our reasons and an offer to both sides to use our best offices to settle the entire dispute. I should be glad to approach Mr. Kaufman with such a proposition."

Several members smiled sardonically. Nobody ranged himself on the side of the Rabbi. A few directors called impatiently for the question. The President, without further remarks, put the motion.

"It is resolved," he stated, "that relief be extended until further order of this Board, to the wife and children of Israel Ginzberg. All in favor will say ' Aye!'"

Ten men sat in silence. Five voices were heard to say "Aye!" Four responses were more or less timid, but Philip's was firm and decided.

"That poor kid. He's going to pay for this," Straus whispered to his neighbor.

"Not if we hold our tongues, as we're supposed to," the other answered. "Kaufman will be delighted with our decision."

"Shall I send for David Gordon?" the President asked—none too happy at the prospect before them.

"One minute, please," Philip requested—burning with a quixotic desire to conceal none of his convictions. "I wish, if you will be so obliging, to have the Secretary directed to make a record of my vote among the minutes. I think, with all due deference, we are making an error, widening the gulf between ourselves and our less fortunate brethren,—no matter how mistaken they may be."

"Is such a record necessary, Dr. Graetz?" Mr. Seligman said, kindly. "You have urged your views upon us. The public will understand we are not unanimous. Those who are known to have dissented will be under fire from both sides."

"I wish it," Philip insisted with finality.

"He's got his nerve," Straus whispered.

"He's stark mad, you mean," was his neighbor's amendment.

"It amounts to the same thing," was Straus' comment.

CHAPTER XIV

A Sentimental Journey

ONE late afternoon, about a week after the Directors' meeting of the Charity Society, anyone who had cared to take the trouble might have seen the talented Rabbi of Beth El sitting all huddled in a disconsolate heap on the staircase leading from the second to the third floor of a bare, uninviting house in the ugliest section of East Baltimore.

It was an altogether unsuitable environment for the spokesman of the most fashionable of the City's Jewish Temples, but his resting place was not more incongruous than his attitude of utter and complete dejection and discouragement. Had he been observed by any of his parishioners, or by the trustees of the Congregations in other cities who had taken envious notice of his talents, there would have been much outraged comment upon his eccentricity. Nobody, however, who saw him seemed to be much interested in his presence there, and he, himself, was for the moment, totally oblivious of what anyone might think of him.

He had found the last week a trying one; so had many of his congregation, particularly those whose interests were in any manner linked with the fortunes of the Pioneer Company. There had been,—to begin with,— the rabid attack made in Ginzberg's name, upon the Charity Society. This had hurt Philip grievously, because the organization had been plausibly made to appear as a mere agency for distributing the largesse of vulgar

187

industrial barons to a pliant, later-day peasantry, whose
alms were to be withheld whenever their attitude ceased
to be one of servile cringing. It was further intimated
that a minority existed upon the Board too intelligent
to accept such a theory, but too intelligent, also, to confuse
the buttered with the unbuttered side of the bread it fed
upon. In this, Philip recognized a thrust at himself, and
he was not allowed to doubt a similar insight on the part
of many others. Evidently, David Gordon had no intention of allowing such a trifle as personal friendship to
impair his plans for the vindication of his client. The
lawyer was acting strictly in accordance with his fiercely-
proclaimed theories of advocacy. The intention of Arthur
Kahn to answer this attack had been overruled by his
colleagues who had sanely counselled the inadvisability
and futility of a further war of words. Philip, who
had contemplated a separate reply, had also allowed
himself to be persuaded to an injured silence, but the
wound smarted all the more because his bruised feelings
had found no vocal or written outlet.

Immediately after this, there followed a series of
sudden attacks, each calculated to add to the distraction
and uproar in the Jewish community. Upon the report of
paid detectives, who had succeeded under Gordon's orders
in securing positions as strike-breakers in the Pioneer
factory, the Company was indicted, once because of an
alleged infraction of the Child Labor Law in the employment of several girl operators under the legal age, and
again because of certain petty neglects of precautions
against fire. To the Company's perfectly veracious assertions that the girls, if they were really as young as
they now claimed to be, had obtained work by deceiving

the employing agent, and that the factory was more carefully guarded against conflagration than most others in the City, David Gordon answered with jeers. The Pioneer Company, he retorted, had displayed no great appreciation of Ginzberg's good intentions. It made a lot of difference, he suggested, whose technicality was being dissected.

The public gave its smiling sympathy to the side which furnished the more diverting entertainment. The Company, by way of retaliation, proceeded to cause the arrest of a number of pickets charged with acts of disorder. These occurrences, according to the version of the prisoners, had been deliberately provoked by the strike-breakers. Most of the alleged law-breakers allowed their cases to be heard by the committing Magistrates and were punished by the imposition of small fines, and were promptly paid. Three, however, were dismissed,—no active participation in any unlawful act upon their part having been disclosed. Next day each one, through David Gordon, filed a damage suit against the Pioneer Company and its chief officers, for false imprisonment and malicious prosecution, claiming huge damages for the indignity. Finally, a well-engineered drive against the Pioneer's stock was made in the local market. The majority holdings of the shares were in the hands of Clarence Kaufman, his family and his colleagues, but there was a fair minority representation held by the general public, and quotation after quotation appeared in the market reports at steadily decreasing prices. Men who purported to know, insisted upon the artificiality of this decline, but others were dubious. They could not be sure of the latent causes of this unfortunate shrinkage in the value of their investment and were sure, at any rate, of the financial strength of the forces intent upon injuring the Company. Many of the more timid threw their holdings upon this falling market and assisted in still further lowering the price of the securities. Those who thus sold their stock at a considerable loss were none too silent in their resentment of the conduct of the managing officers of the Corporation. These harassed gentlemen insisted upon the injustice of such censure, proclaiming loudly the appalling absence of logic involved. Still, calm, well-ordered reasoning is a virtue whose value is never quoted in a disappointing stock market, and a number of well-advertised petty feuds arose among the men whose financial habits had heretofore resulted in harmonious applause of one another's business sagacity and public spirit.

It was all most distressing. Not the least of the disconcerting results of the ugly situation was the effect upon the non-Jewish community. Taking its cue, perhaps, from Gordon's statements, it proceeded to treat the quarrel as a civil war among the "Hebrews," as it preferred to call them, when one of them was present. In vain did anonymous correspondents fill the open letter columns of the newspapers with missives insisting upon the purely economic aspects of the strike, and the enormous number of similar disturbances among Gentiles. The general public could only see rich Jews at war with poor ones, and the attitude of the non-Jewish partisans of either side was distinctly contemptuous.

The less educated of the Gentiles were frank in assuming a definite objectionable quality in these Jews who were somehow different and, therefore, of course, inferior. The more cultured of the non-Jews were willing to base their prejudice upon a certain standard of good taste forever, according to them, unattainable by creatures of Semitic blood, however expensively schooled. Their failure to reach this standard was, once more, evidenced by this disgraceful exhibition of their noisome personal wranglings.

It was this which Philip had feared and to which David Gordon was completely indifferent. To the lawyer, with his Nationalistic ideals, the Jews were a Race whose duty it was to work out their own destiny and develop their own peculiar characteristics as best they might. The Christian might approve, disapprove or ignore—as his fancy happened to dictate. Through all the centuries he had never helped, and after this lapse of time, he could not hinder.

To Philip the whole story as it unrolled itself, with its intense angers, its complete effacement of tolerance and its cruel attacks and reprisals, was a nightmare of agony. His silences were misunderstood as well as his words. He could scarcely meet anyone without some resultant injury to his morbid sensitiveness. He imagined all men and women were thinking of him as a coward because he had failed to justify his gallant words of last Autumn, and yet he knew not what he could do when he found his mind and his emotions waging against each other a war no less bitter than that between Kaufman and the strikers.

How could these men gain freedom without the right to organize,—yet what right had they to prohibit other men to fill their places in peace, if these others so desired? What was to become of Society if they must always work for such a low wage—yet if the industry cannot yield a profit to those who maintain it, would not the most merciful employers simply give place to others less scrupulous? How can one fail to pity the rash mistakes of men driven by abject misery to deeds of violence—yet is not the whole of civilization bound up with the stern maintenance of law and order?

Above all, what part in the midst of relentless enmity can be played by a man who cannot find it in his conscience to pronounce wholesale condemnation upon either faction? It was therefore that Philip was far more miserable than either Clarence Kaufman, feeding his rage in his factory, or Israel Ginzberg, plotting schemes of vengeance in his prison.

The din of this combat and the struggle in his own soul, had the effect of building a wall of isolation around Philip. Nobody meant to be unkind to him. Some few guessed how unhappy he must be, but he was obsessed with a self-conscious certainty of his failure to cope with conditions. He felt deserving of censure which he dreaded, or of pity which was worse. So he avoided as much as he could, the companionship of his judges. He even omitted his customary visits to Ruth. She was genuinely concerned about him and the unrest to which she was sure he was a prey, but he made vague excuses for eluding all her delicate attempts to lead him to share his unhappiness with her. After all, Kaufman was her kinsman. Much of her wealth had been acquired in this business; some of it was still invested there. How could it be otherwise than that she would strive to blind him to all other impressions save those of her clan? It was while this fit of melancholy held him most firmly in its grip that he resolved to make his long-deferred trip to the East Side. Heretofore, he had always been too busily engaged in some social or congregational activity. Now all of his occupations seemed to him to be things of mockery and worthlessness. If he could not help these people whose cause was such a queer blend of a heart-compelling search after happiness and a desperate defiance of common work-a-day practicalities, perhaps at least, he might learn to understand them better, perhaps he might bring to a few of them the knowledge of his all-consuming sympathy.

With no better reasons than these, he had on this cold, damp afternoon, followed the directions of a traffic police-man to take the Madison Avenue car going east, get off at Lloyd Street and walk two squares south. After that, the policeman told him, he might stroll about in any direction he chose, and he would be seeing Baltimore's Ghetto.

Philip had never been abroad but his first impression was one of a foreign atmosphere; not that there was any marked dissimilarity of the architecture of these buildings from those in other sections of the City. The houses here seemed older, perhaps, and the exteriors of most of them shrieked aloud for the ministrations of the painter and the carpenter, but otherwise, they were the ordinary un-adorned brick houses so nearly universal in Baltimore. There were nowhere visible the canyons of lofty tenement houses, with their net work of fire escapes which he had observed in his hasty visits to New York. When he strove to discover the origin of his sense of unfamiliarity and un-Americanism, two things became detached in his mind from the confusion of his ideas. The first was the many-colored shawls worn over the head and shoulders of the girls and women; the second was the overflowing of the community life into the street. The weather was inclement, but the street was full of children, and adults, too, who seemed to have no particular errand there, but to be using it as a combined living-room, nursery and social club-house. Some of the children were even treating it as a dining-room. The air was filled with a lively chatter of voices. Philip's new-found Yiddish stood him in good stead. He overheard much neighborly gossip—most of it about food, some about the growth, ailments and discipline of children, in school and out,—a fair degree of grumbling about landlords, and a word or two about absent men being out of work. Still, the talk, even the grumbling, was cheerful and amazingly intimate. In this casual passing to and fro, Philip, in his capacity as eaves-dropper, acquired several startling bits of information—obstetrical and otherwise. It was certainly a different life from the one in vogue among the members of Beth El, but it did not seem tragic in the slightest degree. Philip had come down-town to have his bruised emotions further harrowed, and was youthful enough, and human enough, to find himself with a subconscious sense of having been defrauded at finding East Baltimore so much less shocking than he had supposed. Perhaps his comfortable friends spoke the truth. These men and women seemed to receive enough of life's necessities to give them as much of happiness as their richer fellow-citizens.

For a few minutes, Philip's mood grew completely capitalistic; but then his wanderings led him into a narrow little court, and he looked up suddenly from his reverie to find himself in the midst of a group of miserably unkempt houses, each one, apparently, with a teeming quota of inhabitants; he peeped into a constricted area-way between two of these slatternly houses, and over a huge mass of repulsive looking refuse he saw the rear of the buildings which faced on the cheerful street down which he had just passed. The view from behind was a revelation to one who had only acquired an impression from the discreet aspect they presented to the outer world. The space between one house and that built immediately behind it was so tiny as to be little more than an interior alley, but these narrow spaces of ground seemed to be the general rubbish heaps of many families. Long flights of rickety wooden stairs covered the rear of the buildings from the ground to the topmost story, telling even unsophisticated Philip that each floor of these structures was used as a sleeping and eating place for many people. Philip's enthusiasm for capitalistic indifference was somewhat shaken. Thereafter, he consciously guided his steps from the main streets into the courts and lanes and by-paths which gave him opportunities to see the hidden side of these houses. He was amazed at some of the things of which he caught fugitive glimpses. Just off the main line of traffic on East Lombard Street he found four dwellings erected in what had once been a side yard, and it appeared as though no one of these buildings enjoyed the dignity of being occupied solely by one family! Now he understood why the life of this district spilled over into the streets.

Yet it was a land of paradoxes. Now and then in the very heart of unspeakable squalor and congestion, Philip would chance across some oasis which bore all the evidences of cleanliness and comfortable living conditions. He began to comprehend the existence among these people, of varying grades of comparative wealth and poverty. They had their own problems of riches and penury, and perhaps, thought Philip, as much envy and hatred was generated by their differences of financial welfare as between factory owner and garment workers; only, and this seemed queer to him, here the rich and the poor lived side by side. He fancied you could not hate so thoroughly the neighbor whose little children you saw each day, at play.

After a long struggle, Philip conquered his self-conscious shyness sufficiently to force himself to enter a few of these buildings. He had a guilty sense of intrusion. He half expected some dark-bearded man to seize him roughly by the shoulder and demand by what authority he came to pry into their homes; but no one molested him. He soon learned why. Each house was the abode of a number of families, and the hallways were used in common by the visitors of all. Therefore, no one could with certainty presume his visit to be one of idle curiosity. The interiors of the houses Philip visited were, in general, much worse than their exteriors, even when observed from the rear. They were gaunt and bare. If the hallways had wall paper at all, it was indescribably filthy. They were utterly cheerless. When an open door gave a glimpse into the rooms, it seemed impossible that such places could be called "home" by anyone; they were merely a few rooms, mainly occupied by rumpled, uninviting beds. They were as primitive as barns without the sense of airiness and tidiness a well-kept barn inspires. Many of these living quarters had beds even in the dining-rooms. Water, in a number of cases, seemed to be brought from a pump in the paved space in the rear, and brought not too often or used too freely. But once again, Philip was struck by the variations in these so-called homes. Here and there, one would be seen which stood out from the others because of its general air of prosperity, and the crude attempts of its occupants to make it attractive. The general effect of a close examination, Philip concluded, was even more depressing than he had supposed; but it did not wear the air of tragedy he demanded! The people who lived in these absurd quarters seemed ridiculously cheerful! The tiny meat and grocery shops which abounded everywhere were filled with customers—to all appearances no more discontented than those who flocked into the department stores in the center of the City. He wondered if they did not know how badly they were being treated! It occurred to Philip to remember how long he had been walking. He was tired. He paused to consider exactly what discoveries he had made and he drew several conclusions from his afternoon. There were too many people in this little town within a town. That was the crux of the trouble. The houses were ugly, but he remembered having been told by one of the older members of his temple that he had been born in this neighborhood, and that, in his childhood, all of the families now most influential and affluent in the Jewish community had lived there. Of course, this had been long before the flood tide of immigration from Russia and Poland had begun. As the immigrant Jews had instinctively sought the vicinity of their more Americanized co-religionists, the latter had, one by one, abandoned these untutored new-comers and left them to form a colony for themselves. How strange and unfamiliar to the ghost of some thrifty, German-Jewish housewife must these cheerless barracks now appear, should she feel moved in the dead of night to visit once more " the glimpses of the moon," and wander among the sleeping scores where she had reigned supreme over her own loved brood. Still, she had managed to live there—the simple-minded, devoted Jewish mother,—keeping her home a happy place of refuge, and training her sons and daughters to become strong and forceful—too strong and forceful, perhaps. So it was not merely the bad houses, as in New York. It was the crowd. It was cramming into these houses, each built originally to shelter one family, an avalanche of people. It was this need for space, and still more space, which had conjured up the hideous back buildings and tenements in the side yards. It was congestion, pure and simple. Why? Why did they huddle together in this fashion? The City itself was vast and unconfined. It could spread out in whichever direction it might desire. Rents in the outlying districts were cheap, and here they were high. As Russian-Jewish families became really Americanized, they too, like their German predecessors, moved on; there were many such,—like David Gordon, for example—in the up-town sections. But the true immigrant remained here. What was the reason?

Philip stopped in his weary stroll as he answered his question. The sound of children babbling in Yiddish came to his ears. That was the reason. Here, these forlorn travelers from a land of persecution, found themselves among friends and fellows. On one side they were girt about with a wall of contemptuous Christian indifference and mockery; on the other side by the positive antagonism, fear and occasional condescension of their Americanized-Jewish brethren. Here was a City of refuge of their own —unlovely, uncomfortable, unwholesome, but none the less, their own! This was the cause, and it forced Philip to the further query: Was not the blame to be laid at the door of himself, and of men like him, who had been ashamed or unwilling to take these waifs by the hand and teach them—by sharing with them the daily round of familiar things—the meaning of life in this America of opportunity?

At this point Philip should really have gone home. He had seen as much as he was capable of understanding in one afternoon, and true to his nature, he had drawn from what he had seen an incentive to the undertaking of a disagreeable duty. He might have gone to his rooms and prepared an inspiring sermon. It was Philip's misfortune to be cursed with a craving to live his sermons—and to make others live them, too.

Therefore, the idea of calling on Mrs. Ginzberg followed as an inevitable corollary of his reasoning. Here was his opportunity for stretching out the hand of fellowship,—doing a difficult duty, proving to his congregation, and the whole community, how little his inaction had been due to a cowardly dread of Clarence Kaufman, and showing the East Side how much his heart was theirs, even if his mind could not altogether approve their methods.

So he made inquiries as to the Ginzbergs' lodging place, and after some difficulty discovered it to be upon the third floor of a large, ugly corner-house. However unprepossessing these quarters might be, they had air and light on two sides, and this argued some intelligence in their selection. The building had an entrance on Lombard Street and another on Albemarle, and it housed a small army of occupants. Nevertheless, everyone in the building knew the Ginzbergs, not only because of the fame achieved by the imprisoned garment worker, but because the family were the proud tenants of the entire third floor, which was, in itself, a title to distinction. Evidently, Ginzberg had been a man of some position and had been forced to maintain appearances. It was also apparent that in his absence his rent was being paid by somebody. Philip climbed wearily to the third floor and tapped timidly at the door. Receiving no answer to his repeated signals, he turned the knob and entered. The room in which he found himself was cold and dismal. It had never been papered but its walls were reasonably clean, although through the broken plaster, the bare laths showed here and there. The room was not dirty. There was nothing definite to be said against it, but there was nothing to be said in its favor, either. In the room immediately beyond, through the open door, could be seen a stout woman with dishevelled hair, seated in a rocking-chair before a coal stove. She was holding a baby in her arms. The woman was crooning to the child in a wailing minor key a single cadence, repeated over and over. Philip found this curious bit of music strangely appealing, in spite of its lack of conventional melody. The infant was palpably less impressed, and broke forth,—as Philip stood there gazing at the picture,—into the fretful wail of misery which betokens physical pain. The Rabbi stepped to the door and asked if he were addressing Mrs. Ginzberg. The woman rose hurriedly with the sick child in her arms. Her cheeks, he noticed, were wet with tears. She had no claims to good looks nor to the outward appearance of intelligence. Probably, the restless mind of her less com-

monplace husband had left her far behind in his struggle toward leadership and Americanism; but Philip saw
something infinitely pathetic about her. She was sordid,
dull and unattractive, but she was unhappy, and in her
woe, he thought he discerned a symbol of the patient, misunderstanding and misunderstood group from which she
had sprung. She demanded eagerly to be told whether he
was " the doctor," and he was fain to admit his adherence
to a profession much less useful to her—at least in her
present predicament. He told her in rather halting Yiddish who he was, and was about to explain why he had
come when to his utter consternation, she turned upon him
in a gale of excited anger and protest. Her voice became
shrill, and her unfamiliar words poured out in a veritable
torrent of undignified abuse. He did not comprehend all
she said; he did not wait to puzzle out the more involved
phrases of her outburst, but he had no difficulty in learning
her opinion of him and of his visit. He was one of the
crowd who were " killing " her husband, who had left her
to care for her poor little children, and now he had been
sent there to gloat over the harm they had done. She was
there all alone, and the one baby was going to die, and she
supposed he was glad and had come to enjoy the sight of
her misery. It was all extremely absurd, but neither of the
actors in the scene was able to perceive its grotesque
humor. In harsh tones and without giving him any opportunity to reply to her harangue, she told him to " get out;"
to leave her to herself in the midst of the despair he
and his kind had brought to pass.

Of course, she was hysterical, and in all probability
she expected him to remain and remonstrate with her as
she deserved; but Philip was not well versed in the ways

THE CHOSEN PEOPLE

of women, and now he was confronted with the triple
barriers of sex, poverty and nationality. He took Mrs.
Ginzberg at her word and quietly retraced his steps and
re-entered the hallway. The woman had been wantonly
cruel to him. She had poured acid into his already fes-
tering wounds. His first intention was to betake his
wretched, useless self to his own rooms and muse upon
the futility of all his endeavors. Then it occurred to him
to consider the case of the sick baby, and the expected
visit of the physician. Perhaps, whether the mother
wished it or not, he could, through the agency of the medical man, supply the little invalid with some comforts it
might otherwise lack. He would await the Doctor's coming and intercept him. He was in no haste, and besides,
this small service would be doing something. So he stood
in the hallway for awhile, and when his weariness made
itself insistently felt, he sat down on the bare, dirty staircase, resting his head on his arms, and his arms on his
knees, wondering why he, with all his high hopes and
unselfish aims, was doomed to see them end in a disaster
in which there was not even a trace of the heroic. How
long he sat there in woe-begone self-abandonment, he did
not know. The shadows grew deeper and the twilight
became dusk, and still he waited. At last someone descending from the Ginzberg rooms stumbled over him and
almost fell. He looked up hastily and in the dim light
was able to see that it was a young woman, dressed in
the trim uniform of a nurse. She appeared no less
surprised than Philip at the encounter.

"What's the matter?" she demanded in business-like
but pleasant accents. "Are you sick?"

A SENTIMENTAL JOURNEY

The Rabbi by this time had risen, and was standing before the nurse, hat in hand.

"I'm all right, thank you," he replied, "I'm sorry I was in your way. I was just resting."

The purity of his accent, his quiet air of good breeding, his clean-shaven cheeks, and the modish cut of his garments, discernible in spite of the dim light, all told her of his quality as a stranger in this building—and in this neighborhood.

"Oh!" she exclaimed, "I beg your pardon. I see you don't belong here!"

"No," he answered, bitterly, "you're quite right. It seems I don't belong here!"

CHAPTER XV

THE STRANGE WOMAN

THE girl and Philip together groped their way down the dusky staircase. There was no compelling reason why he should accompany her, but having endangered her descent by seating himself where he could not fail to be a menace, he felt a dim sense of obligation to return her undamaged to the outside world. She seemed much more capable than himself of eluding whatever perils might be encountered between the third floor and the street, but there are certain definite traditions which inevitably result from being born male or female, so he took her arm and thereby succeeded in handicapping slightly her surefooted progress.

When they reached the threshold of the building, the street lamps were shining and the two looked at each other with frank curiosity. To him, she seemed to " belong there " still less than he did. She was unmistakably Celtic in her ancestry, and her fair hair, blue eyes and piquantly up-tilted bit of a nose, all proclaimed her as an alien to these people among whom she was working. Entirely regardless of whether or not she seemed an appropriate part of her surroundings, she was a pleasant sight to contemplate. She was considerably below the average height, but in her severely tailored uniform her body seemed exquisitely modelled and proportioned. Her features were decidedly irregular, but her face was redeemed from any danger of the commonplace by its unusual mobility. Ideas seemed to course unceasingly through her mind, and with each change of thought her face assumed another aspect. It was impossible to say how it would appear in repose, because it was as ceaseless in its variations as rippling water. One wondered if her lips widened into fugitive little smiles and her eyes grew alternately big or narrow, under their closed lids, as her dreams breathlessly pursued her through the hours of sleep.

Just now, she was regarding Philip with a smile which was an odd mixture of good humor, merriment, conciliation and mockery.

It occurred to him that under all the circumstances, it was his cue to explain his presence on the landing. Even in tenement houses, it must be somewhat out of the daily order of events for well-bred gentlemen to drape themselves on staircases for busy young women to trip over.

" My name is Graetz," he began, holding his hat in his hand, " I was waiting for the doctor. I understand the little Ginzberg baby is ill. I suppose I've been waiting a long time."

" Oh! " she said, her smile almost, but not quite, expanding into laughter. "You're the Rabbi! Your gracious hostess told me all about you, and how she struck a real blow for the rights of outraged labor. I didn't believe her then, but I do now, since she didn't even leave you strength enough for a dignified retreat."

Philip thought her raillery just a trifle ill-timed.

" I wanted to be of some use to the child, no matter how the woman felt," he explained; " that's why I was waiting to intercept the doctor. I'm sorry I got in your way. It seems to be my afternoon for being misplaced."

This time she did laugh, but her mirth had lost its trace of mockery.

" Oh, come! " she urged consolingly, " my shoes must have bruised you as much as Mrs. Ginzberg's tongue. I'll apologize for both women. Mrs. Ginzberg didn't mean any more harm than I did. You shouldn't have run away. You should have been harsh and stern with her—and with me, too. That's the way to deal with nurses and tenement women, and any other kind you may happen to meet."

She turned as though about to go, but he detained her. Perhaps, it was not only because he wanted more information that he was unwilling to lose sight of her so soon.

" Isn't the doctor coming? " he inquired. " How did you get here instead? What's the matter with the baby? Is there anything I can get for it? "

" Good gracious! " she protested. " It's a woman's privilege to be curious! However, the doctor isn't coming at all. There's nothing much the matter with the child. Only, its mother hasn't any sense. Now that I come to think of it, that's a rather serious disease for a baby, isn't it? I came here, instead, because I happen to be a visiting nurse, created for the express purpose of saving trouble for doctors and making trouble for mothers. If the Ginzbergs needed anything, I'd let you get it, just to help you even scores with her, but they don't. So that's all, and it's time to go home, for me, anyhow."

With that she daintily tripped down the front steps, casting a farewell nod to him over her shoulder. He made undue haste to overtake her.

" Mayn't I go with you, as far as the car? " he asked. " It's grown quite dark."

She threw a glance of exaggerated scorn at him.

" Do you need protection? " she inquired. "I don't. A

nurse may go where she must, whenever she must. I suspect other women could, too, but the helpless pose is useful, isn't it? Still, you may come if you want. I take the
Madison Avenue car, and you do, too, I guess."

He would have strolled at a leisurely gait the short distance to Baltimore Street, for he was still tired, and
besides, there were many questions he wished to ask of this
self-reliant young creature; but the pace she set was a
brisk one and she seemed to have a reasonble share of that
curiosity she claimed as a prerogative of her sex.

"What were you doing down here?" she demanded,
suddenly. "If you think it's none of my business, don't
hesitate to tell me so, but I really would like to know."

"I'd like to tell you, too," was his prompt answer,
"maybe you could help me to go about it; but it's a long
story, and we'd be uptown before I got through. Perhaps
you'll give me a hearing when you're not so hurried."

"I'll be glad to," she assured him frankly, "if you care
to spend an hour with a woman who may have to share
a boarding-house parlor with six or seven other ladies,
of more or less doubtful age, and undoubted talent for
neighborhood gossip. The day after you have been there
you may expect to read in the morning "Sun" a detailed
account of your elopement with me under the most disgraceful circumstances. I like to shock them now and
then, but you belong to a demure profession."

"I'll be there tonight," he announced without hesitation, as he went through the form of assisting her to
board the car.

"Dear me," she laughed, "this is your day for rash-
ness. Mrs. Ginzberg and myself within a few hours!"

The car was crowded long before it reached the center

of the city and they found conversation difficult. When it reached Dolphin Street, she sprang up suddenly and with a hasty good-bye, was about to desert him. He darted after her and stood beside her on the pavement.

"You've forgotten to tell me your name," he stated with a sense of triumph in having discovered this confident young woman at fault.

"Indeed, I hadn't forgotten," she answered coolly. "I was trying an experiment, that's all. Now that you have asked—I am Ellen Stewart and I live in that house," pointing as she spoke. "You can't forget it. It's the ugliest one on Dolphin Street."

Promptly at half-past eight, Philip Graetz presented himself at the door of the house so superlatively described, and ordered the untidy-looking negro woman who responded to his ring to take his card to Miss Stewart. The servant eyed him suspiciously, and grudgingly ushered him into a vast room which seemed to have been equipped as a museum of hideous furniture. From the center table, with its walnut legs and marble top on which there reposed an elaborate plush photograph album, to the highly-colored picture on the wall of St. Cecelia among her listening angels, the talented decorator of this interior had not omitted one opportunity to grate upon the sensibilities of anyone with a germ of the æsthetic. Philip glanced about the room with a growing sense of distaste. He sniffed a faint, unpleasant odor, which he identified as a subtle blend of mustiness and cabbage, and he indulged in an instant of self-searching wonder at the caprice which had led him to stray into such surroundings to hold converse with a girl with whom anything like companionship would, in the nature of things, be utterly unsuitable.

THE STRANGE WOMAN

His mood must have mirrored itself rather clearly in his face, for he heard a laugh at the door, and Miss Stewart came into the room, her eyes dancing with amusement.

"There's still time for you to go," she said. "I'll never tell on you, and a dime will seal the servant's lips forever."

Somehow the sight of her, and the sound of her voice, completely removed any lurking desire for retreat which may have lodged in the Rabbi's mind. She looked like a mere wisp of a girl, and a singularly attractive girl, in the flimsy dress for which she had exchanged her nurse's uniform. Her daintiness and charm seemed magnified rather than obscured by these dingy surroundings.

She motioned him to a chair, covered with slippery haircloth, and continued in the same strain:

"You can't say I didn't warn you—but no words could do justice to this, could they? If you could have seen your face! I don't see how Mrs. Ginzberg could have had the heart to turn you out of doors, or I to keep you here."

"I didn't come to look at this room but to talk with you," Philip announced gravely.

"But you can't talk to me without smelling the cabbage, can you?" she asked. "However, talk, learned Sir —I am listening meekly as becomes my inferior sex."

But his first remark was neither tactful, nor what he had intended to say.

"Why do you live in a place like this?" he began. "I can't imagine any surroundings which could have failed so completely to express you—or, at least, what you seem."

Over her mobile face there passed a shade of surprise,

14   209

then one of resentment and injured pride. But before she spoke she had once more resumed her smile of amusement with its lurking tinge of good-humored impertinence.

"Kind sir," she said, " in this year of grace, beautiful ladies may not create a bower of their favorite leaves and flowers, and there await the coming of gallant knights. Our homes are chosen to express not ourselves, but our pay envelopes. These romantic surroundings express my weekly wage with an eloquence even a preacher might envy."

He knew her words were in the nature of a rebuke, but he could think of nothing but the gross injustice of imprisoning such a girl as this in these unlovely walls. He wanted to tell her so, but found himself suddenly bereft of appropriate words. Ellen, however, divined his thought without difficulty, and made haste to quench his impulse of pity.

"Don't you bother about me," she commanded, in matter-of-fact tones, " I do well enough here. I've fixed up my own room to please myself and it isn't often I'm honored by visits from distinguished gentlemen. So I haven't spent much more time than you have under the shadow of St. Cecelia. Now tell me, why did you want to come to see me? It was an odd thing, wasn't it?"

Philip looked at her with a slight sensation of embarrassment. Then, because he felt somewhat afraid of the awkward thought he imagined to be lodged in the minds of both of them, he characteristically forced himself to meet it squarely.

"You mean," he asked, " because I'm a Jew and a Jewish Rabbi, and you are a Gentile?"

She nodded.

"I mean just half of that," she answered; "I haven't any religious prejudices, not having any religion, but of course, you are crammed full of them, or you couldn't be a minister."

He stared at her a moment before replying.

"Do you think, then," he demanded, "no one can believe in a creed, without an antagonism to those who fail to accept it?"

She shrugged her shoulders airily.

"I don't say it couldn't be done," she announced, "but it isn't, and particularly, it isn't done by you Jews. You're the most clannish of all people. In your heart you have already decided upon the superiority of the leftover dinner odors of Jewish boarding-houses."

He refused to laugh at her way of putting things.

"If the Jew is clannish," he argued, "it's because of generations of Christian persecution. If he were to force himself unsought upon his neighbors, you'd say he was lacking in common self-respect; and you would be right."

"Well," she said, "you've certainly profited by the instruction we've given you. If I were to go among all my friends tomorrow and tell them you'd called on me, they might think my taste odd, but they wouldn't be shocked; on the other hand, if you tell your people you came here, without any definite business purpose, they'll believe you're a modern St. Anthony, with the wrong ending to the story. What's worse, they'll make you think so, too."

He was about to protest, but she continued:

"Fortunately, you can urge that you did come on a definite errand. You were going to tell me what you were doing in East Baltimore and you imagined, perhaps, I could help you do it. Go ahead," she commanded.

Under her urging, he told her the entire story of his ministry—of his rosy plans for bringing to bear upon all Jews the spirit of their religion, of the Pioneer strike with its miserable sequel of hatreds and injustices, and of his own inability to bring, either to East Baltimore or to his own people, his message of brotherhood.

She did not smile at his recital, but heard him to the end with an expression varying between the extremes of genuine compassion and sincere respect.

"Now what I want to know," he concluded, "is this: You're not a Jewess, but you work among these people, and they like you and welcome you. Why can't I make them accept me, whose whole life is saturated with Judaism, and a desire to help them?"

"That was the exact problem Jesus Christ was unable to solve," Ellen answered soberly. "Don't be silly enough to be shocked," she added, reading his face, "I didn't say that either to be blasphemous or to appear clever. It would be easy to answer your question by saying the Jews in East Baltimore are glad to see me because I'm there to help them out of a definite physical trouble. When somebody's got a real ache, he doesn't care if it's a Christian or a Mormon who takes it away. Still, that's only part of the truth. I suspect they accept me as an out and out Christian (which I'm not) and find I have good intentions, anyhow,—but to them you're an apostate, and no good intentions can make up for that."

"An apostate!" he repeated, "how can they call me that? Don't I come to them in the name of their own faith, and mine?"

"Yes," she admitted, "but your beardless face, and your mode of speech and your general air of prosperity, all make them believe you have shed as much of your Judaism as you could possibly get rid of, and made a good bargain for yourself by doing it."

This doctrine was so repellent to Philip that he took up the cudgels against it with considerable heat.

"You think, then," he demanded, "the price of understanding, is descending to the level of the people we want to help—to go back to the bondage of all the old superstitions—to pretend to believe in the wickedness of shaving, and the horror of eating milk and meat at the same time—to force women to wear wigs because they happen to be married, and to separate themselves from their husbands while they're at worship? In other words, to lose all the Americanism we've gained in sixty difficult years? If you're right, we can only win the sympathy of the immigrant Jew by ceasing altogether to help him, and becoming just as unfortunate as he, himself, is."

She smiled slightly at his rising vehemence.

"I didn't say I believed these things," she explained. "I'm telling you how I think the others feel. Now that I watch you under the spell of Religion, I'm not sure, if all other Jews are as violent as you, it wasn't a wise provision to shut their women off in some place of safety."

But he was not to be diverted from his quest.

"Do you see any other way out?" he insisted.

"Yes," she affirmed, "but you won't like it any better than the other. My way would be for all of you to stop insisting on your little creeds, with their petty differences. Forget your narrow religion! You're all doing that anyhow, only you're ashamed to admit it.

Encourage yourselves to think of men as men and Americans, and not as Jews at all. Then you've linked yourselves together with all the other men and women in the country who want to have things the way they ought to be."

Philip's whole nature, all his past life, his studies and his dreams rose in passionate protest.

"You can't make men live together in harmony without religion," he declared. "Through religion alone can you make men realize their brotherhood and the love each must cherish for the other."

She smiled a tremulous smile of real pity.

"Yet you tell me yourself," she said, as though she hated to hurt him, "how impossible you have found it to do these things—how cruelly they are bent on maiming one another."

"The fault is with me," he urged, in bitter humility, "with me, and those like me who are too weak to make our listeners learn and practice Truth!"

"It's not!" she exclaimed indignantly; "it's absurd for you to torture yourself about happenings as completely beyond your control as the law of gravitation. You're trying, with your beautiful outworn ideas, to deal with men who are sheer puppets in the hands of forces they don't even understand. You might just as well preach sermons to a hungry wolf about to pounce on a lamb."

"Will it help," Philip asked less enthusiastically, "to let the wolf eat the lamb, without benefit of clergy?"

"If you gave both animals as much to eat as they needed, the wolf would dine elsewhere and the lamb keep out of harm's way," she retorted. "You religionists only confuse the issue; particularly you Jews, who want to be a race apart, as well as a separate creed."

It occurred to Philip to decide that this was a surprising girl. She had ideas, even if they were wrong. She thought things out for herself.

"You believe there is a solution, then?" he asked, less to be enlightened than to plumb fully the recesses of this vigorous young mind.

"Yes," she answered with the same promptness and dogmatism with which David Gordon had answered "Zionism" to a similar question. "The answer is Socialism."

He relished her conclusion a little less than he had Gordon's. Socialism, in his mind, was associated with unkempt, loud-voiced people. The women especially, he felt, should have "bobbed" hair, clumsy shoes, and cigarette stains on their fingers and teeth. To find this delicate, sprite-like Ellen proclaiming such a faith was in itself an ugly contradiction of the proprieties. He felt much as he did when he had once heard a tiny child lisp out its father's crude Atheism.

"I can see," was her comment, "how heartily you disapprove. Still, that's the answer, whether you and your kind like it or not. All the things you preach are totally impossible in the world we have today. Your congregation couldn't practice them if it tried. You can't, yourself. Today, one must eat or be eaten. What's the use of telling me of the beauties of being gobbled up?"

Suddenly she stopped, and began to laugh softly.

"It's silly of me to argue with you," she said. "If I convinced you, your occupation would be gone, wouldn't it?"

" I wouldn't stick to an opinion just to hold my place," he exclaimed indignantly.

" I don't believe you would," she conceded generously; "not consciously, certainly. I didn't mean that. But it would cut the ground from under all your plans and ambitions. That would hurt. Fortunately, nobody ever is convinced of anything by arguments—do you think?"

" What convinced you?" he asked suddenly, following a more personal line of thought.

She wrinkled her brow for an instant as though reflecting.

" I became a Socialist all in one minute," she answered, " I had a patient whose husband worked in a factory. He worked hard, too. His wife needed all sorts of things he couldn't buy her, and he hated Charity. So do I," she broke in sharply and hotly. " When people have a right to Justice, what they're given is Charity. I despise it, whether it's organized or unorganized."

He raised his eyebrows.

" Yet you work for a kind of Charity," he urged.

" I hate it all the worse for that," she rejoined. " I work to earn my bread and the stale odor of cabbage. I've no illusions about my job.

" Well," she went on, " I went to the man who ran the factory where this man worked. I told him the wife would die if there wasn't more money in the pay envelope. He offered me alms. He was a kind man. He proved to me the industry couldn't pay better wages— proved it so even I could have no doubts. Right then and there I decided something had to be done with industry. We've run the World as though Men were made for Commerce, not Commerce for Men!"

He shook his head with the sage wisdom of his years. "It isn't enough to see a flaw in things. One must be sure the remedy isn't worse than the disease."

"No remedy could be worse than this disease," she interrupted. "The patient's dying in agony! There's nothing to be lost by trying any prescription."

She broke off again with capricious suddenness, and smiled.

"Well, I am arguing after all!" she laughed, "but I shan't, any more. Perhaps I'm trying to save you from my dangerous influence, by showing you the worst of me all in one evening. Irreligion, Socialism, St. Cecelia, the plush album, the hair-cloth chair and the cabbage dinner! Your own Board of Trustees couldn't have cared for you more tenderly than I have!"

He said the gallant things he knew so well how to say and then proceeded to ply her with questions about herself, more flattering because of the sincere interest they displayed than his more obvious compliments. She told him of herself with complete frankness. Her father had been the rather prosperous proprietor of a small dry-goods shop in a Pennsylvania town. Her people were perfectly proper and conservative. She had been graduated from a public High School and had come to Baltimore as a student at Goucher College. While she was in her freshman year her father's business, which had for some time been growing steadily worse and worse, suddenly ended in a disastrous collapse.

"Poor Dad," she said, "his little shop went to smash just because it happened to be the year 1908 instead of 1888, but he still blames it on the owners of the department stores and the mail-order houses who snapped up his customers! He believes it was a plot. That's what comes of being religious, and a sound party man in politics!"

Ellen, thrown on her own resources, had matriculated as a pupil nurse at the Johns Hopkins Nursing School,— not, she assured Philip vigorously, because of any silly notions about the nobility of the profession she was entering, but because from the very first, the problem of living would be solved for her. When she completed the course, she had been offered her persent post, and had accepted it, instead of seeking private patients, so that her nights might be free from duty.

" And here I am," she concluded, " aged twenty-five— believing everything my family thinks wicked, and steadily refusing to marry the only young man in my home-town who is willing to forgive my eccentricities. My people are sure that's the worst of all my many crimes. They can't see why I don't like him. He's so well thought of in his Building Association, and I'm not getting a day younger, they tell me. So I don't go home very often. I have a weakness for flattery."

Philip rose to the occasion.

" I should think you would be surfeited with it," he remarked promptly.

" No woman ever was," she informed him demurely. " Still, you've flattered me very acceptably tonight, though I suspect you don't know in just what way,—and I shan't tell you, either. It's no part of a minister's duty to go gadding about pleasing strange women!"

" Oh!" he protested, " I hope you don't mean by that I may not see you again. We've only begun to talk of the things I want to learn. I've had a bad day and, somehow, you've made it end well for me. I may come again, soon, mayn't I?"

She looked at him thoughtfully as he stood before her, prepared to take his leave. Then she smiled.

"Will you be exceedingly angry if I remind you that you're very young and not fit to take care of yourself?"

"There's very little difference in our ages," he answered sharply—slightly nettled by her words.

"Now, you've just proved how young you are," she laughed gaily. "Well," she said, opening the door for him, "you shall do what you please. Only I warn you, if you really become a friend of mine—sooner or later, you'll be sorry—and if you don't——"

"What then?" he asked eagerly.

"Why then," she replied slowly, "it will be I who'll be sorry!"

Before he could answer he found the door closed between them, and he was not certain whether or not the last sound he had heard from within was that of laughter.

CHAPTER XVI

The Appeal to Capital

PHILIP was not so utterly unsophisticated as to view his new-found acquaintanceship with Ellen Stewart without misgivings. He knew perfectly well with what stern frowns conservative Baltimore viewed the companionship of young Jews with Gentiles of the opposite sex. He knew also that whether this restriction had found its origin long years before in Christian intolerance, or in Jewish pride of race, it found today no more eager adherents than among his own people. They held it to be an axiom that if a young woman—whether Christian or Jewess—were willing to encourage acquaintanceship with men of another race, there must be something objectionable about her, either in morals or at least in delicacy. As for men, of course, the rule was the same except in so far as all rules of morals and refinement were subject to some slight relaxation in favor of the superior and less responsible sex. But this greater freedom of action allowed to the lords of creation did not, as a matter of course, apply to Rabbis. A preacher, by virtue of his contract, must be as circumspect in his conduct as the most prudish of ladies, and, at the same time, free from the slightest taint of the effeminate. Congregations of all creeds are accustomed to buy all sorts of shades of perfection when they secure the services of a minister, and no other employers would dare to give open expression to such savage ideas about the exact letter of their bond. Philip, himself, had never before chafed under the rigid regulations to which he was subjected. His tendency had always been toward forcing himself to do what he conceived to be his duty—the more difficult, the better. Therefore, his leanings were decidedly toward an asceticism more monkish than Jewish. He found conventional morality rather easy to practice. His instincitve love of beauty included a fondness for what he considered symmetrical living, and to him all infractions of a well-ordered life, free from anything and everything clandestine, was an excess, and therefore ugly. He had rather approved the custom which set Israel apart from all alien races, even in its care-free meetings of youths and maidens. Such things led to intermarriage—and intermarriage was unreservedly bad. The Jews were the priest-people, the martyr-race. Their long and painful mission was not yet accomplished. There could be no benefit in diluting their heroic blood with strains which were weaker,—or at any rate, unconsecrated.

By all the rules of logic, therefore, Philip should have let Miss Stewart severely alone. As a Jew, as a Rabbi, and as a man half-committed to a marriage with a delightful and highly suitable girl, it was his simple duty to refrain from so dangerous an association as this piquant nurse seemed to promise. For the first time in Philip's well-controlled life, however, his rigid rules of conduct ceased to guide him. He was a Jew and a Rabbi, but his race and his congregation were brutally inflicting upon him, day after day, wounds which caused more pain than he could bear all alone. As for Ruth, he knew his unexplained absence was hurting her, and that fact was an additional source of misery to him; but he could not

resist an uncontrollable repugnance, while this intolerable
strife continued, to resuming his habits of tender intimacy
with this young kinswoman of Clarence Kaufman. He
would not give the semblance of veracity to David
Gordon's coarse newspaper gibe about the buttered side
of his bread. Therefore, in the midst of his congregation,
and in this City whose drift and mystery he had not yet
learned to understand, he was inexpressibly lonely. He
seemed so useless. People liked to hear him talk as
though he were a paid entertainer. Meanwhile, above
his head went the vast current of the City's life and
hatreds; if he were noticed, it was only, he imagined,
with contempt as a negligible, smooth-tongued weakling.
There was not one soul to whom he could pour out the
heart-ache and misery of his boyish disappointment.

Unless—temptation whispered—he chose to make a
confidante—a real friend—of Ellen. She was older than
Ruth—older than himself. More self-reliant, too, and
with a mind wonderfully alert, if less carefully schooled
than Ruth's or his own. She was not afraid of petty
gossip. The companionship could not harm her. It might
even prove a source of happiness. Of course, nothing
lasting or permanent could come of it. To a girl of
her age and freedom from mawkishness that would not
matter. As for himself, who would ever learn of it,
provided he were a bit prudent? In the forum of his
own conscience he knew how free from any trace of the
sentimental their relationship would be. He needed her.
She offered him sympathy and a refuge from his sadden-
ing isolation—all the more because she was not a Jewess
and had, therefore, no part to play in the civil warfare
among the Jewish community.

THE APPEAL TO CAPITAL

So Philip continued to seek out Ellen Stewart and to find with her the only pleasant hours of his day. For her part—she had her own problems of loneliness and no regard whatsoever for any hampering conventions. To her, with her passionate repudiation of sects, creeds and parties, his Judaism made little or no difference except in so far as it tended to narrow his own horizon. She, too, realized the inevitable impossibility of this state of affairs continuing, but she was willing to enjoy the present while it lasted. Her only concern, in fact, was a fear lest his association with her might bring disaster upon him. Therefore, each, without a word to the other on the subject, arranged their meetings with all possible circumspection, and each felt a little ashamed and injured in self-respect, because they were thus slavishly appearing to acknowledge a guilty quality in their innocent relationship.

They talked unceasingly, upon every conceivable subject, and there were few topics upon which they found themselves in agreement. This did not seem to diminish in the least the happiness each found in the other's presence. They differed pleasantly and without bitterness. With all his superior equipment of study and training, he found it almost impossible to convince her of any of his theories. For one thing, she had absolutely no reverence for authority. When he would triumphantly hurl at her pretty head some apt quotation from Huxley confirming his views, she would answer without an instant's hesitation:

" What difference can it make to us what Huxley thought? If a man like Huxley can't make it seem true, there's all the more reason for supposing it isn't."

For Philip's dreams regarding the mission of Israel, she had nothing but scorn.

"Your race," she insisted, "isn't a bit different from any other variety of human flesh, except that it's been inbred so long that all its prominent vices and virtues stand out, sheer, like the typical Jewish nose. If you've got anything to give the world, the way to do it is to mingle yourselves with the rest of men, and mix your wonder-working blood with all of us whom you admit need it so badly."

He explained patiently, yet with enthusiasm, the necessity for the Jew doing his own work unhampered by any confusion of conflicting traditions.

"What special work have you Jews to do in the world?" she demanded sharply.

"We're to bring peace, brotherhood, the recognition of a spirituality in the daily order of life. This shall be the common faith, in one form or another, of all mankind."

She tossed her head impatiently: "Who doesn't aim at that?" she insisted; "the Christian, the Jew, the Mohammedan, even the Atheist, claims the exclusive right to save the world in just this way. I claim it for the Socialist. So you see it's not a matter of religion, at all."

"That's just it," he exclaimed triumphantly, "you all want to do it, but you can't. But we can, because we alone have stood faithful to this ideal through centuries of persecution."

"Why don't you go and do it, then?" she asked. "Now that the persecution is done with, you've done with the ideal, too. Look at your prosperous, well-fed Jew of today. Look at Clarence Kaufman. How much more of brotherhood or spirituality has he than I?"

" It's there," he insisted doggedly. " There's a Jewish idealism under the shell of the man if I could only dig down to it. It's the treatment of the Jews by the Christians—the exclusions, the petty humiliations, the cold, bitter lack of sympathy, which have made the modern Jew what he seems to be."

" I don't believe it," she answered thoughtfully. " If your Jews were what you think, Christian influence could have done them no harm. In America, for fifty odd years, you've been shut out from only the worst side of national life. The schools, the universities, the libraries, the opportunities for public service, are all open to you. You're barred out only from country clubs, summer hotels, and miserable cliques of stupid parasites, where people with too much money gather to do the things working men would be ashamed to imitate. Exclusion from such things should have intensified your idealism. But what have you done? Since you couldn't join the Christian in this folly, you've aped his stupidity among yourselves. You've built up your own little clubs and hotels and made your own little groups of snobs. Bah! men are men, and the sooner they forget their tags and their ridiculous claims to superiority and learn to work together as human beings, the sooner we'll do something worth while with the world."

And from this position she steadfastly refused to budge.

All the talk of this oddly assorted pair was not, however, of creeds and prejudices. They talked of her work and of his, of the books they enjoyed and the ideas which pleased them, and most of all, did they talk of themselves,—freely, constantly, and with unblushing interest

in this all-important subject, after the manner of youths
and maidens—Jew and Gentile—Buddhist and Brahmin
—since Nature's cardinal masterpiece—or blunder—of
Sex was first revealed to a purblind world of males and
females. From these meetings, Philip came with a curious gain and loss of self-respect. He had found someone
who understood and appreciated him—no matter how
much she might differ from his conclusions. All the
more was this true because this understanding woman
was of another race and faith and must unconsciously
have given him her regard in spite of the trammels of an
inherited prejudice and contempt. This gave him strength
and vigor to go about his duties with firmness and
courage—no matter how much or how little his congregation might think of his conduct with regard to the strike.

On the other hand, he carried with him always, a
haunting sense of something in his life clandestine, hidden, almost shameful, and this secret affected subtly
every phase of his thought. He knew he had done nothing evil, yet he was no longer exactly what he seemed.
In a sense, he was a conscious sham, and this knowledge
made him even more than before, morbidly anxious to
avoid all save formal contact with his parishioners.

Among the many stimulating ideas which Philip culled
from his talks with Ellen was this conception of a latent
Jewish idealism dormant in all the race—even the most
sodden. He preached a singularly appealing sermon
sounding this note, and almost immediately thereafter
became possessed with a desire to put his theory into
practice. He would take his faith and his message direct
to Clarence Kaufman. He would awaken him to the
high duties due by him to his race. Single-handed he

would accomplish this miracle and at one stroke vindicate the Religion he loved so fervently, and bring this strife among brothers to a triumphant end. Ellen found it impossible to share his hopes. Perhaps, subconsciously, she had some faint realization of the certainty with which a conclusion of his perplexities would terminate their companionship. Perhaps she was merely more intolerant than he of a man who typified to her the obnoxious thing called "Capital." At any rate, she tried to dissuade Philip from his endeavor.

"You'll never get him to see your point of view," she insisted. "Even if you did, he couldn't afford to admit it now. If you meant to appeal to him, you should have done it at the very beginning, before he had so much to take back."

"I didn't know there was any strike until long after the beginning," Philip objected.

"It was then you lost your chance! Don't bother," she added, almost cynically, "you'll have plenty of strikes to look forward to."

But he refused to be diverted. "What have I to lose?" he argued. "If I fail, I'll merely be proving what you've been maintaining all along about the power of Religion."

"I'm enough of a sportswoman to want your theories to have a real test," she answered, "not one with a foregone conclusion."

He knew this was not her true reason, and his eyes continued to question her.

"Well then," she said in a tone of actual defiance, "if you will have it, I don't want you to lose faith in yourself. When you get through with that man, you'll

be a wretched creature. You'd better leave yourself in a
state of uncertainty. I know I'm silly. I know I've been
right, and you've been wrong, all the time, but a woman's
logic always breaks down somewhere. I'd rather you'd
be happy than be able to see things straight! You were
never born to do both!"

And before he could answer she was gone, leaving him
to make what he could of her mood. He could not but
feel the appeal of her thought for him, yet her words
troubled him, too. Perhaps, even at twenty-five a woman
had not altogether lost her last shreds of sentimentality!

He had no intention, however, of abandoning his
project of an interview with Kaufman. The very next
morning he telephoned that gentleman and made an appointment for the evening. The time was indeed not
well chosen. Gordon's newspaper attacks had grown
more, rather than less, vitriolic. The pleasant thought
had occurred to him of unearthing from the public
records, and exhibiting to an uncharitable world, the
perfectly innocent contributions made at the preceding
election by Mr. Kaufman and sundry other directors of
the Pioneer Company to the campaign fund of the successful candidate for the office of State's Attorney. That
official was an exceedingly popular and entirely well-
meaning gentleman and there were few business men of
his own party of any degree of affluence who had not
offered some substantial assistance in meeting the expenses of his canvass. This had been done in perfect good
faith and without the slightest effort at concealment. In
fact, the statutes required the publication, immediately
after the election, of the names of all such contributors,
together with the amounts they had given, and this re-

quirement had been duly obeyed. Today, however, an advertisement had been published calling attention to these generous free-will offerings and skillfully calculated to induce ribald conjectures regarding the possible connection between the pliancy, in this particular case, of the public prosecutor, and the money with which he had procured his election. Not the least irritating of the characteristics of this adroit bit of authorship was its absolute freedom from a single actual falsehood. Before sundown, six of the most ingenuous lawyers in the City had examined the advertisement microscopically, thirsting for the opportunity to file a libel suit, yet the facts recited were exact, and studiously free from comment. The public was left to infer what it chose, by a man who felt no doubts as to its preference for assuming, without argument, the corruptibility of all politicians, and the infallible habit of money never being disbursed, except to purchase money's worth. There was nothing to be done about it, other than to publish in full the long list of all the other contributors to the fund. Some of the most honored men in the City's public and mercantile life were among those named, but the very lawyers who advised this form of defence knew perfectly well how little effect it would have in preventing a prejudgment of the case of Israel Ginzberg. They swore long and deep at David Gordon, and admired secretly the sinister cleverness of the man.

Clarence Kaufman was still smarting under the effects of this fresh thrust when his young spiritual guide came tapping at his door with admonitions regarding the brotherhood of man and the beauty of forgiveness. The Rabbi, himself, could not but anticipate a hostile reception. When he had read the newspapers that afternoon, he would gladly have postponed his pastoral call, but the appointment had been made and to withdraw now, because his parishioner had been given an additional grievance, would have been, to his mind, more absurd than submission to a flat rebuff.

Therefore, Philip found himself seated in Clarence Kaufman's library awaiting gloomily the entrance of the President of his congregation. The room was not altogether unrepresentative of its owner, although his part in its decoration and equipment had been that of final arbiter rather than originator of ideas. Its furniture was massive and expensive-looking rather than beautiful. Yet there was nothing in the room which could be said to be in actual bad taste. The many books on the shelves, arrayed in their much too-uniform bindings, did not wear a convincing air of having been frequently liberated from their places of imprisonment. One looked involuntarily on the walls for great, gilt, framed paintings of fruit and animals, without, however, finding them. It was the kind of room where one searches minutely for some evidence of the crudity he feels certain he must discover somewhere, and finally confesses with keen disappointment his failure to locate anything more tangible than an indefinable atmosphere.

Into this library there walked slowly the huge frame of Clarence Kaufman, as massive as the furniture, but not modelled with such careful artistry. Tonight he seemed to Philip much older and more careworn than ever before. If the strike had brought hunger and disease into the gaunt tenements of East Baltimore, it had not altogether spared the proprietor of this luxurious home on Eutaw Place. As the two men exchanged greetings, Philip's heart was filled with a great wave of tenderness toward all these blind men who were thus wounding each other and themselves, in their unreasoning fury. In spite of his four and twenty years he felt toward this elderly man and his enemies as though they were heedless, unruly little children who needed to have the jagged stones they were thoughtlessly hurling at each other, taken from them, and themselves led home to be soothed and comforted till their pains had ceased and the hatreds had died out of their hearts.

Clarence Kaufman must have read in the minister's thoughtful face how little of partisanship was in his mind, and he turned to him with sincere warmth.

"My dear Dr. Graetz," he said earnestly in his deep, harsh voice, "I'm glad you've come to talk things over with me."

"I felt I had to," Philip began.

"Yes," Mr. Kaufman continued, "I'm only sorry you didn't come before. I'd have sent for you, except that I didn't want to embarrass you."

Philip perceived a delicacy in this speech much more pronounced than he had expected, in spite of Mr. Kaufman's calm assumption of his Rabbi's subjection to his beck and call. It was not like Philip, however, to stand on a petty question of dignity, so he responded with prompt cordiality.

"I wish you had. I'd have come, anyhow, only I wasn't sure just what I wanted to say to you; but now, I know at least how I want to begin. Do you remember that night last fall at Dr. Frank's home when I said if I felt something wrong was happening in the community which you could remedy, I should come straight to you?"

Kaufman nodded and answered slowly and wearily:

"I told you then I would show you how right I was, or agree to do what you wanted. And now I'm going to show you. It's a long story and a miserable one, but you'll see before I've finished how we've done everything humanly possible to bring these scoundrels to their senses! If there's anything further you can suggest, God knows we'll be glad to try it."

Philip's eyes widened in surprised dismay. After all these weeks, Kaufman's only thought seemed to be the complete rectitude of his actions. The Rabbi had come, apparently, not to teach but to be lessoned. They would never make any progress in such fashion. Very gently, he explained the futility of this method of attacking the problem.

"My dear Mr. Kaufman," he urged, "I think it would be useless to go all over the history of the strike. I've read every statement you've issued and every paper on file at the State Bureau. I'm sure you always acted for the best, as you saw it. Maybe it was best, too, as an abstract proposition. But that isn't what I'm thinking of tonight. You and I are Jews. We love our faith. If you didn't, you wouldn't have given so freely of your time and wealth to the Temple. You surely aren't satisfied with merely having the Temple crowded and prosperous. You want the spirit it stands for to make headway among all Jews and to be respected among non-Jews. Now, we're having a civil war among the Jews, and the Christians are mocking us. We're hurting Judaism in Baltimore—wounding it almost mortally. You're the Captain of one side in this war. Let's assume you've been altogether in the right from the start! but it's our own brothers against whom you've pointed your weapons —the very men we want to teach the meaning of our message. Even a complete victory in such a struggle, would be a disaster we could never completely retrieve, in your lifetime or mine. Can't we make Peace? Isn't any business quarrel a tiny thing compared with the welfare of Judaism, and of God's Truth?"

As Philip spoke, his whole frame reflected the glow of his enthusiasm; he leaned forward in his chair, his eyes flashing, his beautiful voice tender with the sincerity of his appeal.

For several minutes after he had concluded, the President of the Pioneer Company made no reply. His expression was one of bewilderment, as though he had been listening to a discourse in some foreign tongue. Finally, he replied, his guttural tones contrasting unpleasantly with the rich musical intonations of his visitor.

"Doctor, I hardly know how to answer you. You're a splendid talker and I'm not, but you've got to remember this: I didn't start this war, as you call it. I haven't done the things which have turned an ordinary business quarrel, as simple as a dispute about the price of buttons, into a knock-down and drag-out fight. I can't believe that it's my duty to submit to all the abuse and injury this scum of Europe has thrown at me just because they happen to be Jews, like myself. I don't believe Religion means anything like that. If it does, then I don't know anything about Religion and I don't want to."

"But, Mr. Kaufman," Philip pleaded, "just because they are poor and ignorant and in despair, can't you see they are bound to do rash things—yes, cruel and wicked things, for which you can afford to forgive them because you've had the good fortune to have opportunity and wealth. Can't you see," he was about to quote the phrase, " *noblesse oblige* " but hurriedly remembering his auditor might not understand its meaning—he concluded by saying, instead, " Can't you, because of your very superiority, find it in your heart to pardon what you, yourself, could not commit? "

Very slowly and inflexibly, the capitalist shook his head.

" Pardon me, Doctor," he replied, " you're a wonderful young man, as I always said, but you don't know the Russian Jew. How should you? You're decent straight through, and it's natural you should think they're just like you, only without your brains and advantages. That's why I didn't harbor any grudge against you when I heard about your vote at the Charity Society. But you're wrong! The poor and the ignorant aren't the ones who are doing these things. The more education and good living you give them, the more dangerous they are. It's well-fed, college-taught men like Gordon who have turned this little fight into a hell! You wouldn't call him poor or ignorant, would you, any more than you would me? "

" No," Philip hastened to concede, " he's certainly a much brainier man than I feel myself to be, but, Mr. Kaufman, Gordon would be utterly powerless if he didn't have this mass of unhappy, desperate men upon which to work. So it really mounts up to the same thing. If all you say about the immigrant Jew is true, don't you see there's all the more reason why we must lead him to accept our own ideas of what our Religion means? He's in the majority already. The whole future of the Jew in America is in his hands. Do you want to leave him free to develop it without help from us who have had a half century the start of him in this country?"

"No," Kaufman answered, "I don't. That's why you can't give him his way. When a boy is downright bad, you can't discipline him by giving him whatever he happens to want. You punish him. That's what we've got to do with these anarchists. They won't be in the mood for accepting any instruction from you till they learn one lesson:—In America a man has got to obey the Law."

A hundred quick-tempered retorts leaped to Philip's lips, but he repressed them sternly, remembering he had come not to debate, but, if possible, to convince.

"Mr. Kaufman," he began again, "it's idle to treat this as a mere matter of phrases. If you succeed in all you want to do, you'll only reap a harvest of hate for ourselves and for our kind of Judaism. That's why I want to make Peace. Don't you see I only came to you because I'm trying to do the best I know how for the Religion you brought me here to preach? Mere sermons are nothing if the man who preaches them doesn't care what happens among the people he wants to help."

"I know! I know!" Mr. Kaufman said, "I'm sure you want to do what's right, but you can't let your heart run away with your head, either. You ought to be talking these ideas to the other side, not to me. We've always been reasonable."

Philip caught eagerly at the hope his host had not intended to hold out to him.

"I *will* talk to them!" he exclaimed, "just along these lines, if you'll let me say I have your authority to discuss a peace, honorable to both of you."

The factory owner brought his fist crashing down on the mahogany table.

" Go tell them their duty, if you want to—not that they'll listen to you! But for our part, we shall make no more concessions than we've offered from the start. We said we'd arbitrate the wage scale. We couldn't have been fairer than that. Their answer was to kill one of our men. When the Law undertook to punish the criminal who set them at this business of throwing bricks, they weren't willing to trust the courts of their own State like decent citizens, but spent thousands of dollars,— they got, God knows where,—trying to make out we're the criminals instead of the men who teach fools to murder honest workingmen. Let them take back their foul-mouthed lies about how we treated our men like underfed dogs, and worked children in our plant and bribed State's Attorneys, and then they can come back to work if they want. We're still willing to arbitrate the wage scale. We won't go one step further—not if I knew tomorrow their brick-bats would fall on me!"

Philip looked sadly at the angry man across the table.

" Let me say you'll arbitrate the question of the Union, and I'll try, night and day, to bring this thing to an end. I'll try so hard, I'm sure,—I'm sure, I must succeed."

The capitalist was not unmoved by the breathless earnestness of the Rabbi, and his refusal was certainly not easy for him to phrase.

" I can't do it," he insisted; " I pledge you my word I hate to say 'no' to you, but I can't. If we once turn our factory over to the Unions, it won't be our business any more. I won't have it. I won't let a crowd of ragged foreigners dictate to me how I must run my plant. I'd rather close down."

" It isn't as though it were ' your business ' just as

your watch is yours," Philip argued, trying to put into palatable form an economic truth which he felt would, at the best, prove distasteful to Kaufman. "It's too big for that. It's the public's business, partly. And the men who spend their lives in helping to make your product—aren't they concerned at all in the way it's managed?"

"No," Kaufman protested, "that's the idea that is running wild over this country. If the men don't like my methods they can go elsewhere. I can't hold them against their will, can I? If my business goes to smash, they can whistle a tune and walk across the street to a new job. If it's their business, let them finance it. The business is the Capital I furnish."

Philip smiled his most conciliating smile.

"I'm afraid you're wrong there, Mr. Kaufman," he said. "You're partners in a sense, after all. You do furnish the money and the machinery; they wouldn't be much good without labor, nor would the labor be much good without the machines and the capital."

He was about to enlarge upon this text, according to the wisdom he had gleaned from the best books upon the subject, when Clarence Kaufman interrupted.

"There's no use talking that kind of stuff to me," was his unflattering comment, "I can't answer you because I don't understand it. All I know is that if I put my money into a business, I ought to have a right to say on what terms; if you say 'no' I won't put it in at all."

The two men—completely deadlocked—sat together in silence. It was the Rabbi who broke this hush with a final appeal.

"Mr. Kaufman," he begged, determined not to owe his defeat to any mere question of pride, "perhaps I haven't been able to put things as well as I should. Maybe my arguments haven't been the ones I ought to have used. But I know it's right that there should be peace. You know it, too, in your heart. Do it for my sake! Even if you're sure you're giving up too much, do it to save my ministry from failure! It's all my future you hold in your hands!"

Kaufman rose heavily and opening a table drawer, produced some faded old photographs.

"Your work's a success already, Doctor," he said heartily, while he was so engaged, "an enormous success! There's never been any preacher in Baltimore, Jew or Christian, who has scored such a triumph as you have, in so short a time."

Philip's heart sank within him. The man saw no difference whatever between mere applause and actual accomplishment. Where was the Jewish idealism of which he had boasted to Ellen?

Meanwhile, Kaufman returned to the Rabbi's side with the sheaf of photographs in his hand.

"Look here, Doctor," he said; "here are some pictures of my father and mother."

The younger man examined, with interest, these copies of the features of the sturdy, rugged Jew and Jewess of a half century before. Kaufman's parents had been young then, and if the minister might judge from their attitudes and expression, Life had been to them a clear, simple matter of plainly-marked-out duties, with much of anxiety and labor, but with rewards no less definite than its tasks. Both of them, so young and alert when the pictures had been made, had long since tasted of old age, and perhaps lived to wonder dimly regarding the value of all the things they had struggled so valiantly to gain—until, finally, Death had come to blot out whatever vague doubts and surmises their many years had bestowed upon them; on the pictures, however, they were still brimming with youth and vitality, clear-eyed with the realization of the few things they meant to accomplish, and the resolute certainty not to meet defeat.

"These were my parents," Kaufman repeated. "My father came here from Bavaria when he was only eighteen. He couldn't speak one word of English. He borrowed a few dollars from another man who had come from the same village, and bought all sorts of odds and ends of dry-goods and peddled them through the country towns. People laughed at him and played tricks on him. Sometimes he had to sleep by the side of the road. Often he went hungry. He didn't whine about his rights as a human being and the duty of the State to feed him. He kept on working till he'd saved up a few dollars of his own. Then, he and my mother—he'd married by this time—started a little tailor shop on Exeter Street. Here's a picture of the house." He held it out to Philip.

"It's a tenement house, now," the Rabbi reminded him, hoping, while the capitalist was in this gentle mood, to bridge the gulf between him and the modern Ghetto-dwellers.

Kaufman, unheeding, went on with his narrative:

"I was born there," he announced proudly. "At first my father did nothing but mend clothes. Meanwhile, he was learning how to make them. By and by, he saved up enough to buy a few machines. My mother helped in the shop. When they could afford to have a few helpers, they treated them just like part of the family. My mother cooked their meals for them. They were as much interested in their work as my father was. The hum of the sewing machines is the first thing I can remember."

He paused for a minute and then resumed in a firmer tone:

"That little shop is what grew into the Pioneer factory! My father and my mother put every bit of their lives into it. They worked for it, they planned for it, they saved every penny to help it grow. They taught me to feel the same way about it. And now you come here telling me it isn't my business! It is my business! It's got my blood in it, and the blood of my father and mother! I won't let it be looted by a crowd of ignorant law-breakers who would ruin the place tomorrow to make an extra dime a week."

Philip listened with mingled emotions. What force could his abstract theories bring to bear against these warm personal prejudices, woven out of such childhood memories? Yet this idealism he had sought, was there not some germ of it here in the heart of the man's blind, unreasoning refusal to do what was right and just, in this day of changed and complex conditions? He made no reply, sitting there puzzled and dejected.

When the defeated advocate, at length, rose to take his departure, the older man laid his hand kindly on the Rabbi's shoulder.

"Don't you take it to heart so much, Doctor," he counselled; "it's a bad business, of course, but not so bad as it would naturally seem to a young man from a small town, like you. It's not the first strike we've had, and it won't be the last, either. You'll get used to them before long; and we'll teach these fellows their places, sooner or later."

CHAPTER XVII

The Man and the Rabbi

ELLEN'S skepticism regarding the power of Religion in dealing with the conflicting claims of angry men, seemed completely vindicated, yet she displayed a puzzling unwillingness to gloat over the confirmation of her theories. It was a perplexed young minister who came to her for comfort; he had been completely baffled in what he had undertaken, but he felt, more than ever, the certainty of some method—if he could only chance upon it—of bringing about a wholesome kindliness of feeling between men who were all so human, and so warm-hearted behind the armor of their lusts and hates.

Ellen did what she could to stimulate this hope. She seemed to have laid aside her own militant theories that through force alone could Justice be established—no matter how much of pain it might cost to well-meaning soldiers enrolled in the wrong army. She appeared, too, to have lost no little of her spirit of raillery and perverse contradiction. She was evidently trying, with all her might, to save Philip from losing faith in himself and his work, and under her encouragement he bore his failure with an altogether unexpected freedom from despair.

One evening, however, a few days later, Philip was amazed, upon seeking Ellen, to be told of her sudden departure from the City. Without a word of warning to him, she had gone away, leaving no message except the bare statement that she had obtained a brief leave of

16   241

absence from her duties, and would return on the following Monday.

Of course she had a perfect right to come and go as she pleased; nevertheless, Philip was annoyed. At least she might have writen or telephoned him of her intention. He returned to his own apartment, and aimlessly sat down to read. After a few minutes, he became conscious of a total ignorance of the contents of the page before him. He had been thinking about Ellen. He made a vigorous effort to concentrate his attention upon the book he had chosen, but found it an impossible task. Ellen's face, with its saucy smile, and Ellen's voice, with its provokingly disrespectful laughter, would not be banished. Disgusted with himself and not altogether free from anger at the girl for her thoughtless conduct in depriving him so unceremoniously of an evening's companionship, he rather sullenly made ready for sleep; but after his lamp had been extinguished, he found sleep would not come to him. The many ideas he had meant to discuss with Ellen came trooping insistently through his brain and he imagined endless dialogues with her—upon all sorts of personal and abstract subjects. He would certainly find her absence a definite loss to him. Perhaps he had come to rely too much upon her. He must steel himself to go about again among the young people of his own group. Perhaps her unexpected disappearance was not altogether a misfortune. There was Ruth. He had behaved rather badly to her. Since he could find it possible to visit Kaufman, he could not fairly excuse himself for his discourteous neglect of this girl who had been so frank to show him how warmly she regarded his friendship. She wouldn't be human and feminine if she failed to resent it.

Still, he wouldn't find it difficult to regain her favor. Tomorrow night, then, it should be Ruth. He tried to think of the excuses he would offer to her, and of the turn their conversation would take, but persistently and inflexibly the imagined Ruth would shrink in stature and stateliness; her dignified and fastidious dark beauty would be transformed into a piquant, never-to-be-analyzed charm of mischievous blue eyes and gold hair, and it would be Ellen, not Ruth, who appeared before his eyes; an Ellen, too, imperceptibly less matter-of-fact and self-reliant than the one he had known. Her eyes seemed, somehow, with all their mockery, a little more inviting—her mobile lips, more alluring!

He raised his head from the pillow with a sudden shock of surprise and dismay at the images persisting in his mind. He was dumfounded to perceive how small a part, after all, of his desire for Ellen's return was due to his mere wish to talk with her again. Struggle against it as he might, he wanted, with all the force of his long-repressed youth, to clasp her fiercely in his arms, to kiss, and kiss again and again, those rebellious eyes and lips into meekness and submission. He sprang from his bed and relit his lamp. These were strange discoveries to find at the bottom of a Rabbi's mind, certainly not character-istic of himself—disgraceful, in fact! How unutterably humiliated Ellen would be, if she could, by some miracle, know what was happening in his soul! Then the lurking Devil, who from the beginning, has chosen for his favorite pastime the tempting of holy saints and sages—young and old—whispered into his ear a doubt as to Ellen's complete disdain of his new-found mood. Would she be sorry? Would she, with her frank contempt for convention, for social dogma, and for his faith, as well as for the one which should have been her own, pretend a repugnance because he had become conscious of her body as well as her soul?

He paced the narrow room, in an agitated survey of his emotions. He wanted this dainty girl of an alien race; he wanted her quick, untaught mind, her noble scorn of what seemed to her to be false and unjust, but he wanted her appealing, illusive beauty, too—he wanted all of her! He might pretend what he chose, he could not deny what every fibre of his nature cried aloud. He must have felt as he now did for many days, only it needed this crisis to make his own self clear to him. Here was his problem, to be met and dealt with as the man, or the Rabbi, might prove the stronger.

The Rabbi was the first to enter the lists against the mere man. Philip reminded himself with merciless logic of the peril which confronted at once his future and the laborious, carefully-planned years behind him. To what purpose had he spent his days of study and preparation if he were now to fling aside recklessly the tasks he had painfully taught himself to do. What could he make of his life if he should link his career with Ellen's? The pulpit would be closed to him—absolutely and irrevocably. He was unfitted for all other forms of activity. He could write, it was true, but only homilies, exhortations and theological studies. These things would gain no hearing, flowing from the pen of a disgraced Rabbi. He could throw himself with what poor ardor he could artificially kindle, into Ellen's plans for social regeneration. Still, he knew how lukewarm they would ever find him. He was essentially a Jew. He did not want to be anything else.

This broad idea of completely merging his race among all other peoples left him cold and unmoved. There was her Socialism to be worked for, but while he could rise to a pitch of ecstasy in his dreams of realizing Israel's mission, the statistical Utopian plans of Ellen's comrades seemed to him wilful self-delusion—more or less harmful. Unless he paused now, the rest of his life was destined to be spent in busying himself as best he could with useless little tasks, while he lived meagerly upon the scant income his dead father had worked to give him.

The man Philip, thus assailed by the Rabbi Graetz, had not one argument to urge. With the image of Ellen before his eyes, he foreswore logic, and thought instead of the countless men since Adam, who for the sake of some woman's smile, have blithely forsaken their Edens to find with her another Paradise in the desert.

"But would you be happy with her," the Rabbi demanded, "or she with you? What can you hope from such a marriage? You begin with a sacrifice of all your hopes and ambitions—certain to make you moody, sullen and discontented. You haven't one belief in common. It's easy enough to differ good-naturedly about everything you discuss, but when the two of you must bring yourselves to some joint action, how will you force her to follow your plans, or yourself to yield to hers? The friends she has, will have nothing but contempt for you— a Jew and a renegade Jew, at that. Your own friends will shun you as something loathsome. Without work of your own, and with nothing but hostility for your wife's work, how long will your unreasoning Love continue to live? Ellen will not even be able to respect you—a useless, worthless bit of human driftwood, eating the bread you have not earned. If she could find it possible to accomplish the miracle of an undiminished love for a man who was absolutely without any title to regard, you yourself would be always and ever bitterly conscious of her adverse verdict and your own. Suppose children are born to you! That would be the worst of all—a desperate problem and cause of strife between the man and woman who had called them into being, instead of a bond of union and a source of pride. They could never be taught to redeem their father's desertion from his duty—to complete the work he had abandoned to follow the call of personal happiness. Even if their mother should refrain from active opposition, such plans would, in themselves, constitute an unpardonable affront to her, involving so gross an indelicacy, that her blood in her offspring would rise in protest to defeat his purpose. On the other hand, he would find it unspeakably bitter to watch his own sons and daughters completely lost to the heritage of his ancestors—unconscious or indifferent to all the hopes and all the agony which, through the long centuries, generations of Jews had bequeathed to him— Philip Graetz—as the peculiar birthright of his race, to be used, somehow, in marvelous ways,—certainly not to be tossed carelessly to the winds.

The Rabbi found it ridiculously easy to silence the man; but, unfortunately, his victories, won almost without opposition, were also without benefit. The Rabbi could think and argue; but the man, in wounded silence, continued to suffer, and to long unceasingly for the woman he knew only too well he should forget.

The days which followed were for him an unrelieved horror of yearning and conflict. The duty which he frankly recognized, of renouncing Ellen completely and irrevocably, not only laid upon him a sense of tragic loss of something inexpressibly dear to him, but was in addition an active definite pang, attacking at one blow his mind, his emotions and his senses. He must at all cost stifle his boundless yearning for Ellen, and yet he could not. Life without her would be vacant, painful, without incentive, but a future with her would be worse. If he obeyed the Rabbi in him he would have no spirit to go on with the work to which he was pledged; if he obeyed the passionate human impulses now bruising themselves, in impotent revolt against their confining prison bars, there would never again be any work for his restless, ambitious nature to undertake.

Nevertheless, through all the daylight hours of unrelenting struggle, and the sleepless nights of sternly-fought desire, this cruelly-besieged young Philip preserved an unshaken certainty as to the ultimate result of the war in his soul.

Just as confidently as Clarence Kaufman had made sure, sooner or later, of teaching the agitators their places in his annoying industrial conflict, the Rabbi clung to his belief in his ability, at the end of this combat, to emerge, shaken and unhappy, perhaps, but complete victor over his rebel emotions, and undisputed master of himself.

When Monday arrived, however, he did not decide to avoid Ellen. If he considered the possibility of bringing their friendship so abruptly to an end, it was only to reject it without much consideration. It would be unnecessary—needlessly cruel to both of them. If they were to spend the rest of their lives apart, there could be no purpose, certainly, in spoiling the beauty of their memories by a final act of unexplained rudeness. Surely he could trust himself to be with her a few more times, to guide their relationship, gradually, to a stage where they might meet seldom—perhaps never, yet think of each other pleasantly and with earnest regard.

With these resolves fixed firmly in his mind, he went boldly to her home, but when he found himself alone with her, he suddenly forgot all his misgivings, all his unanswerable arguments, all his prudent schemes for their skilfully arranged separation—everything, in fact, except how poignantly he had suffered because of her absence and that now, once again, she was with him.

He grasped tightly the hand she extended in greeting, and murmured in low, half-embarrassed tones:

" I've missed you—missed you tremendously! You'll never know how much I've missed you! "

Her smile seemed tremulous to him. Her fingers, too, trembled in his strong grasp.

An instant later, without either of them knowing how it had come to pass, he had clasped her hungrily in his arms, and the kisses he had dreamed of had become vivid, living actualities. And she had made no effort to thrust him from her.

* * * * * * *

It was Ellen who returned first to the consciousness of other things and other people, in an unsympathetic and censorious world.

She motioned him to a chair, and seated herself at an uncompromising distance from him.

" That's why I went away," she said with seeming irrelevance. He nodded comprehendingly, but with something of awe in his thoughts. Did girls—did Ellen—have such days and nights as those which he had endured? Had he and she, separated by weary miles, been keeping together an unhappy vigil of alternate longings and renunciations?

"That's why I went away," she repeated; "I saw it first—and felt it, too. A woman always does. And that's why I'm going away again."

It was such a sensible termination of the little idyll. Nobody would know. Neither of them had been harmed. She could do her work as well elsewhere as here. Absence would in time lay its healing hand upon the wounds of both. The Rabbi Graetz approved the plan heartily and without reservation. It was precisely what he himself might have urged had it not involved a rather indelicate sacrifice for a man to demand of a woman. The man Philip, however, found the very possibility of her loss intolerable, and it was the man, not the minister, whose spirit, fed upon those never-to-be-forgotten caresses, was now in control.

"No!" he exclaimed, "I can't let you go! How can you bear even to think of it? You can never go away again, without me."

Ellen made an involuntary movement toward his side. Her face told such a story as a man might blithely toss away many things to learn. But she quickly repressed herself.

"What else can we do?" she asked, rather piteously.

The Rabbi part of Philip, with all its keenness of analysis and trappings of the schools, then and there abandoned him and left the mere man to pour out his incoherent, unreasoning wildness, just as though he had been an untaught, unthinking farm-hand or garment worker.

He told her what could be told of his struggles with

himself, of his unquenchable need of her, of his unhappiness; he assured her of his absolute inability to live through such an experience again; he was ready to go away with her, anywhere, and at once. Nothing could matter if he had her. He could do without his work. He could stand the loss of his friends and his reputation. They must be married the very next day and, amid new surroundings, found together a home where they could forget everything except one another.

When he paused for breath, her eyes were moist, but her spirit was unshaken.

"Don't you suppose I've thought of all that, my dear," she asked, "thought of it, and dreamed about it? But it wouldn't work! You've been telling yourself all along it wouldn't; why else have you been so unhappy? I love you for being willing to do it, but I'd hate worse than anything else to have to live beside you and see you trying not to show me how much you blamed me for having ruined your life!"

He protested vehemently against the possibility she spoke of, too vehemently, in fact, to be perfectly convincing. She could only shake her head in despairing certainty.

"Think! Philip—think!" she replied, "I'd hate any man who spoiled my life—no matter if I loved him in the midst of my hate. I won't do to you what I wouldn't let you do to me. We'd have one month of happiness and pay for it, day by day, for a whole lifetime."

"Well, then," Philip exclaimed, passionately, leaping to his feet, "it's worth it! Give it to me! I'm willing to pay."

"But I'm not willing to watch you pay, my dear," she answered very gently. "Don't suppose it's because I'm not fighting with all my strength not to say 'yes' to you, or because I'm too unselfish to have you pay. It's because I know I couldn't bear to watch you do it. I couldn't, and I won't!"

He pointed out to her the inconsistency of her decision with all the ideas she professed. She had a thousand times exclaimed against his intense love of race; she had proclaimed her own utter indifference to all questions of creed or faith; she had no shred of belief in the value of the work to which he was dedicated or the possibility of its producing the slightest results. How then could she attach so much importance to the abandonment by him of his Race, Creed and labors?

She twisted her lips into a curious little smile of tenderness, amusement and pain.

"How funny men are!" she said, "even when they really love you! Can't you see it's not your stupid old work, or your hateful Jews I care about! It's you! I don't believe in your work—not one bit—but I believe in it for you. If I knew you'd never be happy again unless you could blow soap bubbles for the rest of your life, don't you think I'd fight to keep anyone from breaking your pipe? And yet you ask me to break it myself."

"But if I tell you I can be happy!" Philip insisted.

"I'd know you were lying," she answered, "a beautiful lie—the kind I'd want you to tell me—but a lie just the same. You and I weren't made to look on life in the same way—to want the same things from it. Maybe it's because you're a Jew, after all! I can't tell, but I do know how you'd hate me!"

There was a long, unbroken silence. Then Philip sighed miserably.

"Then you're sure there's no hope for us?"

Yet so curious are the odd twists and paradoxes of life and sex, there would certainly have been a hope for Philip had he been just a shade less fine and austere than he actually was; and if one could have fathomed the deepest recesses of the thought of this girl who was willing for his sake to deny to both of them the happiness they craved, one might have been amazed to discover how fervently she wished that coarser strain in him had not been absent. For if it was true—and neither could convincingly deny it—that they could find together an absorbing happiness for a brief month, at the price only of a lasting unhappiness, and that the loss of that month also spelled many years of disappointment and crushed desire, the answer was simple. It was the permanence and the publicity of their union, which would mean his withdrawal from the only activities for which he was fitted. An irregular relationship which might, with care, have been hidden from all the world, would have left him free to do what work he pleased. As long as the two of them found in it a source of happiness it might continue unmarred. When it proved irksome to either, the bond could be gently and noiselessly broken asunder. Had Philip proposed the possibility of such a solution of their problem, Ellen would have welcomed it, not with mere acquiescent submission, but with warm enthusiasm. There were no restraining influences to bid her pause. Her family ties had ceased to have much meaning for her; Religion was to her a pretty myth which Man had long since outgrown; the conventions of Society were fetters to enslave unthinking human beings so that they might be more docile servants of the masters who found profit in the worship of Things as They Are. She had cherished the secret hope of seeing this plan take root in Philip's mind, now when all other schemes for finding happiness had proved fruitless. It was not because she retained any vestiges of what she would have scornfully termed "mid-Victorian prudery" that she gave no hint of her thought to the man she loved with such complete abandon. She could see nothing of dishonor or sin in a frank recognition of what seemed to her the inevitable consequences of a great unselfish affection. But she felt, instinctively, that if she told Philip what was in her mind, she would lose in his eyes something of the charm and delicacy which made him crave her so passionately. She rebelled hotly against this judgment even while she obeyed it. If her love must never end in fulfilment, because of a silly, monkish superstition, nevertheless, she could do nothing or say nothing which might blast it utterly and completely,—making even its memory a thing of ugliness and repulsion. To Philip this possibility of a clandestine and unsanctified union had never occurred—or, at least, if it had ever invaded the outposts of his consciousness—he had banished it with such instant shrinking from the degrading and loathsome possibility, as to cause it to slink completely away into the blackness from which it came. And indeed, for him, such an attitude was the only rational one. His relationship toward his congregation, his duties and himself had already been affected because he had permitted himself the stolen luxury of innocent meetings and pleasant speech with a girl of alien race. He had done nothing for which he could justly blame himself, yet there was a part of his daily round of happenings which he consciously and jealously hid from the eyes of others. His nicely-balanced nature was unable to adjust itself to this slight compromise, without a perceptible loss in enthusiasm and spiritual well-being. It was a true instinct which saved him from the horror of attempting to proclaim to his people his message of faith and justice, while his own soul was secretly steeped in what he would have ever felt to be mortal sin.

So Ellen could only repeat mournfully the absence of any hope of a happy ending for their ill-starred little romance. They settled themselves to a long and fruitless debate of their luckless situation, discussed its unhappy phases for hours, endlessly traveling about in a maze of words. Ever there persisted in Ellen's mind, an illusive hope of the discovery by Philip of the one thread which might lead them out of their labyrinth, together with a crushing certainty that if he could seize upon this thread, he would not be the Philip she had learned to know, and to love.

The long evening came to its end, with Ellen's original resolve still unconquered. She would leave Baltimore. She would speedily put her affairs in order and find work in some other city. She was not strong enough to deny his plea not to be banished from her side during her brief weeks of preparation. But thereafter there should be no opportunities for vacillation and temptation. She would not write to him or tell him where she might be found. The separation was to be complete; but when the minute came for Philip to say good-night, she did not withhold her eyes or her lips from him, and as Philip found his way home in the darkness, he was conscious in the very midst of his woe, of a curiously-illogical sense of sweetness and joy.

CHAPTER XVIII

THE PRICE OF A MAN

DR. FRANK'S machine was waiting at his door. He had bestowed upon his wife, his children and his dinner, an unusually generous allotment of time, and he was anxious to hurry off to the hospital without further delay. In fact, he had already drawn on his heavy driving gloves and turned the knob of the street door when a feminine voice from the library called gently—"Robert!"

The surgeon turned quickly. "Well, Ruth," he asked with crisp pleasantness, "anything I can bring you? I'm off, you see."

Ruth stood among the rich hangings of the library door making a pretty picture, but for once, apparently, too deep in thought to be conscious of her effectiveness.

"I want to talk with you, Rob," she said gravely.

He nodded affably.

"I can very well imagine so, my dear Ruth—Bess says the same thing. As for me, I want to look at you. Meanwhile, neither of us can have what we want, because I have an engagement to look, instead, at a very ugly gentleman's very ugly appendix."

"Please, Robert," Ruth murmured with a compelling air of unusual concern, "you really must find a few minutes for me—it's important. As important," she added, making a palpable effort not to seem too tragic, "as any man's appendix."

"Ah," he smiled with superior masculine tolerance of her trifling feminine concerns, "a lesion of some woman's heart, perhaps?"

But Ruth, tense and anxious, forgot to smile.

" Can't I see you now? " she persisted.

" Not now," he replied, " this is urgent,—honest! I'm late now. Tomorrow! "

She shook her head. " Now! " she demanded. " Tomorrow something else will be urgent and I'll miss my chance again."

" Is it my fault the insides of the people in this town are of such bad quality? " he inquired, and then finding no smiling response to his attempt at pleasantry, he straightway concluded she must, indeed, be in genuine trouble.

" Will you wait up for me? " he asked kindly. " I'll be back about eleven. Will that be time enough? Really, I can't stay now."

" I'll wait," Ruth answered. " Thanks, Robert—I hate to be a nuisance, but——"

Robert actually thought she was going to cry. It seemed an absurd thing for Ruth, of all people, to do—besides, in spite of his surgical training, he hated to see women cry—particularly the women he knew. He patted his pretty young sister-in-law on the shoulder, with such ill-concealed desire to escape before the storm should break that he did succeed in getting a totally unexpected smile from her after all.

* * * * * * *

It was considerably after eleven when Robert returned. He had found more things to be done than he had expected, and he presumed that Ruth, whose matter couldn't have been so vitally urgent, had long since abandoned hope of him and gone to bed.

He entered the house very quietly, and noiselessly crossed the hallway to the library door. All the lights in the room had been extinguished and for an instant Robert could distinguish nothing by the glow of the dim fire in the grate. Then he perceived Ruth nestled in one corner, of a great arm-chair before the hearth, her attitude one of complete dejection. Her head was bowed upon her arms and Robert was once more seized with an alarmed certainty of being called upon to deal with tears. He laid his hand gently on her magnificent dark hair, with the tenderness one finds so much more spontaneous when dealing with attractive and youthful girl-relatives than in giving counsel to far more deserving great-aunts, or male kinsmen of any age. She had not been crying; she welcomed him with a serious, intent smile of gratitude, to his mind utterly uncharacteristic of his wife's spoiled sister.

He looked down upon this pretty young enigma, and wondered whether it would be wiser to try, with bantering words, to coax her back into her accustomed self-control, or to treat her problem, whatever it might be, with a gravity corresponding to her own. It was the latter course which he adopted. She reached up and took the hand he had laid upon her head and held it tightly, for an instant, between both of her own. Such expressions of affection were not frequent with Ruth; she had a real respect and fondness for her brother-in-law,—far greater, in fact, than she bore toward her own sister. Both she and Robert were aware of this, but it was rarely that her feeling for him found any semblance of outward expression. Clearly, something must be wrong with Ruth—and very wrong indeed.

Robert began in his softest and most sympathetic voice —the one which made his patients and his students his enthusiastic slaves:

" You've been unhappy, Ruth, my dear, haven't you ? "
She nodded dumbly, in the dim light.

" Wretched," she said at last, when she found he was
awaiting some response.

Yet her existence during the past weeks had been a
feverish round of gaieties. He could remember no period
when she had been so constantly immersed in such a
bewildering succession of festivities. Robert, in spite of
all this revelry, had not failed to note the defection of the
Rabbi, and he went on to ask gently :

" Is it Philip Graetz ? "

She nodded again, and there was another interval of
silence.

" Don't you want to tell me what's the matter, Ruth ? "
he urged, once more caressing her hair very much as
though she had been one of his children.

" Yes," she said looking up at him and suddenly shak-
ing off her air of lassitude. " It's this strike ! At least,
that's what began it. It made him utterly miserable. It
seemed to disprove all he preached. You remember how
tangled his thoughts were, the night you talked to him
about it ? Well, it got worse with him instead of better,
and then there came this riot at the factory and the murder
of Rosen, and Philip would come here almost every night
to talk things over. It hurt him because I couldn't see
things his way, and of course, I couldn't lie to him."

Either Ruth herself saw something astonishing in this
last sentence, or she thought she detected in Robert's face
an expression of ill-concealed mirth. At any rate, she
interrupted herself to ask in hurt amazement :

" You're not laughing at me, Robert ? You couldn't
be laughing at me, now ? "

"God forbid," Robert answered hastily, and with a kindness greater than Ruth could have hoped. "It's all men and women I'm smiling at, Ruth, and myself, most of all. Don't you suppose I can still remember when I thought I couldn't lie to Bess. And now I think I can hardly tell her the Truth; I don't even know what it means. It takes a long time to find that out, and then you're sorry you know it. Now, you don't know any more than before why I smiled, but you know I wasn't laughing at you. So go on with your story."

But he had broken the thread of her narrative and she struggled unsuccessfully to begin again. He came to her assistance.

"Well," he said, "you felt you had to show him all your little shades of thought because you liked him so much, and you wanted him to understand you, and he didn't understand one bit, and at last he decided that you and Bess and I were all pretty much like our dear relative Clarence Kaufman, from whom we get a good-sized slice of our money. Since then he's stayed away,—that's about it, isn't it?"

She felt he had made her intensely important story seem sadly commonplace. Still, he had certainly guessed the outlines of it.

"That's about it," she repeated.

"Then you've been giving yourself lots of trouble about nothing, my dear child," the surgeon decided, cheerfully. "Even a man with a genius for stirring up mischief like our dear kinsman can't manage to keep his strikes alive forever. Some day—pretty soon, now—this one will come to an end, and our Jewish Don Quixote will find his wind-mill taken away from him, and then, entirely by accident, I'll pick him up some afternoon in my machine, as he's walking home from the University, and drag him in to dinner. That night you'll be prettier than ever, and you'll torment him unmercifully for all the bother he gave you, till he's had an effectual foretaste of the joys of marriage—after which you will, in due time, make a bewitching-looking bride, and thereafter live about as happily as a Rabbi's wife has any right to expect."

By this time she should have caught the contagion of his good humor, but to his surprise, his words seemed to be giving her pain rather than joyousness.

"Ah!" she whispered. "That's what I have been expecting all this time—but not any more! There's somebody else now—another woman!"

"How do you know!" he demanded sharply.

"Never mind," she responded with a furtive expression, which told Robert she had, in all probability, spied on Philip in a manner of which she was not too proud. "I do know,—I'm trusting you not to talk about this to a soul—not even to Bess,—but I've seen him with a girl—not even a Jewess, a working woman of some kind."

Robert still maintained his exasperating air of cheerful incredulity.

"Oh!" he exclaimed, dismissing her discovery airily, "some chance encounter, no doubt; a mere matter of duty."

Her face assumed a smile of sad wisdom. The best and wisest of men, she concluded, were but blind, childish creatures.

"I saw him look at her," she told him after a moment's silence. "There's nothing I wouldn't have given to have him look at me like that—but he never did."

Robert made a gesture of impatient vexation. It would be easy to pretend to Ruth an utter disbelief in her observations, but Ruth was not the girl to have taken another person—even himself—into her confidence without a reasonable certainty of an actual necessity. He knew her well enough to assume definitely that she had made it her business to find out exactly what had become of the man for whom she so frankly admitted her affection, and he had no doubt of her having ferreted out much more than she intended to tell.

He therefore hastily readjusted his ideas to meet this more serious state of facts.

"Then you must wait, my dear Ruth, till he comes back to his senses," he concluded. "Maybe you'll want him then, or maybe you won't; but the final decision will be in your hands. If the girl's not a Jewess, whatever else may happen, the Rabbi of Beth El can't marry her."

"Oh!" Ruth exclaimed, "but, you see, you don't know Philip! He's different. He's the sort who would ruin himself beyond all hope, rather than confess himself afraid of ruin."

"Well, then," Robert replied, "you don't want to be dragged down in his wreckage. We must wait to see whether he can save himself. If he can't——"

"Then I must save him," Ruth announced as though it were the only possible solution of the problem.

"You mean," Robert retorted, "you mean to save him for yourself?"

"Of course," she answered simply, "I haven't tried to pretend anything else."

"I shouldn't think you'd want him, when you feel sure he wants some one else," her brother-in-law urged with as much of reproach in his words as one could use in playing Mentor to a charming girl in such evident distress.

"That's what I told myself at first," she confessed, "but the truth remains: I do want him. No matter how he feels, I want him."

Robert shook his head reprovingly.

"I don't know how to advise you, then," he said; "even if I didn't believe you were wrong, I wouldn't know what to tell you."

"I've thought of a plan," Ruth confided. "I want you to help me, only you mustn't look at me as though I'd shocked you beyond all repair. What makes you think women ought to be patient, resigned animals, willing to fold their hands in meek submission just because the men they happen to care for don't know how to take care of themselves? It's Philip's good I want as much as my own. You, yourself, called his action—ruin. If Bess had been anxious to run off with some disreputable cad, wouldn't you have fought to save her from him—and for yourself? Why shouldn't I?"

Robert had nothing to urge against her vehemence save the conventional prejudices which he was ashamed to put into words, but to which he was none the less devotedly attached.

"I suppose I'm mediæval," he admitted; "you see I married before the days when girls cut their teeth on Bernard Shaw and Ellen Key. So you mustn't mind if I look mildly surprised at the modern attitude. Don't mind me, my dear. I mean it, really. You know, if I can help, you'll make me do it."

"You can help," she told him with an impressiveness

which showed how carefully she had rehearsed her plan. "But this isn't a little thing I'm going to ask. It's enormous. The whole trouble began with this strike. It's that which turned him away from me. It's through the factory I must get him back. I want to get control of the Company and give Philip the opportunity to settle the strike in his own way. It would mean everything to him— not only because of the reputation he'd gain—but in his own mind, too. He would imagine it proved the force of his Religion. He could never desert his faith after that; nor me," she added almost in a whisper.

Robert stared at her a full minute without a word of comment; then he said, brutally:

"It was an alienist you needed to consult—not a surgeon."

"Robert!" she exclaimed, "how can you make fun of me? Don't you see I'm suffering enough?"

"I'm not making fun of you," he answered bluntly. "I think your scheme's mad—or something worse. I hate to hurt you, Ruth; you know I do, but how can you plan deliberately to buy this man? That's what it amounts to; you mean to buy him—body and soul! Do you really want him at such a price?"

She faced Robert without a sign of flinching.

"Yes!" she affirmed boldly, "at that price or any other price I must pay. Now you understand why I must be helped, no matter what you may think of me!"

The surgeon speedily repressed his natural impulse to deliver a sharp lecture, setting forth the limits of his rather indulgent theories regarding life and ethics. Such school-room methods would never do with Ruth. Besides, why debate the morals of her plot when it could so easily be proved to be whimsically impossible! He turned his attention to an analysis of its impracticability.

"Well, I'm not much of a business man," he began patently insinuating, nevertheless, an insight into such affairs far superior to her own, "but it's easy to see how utterly fantastic your scheme is. Even if a fellow had unlimited money to play with——"

She broke into the midst of his objections with a sudden burst of energy. She sprang quickly from her chair, and flashing on the full blaze of lights, pointed to the table, saying in accents of competent self-confidence: "I've got it all worked out. Look here!"

He found the library table covered with neatly-arranged lists of stockholders, columns of tabulated prices, and mysterious computations of all kinds. She forced him to sit down to a study of this mass of data, and seating herself on the arm of his chair began rapidly to outline the ways and means of accomplishing her design.

"If you'll look over these papers you'll see how much stock could be picked up in the open market," she explained. "The price is lower today than ever before, and at a slight advance we could gather in more than I've counted on. Naturally, the cost will advance as we keep on buying, but not very much. You'll see there just how much we could get and what the total expense would amount to. Then, there's the block Bess holds already, and my own shares, and Cousin Fan's, and Cousin Leo's and all the rest that's in the family. All of them, if they were skilfully handled, would turn their holdings over to another member of our own family, and be glad to be out of it. Of course, they'd have no idea why I wanted it. That would leave us with only a shade less than a majority. I know where I could get a hundred shares from two of the directors, and then I'd need just a tiny block from Uncle Clarence himself. He wouldn't have an inkling of how near the edge he really stood, and I'm certain I could wheedle it out of him, particularly if I offered him a girlishly absurd price. You'll find it all worked out here—with every possible mischance provided for."

The neat rows of figures danced bewilderingly before the surgeon's eyes. He had, in truth, no gift for the minutiæ of business. When he attempted the simplest task in addition or multiplication his result was invariably incorrect. He could never succeed in making his bank balance tally with that decided upon by an exasperatingly unimaginative clerk. He blindly invested his surplus earnings in implicit faith, as commanded by an inexorable tyrant of a financier, whose unswerving loyalty he had won while waging on the old man's behalf a long and successful duel with Death. In return, this old gentleman watched over Robert's financial welfare as though he had been a new-born babe. Therefore, he could feel only a dizzy sense of being unequal to the situation, as he lost himself among the maze of Ruth's calculations. He could neither admit nor dispute the soundness of her deductions, because to attempt either would have been to confess how incomprehensible he found them, but his common sense told him two vital things completely disassociated with figures, and therefore, within the grasp of his understanding. The first was the certainty of a magnificently-planned campaign on the part of this decorative young sister-in-law who was so surprisingly more capable than she allowed anyone to imagine.

"It's odd" he mused, "how unexpectedly grand-fathers come back to life!"

His second and much more practical thought related to the absolute certainty of the colossal cost of transforming her hope into actuality.

"Um!" he grunted disgustedly, "such an entertainment as this is a sport for a multi-millionaire!"

She pointed to the footing on one of the long sheets of paper.

"That's what it would take," she announced seriously, "perhaps two or three per cent less—certainly no more!"

The total there set forth smote him with a feeling of real physical pain.

"But that's a fortune, Ruth!" he protested.

"Yes," she admitted quietly, "just about the size of Bess'—or my own. Mine's tied up. I can't get at it, or I wouldn't have bothered you at all. I want to borrow Bess'—all of it. If anything goes wrong, she can have every dollar of mine as soon as I'm old enough to lay my hands on it,—but nothing will go wrong!"

For a moment he was too completely stupefied by the colossal impudence of her proposal to find one word of answer. Meanwhile, she made haste to profit by his silence.

"It sounds like lunacy, I know," she conceded, "but there's really no risk in it at all. When the strike is ended—no matter what terms Philip decides to make—the stock will immediately begin to rise. No one will be able to tell so soon, whether the factory will earn less under its new agreements, and meanwhile, production is bound to increase. Then we'll sell all our holdings as speedily as we can without unsettling the market. We'll have done what we wanted, and have a very respectable profit besides."

" And when the next strike comes, what then? " asked Robert.

" By that time," Ruth began slowly—and then interrupting herself, she said with a sudden flush of embarrassment, " after I've once got Philip, I shall know how to hold him—strikes or no strikes. I'm not worried about that."

Robert caught his breath in a sharp spasm of amazement.

" Ruth! Ruth! " he said reprovingly, " and only a few weeks ago you couldn't find it in your heart to lie to him about a petty shade of opinion."

She faced Robert defiantly.

" I can't help it," she insisted, " I can't give him up! I've tried, and I can't."

He drummed absently on the table for awhile with his fine strong fingers. Then he looked up suddenly—summarizing her demands:

" You mean then, you want me, for purposes which no honest man could approve, to advise my wife, and your sister, to risk every penny she has in the world! "

She had been preparing to meet and repulse his attack.

" I don't ask you to advise her," she urged, " I only want you to let her make her own decision, without any interference from you. I'll attend to Bess. There isn't any risk, I tell you,—and if there were a total loss, my word is good; you know it is. I'll pay back every penny —the day I'm thirty. Money's no good to me if I can't have what I want. In the meantime, what do you care? You make every year more than you can dream of spending, and you always will. Besides, there's my own income. Bess can have that. I'm past caring about dollars and cents."

Robert was not in the mood for smiling, as he would normally have done, at the thought of this luxury-loving Ruth in the grip of drab poverty.

He answered impulsively:

"You know perfectly well, with me, it's not a question of money."

"I know," she agreed without the trace of a mental reservation. Robert had never felt the slightest lack of money, and perhaps this was why his attitude toward it was almost contemptuous. "I know," she repeated.

"But waiving the right and wrong of what you mean to do," he went on, "and the treachery toward Clarence and the rest of your family, which you seem to have ignored altogether——"

She shrugged her shoulders as though to signify the absurdity of his insistence on trifles such as these.

"Even then," he concluded, "it isn't my money for which you're asking. It's Bess', and she has a right to my true opinion. If you wanted my own savings—every bit of them—for something I approved, you know perfectly well you could have them."

She nodded. "Of course! but they wouldn't be enough," she said impatiently, telling him without need for further comment, how much weight she was giving to his discourse about scruples.

"It's the simplest way," she informed him at last, as though bent on making him understand she must gain her end, with or without his help. "If you make up your mind to throw obstacles in my path, you'll merely force me to do something you'd like much less—you and Bess, too, for that matter!"

"What do you mean?" Robert snapped out, wondering

what new vistas were still to be disclosed to him in the mind of this baffling young girl, who had lived all these years in his home, and shown him so little of her inexorable will.

"Arthur Kahn would do this bit of work for me if I asked him to, and promised him his pay," she murmured, twisting her lips into a smile which her brother-in-law found strange, and absolutely repulsive.

"But what possible benefit could you get out of that if you really promised to marry Kahn?" was Robert's wondering query.

The ugly and unfamiliar smile still persisted.

"Promises—engagements to marry—have been broken before this," she answered. "I could make him break it myself—Hate can always find a way!"

The surgeon was genuinely and profoundly shocked.

"I think," he thundered, "I ought to go straight to Clarence Kaufman and warn him of what you intend."

Her laugh was not a pleasant thing to hear.

"Which of us do you suppose he'd believe—you, who have always treated him with such awe and reverence—or Arthur Kahn and myself?"

He shrank away from her in genuine distaste and disgust, but with a sudden change of mood and expression, she laid her hand on his arm and looked into his face with eyes which were brimming with tears.

"Rob! Rob!" she begged, "can't you understand I'm desperate? I can't sit still and see my chance for happiness snatched away. Don't stop being good to me, Rob, just because I'm unhappy enough to clutch at anything! Help me! Don't you see it's because I love him!"

The surgeon, with awkward little caresses, tried his best to comfort her——

At length, he said wearily, as he led her to the door:

"Well, well—try not to worry any more. I'll talk to Bess about it in the morning."

She roused herself quickly to a well reasoned command of herself and him.

"No," she ordered, "not a word—let me talk to Bess first!"

He had not spirit to begin the controversy all over again, and made a mute sign of acquiescence.

As he found his noiseless way up the dark staircase to his wife's room, he was thinking in a puzzled fashion to himself:

"Now, this Graetz chap seems to be a pretty decent sort in a way, but why the devil should any woman want him enough for all that! Ruth, too! above all others! It certainly must be hell to be a woman!"

CHAPTER XIX

The Voice of Duty

Ruth slept but little during the night following her disturbing discussion with Robert, and as she nodded to her reflected image in her mirror next morning, she smiled at the little tell-tale marks of fatigue and anxiety, with much the same appreciation as a noted actress might exhibit after having evolved an exceptionally clever stroke in her " make-up." In a becomingly subdued morning negligee, she looked the exact part she was about to enact when she should creep into her sister's room. Sitting on the edge of her bed while Bess sipped her coffee and nibbled at her roll, she would make of her a whole-souled, devoted ally. Bess would be much easier to manage than Robert had been. There was a gleam of excitement in the girl's eyes, but she never seriously contemplated the possibility of failing to mold her indulgent sister to her will.

Nor was her confidence misplaced. An hour later, Ruth, more than ever spent and unstrung, but completely triumphant, emerged from Bess' room and walked to the telephone. She lifted the receiver from its hook but replaced it again without calling for a number. A note would be better, after all, she concluded. It would save Philip from the exhibition of an embarrassment which he would unconsciously resent, after the manner of men. Besides, it would leave him no opportunity for evasion or excuse. So she carefully penned a most artful little letter, telling him simply, but with a latent quality of mystery, of her discovery of a circumstance which could be made of inestimable value to his own ministry, and to the entire Jewish community. Though it could not safely be committed to writing, she would vouch, unhesitatingly, for his interest in its details. It was the very thing for which he had been seeking. She would therefore hope to see him that evening between eight and nine, and in the event of his having some prior engagement, she would detain him for only the briefest possible interval of time.

There was much of thought and a little deliberate cruelty concealed between the lines of this innocent-looking note. It would perhaps have been more business-like to have waited until her plan for the seizure of control of the Pioneer Company had been consummated, before mentioning the subject to the Rabbi. Ruth, however, had her own ideas relating to the way of a man with a maid, and the possible complications which might develop within a single brief hour of uninterrupted love making. Even now, her interference might come too late, and she determined he should never again see this objectionable woman without the definite thought in his mind of the work he could certainly accomplish, in the immediate future, provided his movements were unhampered by a compromising affection for this unsuitable girl.

She might also have granted him an interview in the late afternoon had she wished, but it was her premeditated desire to interfere, if she could, with his plans for an evening which she felt, instintcively, revolved around this mysterious woman. He could not refuse to come; she had stressed too insistently the call of duty, and concealed too thoroughly any personal interest. And besides, what she had written expressed the exact shade of dignity she wished to display, without a perceptible shadow of offended pique. Ruth was, on the whole, exceeding well-pleased with her composition. She summoned a servant, bade him deliver the letter to Philip in person, and thereafter, with a wise realization that her pallor and languor, while eminently suitable for an interview with Bess, were the exact opposite of what would be needed when Philip should arrive, she returned to her own room, and slept soundly until late in the afternoon. If her forceful grandfather had indeed returned to earth, he seemed in no hurry to vanish once more into the land of shades.

The first of her calculations proved unerring. Her summons threw the Rabbi into a state of uncomfortable vexation, flavored, nevertheless, with a compelling curiosity. Ellen was in the throes of plans for departure. Her determination to tear up their companionship by the roots had not wavered, and their hours together were filled for each of them with a mingled sweetness and misery which left them unnerved and sorrowful. Still, neither of them was willing to forego one minute of these precious evenings. Above all things, Philip would have wished to avoid Ruth, particularly now when his heart was sore with the burden of a thousand comparisons and empty reflections upon the absurd incongruities between the things we want and the things we can obtain. But Ruth's letter left him no possible alternative. No matter what he might endure, he could not altogether ignore the voice of Duty. There was nothing to be done save to send Ellen a word of explanation and a promise to come to her later in the evening, and to present himself duly at Ruth's home.

His pretty hostess received him with a charming graciousness which was subtly designed to put her visitor at ease. She had spared no pains to appear at her best, and in her conversation also, she skilfully avoided all dangerous places. She was guilty of no crude reproaches regarding his prolonged absence, nor did she imply, even faintly, having languished unhappily under the shadow of his neglect. She was cordial but not effusive; since, to ignore altogether the unexplained break in their relations would have been too marked an insincerity, she said with apparent simple frankness that she had understood perfectly how troubled he had been by this strike at the Pioneer factory, and how natural she thought it that he should have come to find his frequent visits to her home a source of misconstruction and embarrassment.

In this manner she relieved him of the entire burden of the explanations and apologies he had dreaded, and then without giving him an opportunity to commit himself to any polite falsehood, of which he might later have repented, and for which he would doubtless have proceeded to blame her, she plunged at once into the reason for tonight's conference.

"It's because of this labor war, of course," she informed him. "I've spent ever so many hours thinking about it, and what you have said about it. I suppose it's hard for me to see all these questions in your detached, clear manner; but I'm certain you're right, after all, and I believe things ought to be arranged by some one like yourself whose only interest is in doing justice to both sides."

He fancied then, he had been summoned merely to hear her recantation, and behind his courteous protestations of pleasure in her acceptance of his views, there was a huge element of annoyance at this wasted time he could have spent to so much better advantage.

She hurried on, however, to the climax she had in store for him.

"Of course, your own point of view is unchanged?" she asked. "You still want to bring to bear on the problem the power of Religion and of Jewish Ethics?"

"Of course," he repeated, "I've made all kinds of attempts to do this. I spent an evening with Mr. Kaufman last week in the effort to persuade him to let me settle the trouble. I found him absolutely unresponsive."

She leaned forward in her chair in an attitude of eager solicitude.

"I knew that," she told him. "I think it was that which sharpened my wits, and now I've found a way to give you the opportunity to bring the strike to an end, upon whatever terms you think fair."

The air of well-bred, but unexcited, interest he had hitherto worn dropped from him, and he stared at the girl in startled amazement.

"I—I don't think I quite understand," he stammered.

"I'll tell you all about it," she said happily, "only it must be a dark, deep secret for a week or two, between the two of us. That's understood, isn't it?"

She had already begun to weave about him the web of a hundred threads of common interests and important confidences.

"Of course," he answered impatiently.

"Well, then," she explained, "the whole idea is really perfectly simple. I only wonder neither of us thought of it before. I'm going to buy a controlling interest in the factory. When I get it, you won't find me as unresponsive as Uncle Clarence. I shall want you to see the people on the other side, find out just what they ought to have, and promise it to them."

THE CHOSEN PEOPLE

In one swift instant, the whole effect upon his life of such a programme became clear to Philip. It was a colossal opportunity—not only for himself, but for the men and women who fed their hard-driven lives into the hungry maw of the garment making machines; a victory for his Religion, too, whose power in the turmoil of the market place, he himself, had almost begun to doubt. On the other hand, it committed him forever to his faith, and it severed him, forever, from Ellen. Only as a Jew and a Rabbi, could his domination of this huge hive of industry be made significant. Only as an experiment in Socialized Judaism, could its success mean anything more than a mere truce in the endless antagonism of Capital and Labor. Then there was Ruth herself, this unthinking, care-free girl, who was blithely planning to stake a fortune upon his devotion to the cause he had so often voiced in fiery words. How was he to deal with her? It was this last thought which first found expression in words.

"What made you decide to do such a tremendous thing, Ruth?" he demanded breathlessly.

"It was your sermons, Philip. Somehow they made me feel I *had* to help!" murmured this girl, who only a month or two ago had been burning with a passion to lay bare before him each of her little weaknesses and sins! And, even now, her spirit raged within her at what she was doing; but she had tried truth and nobility, and they had failed her, while the devious windings she now trod promised her all she asked of life. She would atone somehow! She would become the thing she now pretended; but no matter what might happen, she would not go on with living, empty-handed.

If she had told the truth to her minister, whose task it

THE VOICE OF DUTY

was to love erring human nature all the more because of
its pitiable shortcomings, he would have turned from
her in disgust. As it was, he could only look into her
shining eyes, touched and saddened by her sweet faith,
and unquestioning willingness to place all her dower of
wealth and opportunity into his hands to be used to bring
balm to the pain and fever of a suffering World.

"Aren't you glad?" she asked suddenly, "I thought it
would make you happy—as happy as it does me!"

"It makes me solemn," he responded, and in truth it
did. "I shall need to be wiser and better than I know
how, not to fall short of what you've a right to demand."

"No! no!" she insisted gaily, "you musn't think of
it like that! Remember all these poor silly creatures who
only ask to be treated fairly; and that's the very thing—
the only thing—you, with the power in your hands, will
want. You'll find it a kind of triumph—not only for yourself—but for everything you believe in. It will be wonderful,—almost like a sacrament!"

She was speaking his own language to him, binding
around him the weight of an obligation he knew not how
to refuse, and yet his thoughts were tossed about in a very
tempest of misgivings and despair. What would this generous girl feel if she could know the price she was wringing
from him? If only Ellen could have been able to hold out
to him such hopes, to mingle the gift of herself with such a
boundless fulfillment of his dearest ambitions! But now,
more than ever, to cleave to the woman he loved would
brand him as a renegade of the most despicable type—
false not merely to a cause or a creed, but to the possibility
of a unique service to man and to God.

Ruth understood too well the perils of anti-climax to

277

risk detaining him much longer; she repressed, without pity, her own insistent longing for an evening full of joyous personalities, and pleading another engagement of long standing, she sent him away. She commanded him to proceed to work the very next day, guarding, however, with the most jealous care the secret of the method by which he intended to put into effect whatever compromise he might agree upon. Those with whom he discussed terms might suppose him to be an emissary of Kaufman, or an impecunious free lance with a blind belief in his persuasive power to induce the acceptance of just conditions—or they might believe whatever they chose, so long as they had no inkling of the actual plot. Such publicity would, of course, have made her project impossible. She realized perfectly well the danger to which she was exposing her delicately-adjusted scheme by sending the Rabbi thus prematurely, to learn the real sentiments of the representatives of the workers. She was, however, much more interested in her plans for the recapture and complete subjugation of Philip than in the actual termination of the strike, and she was only too cognizant of the urgency of compelling his interest and enlisting his personal loyalty, without one instant's further delay.

As Ruth reviewed her evening's work, after Philip had gone, she found no difficulty in justifying to herself each step she had so succcessfully trodden. For awhile, he would be unhappy, of course; Ruth was genuinely concerned about that; with all the force of her strong young nature she wished she could have been given the task to calm, this night, his restless misery, and soothe his pain; but she repeated to herself how surely she was doing for Philip precisely what was best for him. She was saving his reputation and his promising career from irreparable ruin. At the same time, to ease his heartache, she was giving him the work he loved to do, and in the future she, herself, would compensate him a thousand times over, for all she had taken from him. She would make this man for whom she had been willing to fight, happy beyond all imaginings. She smiled to herself as she thought of the myriads of delicious joys she would shower upon him.

For the unknown woman who was also, perhaps, to suffer as the result of this night's work, Ruth had nothing save cold, contemptuous hatred. It was not like Philip, she told herself, to have drifted, without expert guidance, into such an ugly situation. The woman, no doubt, was thoroughly bad, and diabolically artful. Ruth made no effort to conceal from herself her hope that the woman's share of the anguish might be keen and bitter, though she decided regretfully upon the improbability of such a result. Of course, this Christian girl could not really care about him; she was merely amusing herself, ministering to her vanity, taking a Christian's pride in humiliating and torturing a Jew. Ruth hated her frankly and with a self-righteous, satisfying hate. The woman had been bent on making as much mischief as she could; she had already done her share. As Ruth remembered the total wreck of all the pleasant, self-satisfying illusions she had formerly cherished regarding her own character, as she thought of the ugly tissue of treachery she had set herself to spin,— of the depths of depravity into which this woman's wanton cruelty had forced her,—depravity so dire as to have caused even kind-hearted, tolerant Robert to think of her conduct as repulsive—she charged each one of her own desperate impulses to the score of this Ellen she had never met, and could imagine no punishment too ferocious to be inflicted upon her.

While Ruth sat in her dainty room alternately giving herself up to thoughts of the tenderest love and the most ruthless revenge, Ellen in her bare, ugly boarding house, waited in vain, far into the night, for Philip's coming. For the first time he had failed her. He had chosen to forego one of the last of the few poor meetings which lay between them and a silence which was never to be broken. Philip had made his way almost unconsciously from the Frank home towards the house on Dolphin Street where he knew Ellen would be waiting to welcome him; but when he was nearly opposite her door, he had found himself unable to enter, and had continued aimlessly to wander toward the center of the City.

He was in a fever of unrest, which he found himself equally incapable of understanding or controlling. Ellen was going away. He was not to follow her—now or later; that had been determined upon and presumably accepted as inevitable. Why then should be be moved to such unutterable anguish by a happening, the only effect of which was to set the seal of certainty upon Ellen's resolve? Had he, after all, been clinging to some vague, unexpressed hope that at the very last, human weakness would prove stronger than sage expediency? Had this been the secret of the mysterious happiness he had found with Ellen, even in the midst of their sorrow? Had he expected her to relent and remain, or did he foresee, at the end, a reckless snapping of his own bonds and a fiery insistence on setting forth with her—no matter what should be the consequence to his work, his faith, or himself?

THE VOICE OF DUTY

He did not know. He only knew he had this night been called to embark upon a task which was, for him at least, as intimately linked with his Judaism and his Rabbinate as the soul is wedded to the body. If he accepted his duty he must do it as the preacher of the faith of Israel. If now, or at any time hereafter, he should desire to brave the scorn and reproaches of his own people, he would be tossing away his golden opportunity to establish God's peace and justice in the hum of the busy factory, as well as in the hush of the stately synagogue. Somehow, by what means he could not know—he might find it possible to avoid entangling himself with Ruth, but Ellen would be lost to him beyond all hope, as surely as though he had imprisoned himself within monastery walls.

Well, then, he thought, as he walked wearily on through the cold electric brilliance of Baltimore Street, suppose he were to obey the call of his surging pulses, and forget this austere, unsatisfying ideal of Duty, which made more, and ever more, insatiable demands upon the man who chose to give himself to the service of others, but dared still to hope for some poor crumbs of happiness for himself. Eventually, the strike would end without him. If Religion meant what he believed, did it really depend on the strength of his frail arm and the melody of his faint voice? The world was teeming with problems too knotty for his bewildered brain; was it not presumptuous for him to imagine they would go unsolved if he turned aside from their consideration? Who was he, to be sure of God's purposes? What is best for Man is a thing shrouded in mystery. Of only one thing could he be sure. There was a woman whom he wanted—wanted with all his soul and with all his heart, and with all his might, and he was about to lose her because of some nebulous, ill-defined thing called Duty, which might, in the end, prove only a delusion and a snare.

By this time the Rabbi's unguided steps were leading him, with the certainty of movement of a somnambulist, unerringly to the Jewish East Side Quarter, and to the corner where he and Ellen had first met, only a few weeks before. He looked up suddenly, and with a start of surprise, recognized the spot. How much struggle, pain and joy he had lived through since that afternoon only a little while ago—as men measure time, crudely, with clocks and calendars.

Why should he not drink to the dregs the cup already at his lips? The God who had created him in this guise, and filled his soul with these fierce yearnings for a personal happiness, must have known what was to be the result of the elements He had chosen to blend in his making! Was it not a form of Atheism thus to contend, with his man-made, little scruples, against the force of God?

It was now long after midnight. The squalid street was dingy and deserted. As the minister stood there, aching with the intensity of the warfare being waged in his tired brain, he tried in vain to feel the claims upon him of his sleeping brethren who lay huddled together in desolate, spirit-quenching poverty behind these forbidding walls which rose up out of the dark, round about him on every side. He had come to these people in sunnier hours and they had treated him as an alien—as more of an alien than Ellen. He had yearned to pour out the richness of his life and his learning in loving service and they had met him with contemptuous indifference. It would always be so. He

would never find among them sympathy or even comprehension; and it was for these creatures who scorned him
that he was to give up the best of life; he was to offer
himself as a sacrifice for men and women who would not
even know of his deed!

In the midst of his musings, the sharp, discordant cry
of an infant smote his ear. Its sound was slightly muffled
—the windows on all sides being tightly sealed, in defiance
of all the precepts of hygiene so glibly mouthed by fortunate individuals to whom each fragment of coal does not
present a problem in finance. This infant's despairing,
desolate wail set the Rabbi's tense nerves aquiver. In all
likelihood there was nothing the matter with the child, but
it cried as though its sufferings were cruel beyond all
endurance, and as if, in all the world, there was no one
to comprehend its despair. Philip walked hastily away
and did not pause until he could no longer hear its sobbing. Then he stood still, but he could not rid his imagination of the fancied sound of the childish weeping. He
imagined some little waif crying, in an agony of pain and
dread, in the darkness with no one to hearken to his call
or to comfort his tiny, frightened soul. The thought
straightway flashed into Philip's morbid mind of the sym-
bolical character of the baby's cry. His people, too, were
calling to him out of the darkness. They were in anguish
and in terror. The things they craved were perhaps no
better suited to their needs than the demands of a sick
child. The aid he was able to bring, might be worse than
useless, but they were weeping and in despair and he who
had promised to live and die for their welfare had been
about to desert them in their hour of blackness and spend
his days in a happiness stolen from his fellows!

THE CHOSEN PEOPLE

He had turned westward on Pratt Street with a half-formed idea of returning toward the heart of the City and thence to his home. Trudging along he recalled, through some freak of memory, the stories he had been told of a famous battle which had once been waged where he now stood—a significant prelude to the long years of relentless warefare between the States.

The street which now lay empty and silent had then been vibrant with the tramp of armed men, marching through present danger to cope with a still greater peril in the South. In the ears of these intrepid men from the North had rung the shrieks and curses of thousands who felt the presence upon Maryland soil of these invaders to be a strain harder to bear than death itself. Soon, instead of mere angry words, deadlier tokens of hate had been hurled against the strangers. Out of the dense crowd which lined the roadway rifle shots had gone speeding into the ranks of the soldiers, only to be answered by the rattle of volleys of musketry. The ground upon which the Rabbi trod had been sanctified by the blood of martyrs, who, dying by each other's hand, had none the less yielded up their lives for the same idea. To each one who died, some abstract principle, but dimly understood, had been far more precious than the mere physical routine of keeping alive!

Tired as he was, the minister's gait unconsciously assumed a martial stride as he pictured to himself this scene of fifty-five years ago! Fifty-five years!—and still this story of heroism was fraught with untarnished meaning and pathos, because the men who had died here on Pratt Street, had given voice to the hope poor, bewildered mankind loves best to cherish; the faith in the beauty and purpose of a lifetime of loyalty to one's beliefs, and of a cheerfully-accepted death rather than their surrender.

Yet each of these men who here passed from life on that April morning had known the ecstasy of some woman's love, and had sacrificed that, too, with all the rest of glad, youthful existence. Each of them had suffered her pain as well as his own, as he had unclasped her soft arms from around him and hurried off to the grim embrace of Death.

What answer was Philip to make to his accusing conscience through all the long years still before him, when he should be called to explain why he had shirked what all these men had blithely dared?

True, it was easier to give one's life among cheering comrades, in one swift impulse of emotion, than to dole it out, day-by-day, in prosaic solitude and soul-numbing doubts, but these men who had died to preserve a Union or to defend the liberties of their native State, were mere random artisans or plow-boys, not men like himself who had schooled themselves during years of preparation for the coming of a crisis. And he, Philip, was besides, one of the Priest people of God! It was but fair that more should be demanded of him, and with God's help, he, too, would answer the bugle call of duty! God's voice, speaking through his trembling lips, had inspired a young and heedless girl to devote her wealth to the service of Truth; tomorrow, like a prophet of old, it was to be his privilege to stand between two armies of angry kinsmen and bid them throw down their weapons and work together for peace and Justice, in the name of the great Jehovah! Nay, more, it would be his marvelous task to force these bitter enemies to keep the compact after having made it, and to serve as an example of equity and brotherly love to all mankind. It was a mission worth dying for, and gladly, too. It was worth living a wounded, crippled life to do this thing. Countless little children, like the infant he had heard crying in the night, would have the currents of their lives diverted to the left or the right according to his weakness or his loyalty.

Besides, with this haunting memory of the desertion of a supreme opportunity, his life, even with Ellen, would be like that of Cain—a wanderer upon the earth, fleeing from the knowledge of having killed the noblest part of his own self. The fate he must accept was more cruel than that of Jephthah, whose vows had forced him to the sacrifice of a mere daughter; but like Jephthah, the welfare of his people was at stake.

He had heard in the night their cry of pain and misery; he could bring them to peace through the God he served. His pity for them was greater than his pity for his own wounds. He would not fail them. He, too, like his ancestors, would know how to suffer for the faith that was in him!

CHAPTER XX

THE APPEAL TO ORGANIZED LABOR

PHILIP began the first day of his career of renunciation and self-immolation, with a bold concession to the unlawful manner of living he had determined to abandon. In the broad daylight of the morning, he went directly to Ellen's house, without giving one thought to the possibilities of detection. He could not permit her to go about her work, all through the long day, without some word from him to explain how little of indifference or neglect there had been in his absence of the night before. From her doorway he had walked with her the entire distance into East Baltimore, not even taking the trouble to avoid the more congested thoroughfares. All of which merely demonstrates the criminal imprudence ·which logically flows from a firm faith in one's own innocence! There is nothing like a little chastening guilt to teach a man how to become a pattern of cautious respectability.

This morning, the Rabbi had no room in his mind for cares about petty gossip. He told Ellen everything of his adventure of the night before—withholding no detail, except the prologue of his former tender interest in Ruth, and his own surmises regarding the hopes his fair parishioner might indulge for the future. Even the most veracious of men and ministers must retain some shreds and patches of decent reticence. Ellen listened to his story with few interruptions. She was sufficiently a woman to presume an additional motive on the part of Ruth other than the one so becomingly displayed. Of course, this young Jewess was merely using a particularly adroit method of dazzling the young Rabbi with the power of her vulgar money—money which, Ellen reflected bitterly, had all been earned by the efforts of others, and which this rich young idler had done absolutely nothing to deserve.

For a minute, in spite of all her tediously worked out conclusions, Ellen felt sweeping over her a wild, angry impulse to match her wits against those of this arrogant daughter of a line of parasites. She could make her understand how many other things there were in the world besides bags of gold! If she would but nerve herself to a struggle for Philip she felt sure the victory would be with her—despite the handicaps of race, poverty and tradition.

Then she looked at Philip's haggard, care-worn face and the hot, unreasoning desire for combat died within her. What a night this boy must have endured! And how many more like it he would still have to face if she led him away in triumph as a trophy of her feminine skill,—worse nights, in fact, because the last had ended, so he imagined, in a somber kind of victory while those to come would be dedicated to fruitless regrets. She would awaken in the night time, and turning quietly around so he might not become aware of her scrutiny, she would see in the dim shadows, his features set in that tense, twisted look of misery—his sleepless eyes dull with the frank recognition of a wasted life; and all the while, in the silence, she would be able to read his unspoken words saying, over and over and over, how it was she, Ellen, who had lured him to this doom of perpetual exile from everything he cherished.

THE APPEAL TO ORGANIZED LABOR

As they strolled slowly along, she spoke to him, now and then, in short sentences of gentle sympathy lest he might guess how much his narrative was hurting her. She was no longer giving her attention to what he was saying, but with the passing of each minute her own ideas became more clearly defined.

What would be the use of her victory when it must be bought at such a price? How could this empty-headed little Jewess, with her simpering airs and graces, and her jingling money, matter to her? What possible consolation would she find in teaching her the lesson she deserved? It was the man she cared about. This theatrical game of Ruth's was after all nothing but an incident. Sooner or later, something like this must in one way or another have come to pass, to make clear the sharp distinction between his kind of life and hers. By arts she detested, Ellen could, if she chose, enslave his senses for a few, brief days. Now she knew with certainty what she had always told herself: that she could never entwine his spirit with her own,—not even for those few hours of which she had dreamed. She would have been satisfied with that. If for the tiniest space of time she could have made certain of her conquest of every bit of him—the complete union of his nature with her own—she could have reconciled herself to the swift lapse of her short, glorious hour. But this morning, in the dull grayness and chill, she knew beyond all peradventure the ugly truth. She could ensnare, if she would, the weaker part of him only by lulling into slumber the stronger half of his sensitive being. And even then, there must soon arrive a horrified hour of awakening.

With the swiftness of thought as rapid as the play

of light and shade upon her mobile face, her decision was made. These ebbs and flows of hope and despair, these meetings at night with their words of sober renunciation, and their kisses and caresses of an intensity in which there was much more of sharp pain than of joyous tenderness, could mean nothing further to them but added torment—and temptation, too! She would end it, once and for all, without another day's delay. There should be no scene of farewell to blur with foolish, incoherent words, and uncharacteristic tears, the happiness of their memories. After they should go their separate ways this morning, she would not see him again. She could go away as well today as a few days hence. By nightfall she would be beyond his seeking.

All unconscious of the fate in store for him, Philip accompanied Ellen to the door of the East Side branch office of the Medical Service Society which employed her, and there he left her. If she held his hand for an instant longer than was usual at their moments of casual separation—if there was a deeper seriousnes in her voice and her smile—he attributed these things to the earnestness of their conversation and to the sweetness of her comprehension of his problem. He meant to see her tonight; they would talk further of his plans and of hers. Meanwhile, his work was with the garment makers, and without further delay, he made his way to their headquarters.

It was then almost ten o'clock in the morning. Philip, with his ready-made ideas regarding the industrious habits of the working class, and his failure to distinguish between laboring men and labor leaders, had assumed the certainty of the men he sought having reported for duty hours ago. He was usually at work long before this time and was accustomed to reproach himself, now and then, with indolence; he was therefore both surprised and a little annoyed to find the offices of the Union deserted except for the presence of a totally indifferent office boy, intently devouring a questionable morsel of paper-bound fiction. The uncarpeted floors of the offices were littered with scraps of paper and fragments of burnt-out cigars; a distasteful smell of stale tobacco, garlic and a not-too-carefully-scrubbed little boy, caused the most unpleasant sensations to assail Philip, already slightly unsteady as a result of his sleepless night. Every window, of course, was uncompromisingly closed.

The little boy honored the Rabbi with only the most casual of glances, and went on busily ministering to his hunger for literature. Philip walked to the window and threw it wide open, taking deep breaths of the cool air, and finding himself promptly revived. At the same time, he succeeded in securing the attention of the boy in a way which simple words would never have obtained for him. The hero of the tale the boy was reading was at that very instant leaping boldly from the roof of one tenement house to the fire escape of another, to defeat the dastardly purposes of a band of ruthless assassins. The youthful connoisseur of narrative detected in himself a rather striking resemblance to the dauntless and acrobatic protagonist of this epic; nevertheless, the cold air from the open window distressed him; perhaps the feats of daring he admired had been performed in the balminess of summer. At any rate, he turned to Philip and said pertly:

"Hey, Mister! don't you know it's still winter? Real money—they pay for coal to heat this place."

Philip lowered the window, without a word of protest. After all, his action in raising it had been arbitrary.

Then he asked the boy, who was in charge of the head-quarters.

"Me," the youngster responded, with a delightful sense of his own importance, but he did condescend to furnish further scraps of information. Nobody came down to these rooms until after what the boy called "dinner time," by which term he meant to identify the noon hour. Thereafter the officers might be expected to stroll in, at indefinite times, during the early afternoon. To the Rabbi's disappointed exclamations of surprise, the boy contented himself with the rather contemptuous reply that if Philip had known anything at all regarding the habits of such gentlemen as his employers, he would realize the necessity of their presence at headquarters every night until very late. "They gotta sleep some time!" their small advocate had declared belligerently.

So Philip was left with an entire forenoon of enforced leisure, and no inclination whatever for enjoying it. Only a few blocks away—or a few "squares" as everyone in Baltimore would have phrased it—there was a thriving Jewish Settlement House whose workers would have been proud to exhibit their activities to the Rabbi.

This morning, however, found him with no strength for courteous inspection and the display of a polite enthusiasm over each marvel presented for his approval. Ordinarily, he would have enjoyed wandering up and down the streets, with eyes and ears alert to learn what he might of the life of the people who were, at one and the same time, his fellow-Jews, and strangers less comprehensible than the up-town Gentiles. To-day, he was too weary from his pilgrimage of the night before, to undertake such an adventure, even had he not been a victim of a great desire to avoid being left alone with his own thoughts. There were motion-picture parlors plentifully strewn throughout the neighborhood, where the legends thrown on the screen were printed in Yiddish. He might have improved his acquaintance with the dialect by such an essay of frivolity, but he rather prided himself upon a fastidious dislike of motion-pictures, even at their best.

At last he decided to ride up-town to the Hopkins Library, and there he lost himself until lunch time over a translation of Dante's "New Life"—learning how another man, long since mingled with the dust, had drawn inspiration and courage from the soul of a woman whose warm human companionship he had been condemned never to know.

In the afternoon he again presented himself at the headquarters of the strikers and this time the rooms, in vivid contrast to their former state of empty dreariness, were agog with the confusion of hurried messengers and excited conferences. Philip, after submitting to a number of preliminary challenges, found himself in an inner room where six or seven men were grouped about a long, dirty, pine-wood table littered with a mass of papers, among which each one seemed to be struggling anxiously and hopelessly to rescue some misplaced document. All of them, in this stuffy room, were arrayed in hats of varying degrees of shabbiness, and most of them were heavily bearded.

When Philip entered, they all seemed to be talking at the same time, and so incoherently as to leave him in some doubt as to what language was being spoken.

When his hosts became conscious of his presence, one of them, speaking English with a marked accent, but with an almost perfect grammatical precision, demanded of him the purpose of his visit.

THE CHOSEN PEOPLE

The Rabbi, standing at the foot of the table, replied to this question.

"My name is Philip Graetz," he informed them, "I'm the Rabbi of the Temple Beth El."

There was certainly no outburst of cordiality at the announcement, but one of the men arose and placed a chair for Philip and invited him, with some semblance of heartiness, to be seated. The Rabbi would have preferred to stand; he talked more fluently when he was on his feet, but he deemed it unwise to reject this little act of friendliness, so he accepted the chair and continued:

"I've been thinking a long time about your strike, and remembering that most of your men are Jews,— just like myself, and the men who own the Pioneer factory. Our Religion tells us Jews ought to live at peace with each other. I think I've found a way to make peace on fair terms if you leaders will help me. I can't tell you yet just how I mean to do it, but if you and I can agree on a settlement, I give you my word I can put it through; and remember, I don't want anything except what's just to both sides,",

There followed a buzz of guttural syllables, as Philip's words were translated for the benefit of the few who could not comprehend him. Then, after a whispered conversation between several of the men, the one who had first spoken turned to Philip and asked bluntly:

"Do you come here from Mr. Kaufman?"

"No," Philip answered. "I represent nobody but myself. That ought to make it all the easier for us to work together. All I want is to send the men back to the factory with an agreement that shall be perfectly fair. If we can decide what is fair, I've got a plan to make the Pioneer Company accept it."

Again there was a murmur of confused words,— louder and more articulate than before. Philip recognized one or two phrases and heard the name of Kaufman repeated several times.

"I can understand Yiddish," he announced, with a shadow of pardonable pride—harboring no doubt of a more genial reception because of this possession of a common language.

He was greatly surprised, therefore, when immediately upon learing of his unexpected ability to deal with their dialect, the entire group abandoned their places at the table and gathered into an excited knot in the farthest corner of the room. No one seemed, in the slightest degree, to be concious of any discourtesy in this proceeding. They had something to discuss which, for many reasons, this stranger ought not to overhear, and they consequently, without the semblance of an apology, set about discussing it.

The man who had first spoken seemed to be contending earnestly against most of the others. Apparently, the debate developed no small amount of heat and personal acrimony. The speakers gesticulated wildly, and several times a grimy finger was pointed accusingly at the waiting Rabbi.

Their deliberations came to an end as unexpectedly as they had begun. The men returned to their seats at the table, and their spokesman addressing Philip, thanked him for the interest he had shown in their trouble and added— patently without having been authorized to do so—his belief in the possiblity of some settlement through the Rabbi's kind efforts. The strikers, for their part, like Dr. Graetz, wanted nothing in all the world except what was just and right. The committee would ask the

THE CHOSEN PEOPLE

" Reverend Doctor " (the speaker rolled this unctuous phrase lovingly under his tongue) to take up this matter in detail with Mr. David Gordon whose offices were in the Atlantic Trust Building. Mr. Gordon understood exactly what the strikers needed. The man ended by invoking upon Philip an ornate blessing for his pious solicitude for the cause of the poor and oppressed.

Philip returned to the street and boarded a car, with a sense of relief. There was nothing tangible of which he had cause to complain. He had been given some sort of hearing, had received fair words in exchange, and had been referred to a practical man with whom it would be easier to deal than these puzzling, black-bearded men with whom he found it so difficult to remember his kinship.

Yet he would have much preferred to have remained with this committee until late at night in earnest but good-humored dispute over the merits of their demands, if only they would have given some sign of acceptance of him as a friend who was there to learn their needs and to give them, with generous heartiness, whatever help he could. Instead, they had viewed him with frank suspicion, questioned his motives, and sent him, in the end, to some-one whom they believed sufficiently clever to distinguish whether he was, in truth, a friend, a spy or an ambas-sador,—someone who would know how to utilize his aid or to render harmless his hostility, as the circumstances should indicate.

Philip's next duty was to report to Ruth the outcome of the first day's skirmish, and this he did before return-ing to his own rooms. The girl had spent the day in vigorous, well-devised and skillfully-executed operations for financing, without publicity, the cost of the huge purchases of stock she planned to begin upon the morrow.

She had, so far, performed her share of the work without a single untoward incident, and the coming of twilight found her as unwearied and enthusiastic as if she had been motoring in the Park. She was painfully impressed by the ravages which the last night and day had worked upon Philip. She had no difficulty in guessing the cause, but she was wise enough not only to say nothing about his ashen cheeks and the deep circles under his eyes, but, in addition, to lend an air of plausibility to his belief that she had found no opportunity to perceive anything unusual in his appearance. With this idea in mind, she led him swiftly from the lighted hallway into the dusk of the library, and there he told her of what he had already accomplished and of his projected interview with Gordon next day. She gave a moment's consideration to the thought of urging him to see the lawyer that very night, thus separating him a second time from the influence of the woman from whose clutches she meant to rescue him; but when she remembered his air of complete exhaustion, and his look of hopeless misery, she could not find it in her heart to add to the weight of his unhappiness.

Therefore, Philip had returned to his own rooms, telephoned the lawyer making an appointment for the following morning, and completed a solitary dinner, preparatory to a visit to Ellen, when a note from her was brought to him. The hour when it was to be delivered had been marked on the envelope and the letter itself was a thing of only a few lines. She had written:

"MY DEAR:

We have reached the time—you have known it as well as I—when our hours together have come to hold less of joy than of pain. When I made sure of this, I determined there should be no more of them, and when this note reaches you I shall be gone. You would have found no comfort in bidding me farewell. There are a thousand things I would have wished to say to you—but you know them all, already, or if you don't, you could never have understood them. It would be silly to tell you to forget me; it is almost as silly to urge you to remember only the happiness we found together; but try to do it, anyhow, because it's I who ask it of you!   Ellen."

Philip sat perfectly still for a long time, his eyes fixed upon the letter. So his romance was over. He was surprised to find, in himself, no increased intensity of suffering. This was what he had been nerving himself to meet for days, and now when it had come, he felt numb, almost stupidly insensible. His capacity for all emotion had been stretched to the breaking point. To his dull eyes life seemed to stretch out endlessly before him with nothing of brightness in it, but with nothing more of horror potent enough to do him further injury. He was even concious of a sense of relief at having arrived, after all this fever, at a state of languid indifference to anything Fate might choose to inflict. There would be no more of struggle, no more of vain desire, no more of beating one's wings desperately against the cage of Duty.

He was done with Youth and all its frantic hopes and disillusions; his mind and his body were too unutterably weary to care what was in store for him.

With Ellen's letter in his hand, he flung himself, fully dressed as he was, face downward upon his bed and lay there for hours perfectly motionless, his mind possessed by a kaleidoscopic jumble of incoherent fancies and memories until his crushing exhaustion brought its own anæsthetic, and gave him the boon of Sleep.

CHAPTER XXI

A MATTER OF DEFINITION

PHILIP arose next morning, after many hours of slumber, feeling precisely as though someone very near to him had died, after a long and agonizing illness. He could not rid himself of a sense of irreparable loss, but, on the other hand, he perceived with perfect clarity how little of consolation there would have been in postponing the inevitable disaster.

Meanwhile, the world's work must go on, no matter over whose dead hopes it passed, and for him the most important part of the world's work was the ending of the strike at the Pioneer factory.

He found himself unable to walk down town, remembering as he did, so vividly, how he and Ellen had passed down these streets together only the day before. There were a thousand irrelevant recollections of her words, her face, and her little mannerisms which kept crowding unsought into his thoughts. He did not endeavor to push them aside. After all, what else of her was left to him?

He hailed a street car, but noticing through its windows several of his acquaintances, he returned hurriedly to the sidewalk and let it pass on without him, thereby provoking a broadside of profanity from the exasperated motorman. Yet he had fancied what he desired most was to forget himself among a crowd of people!

Finally he yielded to the wanton extravagance of being driven to the Atlantic Trust Building in a taxicab. He knew he was more than a little absurd, but he did not greatly care.

Thanks to the " taxi " he had not needed, he arrived in Gordon's busy offices some minutes before the hour of his appointment, and sat impatiently in the reception room pretending to read a newspaper.

When his turn came, he was shown into David's consultation room and found him seated at a big work table, on which lay neatly arranged piles of books and papers. The room was severe in its freedom from all ornamentation, but it was nevertheless a cheerful work-place, with its great windows, and its air of comfortable spaciousness.

As the two men shook hands, the lawyer cast at Philip a glance of rapid appraisal. The boy didn't look well. Evidently, this strike was getting on his nerves. It was a pity that a perverse Destiny made it necessary for fragile pitchers to go to the well!

" Good morning, Doctor," the lawyer said briskly. " The committee telephoned me all about your visit to them. I'm sorry you will persist in meddling in this grimy strike of ours—but here you are! "

" Sorry? " Philip repeated in a questioning tone.

" Yes, of course," David answered emphatically. " I told you before, you haven't the temperament for such rough sport. Look at yourself! You're as seedy and forlorn looking as if you'd been on a three days' debauch, while I'm as chipper as the handsome young man who stands in the front row of one of Mr. Kaufman's clothing advertisements. Yet I represent the sobbing victims in this tragedy, while all your overfed people are hopelessly testing out plans to ' eat and grow thin.' You ought to keep your fingers out of reach of the flames! "

A MATTER OF DEFINITION

Philip, who had come here to forget a real sorrow in a great mission, was in no humor for such ill-timed chatter. He replied with unusual tartness:

"You seem to have had no scruples about burning my fingers the only time you got the chance!"

"You mean after the Charity meeting?" asked David, smiling. "My dear Doctor," he added, "you will never realize how forbearing I've really been to you. I could have made use of you in this mess, in ways of which your innocent young mind could never conceive. The angel in me strove with the artist, and it was the artist who came to grief. Honestly, it's downright cruel of you to make of yourself a constant source of temptation to a man like me whose morals were never particularly strong to begin with."

If there was anything mildly amusing in David's words, Philip was not in the mood to perceive it.

"I've come, then," he said uncompromisingly, "to tempt you some more. If you find pleasure in making well-intentioned people ridiculous, you shall have another chance."

David regarded him with an air of puzzled good-will.

"All right," he assented after a minute, "I've been trying—if you'd been able to understand—to give you a chance to get out of this present little spasm with a good grace. You could have blamed it on me—said I was insulting from the very beginning. But you won't have it. Tell me your latest rosy dream, and your troubles will begin afresh."

"I presume you don't want to talk to me in confidence?" Philip suggested.

"Not about this affair," David announced bluntly.

"You saw the committee yesterday afternoon. Did they strike you as men to whom one could send a message saying 'Dr. Graetz called—we talked secrets together. If anything comes of it, I'll tell you?' If you wanted a confidential conference, you should have come to me first."

Philip nodded in acquiescence; he saw the reasonableness of the lawyer's position.

"I didn't stop to realize," he admitted by way of apology, "the type of men we'd have to deal with."

"No," David agreed, "we're in a bad way there. The strikers have a huge streak of the fool in them, and the owners, of the knave. So we have to play with the cards on the table—unless you prefer not to play at all," he concluded.

Philip made a gesture of determination. He had no intention of being frightened from his duty.

"Then talk away," David commanded. "Only remember to say nothing to me you are unwilling to have shouted from the house tops, and if you forget, and thereby get another bruise, remember how the villain of the plot, touched by your girlish purity, tried in vain after your guileless visit to his rooms to 'save your honor.'"

After which flippant, but not meaningless, warning Philip began,—speaking deliberately and slowly:

"You have to take part of my message on faith. To begin with, bear in mind I represent nobody but myself; but I have worked out a method of forcing the consent of the Pioneer Company to any agreement with the strikers to which I find it possible to give my own approval. The only thing necessary is for the strikers and myself to reach such terms."

A MATTER OF DEFINITION

The lawyer considered Philip's remarks gravely before replying.

"You're sure you don't care to give any further details?" he inquired.

"No. If I did it would make the success of my plan impossible," the Rabbi insisted firmly.

"Let me ask you one other question," the lawyer went on. "When you say you represent no one else, you are using an equivocal expression. I don't represent the Union. They have paid me no fee, and my only formal client in this affair is Ginzberg; but I have the means to force the Union to do exactly what I demand—within reasonable limits, of course. Now, I take it for granted you aren't going to put the screws on the Pioneer people all by yourself. Tell me as a man of honor—which I know you to be —whether your confidence in your ability to have your agreement ratified is an actual fact, or whether you are merely going to rely on pretty preachments to them about what their religious duty is. If that is what's in your head, you're wasting my exceedingly expensive morning."

Philip, without hesitation, gave him the assurance he desired.

"I am not basing my plans on persuasion at all. There will be no question whatever about my power to do what I promise. There is a bare chance of my calculations going awry, but it's extremely remote, and by the time we come to put our settlement into formal shape, I'll be able to give you an absolute, binding contract. If the scheme breaks down before then, I'll tell you at once. I don't see how it can, unless you talk too freely about my confidence in my ability to put the agreement through.

I take it, though, you're as anxious to end this trouble as
I am."

David smiled:—

"Almost," he replied, "perhaps not quite. I haven't
come to the point where I'd agree to a surrender."

"I don't want you to," Philip said. "I wouldn't accept
a flat surrender from you if you wished to make it. I'm
here to agree on terms which are fair—and which will
last!"

"Good," exclaimed David, "only your idea of the
meaning of the word 'fair' may not be the same as the
one in vogue in East Baltimore. Still—we'll see!"

"Don't you want an affidavit that I haven't come from
Mr. Kaufman?" Philip asked, with a trace of malice, remembering the suspicions of the committee. "Your
friends didn't seem to be satisfied with my bare word."

"Pooh," David retorted lightly, "I know you don't
come from Kaufman because you say you only want
what's fair. Besides, you insult me when you suppose
I reason like the people you saw yesterday. What do I
care whether you come from Kaufman or the devil himself if you can execute the kind of agreement I want? I
can take care of myself. As for the chance of your being
a spy, those poor fools were just flattering you. I can't
play the hypocrite like that."

Philip allowed himself to be betrayed into a watery
smile.

"Let's get down to definite terms then," the lawyer
resumed, laying a blank sheet of paper before him. "First
of all, the Company must co-operate with me in obtaining the release of Ginzberg. I shan't let him be the scapegoat!"

"I'm satisfied," Philip conceded immediately, "I have no wish to cause further suffering to anybody."

"Why, you speak as 'one having authority, and not as the Scribes and Pharisees,'" David quoted irreverently. "Second," he went on, "in some form or other, you've got to recognize the Union. You can see there couldn't be any peace without this."

"I never had any other idea," Philip agreed.

"Good," exclaimed David, "we're getting on capitally. The question of the form of recognition is full of details. We can take them up later since we agree on the main principle. Now the piece-work scale, over which the trouble began; of course, there must be some adjustment of that."

"I'm willing to refer the whole question of a scale to competent authorities," was Philip's decision. "We can both bind ourselves to abide by their action. While they investigate we can go back to the scale which was used before. It oughtn't to take long."

David frowned. "Why drag in a new element of uncertainty?" he argued. "You and I can agree on modifications, here and now, and leave no loose ends to get tangled up later."

"No," was Philip's peremptory conclusion, "I don't understand the first thing about a piece-work scale and if I agreed to any such plan as yours, I'd simply be inviting the Union to dictate whatever it wanted. I must be fair to both sides."

"We could use the scale in force in the Alpha Clothing Company's plant," the lawyer argued persuasively; "it works there. They make about the same grade of garment."

"No," Philip repeated, with emphasis, "I don't know whether their scale is fair or not. It may work there today and cause a strike tomorrow. I'm not satisfied to gulp down a dose about which I know neither the contents nor the men who mixed it. We will have a new scale written by men in whom both of us have complete confidence. The Company will shoulder the expense. You can pick all three of these men yourself, provided I retain a veto power on the names you select. Certainly, nothing could be fairer than that!"

David's expression began to take on a new quality of respect for the Rabbi. This boy was clearly not without some promise. After all, the lawyer decided, there was something in being a Jew which even reformed Judaism could not kill!

"Well," he grumbled, "I guess I'll have to let you have your way. Three men to prepare the new scale; we select them, subject to your rejection. You pay. The old prices to apply until their report. Is that understood?"

"That's right," Philip said, taking the initiative. "The next thing is that all the damage suits against the Company must be dismissed."

David made a grimace which seemed to indicate a half-humorous chagrin.

"Oh, come," he complained, "the Company can settle them very cheaply. They really form no part of an agreement between the strikers and the Pioneer. You leave those to the Company's lawyers."

Once more the Rabbi refused to be cajoled.

"Neither does the suit between the State of Maryland and your client Ginzberg form part of such a settlement, if you want to stand on formalities. I'm not counting the money to be saved or spent. Those suits were brought as moves in the strike, and now that we're ending the strike the cases must be abandoned."

David stared at Philip for a minute as though trying to discover whether a determind show of opposition would be apt to shake his resolution. Then apparently deciding the young idealist was not to be budged from his position —and remembering the comparative unimportance of the matter—he allowed himself to smile, and imitating the dialect of a negro servant, to exclaim in tones of exaggerated terror and respect:

"All right! boss! All right, jes' as you say, boss!"

"It's only fair," Philip remarked coolly, as though closing this phase of their negotiations.

David permitted himself the luxury of a little lecture to this professional teacher of ethics.

"I suppose it is," he told him, "and we'll let it stand as you wish. But you've got to remember one thing— disputes like these (or any other kind, for that matter), can't always be adjusted according to cold, Sabbath-School dogmas of abstract justice. There must be a reasonable degree of give and take, not based on any theories at all except the fighting man's genial desire to carry home a bit of his foeman's skin, to exhibit as a trophy to the admiring women-folk. After you get that idea well into your mind, I'm afraid you'll make a shrewd trader, some day, in spite of yourself."

Philip shook his head. "I hate fighting," he admitted, "and I don't like trade much better."

"You'll deserve just so much more credit if you do learn to fight reasonably well," was the lawyer's comment.

"As for trade, it is only a less boyish form of fighting. However, to return to our job—what else do you want?"

"I'd like some provision for a permanent board of arbitration for the adjustment of any future disputes as they may arise." Philip, forgetful for a moment of himself and his intimate unhappiness, put into his words some faint glow of his habitual enthusiasm.

"Ah!" sighed David, "I was expecting the visionary in you to crop out somewhere. Well, I'll talk your thought over with our crowd, and see what can be done, but you mustn't indulge too many hopes. Working men can't rake up any uncontrollable affection for arbitration tribunals. They have such a noticeable habit of seeing the employers' point of view!"

"Perhaps," the Rabbi struck in sharply, "that's because the working man's demands are so often unfair."

"Perhaps," David conceded cheerfully. "Anyhow, the laborer perceives how the decisions affect him and he prefers his own crude weapons."

"But arbitration is the only sensible way," Philip began dogmatically.

"Logical, you mean—not sensible," David interrupted. "You will forget the difference. The laborers' demands are very often unjust as you so unhesitatingly remarked. Therefore, logical people refuse them—arbitration boards, oftenest of all. But it isn't always sense, to deny an unjust demand."

"I can't see it," Philip protested. "The laboring man and his employer have each a right to exact justice—neither more nor less."

"You don't know what you mean by that word," David answered. "Nobody does—the Judges least of all. Look here! Everybody has a peculiar desire to live more comfortably next year than he did last year. It isn't rational. It may be bad for the soul,—stressing as it does the things of the flesh instead of the spirit. Still it's prevalent. Even I allow myself to become influenced by it. Now, this instinct isn't so baffling for the employer. He adds a few cents on to the price of the article he sells, or shaves a little more than a few cents worth from its quality, and behold, next year's automobile has been paid for, and no one has been sufficiently injured to get up and howl. The laboring man has no one to squeeze but his boss. If he wants some absurd little luxury, there's only one paymaster for him to browbeat."

Philip's dissent was expressed in terms of orthodox economics.

" The true interest of the employer and his employees is identical," was his thesis. " Neither can inflict an injury on the other without damaging himself."

David snorted scornfully.

" The true interest of myself and the lawyer on the other side of my case is identical. We're both interested in having litigation continued according to the rules we know, and keeping it reasonably expensive. That doesn't prevent me from sitting up nights trying to outwit him ! "

Philip was interested and would have been glad to probe more deeply into the subject. But David, recalling, perhaps, how much time they had already been closeted together, began to check off on his memorandum sheet the points they had agreed upon, and seemed anxious to bring the conference to a close.

" I'll make a detailed draft of the whole thing," he

promised, "and submit it to you in a day or two. We seem to be pretty close together. Of course, there'll still be odds and ends where each of us will have to use some forbearance. The rights in your shop, for example, of the officers of the Union."

"We won't quarrel there," was the Rabbi's confident prophecy. "I want the Union to have a fair share of power, and to accept a corresponding amount of responsibility."

David, this time, did not allow himself to smile. He saw a chance of wresting, through the Rabbi's academic theories, a substantial advantage for the men he was representing, and he merely nodded.

"I'll see what I can frame up along those lines," he stated with a grim, hidden meaning.

"Good!" Philip said, reaching for his hat. "I guess that's about all. Telephone me when you want me again. I'll hold myself subject to your call."

"Thank you," David responded. "I believe we've done a good morning's work. I'll try to be vague with the strikers for the present. Only I may assure them, of course, if we agree on a peace, there are no exceptions to be made because of anybody's activity during the strike? Everybody gets his old place back; that's your understanding, isn't it?"

Philip stopped to consider. He really had only the most nebulous ideas regarding the actual management of the plant.

"That's elementary," David added, surprised at the Rabbi's delay.

"Of course," Philip said slowly, "nobody is to be barred from work because of anything he did during the

310

strike. I never considered such a thing; but about his *old* job, I don't know. I'll have to find out about that. Lots of these places have been filled by new men. We'll have to expand a bit to take care of all of them. Your men may not be able to return in a body; but that won't matter. Tell them they're to have their old jobs, or others, at just as good wages. And if there's delay in putting them to work, they shall be paid in the meantime."

The young man waited confidently for the acknowledgment of his marked generosity. He was surprised to find David looking at him in blank amazement.

" Why, you are not thinking of giving permanent employment to the strikebreakers? " he exploded, incredulously. " You don't expect our men to work side by side with these ' scabs?' It can't be done! You might just as well try to mix oil and water."

Philip set his lips in a stern line of unyielding determination.

" What else did you expect? " he demanded. " I told you I intended to deal fairly with all interests. I've certainly shown you that much. The Pioneer Company brought these people to their plant—many of them from Rochester and New York. I don't say they should have, but they did. These ' scabs '—as you call them—were begged to work there when there was some danger in doing it. Now I don't intend to turn them adrift to hunt around for new jobs, or to starve. It would be abhorrent. I won't do it! "

David's expression was one of mock-heroic despair.

" It's no use," he groaned. " You're incorrigible! Are you perfectly serious? Because, if you are, we might as well stop work here and now."

Philip began to argue the point, volubly and with a sincere conviction in the absolute rectitude of his position. David broke into his discourse with scant ceremony.

"There's not a bit of use in your talking about it!" he announced. "What you suggest is less possible than electing Kaufman as President, on the Socialist ticket. The more you listen to yourself the less open to reason you'll be, and you've got to hear reason. It would be a pity to break things off at this stage. My waiting-room is jammed. I can't talk to you any longer, now. Come back in three hours and I'll try to corrupt you enough to make you forget this little scruple."

In three hours to the minute, Philip returned and David, eyeing him with his peculiar disconcerting smile, began to belabor him with plausible words.

"I told you this morning," the lawyer explained, "the impossibility of following pretty words and phrases in dealing with the passions of angry men. This word 'justice' has gone to your head. You're reeling drunk with it. I'll grant you without argument the hardship upon these strikebreakers of turning them adrift; but this is not a world of love-making between enemies. These 'scabs' came here knowing perfectly well the chances they took. Theirs is the fortune of war. You've got to choose between hurting them and hurting the strikers."

Philip could not accept this as a fair statement of his alternative. The strikers could come back to work and the new employees could work beside them. Neither need suffer. Only stubbornness prevented such a solution.

"But if they're made that way," the lawyer thundered, "what are you going to do about it? Tell them how naughty they are! You might as well tell them how thriftless they are to marry and beget children, when you could prove by the simplest arithmetic how little they can afford such an indulgence! You've got to deal with men as they are! They won't go back to work unless you discharge these people, and you've just got to make up your mind to it!"

Philip felt sure David could make them see the cruelty of such a demand if he set himself to the task. He, himself, he added, would be able to do it if they could be brought to think of him as a friend.

"It's ideas like these," David insisted brutally, "which will always keep them from thinking of you as anything but a stranger. What do they care if they're cruel or not? They want to hurt these 'scabs!' They believe the one business in life of a 'scab' is to take the bread from honest men's mouths!"

"But you know better," Philip reproved. "You know the strikebreaker, like the Union man, works because he's hungry and his wife and babies are hungry."

"Can't you understand," Davided demanded, "it isn't a question of what I see? I'm not the man who is going to press vests for Kaufman, any more than you are. If these fellows had sense enough to grasp your fine distinctions, they'd be preaching sermons or practicing law, instead of pressing vests."

Still, Philip remained unmoved. The discussion began, to David's disgust, to go around and around in a circle, the Rabbi insisting upon the sinfulness of the ejection of the strikebreakers, the lawyer emphasizing the impossibility of peace on any other basis. At last, Philip, unable to make any headway in a debate where neither opponent was willing to concede the truth of what the other assumed to be axiomatic, made an effort to bring this fruitless exchange of words to an end.

"Mr. Gordon," he said quietly, "I don't seem able to make you understand that I consider an unjust peace as bad as no peace at all."

"Exactly!" Gordon snapped out, "because you're thinking of what you call 'justice' and I'm thinking of suffering men and women."

"Which set of men and women?" Philip could not resist asking.

"The largest number," David answered. "It's a school-boy's problem in mathematics!"

Philip continued: "Of course, this won't make any difference in your point of view, but I've made enormous sacrifices to put myself in a position to end this strike. I've paid a price I couldn't have believed possible. Wouldn't it seem strange to you if I'd be willing to have gone through all this for something which seemed to be base and degrading, instead of a work I could be proud of? If I've forced myself to do this because I thought it a duty, haven't I a right to expect others to rise above a blind, angry prejudice?"

David was swept from his habitual pose by this frank, boyish appeal. He rose and laid his hand on the Rabbi's shoulder.

"Would it help you to tell me about it—in confidence, this time?" he suggested, with a gentleness so unexpected as to startle his visitor.

Philip shook his head sadly. His wound was not such as could be bared to anyone. "It's too late," he replied; "thanks, just the same. I wasn't making a play for sympathy, but you see what I mean?"

A MATTER OF DEFINITION

"Yes, I see," the lawyer said gravely, "but if your pain has led you to do something for other men and women who are unhappy, don't let it be wasted in idle wishing. You can't do the things you want to do. Do the next best thing! Do it even if you have to add to your other sacrifices some of your theories of what ought to be done!"

Philip considered the question for a long time in silence. Then he rose, suddenly, and said:

"I'm sorry. I can't do it. I would if I could, but I think it would be better to close the plant altogether. If your people can be made happy only by doing this cruelty to the others, I don't think they've any right to happiness. At any rate, I couldn't have a part in bringing it about."

The two men stood side by side, regarding each other seriously. At last David spoke:

"I'll go as far as I can to prevent what I'm sure is going to happen. I'll urge the strikers to accept your condition. I'll argue for it although I think it's unwise, foolish, and sure to cause a recurrence of the trouble, pretty soon. But I shan't try to force it on them. That would be wrong. I'll do what I can, but it won't work. It's against human nature."

To Philip there came a swift inspiration.

"You may tell them still more," he urged. "We'll make the strikebreakers join the Union as the price of their retention. Surely, that ought to satisfy your committee; but they must be treated decently in the Union, and out of it."

David grasped the Rabbi's hand.

"You're a good fellow, Doctor, but you don't know much about the curious animal known as Man; the strikers would think their Union polluted by these people. They'd

315

hate them all the more if they were forced on them. They'd treat them like dogs. No, that scheme won't do. I'll talk it over with our crowd and let you hear from me."

Philip went directly to Ruth's home to warn her to buy no more stock until this cloud should be dissipated. The report he made to her threw her plans into a state of complete confusion. She was not concerned because of the shares she had already bought. She could dispose of them without appreciable loss, or better still, hold them and profit by the rise which was sure to come when the strike should, some day, be brought to an end. It was Philip himself about whom she was troubled. She did not know, of course, of Ellen's departure. All she was able to foresee was the complete wreck of her carefully-prepared device for capturing and holding Philip's interest. If he should abandon his efforts to effect a settlement, she would have no further excuses for these daily consultations—no more important secrets to be shared with him— no claim on his gratitude save the faint one of her good intentions. Above all, she would have lost the power of separating him from the alien woman for whom he had betrayed an absurd infatuation.

To Ruth, the Rabbi's scruples regarding the discharge of the strikebreakers seemed absurdly unimportant. She would cheerfully have pensioned them for life or had them boiled in oil, to accomplish her designs. There weren't many of them after all. Philip—lovable as he was—certainly was an uncomfortable sort of man.

She could not, however, allow one of these disconcerting reflections to escape in words, and this restriction was the most irritating part of it all. Any argument she might urge for the abandonment of his position would identify her in his mind as a girl incapable of a real devotion to

Truth and Justice. Also, it would imply an adverse criticism upon his judgment, and no man, she reflected, is broad enough to tolerate that.

So she was forced to content herself with mere expressions of sympathy and hopes for the ultimate adjustment of the dispute. She hinted vaguely at some compromise whereby the strikebreakers might be discharged with a secret agreement on the part of the Company to continue the payment of wages to them until they should have found employment elsewhere; but Philip rejected the idea indignantly. There was a real principle involved in an employer being loyal to the men who had been loyal to him; he would not yield this point—no matter what happened. It would be cowardly, irreligious and a bad beginning for the administration of an industry upon the basis of Equity and Fair Dealing.

With this unsatisfactory condition of affairs, Ruth was obliged to content herself. She awaited with such slight patience as she could command, the result of further meetings between Philip and David Gordon. Here, again, her hopes proved futile. The strikers absolutely and contemptuously refused to work, side by side, with men they believed to be professional strikebreakers. In vain David argued the probability of the speedy flight of such unreliable birds of passage; without avail he hinted at valuable concessions he might obtain from this guileless young Rabbi—concessions which could never be wrung from hard-headed business men. The strikers remained as obdurate as Philip himself. Ruth made no further efforts to wrest the control of the Company from Clarence Kaufman, and the miniature civil war, with its newspaper sensations and its petty outbursts of disorder, continued its course, as before.

Ruth, who made it her business to glean some secret data regarding Philip's routine of life, soon indulged a reasonable certainty of a break in his visits to the "objectionable woman." That was something gained, to be sure. Still, he displayed no desire to spend much time with Ruth—or with anyone else for that matter. Inwardly his spirit was raging at the monstrous irony of which he felt himself the victim. He had been led to believe in his special fitness for a great mission; his opportunity had come to him; he had accepted it without a suspicion of its spurious quality,—embraced it with what now turned out to be grotesque posturings and grandiloquent phrases; he had paid for it grievously in the loss of Ellen, and when he had laid down the price, he found he had been tricked,—made colossally ridiculous, like some poor, stupid boy, at a country fair, who is led to part with all his precious savings for a brightly-gilded block of worthless iron, and hears nothing but peals of laughter when he tells the story of his tragedy. Even the mechanism of his failure seemed absurd to the unhappy minister. It was his devotion to the cause of Justice which had made it impossible for him to accomplish Justice; because he wanted to serve all men he was unable to serve any. It was the best in him, and not the worst, which had been his undoing.

He had said something like this, in the bitterness of his disappointment, to David Gordon, when they had parted at the end of their final, unsuccessful interview. David had favored him with his cryptic smile, and answered:

"My dear Doctor, the stag is a beautiful and poetic animal. If you were to yoke him to a cart with an ox, he'd die; and he wouldn't help the ox much, either!"

CHAPTER XXII

THE HAPPY ENDING

ONE afternoon, about a fortnight after Philip's unsuccessful attempt to act as peace-maker, David Gordon sprang from a street-car before it had come to a full stop, and hurried up the steps of the most fashionable and exclusive club in the City.

It was a wonderful afternoon, holding the first promise of the advent of Spring. Although the air was still cool, there was a hint of Winter's end, in the brilliant sunshine, in the budding trees which lined North Charles Street, and in the dainty costumes of the pretty girls who strolled along the Avenue. It was one of those day when Baltimore deserves, and receives, a free pardon for any crimes its climate may perpetrate in the midst of Summer or Winter.

David, however, seemed completely insensible to the beauty of his surroundings. The Club he was entering was one of which he knew perfectly well he could never become a member—no matter to what other distinctions he might rise. Within its walls there was enforced an unwritten law which proclaimed a Christian imbecile a more appropriate member than a Jewish sage—assuming there was such a creature. David was unable to cherish any resentment at this state of affairs. His feelings toward the Club and the civic aspirations which gave it birth, were no more cordial or respectful than the Club's toward him.

As he entered its sacred portals and hurriedly ordered the door-man to announce him to Mr. Frame, he was not even conscious of any increased importance in standing within these superlatively-genteel precincts. He merely wondered why busy and important men, like Frame, cared to lounge around such places, talking to pinheaded manikins.

He was led into a private room where four men, considerably beyond middle age, were seated around a table. All of them were smoking fat cigars, and the figures of three of them seemed to have been patterned after the cigars, or the cigars selected to conform with their figures. The fourth man, John Frame, was as lean as David. Whatever might be alleged against the gross tonnage of this quartet, no one of them had a commonplace face; the waiter who served them would probably have exclaimed, in reverent wonder, on the aggregate number of million dollars represented when they sat down to dine together; they, themselves, if they had not learned from their wives and daughters the bad taste of anything approaching vulgar boasting, would have preferred to direct attention to the ability of their combined number to make any business man in the City do their bidding after a more or less extended course of such agreeable persuasion, by word and deed, as they knew how to administer.

When David Gordon entered the room and the door had been closed behind him, none of the four arose, nor was anyone sufficiently formal to invite him to sit down. David drew a chair to the table without waiting to be asked. He himself was no great believer in ceremony, and it pleased him to be convinced that these financial potentates had as bad manners as his own.

" Gordon," began Mr. Frame, " we've sent for you

because you are a practical man. We've all done business with you before, and we know you can understand sense when you hear it, and put things across." He paused, awaiting some bashful acknowledgment of this glowing tribute. It came promptly.

"Thanks," David replied, with his elusive smile. "You would certainly note my blushes—only we have such swarthy complexions—we Jews!"

Somebody gasped at such a flagrant tone of disrespect, but Frame rather liked Gordon's impudence, and David was perfectly well aware of the fact.

"Won't you have a drink?" one of the other men suggested by way of interlude.

"No," David answered, smiling again, "thanks just the same. I don't drink at all, but if I did, I wouldn't now."

Nobody remembered to offer him a cigar and he calmly drew one of his own from his case and proceeded to light it. Mr. Frame resumed his remarks:

"Well, Gordon, we've come to the conclusion this Pioneer strike has been going on long enough,—too long! It's beginning to hurt business, generally. It's threatening to keep Capital out of the City—particularly now when all sorts of financial operations are under way. It's got to stop. I don't know where all the money the strikers have used has come from, but I suppose whoever's putting it up could reconcile himself to the pain of having his sport spoiled."

He looked at David narrowly as though he might perhaps learn something interesting about the contributions to the expenses of the strike, but David merely continued to wear his exasperating smile.

Mr. Frame swiftly re-enforced his determination with

21   321

the recollection of the banks he controlled and the avenues of commerce he dominated; he cast a swift glance around the table at his colleagues with their similar titles to power.

"We've decided!" he repeated. "The thing's got to stop."

"You make me very happy, gentlemen," was the lawyer's comment. "I myself have always pushed my love for peace and conciliation to a point almost absurd. But I have no influence whatever over Mr. Kaufman. I think you should have spoken to him. It surprises me sometimes to reflect how a man and a merchant can be so stubborn."

Frame smiled meaningly.

"He's a little less stubborn than he was yesterday. I had a talk with him. The four of us control, directly or indirectly, all his banking connections. We had a mighty serious sort of talk. That's why I sent for you."

David nodded.

"Of course," Frame went on, "Kaufman's a big customer of the banks, and his industry is important to the City. He has to make some concessions, but we don't intend to have him humiliated. You understand?"

David nodded again.

"Humiliating Kaufman wouldn't interest me," he observed. "No one could be sure he hadn't done it to himself. Give me the things I want, and he can advertise the result as a glorious victory!"

"You can't have all you want, and neither can he," was Frame's flat ultimatum. "You've got sense enough to know that. That's why we sent for you. You've known that for weeks."

"Very well, sir!" David said briskly. "You gentlemen are too big to haggle with. Tell me what I can get, and I'll tell you without a minute's delay whether I'll accept it."

"That's the kind of talk I like to hear," Frame exclaimed. "You can force your men to stand behind your agreements, I take it?"

"I'm like the Czar," David said; "my word is absolute law, but if I stretch my despotism too far, I'm apt to lose my head."

"Suppose you tell us then how far you can stretch it," demanded Frame.

"Very well," began David, "to begin with, Kaufman recognizes the Union. There's no avoiding that!"

"Wait a minute," Frame interrupted. "It depends on what you mean. He's got to recognize the Union. The other clothing men have all come to it, but we won't force Kaufman to have a closed shop. That's a step we'll never take. If it's your idea to shut everyone but Union men out of the plant, we might just as well stop talking here and now!"

A stupider man would have pretended to insist on his full demand in the hope of thereby gaining the largest possible fragment of what he had claimed. David took exactly the opposite course.

"No need to argue it, Mr. Frame," he conceded; "I never expected anything so drastic—an open shop, of course, but with a few assurances. If our settlement went no further, what reason would we have to expect Kaufman ever to employ a Union man as long as he could find another?"

"None whatever," admitted Mr. Frame frankly; "he'd be a fool if he did."

"Just so," David said, "and he isn't a fool—at least not that kind. An open shop then, with an agreement for the employment, at all times, of seventy-five per cent. of Union members, provided the Union can furnish them —no man to be discharged because of his Union activities —how's that?"

"The percentage is too high," struck in one of the other capitalists indignantly. "Seventy-five per cent!"

"Sixty, then," was David's genial correction. He had expected to be cut down to fifty, and was more than satisfied when his suggestion was accepted.

"Well, there's so much accomplished," said Frame. "What's next?"

"The strikebreakers have got to go," David insisted— and then before any of his judges should have committed himself to an opinion, he continued: "I'm urging this as much for the sake of the general welfare as our own. You know they're a dangerous set of men. The City will be better without them. Besides, if you make us give in on this point, you'll have all your trouble over again in a month. These 'scabs' will get along with the strikers about as peacefully as a match and a keg of gunpowder."

The four men shook their heads sagely. They had no desire to have this disturbance to settle a second time. The lawyer gave a whimsical thought to Philip Graetz, and his theories about Justice, and passed on to the next question.

"The new wage scale," he began——

"That wage scale is all right," interrupted one of the men who had not yet spoken, "I've gone through it from top to bottom. It's the most liberal in town. My judgment is not to press Kaufman on that. Good Lord! the man's got some rights."

THE HAPPY ENDING

The point was argued at considerable length. David was not able to point out anything particularly unfair about the proposed scheme of wages. He could only stress the inability of the workers to understand its rather complicated terms, and speak of the consequent distrust with which they regarded it.

"Very good, then," was Frame's brutal way of ending the discussion, "get it translated into the jargon they talk, or hire a school-teacher to explain it to them. The wage scale stands."

David finally yielded the point, realizing how untenable his position would be if the strike continued upon that single issue. He complained that he was receiving harsher treatment upon this point than if he had been dealing directly with the Pioneer Company, Kaufman having always been willing to arbitrate the matter of wages, but the four unanimously tossed at him the same argument he had used against Philip.

"No arbitration!" they all cried stridently. "We want to get done with the whole thing,—now, without delays."

One by one, the various items in the dispute were thus adjusted. At the very end, David remarked casually:

"Of course, the prosecution of Ginzberg is to be dropped. I nearly forgot to mention it."

"I don't know," Frame hesitated. "Law and order, you know—Capital is exceedingly timid——"

"Capitalists aren't—and they've no legitimate excuse for being too squeamish, either," David retorted dryly. "Look here, gentlemen, I've promised this man his liberty. He's got to have it. That's my price."

"Really," one of the men said coldly, "I can't see

any direct connection between this lawbreaker and the merits of the strike we're trying to settle."

"Maybe I can make it more apparent," was David's instant reply. " My idea of keeping my promise to Ginzberg obliges me to print a statement on the front page of the morning papers, at least once a week, so long as he remains in prison. Perhaps the continuation of this policy might cause timid Capital to become actually hysterical."

"Well! well!" was Mr. Frame's soothing conclusion, " after all, it's not highly important. You don't make any demands, do you, about this other fellow—what's his name—the one who threw the brick?"

"Clutsky," David answered. " No, he's past helping, and besides, he's no client of mine."

"All right," Frame decided. " We can play up this business of Law and Order with him. But will the State's Attorney and the Court let your man go?"

"That's my part of the job," was David's confident assurance. " They'll be glad to drop the case if the Pioneer people ask it. They'll jump at a chance to get out of the mess with credit. No jury would ever convict Ginzberg, after all this hue and cry."

There was an instant's pause. Then Frame declared crisply:

"That's about all, then." He rang a bell sharply and when the attendant responded, he ordered:

"Boy, call up the Pioneer Clothing Company, and tell Mr. Clarence Kaufman I want him here, at once."

"Hadn't we better go to my office?" David suggested. "We'll want stenographers."

"No, get them here," Frame commanded, " and silent ones, too. None of us wants to be known in this affair." The others shook their heads in emphatic acquiescence.

THE HAPPY ENDING

Kaufman appeared promptly, duly attended by two of David's professional colleagues. The clothing manufacturer, if the truth must be told, was more than a little awed and flattered by his presence in this Citadel of Non-Jewish gentility,—particularly when, to prevent the necessity of an adjournment, all the parties to this treaty sat down to a hasty meal within this holy of holies of Social aspiration. David, illogically, found himself much more disgusted than amused at this transparent display of snobbishness, even though Kaufman's mood increased to an unexpected degree the man's pliability.

There was a mass of work to be done, and most of it was accomplished by David Gordon. Documents were dictated, corrected and dictated again. There were hurried trips to be made in motors to the headquarters of the strikers—to the houses of several officers of the Pioneer Company, to the home of the State's Attorney and with that officer to the dwelling of one of the Judges of the Court.

It was nearly midnight when the settlement, in all its details, was fully consummated. A spirit of general forbearance and forgiveness settled upon the ill-assorted group of Jews and Gentiles like a warm and sticky fog. They all shook hands with each other in amiable toleration. Even Kaufman, after having finally reconciled himself to the nauseating dose held to his lips by these overlords of industry, found the prospect of peace not without its allurement. He held out his hand to David Gordon who accepted it with the same inscrutable smile he had worn since these felicitations began.

"Well, Mr. Gordon," Kaufman told him in his harsh, guttural tones, "you've made a lot of trouble for

me and you've called me some hard names, but I don't
bear you any grudge. After all, it was your business to
fight me! I ought to have had you on my staff of
lawyers! I'd have found it cheaper, no matter what your
fees are!"

And David continued to smile enigmatically, and to
accept congratulations from everyone in the room, upon
his masterly handling of the whole affair from beginning
to end.

Just as some one made a movement toward the door,
David Gordon called for silence.

"Gentlemen," he said, "there's one more thing to be
done. Some statement should be prepared and given to
the press. They're sure to print a long story about this
agreement. We may as well give it to them the way we
want it to appear."

He began without delay to dictate a comprehensive but
interesting account of the termination of the long struggle,
and of the terms which each side had agreed to accept. As
he was about to conclude the article, he paused and
declared:

"It's sense to say something about the manner in which
we happened to meet to discuss a possible settlement. If
you don't, you'll merely open the door to a flood of newspaper surmise and gossip."

"Leave me out of it!" was Frame's peremptory command, which was echoed, without hesitation, by his three
companions.

Kaufman's counsel looked at David hopefully. They
were as willing to be mentioned as the financiers appeared
desirous of wrapping themselves in mystery.

"Of course, I could say we lawyers met informally and

arranged the thing," was David's doubtful comment, " but you know, perfectly well, nobody would believe it."

At this point, Kaufman rose to the occasion.

" I think," he volunteered, " it would be just what you want, and a very pleasant thing besides, to give some credit for this agreement to Dr. Graetz—our Rabbi, you know. He's worked very hard for peace ; he came to see me and tried to persuade me to it, and he went to the strikers, too, on the same errand, I've been told. This quarrel has bothered him a lot and I'm sure he'd like to think he helped to end it. He did, too," Kaufman added, really becoming convinced as he spoke. " His arguments have had great weight with me ! "

" The very thing ! " everybody agreed, though Kaufman's attorneys said it rather disconsolately.

David Gordon, before he began dictating the paragraph which put Kaufman's thought into appropriate words, gave vent to an odd little chuckle which was not altogether indicative of mirth. It was David's audible expression of his ability to see and appreciate the irony of existence in general, and of Rabbis, clothing merchants and labor disputes in particular.

CHAPTER XXIII

GOD'S WORK

PROMPTLY at ten o'clock on the morning following the settlement of the strike, Mr. Israel Ginzberg, accompanied by his attorney, appeared in the Criminal Court where he pleaded guilty to an indictment for " inciting to riot," and was paroled into the custody of his own counsel for a period of two years. The more serious charges against him were dismissed, and as he stood in the corridor of the Court House accepting the noisy congratulations of his friends, he felt himself to be, indeed, something of a public character.

During the same morning, Ruth Hartman, in spite of several pressing engagements with dressmakers and milliners, found no great difficulty, with the aid of her motor car and the telephone, in disposing of all her accumulations of Pioneer stock. Her winnings amounted to a tidy little sum, but she was not in the slightest degree elated by the outcome of her adventure. She had not succeeded in what she had set out to accomplish. A lapful of gold instead, seemed to her but poor consolation.

There was still another consequence, and a rather curious one, which resulted from the sudden truce in the labor war. Philip Graetz awoke, much to his amazement, to find himself once more restored to all the popularity he had enjoyed during the first days of his ministry. If anything, his position was even more enviable than in those early days, for most of his former triumphs had been based upon mere promise, while now the community regarded him as a man of remarkable achievement.

GOD'S WORK

The Rabbi's first reaction to this strange verdict of the sapient public was one of sheer bewilderment. The late Lord Byron, when he awoke to find himself famous, accepted the situation with cheerful alacrity, and his example has been faithfully followed ever since by each and every politician, scribbler, actor or criminal who succeeds in imprinting his deathless name upon a page of newspaper; but the aristocratic poet had one enormous advantage over Philip. He was in thorough agreement with the gratifying opinion of his indulgent critics—not only regarding his own genius, but upon the sterling worth of the particular bit of work which mankind delighted to honor. Philip was more doubtful.

He acknowledged one telephone call after another with the simple statement that he had worked as faithfully as he could to bring about a state of good feeling, but had at no time been given any cause to believe he had made much of an impression upon either side. His acquaintances, and the public generally, calmly brushed these remarks aside as evidence of a rather becoming modesty. Since the head of the Pioneer Company and the representative of the Unions united in attributing to the minister the impulse toward Peace, and he himself had been forced to admit his efforts in that direction, what else were they to infer?

Philip did not know how much or how little influence his unsuccessful appeals to Kaufman and to Gordon might have had. Perhaps his insistent pleadings, even though repulsed, had left each of the combatants with a lurking desire to yield to these entreaties, though not in the precise way the Rabbi had desired.

He might therefore have been perfectly contented to

listen gratefully to the soothing sound of the universal
applause which was his—whether justly or through some
incomprehensible error—had the settlement commended
itself to him. Its terms, however, he considered nothing
less than abhorrent. He would almost have preferred a
continuance of the quarrel.

The recognition of the Union, to his mind, was a
mere empty flourish of phrases. The right to organize was
conceded, but the Union men were to work side by side
with non-Union operators. The result combined, so the
Rabbi thought, all the disadvantages of a "closed shop,"
and one where no organization was tolerated. The Union
would have some power—just enough to make mischief—
and no real responsibility. Between the two classes of
workers, there would be friction from the very beginning.

The strikebreakers had been abandoned without a
qualm. That, in itself, was enough, in the opinion of
Philip, to brand the whole scheme as a conscienceless
betrayal of all principle.

There was no provision for the peaceful adjustment of
future disputes. Sooner or later, all this misery must be
lived through again. The wage scale had been adopted
without any inquiry as to whether it was fair or not.
Finally, the disposal of the case of Ginzberg seemed to
him, in its iniquity, to typify the spirit which animated the
whole transaction. After all the man's poses as an innocent martyr, after all the fiery invective which had been
published in his name, he had confessed in open Court
his guilt of an offense, which, if committed, made him
morally responsible for the blotting out of a human life.
And thereupon he had gone scot free, while for poor,
friendless Clutsky there was in store a long and rigorous

GOD'S WORK

punishment! It was monstrous—all of it. And people fixed the responsibility of it on him! Only they didn't blame him as they should have done if it had really been his work; they lauded him to the skies!

He remained all morning in his rooms trying to adjust his thoughts to the palpably absurd situation in which he found himself. Meanwhile, over the telephone, there continued to trickle a steady stream of felicitations from Gentiles, as well as Jews. There were but two courses open 'to him; one was to be silent, and let people believe what pleased them; the other was to repudiate, with all the scorn it deserved, this disgraceful Peace.

His first inclination was toward a policy of protest. That was what ought to be done, and what he wanted to do. He could crush into one intense sermon all the indignation he had concealed, all the disappointment he had endured and all the soreness of heart and bitterness of bereavement he had felt because of the loss to him of the woman he loved. He could excoriate these smug, complacent creatures who were happy now, because there would be no more disturbing clamor; he could hurl at them the thunder of his eloquence in a way which would shake them, for a minute at least, out of their disgusting ecstasy of self-worship. The rich, with their brutal selfishness, the poor, with their brutal stupidity, the cautious, with their ignoble prudence, Russian Jew and German Jew,—Orthodox and Reformed —Zionist and non-Zionist, he would tell every one of them how base and cowardly had been their conduct in this crisis, and how little of worth and decency there was in them. The Gentiles, too, who had stood aside and sneered at this enactment by the despised Jews, of the drama so often played by the holiest of their church wardens! He would not omit to hold up to them a mirror in which they might view and appreciate their grotesque deformities.

He sat down to draft such a sermon, and page after page of it accumulated on his desk—despite the interruptions of the telephone. He would turn from this vitriolic manuscript, born of his aching sorrow and his burning indignation, to answer civilly the well-meant greetings of the very people of whom he wrote. He had no idea, himself, whether the man at the telephone or the one at the desk was the real Philip.

While he was at luncheon in the grill of his apartment hotel, he was interrupted, again and again, by men who slapped him on the back, and women who daintily pressed his finger tips as they assured him of his own remarkable qualities, and refused to consider seriously his constantly repeated refrain of how small a part he had really played in the achievement they praised.

The noon newspapers were delivered to him while he was still at luncheon and he found in two of them editorial commendation of his activities. Both journals congratulated the City upon the possession of a spiritual leader whose deeds as well as his words were examples in practical religion.

Much more disturbing to the young Rabbi of Beth El were the " human interest stories " which decorated the newspapers. They told of the unrestrained happiness among the strikers and their wives and children, at the passing of their days of famine. Philip assumed, with a credulity which would have rejoiced the hearts of the space writers who penned them, the literal truth of these masterpieces of restrained pathos. They were, in fact, exceedingly well done, and with so exact a correspondence to actual conditions that the incidents recounted might really have happened had the characters described been gifted with a proper sense of dramatic values. These newspaper sketches, however, smote Philip with renewed doubts. He had been willing, almost axious, to cast away his newly-regained laurels. But this Peace—no matter how degrading—would bring bread to the hungry, safety to the endangered and good-will to those whose souls were full of hate. Ought he to banish it, even if he could? He returned to his study but added no more to the epoch-making sermon. Instead, he tried to decide what he really ought to do. The settlement of the strike was now an accomplished fact. People believed he had been instrumental in bringing it to pass. His own influence for wiser and fairer settlements, in the future, might be strengthened if he were willing to endure the responsibility for this one. He sprang from his chair in angry impatience. Always, it appeared, one's opportunities for usefulness hereafter, must be paid for by doing something vile today; standing unyieldingly for Truth, here and now, meant never having the chance again! That was the lesson he had learned from this strike and his efforts to bring it to an honorable end.

Was it all worth the trouble? he asked himself. He had sacrificed his work, his effort and Ellen to do what he believed to be right and necessary. All these things had counted for nothing, and people had looked at him askance. Then while he lay exhausted and helpless, others had done a wrong and useless thing, and every voice was lifted to him, Philip Graetz, in a mad chorus of love and gratitude. The minister smiled unpleasantly. Uptown and downtown, human animals were silly fools—and that was the truth. Was it worth spending one's life to toss words to such creatures, who could not comprehend, and—still worse—had no wish to comprehend. They would be just as happy or miserable if left to themselves; while he, at least, would be free,—free to do what he would, and go where he pleased—to look at life instead of ceaselessly trying to mold it; to seek for and find Ellen, he whispered to himself, half guiltily.

Then he shook off defiantly this feeling of guilt, and looked without shrinking into his own mind. He had accepted her loss in good faith; he had reconciled himself to his duty so long as he had found in it the hope of accomplishment; even after his failure to deal with David Gordon, he had gone steadfastly on with his work, clothed in the dignity of an earnest, though unsuccessful, effort. But today he was possessed by an overwhelming skepticism. Why try to change these besotted beasts? This was the mode of life they enjoyed! An event occurred, dripping with cynical wickedness; they hailed its advent as the happiest of tidings.

He was not merely useless here; he was actually in the way—making men uncomfortable with ideals they did not want. Meanwhile, somewhere in the world there was Ellen, missing his presence with the same poignancy as he did hers, recalling each trick of his speech and gesture, each of his thoughts and hopes, each of his caresses, too. Where she might be, he could not know, but he never doubted he could find her. The longing of each for the other, if he could only burst asunder his prison bars, would surely guide them to their lovers' meeting at the journey's end.

The whole afternoon drifted by in such unprofitable

GOD'S WORK

musing; the members of his congregation were priding
themselves on the lucky chance which had called him to
minister to them; other Temples in Baltimore and elsewhere were thinking of Beth El with envy. Even the East
Side regarded him with kindliness. Had he chosen to
step from the door of his hotel and walk the length of
Eutaw Place, his progress would have partaken of the
nature of a small ovation. Yet the hero of the day chose
to remain locked in his own study, lost in misanthropic
reflections about the emptiness of what men call failure or
success,—reflections only relieved, now and then, by some
fleeting memory of Ellen's sudden, unexpected smile in
the midst of tender seriousness, or her equally unexpected
sweet gravity in an interval of laughter.

As twilight settled down upon the City, a visitor was
announced. It was a newspaper man. The notion had
occurred to a resourceful editor to print the opinions upon
all disputed questions of Sociology of this young minister
now occupying the center of the stage. To obtain this
interview, he had diplomatically selected one of the few
Jews on his staff—a member of Philip's own congregation,
—whose name was Joseph Adler. Adler was generally
accorded in the Jewish community a position somewhat
higher than his importance to his paper, and the size of
his salary, would have earned for him. He was the son
of affluent parents, had received an expensive education,
and was supposed to be doing journalistic work as a prelude to something exceedingly important—and vague—
particularly vague to the young gentleman himself. He
welcomed heartily this evening's assignment, since he was
a born gossip and yearned to be able to recount next day,
and for several days thereafter, some little reminiscence

of his reception by the popular preacher, thereby identifying himself as one of Philip's closest intimates.

This evening, however, he seemed doomed to disappointment. Philip received him with his habitual courtesy, but flatly declined to talk for publication. He apologized graciously for his refusal, but left no doubts of its finality. Adler employed, in turn, all his arts of flattery and entreaty, but with no effect. Philip explained his lack of opportunity to give careful thought to the subjects upon which his views were requested, and his unwillingness to become responsible for any ill-considered statements.

None the less, he said, he was glad to see Mr. Adler, and would always enjoy having him stop in his rooms whenever he was in the mood.

Nearly all of Philip's lies were of this merciful variety. This one brought its own punishment in the shape of Adler's deferred departure. He deluged the Rabbi with odds and ends of newspaper gossip upon a host of unrelated subjects, and was not a whit discouraged at his host's lack of curiosity or enthusiasm.

At last, he rose to go, saying he was about to seek an interview with David Gordon.

"He's always good to the newspaper boys," Adler said, rather significantly.

Philip thought the lawyer had good reasons for this cordiality, but his response was non-committal and polite.

"It's been a great thing for him, this strike," Adler volunteered, "not only in reputation—but they say his fee runs way into five figures."

Philip expressed a surprise not wholly perfunctory.

"Indeed, yes!" the newspaper man rambled on, in no apparent hurry to be off. "You know," he said, lowering his voice to a confidential key, " I had a wonderful story about Gordon's fee and who was paying it—but the Chief wouldn't use it, 'cause it couldn't be verified."

This time Philip's thirst for information had lost its languid quality, and he asked boldly for more details.

" You mustn't breathe a word of it to a soul, Doctor," Adler cautioned. " I wouldn't tell it to anyone else around here, though it's common gossip now in all the newspaper offices. We're all sure it was Max Hirsch who brought Gordon into the case and put up a lot of the strikers' fund besides."

Philip's world reeled under him. Hirsch was the guiding spirit of the Alpha Clothing Company, one of the Pioneer's most vigorous competitors. It also happened that Hirsch, like Kaufman, drew his religious inspiration from Beth El.

" Why on earth," Philip demanded, excitedly, " should Hirsch want to do such an unheard-of thing? "

" It's not so unheard-of," Adler replied coolly. " The Pioneer has been fighting the Alpha for years, using every dirty trick it could think of to edge them out of good business. This season, I reckon the Pioneer's sales dropped off. Besides, Kaufman's was the only plant in town that was free from the Unions. Now they're all in the same boat. Maybe some of the other houses chipped in a dollar or two, besides."

The Rabbi listened with ill-concealed horror to Adler's glib chatter.

" I don't believe it," he exclaimed at last, in low, excited tones.

" Well, I don't say it's true," the newspaper man made haste to say, " we couldn't verify it. Gordon's too keen to let anyone prove anything he doesn't want known. But it's the gossip of the office. And Hirsch has gone to Gordon's house, at nights, pretty often the last few months. Dave's been his lawyer for years. Still," he concluded, with amiable philosophy, "what's the difference? It's all over now, and Gordon did a good job, no matter who paid him!"

Philip could not trust himself to answer this heresy, and Adler finally succeeded in making his exit, saying as he left:

"Well, good-bye, Doctor. I came to interview you, but you seem to have turned the tables on me."

Philip left to himself, faced this new possibility with positive loathing. It was idle, vicious rumor, of course, engendered in the minds of office underlings with a perverted taste for slander. He had compromised his dignity in encouraging this murderer of reputations to repeat such poisonous stuff to him. Persistently, nevertheless, the thought recurred to him:

"Suppose it's true! Is it so improbable, after all? Why has Gordon been so secretive about the identity of his employer? Suppose it's true!"

If it were really true, Philip concluded there was nothing in mankind or womankind one might trust! Everything they did or thought was vile and base! Those confiding wretches—like himself—who had no share in the carnival of treachery and corruption were the senseless dupes of the others. All the strike, with its life-like stage-setting of pathos and heroism, had been nothing but an idle mummery, enacted by fools, to serve the money-looting ambitions of knaves.

He had been the most credulous of all the innocents—

not only because he had, with never a suspicion, allowed himself to be used as one of the puppets,—others had done that. The deluded strikers had gone hungry, as incidents in the strategy of this private war between Hirsch and Kaufman. But the Rabbi had suffered all the strikers had suffered, and more. Like them, he had made his sacrifice of personal happiness, but he had, in addition, staked the whole of his enthusiasm, every vestige of his faith in himself and his work, in playing a man's part in this struggle. Now, when he had emerged from the thick of the noise and the din, battered and wounded, and with no consolation save the knowlege that he had remained true to his own standards, he was to be told that the whole affair had been nothing but a gigantic entertainment, arranged, like a battle of unwilling gladiators, for the august pleasure of a wealthy patron of such spectacles.

It was monstrous! And Philip, rapidly working himself into a frenzy, almost hysterical, decided flatly, if this story were true, he was done with his ministry, and with these people who could seem so kind and warm-hearted and yet engage in deeds so far beyond the pale of forgiveness.

He would preach the sermon which lay uncompleted on his desk. He would end it by putting his suspicion into words. The flaming indictment should end with his resignation. He would tell them how they had robbed him, in these brief months, of his belief in himself and all other men, as well as in the God who could be guilty of their creation. Then he would· go—whether he found Ellen or not,—he would remain here no longer, breathing the same polluted air with Hirsch and Kaufman and David Gordon.

It was David's conduct which rankled most. In spite

of the man's affectation of cynicism, the Rabbi had believed in his breadth of vision, his underlying sincerity, his unselfish willingness to fight a good fight for the weaker cause. He was the more deceived! It was Gordon who had done him the worst wrong of all! He was the arch-traitor, the master conspirator!—always supposing, of course, this tale to be true!

Even in his rapidly-increasing excitement, Philip remembered the injustice of forming his judgment without knowing whether or not the story was a mere scurrilous falsehood.

Of course, he could find out sooner or later. He would allow himself no rest until he had; but he could not bear the suspense another hour. One way or the other, he must learn the actual truth and decide whether he was to live his life in a world of lies and cruelties, or among men who had some standards of honor, however crude.

He would talk to Gordon. He would tear the man's secret from his heart. An he would do this now—this very night. He hurried from his hotel to Gordon's home and demanded, in tones of insistent eagerness, an immediate audience with the lawyer. The servant eyed this importunate visitor with frank astonishment; but Philip was in no mood for delay. He had a right to be here. Gordon owed him a debt of explanation upon which the whole of the minister's future happiness depended. He had come, in no temper of mild indulgence, to claim its payment.

The servant who had left the Rabbi standing in the hallway, returned saying his master was now engaged in consultation with an important client. If Dr. Graetz would return at nine o'clock he would be glad to receive him.

Philip, most reluctantly, suffered himself to be turned away. He must submit to a further delay of more than an hour! Morever, why had not Gordon suggested his awaiting his leisure in his home, instead of thrusting him inhospitably into the street? It was suspicious, certainly! Someone was with him whom he didn't want the Rabbi to meet, someone who wouldn't come to the lawyer's office for fear of observation. Hirsch, of course. Hadn't Adler said Kaufman's rival had been coming there at nights? The thing was palpably clear. Philip walked up and down Madison Avenue at a rapid, irregular gait, lashing himself into an ever rising flood of nervousness and frenzy.

As he walked, a most uncharacteristic impulse seized him in its grasp. He would play the spy. He would secrete himself in the shadow of the house adjoining Gordon's and discover what manner of visitor the lawyer chose to entertain. The angle of the wall made a patch of inky blackness. No one would ever know of his presence there, and as this mysterious client walked from the entrance of the apartment house in the side yard, to the pavement of Madison Avenue, he would pass within a few feet of the minister. If it were Hirsch, he could not fail to recognize him. Philip, even in this abnormal key of excitement, did not persuade himself to such a step without some qualms; but he silenced them effectively. Who else had scruples in this world of detestable intrigue? Besides, he was only seeking to learn what it was his right to know. He stifled his misgivings and remained hidden at his point of vantage.

After many minutes, the door suddenly opened, but the lights in the hallway and vestibule had at the same instant been extinguished. Philip, in that brief instant of attempting to adjust his vision to the increased darkness, could see nothing more than the uncertain outline of a bulky, male figure descending the steps. The man, however, must pass him on his way to the street, and the Rabbi crouched breathlessly against the dark wall. To his surprise and consternation, the visitor, instead of turning to the front of the building, made his way rapidly in the opposite direction, and vanished through a little lattice gate which led into a court-yard abutting upon the lane in the rear of the house!

The lattice gate clicked behind him, indicating the probable presence of a spring lock. To pursue the man was, therefore, impossible, without regard to the madness of such an indiscretion. To intercept him in the lane, or "alley," as Baltimore parlance terms it, involved a flight along half the exterior of the block, without any certainty as to whether the man had found his outlet toward the North or the South. This, in spite of its wild indecorum, Philip attempted, but when he reached the dark outlet of the alley into the side street, there was nothing to be seen. The man may have turned in the opposite direction, or Philip's pace, though it left him breathless and exhausted, may have been too slow. His essay in espionage had brought him nothing but a fluttering pulse and a burning sense of humiliation.

Still, he reflected, as he made his way back to Gordon's house, there could be no reasonable doubt as to the lawyer's guilt. Why else should his client slink from his door like a house-breaker seeking refuge from the light? The man had been Hirsch! The precious pair had suspected him of such dishonorable eavesdropping as they would have adopted as a matter of course. (Somehow the fact that he had not disappointed such an expectation, did not occur to Philip.) They had schemed to elude him. Now that he reviewed his impressions, he found it less difficult to persuade himself of some resemblance to the clothing manufacturer, in the height or gait of the dark bulk of the man upon whom he had spied.

The Rabbi burst into Gordon's study like an avenging spirit. He did not accept the hand held out to him in welcome, nor seat himself in a deep chair toward which the lawyer pointed. He was ashen pale, and there was an unearthly glint in his eyes.

"What's the matter?" asked David. "You look as though you'd seen a ghost."

"I've seen worse things," began Philip in shrill excitement. "I've come to ask you about them—and about yourself. I know now who paid you to tear this town into shreds and to make blind fools like Ginzberg and myself wish they were ghosts! I came to ask you to teach me how people can go on living when they do such things, and when they believe everyone else would do them, too, if they only knew the trick!"

The lawyer stared at his distraught visitor without answering. He seemed to be trying to make sure whether he was altogether mad.

"Sit down," he commanded at last, in tones of uncompromising sternness.

"Answer me!" was Philip's hysterical demand. "You could use all of us as pawns in the game your boss hired you to play. Some of us gave up bread, and one laid down his life and I threw away something better than either. And you made us all prance around as you pulled the strings. We covered up our sore hearts with what we thought were wonderfully heroic words and deeds, while you and he sat behind a closed door chuckling as you figured up how many dollars you could make by it all! I want to know how it feels to be like that, so I can try it, too."

Gordon sat down and looked at the Rabbi with the expression of a man who has been saddled with the responsibility of a sick child.

"Tell me," he urged patiently, "what has upset you in this way?"

"Don't pose with me any longer," the Rabbi exclaimed in the same shrill, unnatural voice. "I know all about you and Hirsch, and I for one won't stand it. I'm going to shriek it from the house-tops, and after that, I'm done with you and him and all your kind. If there's nobody in the world but fools and rascals, I shan't be one of the fools any longer."

"You don't seem to be able to help being," David retorted, dropping, at last, his attitude of concern. "You're talking gibberish. If you know anything you care to shriek, you've chosen the wrong audience. I have no taste for melodrama."

"I do know something," Philip insisted. "I know it was Hirsch who paid your fee. I know he was here this very night."

David indulged in his cryptic smile.

"You're on the verge, my dear Graetz," he warned, "of making yourself extremely ridiculous. When it comes to a matter of actual facts, you know nothing. I doubt if you'd care to shriek from the house-tops the methods you use of reaching your hare-brained guesses."

"Oh, you're clever enough," Philip sneered; "you

arrange things so you don't get caught red-handed!"

"Really, Doctor," David said coldly, apparently at the end of his forbearance, "until tonight, I prided myself upon the superlative quality of my bad manners. You can hardly expect me to assist you in robbing me of these laurels. For tonight, at least, I'm afraid we haven't anything further to say to one another."

The lawyer rose significantly. Philip felt himself about to be dismissed without a word of absolute certainty to silence or confirm his torturing suspicions—to tell him whether or not he should tear up the roots of his life and his ministry. His unstable emotions swept him suddenly from his passion of burning indignation to a burst of pathetic despair.

"For God's sake, Gordon," he begged, "tell me the truth! Don't you see I can't go on in this way? Tell me if the whole thing has been a hideous joke, and if it has, let me get away from these lepers, while I'm still sane. I couldn't stand it here any longer; I couldn't!"

"So far as I am concerned, the thing has been anything but a joke," was David's grave assurance. "What else do you want to know?"

"I want to know who paid you," Philip asked breathlessly. "If you'll tell me, I'll never repeat it so long as I live. I don't want to punish anybody any longer. It's for myself I'm asking. I tell you I must know!"

David met his eagerness with a stern but not unsympathetic kindness.

"There are some things a lawyer may not do—not even to save a friend (or himself, either), from suicide or worse. One of these things is the betrayal of his client's secrets."

"It's a strange sense of honor you lawyers have," Philip answered, flaming up again, in his disappointment. "There's nothing too bad for you to do if it helps the man who can pay you; you know nothing of fair dealing, or courage or fidelity except what a slave shows for his master!"

If he expected to reawaken David's indignation he found himself altogether unsuccessful.

"There's a kernel of truth in that," David conceded thoughtfully. "Yet even to you chivalrous noblemen the mercenary soldier has his uses. There's a monument at Lucerne, I believe, to a group of them who died at Paris, to save the life of a stupid French King. The oddest part of it is that the sculptor was the same one who did the figure of Christ you saw at the Hopkins Hospital!"

Philip considered for a moment the force of David's thought. Clearly no matter what else might be said of him, this lawyer was no vulgar, heedless wage-earner; but did not the strength of his mind and the vigor of his perceptions make it all the worse for him to lend himself to Hirsch's evil purposes?

The Rabbi therefore returned to the attack—though less violently than before.

"Then you aren't going to tell me?" was his challenge.

"No," David responded. "You see how impossible it is and how useless. Suppose I were to say to you—which I'm not doing, remember—it was not Hirsch. Immediately, you'd begin to grope about for some other name. If I were to tell you the right one, you would at once begin to analyze his motives which might fail to commend themselves to your nice sense of delicacy. I can't do it, but I'll do something better for you, if you care to have me."

"What else can you do for me?" Philip inquired in sullen dejection.

"I can show you," David answered promptly, "of how little importance it is who paid this money, or why he did it. It has not the weight of a feather in the balance of my life, and it shouldn't have in yours."

Philip's expression was one of open-mouthed incredulity.

"Not matter!" he stammered. "Not matter, whether the whole fight was done to sell a few more suits of clothes or really to help men and women! Not matter whether it was an act of devotion or of treachery! Why, you're talking drivelling idiocy!"

"Let's talk sense," David began, "not mere high-sounding phrases. And let me ask you a question or two. You haven't much respect for Kaufman's money. You have suspicions, now, of Hirsch's. There really are a few more in your congregation I might speak of. Did you think worse of yourself or your work for taking the salary they paid you?"

"That's different," protested the Rabbi, "even if I can bring myself to keep on taking their money. No matter who paid me I was trying to do God's work! You were doing Hirsch's—or somebody's like him."

"God's work," Gordon repeated, smiling gently. "Well, let's assume, for the sake of argument, you're right. Is your idea of God so narrow as to believe His work only gets done in a ministerial way? There's so much more work done in offices and factories than in churches and synagogues, I should think, as a partisan of Religion, you'd want to claim some of it. Now listen, I'm not trying to quibble. I can see you're in a bad way, and

I'm just fool enough not to be willing to let you make your own kind of a mess of things. What you call God's work, I was doing, too, without any mawkish ideas about ways and means. It doesn't take a saint to do it. On the contrary, it usually gets done by sinners. And it always gets paid for by sinners; you admit it even in your own case. Does it matter? On the contrary, to use your own mode of thinking, if God can have His purposes worked out for Him, and use the money and the efforts of the devil to gain His ends, it's a genuine tribute to His superior wisdom."

The minister gasped, and swallowed several times before he collected his thoughts sufficiently to answer.

Finally he said: " I think I see what you mean. I'm sure you don't mean to be irreverent."

" I certainly don't," the lawyer interrupted. " I'm really trying to be just the opposite, and to help you, besides, to get your balance."

" Thanks," was Philip's brief but not disdainful acknowledgment. " You mean, I take it, your work was useful, and had a purpose, no matter how you happened to get the chance to do it, and no matter whether the man who gave you the chance understood its real purpose, or cared."

" That's about it," David agreed. " If you're going to deal with men, you've got to begin realizing how little they guess what their acts mean. They do what you call ' God's work '—and what I call something else—without knowing it, sometimes even while believing they're thwarting it! It's the man who can see what is needed, and use what comes to his hand without a prim, lady-like fastidiousness who does the most building."

" But even if you're right about your means," the minister objected, " can you build, according to your design, with such men for partners? This strike,—for example,—you had to settle it in a way which you know was bad."

" Indeed, I don't know that," David quickly interposed. " It wasn't ideal. It was better. It was the best settlement we could get under the circumstances. You can't do the work of fifty years in a few months. If you did, it would topple over in the first breeze. But we did better. We laid a foundation. As you say, it cost hunger and tears, and a bit of blood, besides. Just the same, the foundation is there!"

" You'll have the whole thing over again in two years," was the Rabbi's disgusted prophecy.

" I hope so," David replied cheerfully. " Without strife there's no progress!"

Philip, without warning, sprang from his seat and began to walk about the room.

" Perhaps you're right!" he said. " Perhaps you're right about it all, but to me, everything's in a jumble. I know what I think ought to be done, and I know what I think is bad and evil. I don't understand how to mix these things up, and use the things I hate in doing the things I want."

" If you believe in God," David insisted, " you must know He made such a curious mixture every time He created a man or woman."

Philip kept on pacing the floor, as before.

" Perhaps you're right," he repeated. " Anyhow, it's all too much for me! I came here thinking you were a fiend incarnate. Now I don't know what to think about you or anyone or anything, except myself. As for me—I'm not fit to deal with these things. You must see it yourself. They eat into my soul, and I do no good—do harm, maybe. I'm going to quit!"

The lawyer left him to his monotonous walk between wall and wall, for an appreciable interval of time before he inquired pointedly:

"What else, worth while, do you think you can do?"

"Nothing!" was Philip's frank confession. "I'm a misfit. There's something wrong with me."

"What will you do then?" came the next question, "just vegetate until you decay and die?"

"Yes," the minister answered bitterly.

"I'll be damned if you do!" David exploded suddenly. "Look here;" he went on, "I'm not a child. There's more to all this than Hirsch and Kaufman and the strike. Even if you'd made a flat failure of it—which you haven't—one doesn't quit at twenty-four, because he couldn't win the first skirmish. You've talked odds and ends, about what all this cost you! It was a woman you meant, wasn't it?"

Philip made no answer whatever.

"A Christian," David continued confidently. "You stuck to your job when you found you couldn't have both!"

"What makes you imagine——" the minister began weakly.

"Don't try to lie," David orderd. "You don't do it well; besides, I'm no babbler. It doesn't take much of an imagination for me to guess what's the matter with you. Don't you suppose I've ever been twenty-four myself!"

He sat silent for a minute, musing. At last, he took up his thoughts where he had laid them down.

"I could tell you about my own boyhood and what came after it, if I wanted. It wouldn't strike you as a happy story. Maybe you'd think it even harsher than your own. Everybody in this genial City doesn't spend his time trying to make life easy for a penniless Russian Jew boy, with a craving to live and work like his betters.—— But what's the use? There's no one who's worth the room he takes up on earth, who hasn't had his bad times. The question is—what are you going to do about it?"

Philip still made no answer, and David, noticing his shy unwillingness to speak of his tragedy, went on with his consideration of the younger man's problem.

"Perhaps you didn't know it, but you came here looking for an excuse. If your work wasn't worth the sacrifice, you might as well have the woman. Now you may admit it or not, but your excuse is gone. You must stick to your job!"

This time, Philip forced himself to give thoughts words.

"I don't know—I don't agree with all you've said. Besides, if it's true, I don't know how to work in this kind of world. How can you, of all men, urge me? You don't believe in my work! You never did! You don't believe in Religion at all!"

"I don't," the lawyer admitted without an instant's hesitation. "I don't, for myself; but I believe in it for you, and I believe in you, too, in spite of all the things you've done and said to make me fear you were nothing but a dreamer. Besides, there's one thing more I do believe in—the Jew. There's something about us—I don't know what—that the world needs. You've got one phase of it, with your beautiful, impossible visions; I've got

23 353

another with my hard, practical will. I and my kind have to fight against you and your kind, but they need us both, and I shan't let you shirk!"

The Rabbi made no effort to hide his astonishment at this unexpected display of sentiment coming, as it did, from David Gordon.

"I can hear you think!" Gordon laughed. "I know it's queer for me to be preaching like this to a preacher! But it's sense I'm talking. You're a Jew. You can't hide it and you can't escape it. You may try to run away from yourself, but you'll only be a pitiable, contemptible Jew, instead of a decent one. If you choose this woman instead of your Race, you're forever lost to us—to yourself, too. If she's what you think her, she's too good to be tied to the thing you'll become. You made your choice once, and it was the right one; stick to it! Go back to your job!"

"What can I do?" asked Philip. "I don't believe in people any more."

"Believe something sane about them, then," David answered. "You were sure they were all essentially good. Well, they aren't. Learn, if you can, to like them even when they're bad; make them do what's best for them whether they want to or not, only don't try to cram it down their throats. Let them think they're being fed on delicious, forbidden fruit, while all the time, without knowing it, you're giving them physic in doses too small for them to taste, but sure, after years of treatment, to do the work."

"In other words," exclaimed Philip indignantly, "make myself over. Learn to lie and flatter and pretend, like the rest—learn to make people do what I want by seeming to do what they want!"

" Just so ! " was David's genial commendation. " You needn't be afraid of losing too much of your present self. Try to think a little less of your beautiful, white virtue ! A man can't do much good until he forgets how good he really is ! "

Philip shook his head doubtfully. " I don't believe I can do it," he murmured.

" You must," the lawyer assured him. " I shan't let you do anything else ! Can't you see what I have in mind ? As a result of somebody's blunder, you've become an influence here in Baltimore, in all Jewry—maybe. People believe you make things happen—settle strikes, and such little matters. I know better. So do you, but they don't. Wouldn't it be criminal to throw away such a chance ? Think what you might do next time ! A man with a dream, learning, bit by bit, to make it come true ! The more you've paid to stand where you are, the less you can afford to run away now ! "

" Is it a promise ? " the lawyer asked suddenly.

" I'll think about it," Philip responded slowly. " By the time my next chance came, perhaps I wouldn't want to seize it ! "

He rose in preparation for his departure ; midnight had long since come and gone.

David eyed him narrowly.

" Do you sleep here, or do I sleep in your rooms ? " he inquired, in matter-of-fact tones.

" Why, neither," Philip replied, recognizing gratefully David's solicitude. " You mustn't think I don't understand and appreciate——"

" Rot ! " struck in David. " Do you think I'm fool enough to lose a useful, up-town ally ? How do I know what kind of a successor to you, Kaufman may pick? I'm going to cling to you like a shadow. I'm going to feed you and make you go to sleep at nights. I may even degrade myself by setting foot in your Temple to keep you from talking pulpit rubbish! And tonight, since I suppose my pajamas wouldn't fit you, I shall go with you!"

The lawyer had his way. As the two of them walked up Eutaw Place together, they encountered a gay party of young men and women returning home from a dance.

"Look!" whispered a young girl to her escort, "there goes Dr. Graetz with David Gordon."

"Yes," he answered, "I suppose they'll see a lot of one another since they settled this Pioneer strike."

"Wasn't it splendid of Dr. Graetz?" said the girl. "Still, do you think he ought to make a companion of this awful Gordon man? Besides all the rest, he's a Russian, you know!"

CHAPTER XXIV

A Prophet Listens to Reason

"With faith in our hearts, O God, have we entered Thy house!"

It was the Sabbath morning, and Philip Graetz, standing in his pulpit, faced his congregation and spoke in his own musical, appealing way, the familiar words of the beautiful ritual.

The Temple Beth El was not, as on the afternoon of Atonement Day, filled to overflowing. It was Saturday, and there were more than a few vacant places which told significantly of husbands, brothers and sons whose prayer, if made at all, was expressed in terms of labor. Still, the congregation was certainly not a small one. Since the last service, the Rabbi had achieved his remarkable triumph in the settlement of the Pioneer controversy, and there were many men who deemed it worth while to abandon their daily tasks to discover whether their minister, in his sermon, would make any reference to his experience. Those who liked him best, hoped he would preserve a discreet silence on the subject. The quarrel had left wounds enough. Philip, in bringing about Peace, had done a deed of which a man might well boast, but, therefore, he would be all the wiser to refrain from its mention. There was no way it could be discussed without bestowing censure somewhere.

And before these people stood Philip, telling in his vibrant voice how they had gathered together with faith in their hearts. His first words smote him with a sense of mockery and deception. He had not come there, this morning, with a heart glowing with enthusiasm. He was there to begin a new role of stratagem and casuistry. Never again was he to lay his soul bare before his people and his God, as he had done at this altar in the passionate fervor of Atonement Day. Then he was quivering with a divine inspiration. He had dedicated himself freely and joyously to all that was beautiful and holy. Now he had been taught to believe God himself could find no use for such impracticable seeking after Him. It must be done by devious paths, with a thought all the while to the snares of men. It began with lies—this new mode of ministering to one's people. Where would it end?

With this undercurrent of protest and doubt in his thoughts, Philip read the Sabbath service. No one appeared to perceive the slightest variation in tone or gesture, to tell them of the new Rabbi who had usurped the place of the young enthusiast they had chosen. No one, that is, except perhaps David Gordon, who had slipped into a pew at the very rear of the building, and sat there half hidden by a pillar, watching his pupil with his peculiar cryptic smile.

The minister as he read, indulged an illogical surprise to find how little of his new mood was perceptible to his auditors. He felt, since they were so blind, God Himself should resent this intrusion into His sacred place of this impious stranger, and cast him headlong forth. He almost wished He would.

While the choir burst forth into a melodious chant, Philip remembered that he might still, if he chose, refuse to surrender his beautiful idealism. There was still a sermon to be preached. He was free to pour forth the thoughts which to him were Truth, and always would be. Kaufman was there, Hirsch was there, and so was Gordon.

358

A PROPHET LISTENS TO REASON

Ruth was there, too—intent, and looking up at him with her great, dark eyes. Could it be the law of life that prudence was a more precious thing than courage?

If a man stood in God's presence and lived a lie—even a well-meaning lie—would God ever again trust him with the flaming sword of His Justice?

If the sermon had been spoken at that instant, Philip's ministry would then have ended; but the organ continued to peal forth its throbbing harmony, and the Rabbi continued to struggle with his thoughts as he sat there in the full view of his congregation, who supposed his spirit to be thrilled with the happiness of his victory and his people's gratitude.

These were his people, after all. Even in the few months he had been with them, he had shared so many of their griefs and tried to help them in so many of their perplexities! On the right, sat the children whom he was, next week, to confirm in the faith of their fathers—unless next week should come, and find him gone! The boys and girls would be sorry. There was no pretence in their fondness for him. Nor in that of their parents either, he was forced to admit, even if he could not make them think of God and Man as he did. Ah! well, who was he, after all his failures and incompetency, to turn away from men and women because they did not measure up to his standards? How could he disdain any man, whatever he may have said or done?

In this state of deep dejection, Philip rose to preach his sermon. There was mirrored in his discourse a curious mixture of his new mood and his old. He spoke of ideals, and how one must never lose sight of them, but he spoke also of tolerance for all men—even those who fought to make these very ideals impossible of fulfilment.

He told of the need for Religion and Judaism—in every activity of commerce and endeavor, but he allowed the idea to creep into his discourse of the wrongfulness of a militant effort on the part of anyone in spiritual authority, to obtain, by force, what could only be gained through an appeal to conscience.

He talked on in this manner, voicing empty, meaningless phrases, until his discourse had consumed nearly half an hour, and then concluding with a sonorous platitude, he returned to his seat. Once more the organ and the choir flooded the stately building with music. Philip examined the faces of his congregation. No one seemed to have detected any change in his doctrine; on the contrary, the decorous rustle, which in a house of worship takes the place of applause, was, if anything, slightly more prolonged and enthusiastic than usual. Did nothing matter in this most paradoxical of all paradoxical worlds?

Yes, he mattered to himself. He must matter a little, besides, to what men called God. Otherwise, how could one go on living?

If men could not understand, then God must understand doubly, and give him strength to go on, as he must, with his task, lacking even the poor solace of his own approval.

As on Atonement Day, his exultation had found voice in prayer, so this morning in his bewilderment and doubt, he rose and cried, almost with a sob in his voice:

"Great Spirit of the Universe, whom none of us may comprehend, and whose will we seek in vain to know, be with us as we tread the difficult mazes through which we wander in the wilderness called Life.

"Help us in our blindness and our ignorance to learn Thy purpose and to do it.

A PROPHET LISTENS TO REASON

" Help us also in our frantic yearning toward the distant light, to deal gently with our surging brothers and sisters who seem, in their haste, to crowd us back into the deeper darkness.

" Give us, we pray, a measure of Thy Divine Love which looks upon our weakness and our sin with an all-forgiving compassion.

" When Moses, Thy servant of old, after all he had yielded up of soft Egyptian ease and the warm human happiness of hearth and home, learned of his unworthiness to enter the Land of Promise, Thou didst so fill his heart with Thine own Spirit that he did not in his bitterness of woe abandon Thy people to their fate. He was given strength to bear with their murmurings through the long years in the Wilderness, teaching them to know Thy Holy Law, and to be ready for the Glorious Destiny he was never to share.

" Help me, too, O all-wise Father, as we seek, through desolate wastes, the land we know not, and into which I may not enter, to be faithful to my trust even when I fail to comprehend its meaning. May I minister to these, Thy Priest People, in love and tenderness, even if, perchance, they murmur against Thee. So that in the end—not we, but our children's children may behold that day when Thy promise shall be fulfilled—and through Israel, Thy blessing and Thy truth, shall become known to all the Nations."

* * * * * * * *

David Gordon, plunged deep in thought, forgot completely his crafty scheme to escape quietly from the Temple during the benediction, and thus avoid all inconvenient notice. It happened, therefore, that as he stood in the portico, he found himself next to Clarence Kaufman who, under the double spell of the Divine Service and the recent truce in the labor war, felt moved to hold out his hand in friendly greeting.

"Good morning, Mr. Gordon," he said effusively. "I'm glad to see you here. You should come oftener."

He spoke as one having a vested interest in the hospitality of the House of God. David gave him his characteristic, exasperating smile.

"Wasn't it a splendid sermon?" Kaufman went on, as though he defied this connoisseur of speech to deny it. "Inspiring, I call it!"

"Just the right word, Mr. Kaufman," answered David, without the slightest change of expression. "But the best of it is this: Dr. Graetz will preach a better one ten years from today."

After which, the lawyer slowly wedged his way through the throng, intending to hasten back to his busy office. On the pavement, however, he came unexpectedly face to face with Ruth, and he paused and bowed.

"Well, David Gordon," she exclaimed, "you're the last man I should have expected to fall under the spell of a Rabbi."

"I am the last one," he replied; "it only happened this morning. Still, it's a brilliant achievement for Graetz. Anyone might convert a Christian to Judaism—but a Jew! It's never been heard of before!"

She laughed gaily as she answered:

"I can understand how he did it, after you once got here. But how he succeeded in making you come, passes my understanding!"

"Oh!" David said, with an air of deep mystery. "He really can't claim any credit for that. I was on an errand of the devil's when I strayed into the House of the Lord. To tell the truth, I came on important business!"

A PROPHET LISTENS TO REASON

Ruth's expression hovered between shocked amusement and equally shocked indignation. Before she could give voice to either one or the other, however, she noticed Philip on the edge of the crowd, and forgot all about David and his blasphemies, as she threw the minister a radiant glance across the space which separated them. Philip moved steadily toward her, stopping now and then to acknowledge the greetings of one of his admiring flock.

None of this unspoken drama was lost on David. He smiled his inscrutable smile and turning to go, said to the girl:

" You see, I am more candid than you, Miss Hartman. Even if I were clever enough to guess, I'm sure you'd never admit—to me or to anyone else—just what bit of business brought you to Temple this morning! "

Before Ruth could express her very genuine annoyance at David's impertinence, he had crossed the street, and Philip's slow progress had brought him to her side.

The lawyer, from his point of vantage on the opposite side of the parkway, observed them intently as the two walked down the street together.

Evidently, something in the situation appealed to David's peculiar sense of the ironic, for his habitual cryptic smile seemed insufficient to do justice to the occasion, and he gave vent to the odd throaty chuckle he reserved for those supreme moments when he tasted the full flavor of his philosophy.

But when the sound had died away, he stood there for an instant—his face grave and thoughtful—as though he were trying to puzzle out some important problem.

Then he turned, and shrugging his shoulders, hurried on.

Finis.